TROUBLE with LOVE

ROSEMARY DUN

The Book Guild

First published in Great Britain in 2016 by Sphere

Second Edition published in Great Britain in 2025 by
The Book Guild Ltd
Unit E2 Airfield Business Park,
Harrison Road, Market Harborough,
Leicestershire. LE16 7UL
Tel: 0116 2792299
www.bookguild.co.uk
Email: info@bookguild.co.uk
X: @bookguild

Copyright © 2025 Rosemary Dun

The right of Rosemary Dun to be identified as the author of this
work has been asserted by them in accordance with the
Copyright, Design and Patents Act 1988.

All rights reserved. No part of this publication may be
reproduced, transmitted, or stored in a retrieval system, in any form or by any means,
without permission in writing from the publisher, nor be otherwise circulated in
any form of binding or cover other than that in which it is published and without
a similar condition being imposed on the subsequent purchaser.

The manufacturer's authorised representative in the EU
for product safety is Authorised Rep Compliance Ltd,
71 Lower Baggot Street, Dublin D02 P593 Ireland
(www.arccompliance.com)

This work is entirely fictitious and bears no resemblance to any persons living or dead.

Typeset in 11pt Minion Pro

Printed and bound in Great Britain by 4edge Limited

ISBN 978 1835742 082

British Library Cataloguing in Publication Data.
A catalogue record for this book is available from the British Library.

The TROUBLE with LOVE

For Queenie

Prologue

Springtime, and up and down the Western Isles of Europe, ribbon-like glass eels arrive on a migration which begins deep within the doldrums of the Sargasso Sea. On tidal swells some wash up the River Avon – where they grow into elvers – and travel on past the old Roman docks at Sea Mills to navigate twists and turns and pass underneath Brunel's suspension bridge, where many moons ago an Edwardian lady threw herself off its parapet, her billowing skirts opening like a parachute, landing her safely on the water below. These elvers continue their way upstream, some ending in Bristol's docks, where the unlucky are picked off by angling cormorants as others make their way along The Cut up to where the river narrows and otters fish for bigger prey and kingfishers spear sticklebacks.

These plucky elvers hide in mudholes, cracks and burrows, where they mature into large brown eels biding their time until one stormy October night, urged on by Atlantic trade winds and a full moon, they are said to haul themselves up out of the water to clamber across land in search of the waterways that will transport *them back to the spawning grounds of the Sargasso, where the monster Kraken lurks. It is then that the waters squirm with sleek fat eels, come together in writhing masses, thick as the sargassum weed that winds around them.*

1
High Tide, April 2014

It will all end in tears, Polly's friend would say. Later. But Polly knew best. Nonsense, she insisted. If you think about it, it's practically perfect. For what could be more liberating than knowing when and why it was all going to end?

*

Polly's shop *Cutie Pie* sat on the side of a steep Bristol hill famous for its trendy independent shops, and just up from Banksy's mural of a naked man hanging by his fingertips from the ledge of his married lover's window. The shop was as bright and as cheerful as Polly. Those in the know would pop into this emporium of punk-slash-rockabilly-slash-'50s-pinup to buy a dress or a shirt or frou-frou skirt, or a bright pink fake leopardskin jacket, safe in the knowledge that they'd be unlikely to bump into anyone else wearing the same outfit, for Cutie Pie shop specialised in the witty and wacky. This shop was guaranteed to brighten your day with its clash of colours and hip yet accessible style. This shop could make you smile. It was the realisation of Polly's dream of running her own business on her favourite street close to Bristol's historic docks. Coming to work each day was a joy.

Time for some cheerful tunes, she thought. *Let's get that sun shining!* Into her CD player she slid Georgie Fame's "Sunny" and began to sing along as she fiddled with her window display.

Outside, a strong south-westerly gusted, lifting girls' skirts and turning umbrellas inside out. She was half expecting Mary Poppins to come floating down when her attention was drawn to a man chasing a pirate hat as it bounced in a most jaunty fashion along the street. Incongruously dressed in a frock coat and long boots, he pawed at the hat as it changed direction, threatening to head out into a busy stream of traffic. Just in time, he stamped on it, picked it up, shook it out and turned around to – yes – catch Polly gawping at him through her shop window. Flustered, she attempted to look away as he gave her a little bow.

'Oh crap,' she muttered, 'it's him!' and thought to duck down behind her counter but it was too late. So, instead, she feigned being busy.

"Ping" went her doorbell. And there he was. Johnny-Depp-pirate-hat in hand. The hunk who'd bid against her at the auction.

*

Two weeks earlier and Polly and Mel were on a mission. They'd met up outside Bristol Auction House, housed in a building that squatted in one of the tiniest back streets off Bristol's harbourside. Polly wore a vintage cream coat which she slipped off, revealing a pink dress covered with a cupcakes pattern and topped by a raspberry-coloured crocheted cardigan. 'I see you've come as a raspberry cupcake today,' quipped Mel, as Polly draped her coat over her arm.

'Whereas you're more Cruella de vil.'

'I hardly think so, Missy.' Mel wore a sharp black trouser suit with cigarette pants, tailored jacket and freshly ironed white polka-dot shirt (no Dalmatians killed in the making of).

Polly leant forward to give her very best friend in the world a kiss on the cheek.

'Gerroff, lezzer!' said Mel, as she smoothed her just-below-the-ear-choppy-blonde bob. 'You'd better not have left any red lippie on my face.'

'Hold still.' Polly pulled a tissue from her bag, gave it a lick, wiping the mark she'd deposited on her friend's soft cheek. 'Thanks for coming with me,' she said. 'Truly.'

'Stop calling me Truly!' Mel grinned at her. 'You know how much I love slumming it with you arty types.'

They linked arms and waltzed in, finding places near the front where they settled on a battered leather sofa in the already packed auction house. The auction was well under way and they were just in time. For there he was. The man of her dreams. Looking a tad flaky, it was true, and his clothes had seen better days.

'Go on, then,' Mel hissed in her ear. 'Don't let him get away.'

So Polly stuck up her hand.

'One hundred and eighty pounds to the pretty lady with the auburn hair.' The auctioneer smiled what Polly considered more than a professional smile at her.

'Oh, give me strength,' muttered Mel, who'd spotted the auctioneer's leer.

'Two hundred pounds for the pirate!' came a male voice from somewhere behind the pillar. Polly craned her neck but couldn't see who it was.

'Bugger. We've got competition,' hissed Mel.

But Polly was not to be thwarted. And certainly not by a man so cowardly that he had to hide behind a pillar. She wanted this life-sized figure of a pirate for her shop. And no man was going to get in her way!

'Two hundred and fifty!' she shouted, as Mel shot her a look of… pride, it might have been, or caution more like, for they'd agreed not to go over the two hundred mark.

The auctioneer cast his eye towards the pillar, but no counterbid was forthcoming, so he brought his gavel down.

'Sold!' And Polly hold up her auction number.

Out in the yard, she was just buying two coffees from a van when there, coming around the corner of the auction house – as if locked in some slow-mo Diet Coke commercial – strode a man in dark curly-haired gorgeousness.

He stopped in front of her and held out his hand. 'Spike Monaghan.'

(*For God's sake, Polly, close your mouth.*) 'Hello,' was all she could manage.

'I'm hoping I'll be getting visitation rights,' he said, with a soft Irish lilt as he beamed an expansive friendly smile at her.

'Sorry?' Her brain wasn't doing catch-up very well as it still appeared to have its tongue hanging out. (*He wants to visit me?*)

'The pirate?' he said. 'Fair play to you outbidding me like that. I'd be interested to see where you're going to put him.' He released her hand. 'I didn't quite catch your name?'

'Right. Yes. Polly. Park Street. Shop. Cutie Pie.' Polly appeared to have lost the knack of joined-up speaking.

'Excellent.' He walked backwards a few paces then gave her a cheery wave as he headed off for the main road.

And that had been that. She'd not thought she'd see him again, had nearly (okay, not quite) forgotten him, and yet here he was. In her shop. With a dead cheeky grin on his face.

'Hello again,' he said, ruffling his hair. 'Don't you just hate hats! Look at me now. I've got the terrible hat hair.'

She gawped at him – not used to seeing a pirate in her shop… unless you counted her shop pirate, Cap'n Jack, which she did not.

'Do you not remember me?'

'Yes,' she managed to get out. Of course she remembered him. All her nerve endings were already going – boing – and standing to attention. 'You were my rival for my pirate, here,' she said – gesturing.

'And very sad I was to miss out on him,' giving Cap'n Jack a pat on the shoulder. 'Was hoping to buy him for a friend of mine who – you know – does pirate tours around the docks? He's off sick today – hence the pirate costume.' He indicated his get-up. 'D'you like it? I'm standing in for him, you see.' He leant forward. 'And before you go asking me, no, he isn't off with the scurvy.'

Blank face from Polly.

'Geddit? No?' He stood up to his full height. 'Pirate? Scurvy?'

Over six foot tall, she reckoned… *Hmm… six foot two…?*

'Just as well I'm not a comedian,' he added. 'So.' Another cheeky grin. 'Have I gone overboard with this lot – if you'll excuse the pun. Is that what you're thinking? But I do like the dressing-up, and…' (he was definitely giving her the once-over) '…judging by the looks of you and your fine shop, I'd say you like the dressing-up too.'

He wore such an air of amusement that even his sticking-up hair appeared most tickled. And it was, she noted, the kind of hair made for running your fingers through. If you had a penchant for that sort of thing – which Polly most definitely had.

'I guess so…'

'That's a wicked dress you've got on there,' he said, holding her startled gaze for a moment longer than was absolutely necessary. 'Very nice. The shop too. Way cool.'

'Yes, well.' She tried to affect an I'm-in-charge-this-is-my-shop kind of air, but didn't quite mange it, due to the fact that she was trying terribly hard not to smile. 'Did you come in for anything in particular?'

'Apart from my visitation rights, you mean, Polly? It is Polly, isn't it?'

She coloured up.

'I could ask for change for the meter? As a reason for popping in. Would that help? Only I don't have a car…'

Oh, he's charming, isn't he. And we all know that charming, good-looking blokes spell "trouble"…

'Tell you what,' his eyes alighting on a tie rack, 'how's about I take one of these fine fellas?' He waved a black tie covered with cavorting skeletons in her general direction. 'This one here could come in handy for scaring away awkward customers. Should I have any.' He held it up to his shirt. 'What do you think?'

'Looks great.' She gathered her composure. 'It's a Mexican Day of the Dead design. It's a major Mexican festival?'

'Is it, now? Amazing the things you can learn. I'll take it!'

'Good choice.' (He was giving her a quizzical look). 'Of tie,' she added. Flustered. She hadn't said anything daft, had she? Then why was he looking at her like that?

'Why don't I give you my card? Because,' he said, his face deadpan, 'you never know when you might be in need of a stripper.'

She stopped mid-ringing up his purchase. 'I'm sorry…?'

'Ha! Your face!' A big grin on his. 'Got ya! Sorry. Couldn't resist the whole stripping thing. Is what I do, you see.' He pointed at his card. 'Not the full monty – if that's what you're thinking – jeez, no. If you look at my card, you'll see that I strip floors, and sand them.'

She looked at his card. It did.

'One of my many jobs. That and restoring furniture, doing up boats, writing music reviews for *West is Best*… Do you get that magazine?'

She seemed to have lost the power of speech once more, and merely shook her head.

'Don't mind me, Polly. Polly… Is that why you have a pirate? So's you can do the whole "Pretty Polly" "Pieces of eight" parrot kind of thing?'

She wondered if he was taking the piss, and if he was hyperactive.

'I'll shut up, shall I? It's the nerves. I tend to gabble when I'm nervous. I do apologise.' Taking the proffered bag, he executed a long theatrical bow. 'Tell you what,' slapping his forehead, 'I've an excellent idea. Why don't I take you out for a drink tonight? To prove how I've not escaped from an asylum for the piratically insane! What do you think? Do say yes, Polly. Pretty please.'

Seeing as he asked so charmingly, and she couldn't see any other way to get him out of the shop, she said yes. After all, what harm could it do?

2

It wasn't as if he wasn't straight with her from the start, as near the end of the most entertaining first date she'd ever had, he took her hand in his and said, 'I'd really like to see you again.'

'Good. Me too,' she answered, turning her face up for a kiss that didn't come.

'Hang on,' he said, gently pushing her away to arm's length. 'I haven't finished. There's more.' He sounded unsure. 'This is tricky.'

'Go on.' She gave him a quizzical look as they stood on the Downs, next to Clifton Suspension Bridge. The night had that clean, freshly washed smell it gets after rain, when the roads shine darkly silver in the light of streetlamps and a watery moon.

'The thing is,' he began, and her heart sank, because, let's face it, nothing good ever begins with "The Thing Is".

'I do like you, Polly,' he was saying. 'Who wouldn't? You're great. Dead sexy...'

'Yes...?' *Okay. Not sounding so bad. Could say promising*

even. And he does have very kissable lips. She leant towards him, still hoping for that smooch.

'It's just… ohhh…' He turned away, shoving his hands in his pockets, then turned back. 'Maybe this was a bad idea after all.'

'What do you mean?' she said, oblivious to the cars creeping across the bridge from Bristol to Somerset and back. 'I don't understand.'

Hadn't they had a great evening, the two of them? Doing their small pub crawl around Clifton village? Laughing, chatting, getting along? Did she not scrub up well, with her hair fastened up, a few tendrils escaping here and there to give a sultry rather than dragged-through-a-hedge-backwards look, and her figure shown off to its advantage by a clinging vintage frock pulled together with a genuine Vivienne Westwood jacket? Did he not fancy her at all, then?

'I'm guessing this is a terrible way to end a first date, Polly. But it's best to get it out in the open.'

What? What? He's not going to say he's married, is he?

'Why don't we sit over here.' He wiped a bench with the sleeve of his jacket so they could both sit down. 'Okay. Deep breath.' He turned to face her. 'To cut to the chase. I'm emigrating to Australia. There. I've said it. I am emigrating to Australia, Polly. In October.' He stretched his long legs out in front of him as she let it sink in.

'You see,' he continued, twisting around on the bench so they were face to face. 'it's been a dream of mine for so long. I've an uncle over there. Mum's brother, Dermot. He's got me a job helping with his property development company. Doing up old houses. Erecting flatpack homes. Don't laugh. I know. Flatpack houses sounds mad, doesn't it? But they have that kind of thing in Oz.'

'Oh. Right.' She tried to concentrate as questions bombarded her – when? Why? What did this mean? Rain dripped on the top of their heads from an overhanging beech tree as she fidgeted with the strap of her handbag.

'Will you stop your fidgeting, there, and tell me what you think.'

She let go of her bag. 'Think about what? The frankly insane idea of building a house with an allen key?'

'No, Polly. What I'm suggesting is that we see each other until I leave. I know it's a big ask – but I'd really like to…' and here he gave her a sheepish grin. 'I know it's only six months away. But a lot can happen… After all, if we were teenagers – which clearly we're not – then six months would practically rank as being engaged. Not that I'm suggesting…' He smiled another of his twinkly smiles. 'You know what I'm saying, here.'

'I do…' and then she added quickly '…know what you're saying.'

He tipped his head back to gaze up at a sky dappled with cloud.

'Shall we give it a go, then, Polly? See what happens?'

'Why not,' she said, giving him an uncertain smile. 'October *is* a long way away.'

Overhead, a seagull wheeled in the sky as he (finally, she thought) leant in to kiss her, and she slid into him so that they were entwined in a sweet kiss. When she opened her eyes, he was gazing down at her.

'Glad that's settled,' he said. 'If you're sure?'

'We're both grown-ups, aren't we?'

'I certainly hope so,' he said, pulling her to her feet, 'with what I've got in mind.'

And they hurried down the hill to her house.

*

The following evening, she met Mel for an after-work drink – so that Mel could get the lowdown.

'You're just too cynical,' Polly was saying, as she took a sip of her cider. 'It will not end in tears. Anyway – c'mon – who would you pick to play you in a movie? If you had to?'

'That's easy. Ripley from *Alien*. But don't change the subject.'

'Honestly, will you stop giving me that look. So he's leaving after six months. No big deal. Really.'

'Hmm.'

They were sitting at a weather-beaten table outside The Nova Scotia pub; Polly's local at the end of her road. Inside was packed to its tobacco-stained rafters with ferrymen, tipsy women and grungy gruff-voiced men nursing their pints. The two friends needed to talk, so they'd taken their drinks outside, the surprising spring weather having cleared to bestow an evening warm with the promise of summer.

Mel gave her a typical Mel look. 'I don't want to see you get hurt, that's all.'

'I won't. Both Spike and I are cool with it all. I've told him it's fine – I'm not looking for anything heavy, am I? Especially not after Paolo the Klingon.' (So called because he was clingy.) 'Look, Spike's younger than me, he's got itchy feet... it would never work if he stayed. So, there's no need to worry. Everything's cool. We both know the score. We talked it through last night.'

'I'll bet you did, you dirty cow. So how was he? You know... in bed? The full details, please.'

'Shut up.' Polly gave her a playful shove.

'Seriously, though.' Mel gave her friend's hand a heartfelt squeeze. 'I do think it's all very convenient for him. This whole going off to Australia does rather let him off the hook, doesn't it? He gets to have his fun with no danger of commitment.' She put down her glass. 'A classic case of having his cake and eating it, if you ask me.'

Polly sighed. 'It cuts both ways as I'm not into anything long term, either, don't forget.'

Mel gave her an oh-yeah glance. She took a sip of her pint and then licked the Guinness moustache from her upper lip. 'Hmm,' she said, giving Polly one of her looks. The one that was all about what Mel considered to be Polly's "failure to commit".

She knew Mel considered her commitment issues to be all Polly's mother's fault – had told her so on numerous occasions. But Polly didn't hold with psychobabble claptrap. She was a modern woman with choices. So what if she hated the feeling of being tied down? Or owned? In her book, marriage was outmoded. If she ever did decide to give it a go, she'd opt for the Tim Burton/ Helena Bonham Carter model of living in adjoining houses.

'Remind me – when is he leaving?' said Mel.

Polly leant back as a breeze, coming off the water, caressed her hair and then blew it across her face. 'October. It'll be October.' She sat up and beamed at her friend. 'Can't you see, Mel? There'll be no tearful breakups and no messy endings?'

'Hmm,' said Mel. Again.

3

Spike spent the Saturday night at her house. After a cup of tea and a round of bacon sandwiches, which Spike made while she had a doze, he ordered her to get up – 'C'mon, Polly. 'Tis a glorious Sunday morning, and I've got something to show you. Not that. Honestly, you've a one-track mind.' He pulled her to her feet and smacked her bottom.

'Oi!'

'Hurry up there. We're off to catch a ferry.'

'Why? Where are we going?'

'Will you not wait and see.' And he planted a kiss on her forehead.

Polly wasn't daft. She knew she was sliding down the helter-skelter of falling in love but rationalised that all would be fine. The two of them hopped on board a ferry close to where her back yard met the river's footpath. She couldn't remember the last time she'd been on one. A bit like when she lived in London and never bothered to visit Madame Tussauds or the

Tower of London. God forbid. Now that she was on board the gaily painted yellow and blue boat, she resolved to do ferry trips more often. She felt as giddy and excited as when she and Mel had gone on a school trip to Longleat House with the prospect that they might see an actual ghost, or that a real lion might escape and gobble up their classmate Natalie Wong (nicknamed Natalie Pong because of her BO), or that the Marquess of Bath – stunned by their beauty – might invite them to become his latest wifelets.

Yes, this was a grand way to see the river and harbourside, especially on a mild spring day like today. She positively glowed with the after-effects of great sex and a good-looking man by her side – even if he was trying to dangle his hand in the water when he'd already been told, 'Best not do that, sir.' Polly was delighted to see the ferryman wore an actual fisherman's cap and navy jumper. She couldn't squeal out loud (after all, she wasn't thirteen anymore), but did so in her head.

Spike took a photograph of her with his phone. 'God, I must look a right mess,' she said, even though she was happy with the way her hair was wild and bright orange in the sun, and how her clothes just seemed to slink onto her body.

'Aren't you the gorgeous one,' he murmured, and she wasn't sure she'd ever felt more sexy or alive.

They chugged past chi-chi new-build riverside apartments, and a jetty to the left on which a cormorant sat preening itself and then stretched upright in a crucifixion pose, its wing feathers spread like washing pegged out on a line. Up ahead, another black cormorant bobbed on the water – she watched as it flexed its long black neck like some haughty queen – then, quick as a blink, dove straight into the water. Where it entered, the river's surface danced in slivers. She pointed. 'Did you see that bird?'

'What bird, where?' he said.

The Trouble With Love

And then – there! Further along, the bird popped up like an emergency buoy suddenly released from a scuppered ship. Held fast in its beak was a long, wriggling, almost transparent ribbon-like creature. *Looks like one of those eel thingies...*

'Have you ever been on the *Matthew*?' Spike was asking, as they pulled alongside the dark honey-coloured replica of the wooden ship that once carried John Cabot and his crew on their voyage to discover America, long before Christopher Columbus. She marvelled at how tiny it was, and shook her head – no, she hadn't been on board – maybe one day. The ferry docked to let people off and others on.

'Nearly there,' said Spike.

She smiled at him, not minding that he had a surprise in store for her, because Polly loved surprises. Not for her the rattling of Christmas presents to try and discern what was inside. She was all for delayed gratification.

'Can't wait,' she said, as he squeezed her arm and touched her knee with his. The ferry leisurely continued its journey through the swing bridge, on past giraffe-like cranes outside the M-shed and harbourside bars and restaurants. Passing another ferry, theirs tipped slightly in the water and ploughed towards a group of juvenile seagulls hanging around in a gang on top of the water, their dirty grey-speckled weave of feathers patterned like fish scales. *Is that why they're called herring gulls?* she wondered, as the birds did their tippy-toe running along the surface then took flight to make way for the boat.

The ferry shushed and slurped along, until Spike announced, 'This is where we get off,' just as they approached a line of four barges and a small landing stage. 'Here, give me your hand.'

*

'What do you think?' Spike had stopped on the towpath, next to a dilapidated mostly pea green-painted barge that reminded Polly of "The Owl and the Pussycat".

'Is this the surprise?' she said, waiting to be enlightened further.

'Yes. She's my boat. I'm doing her up before… well, anyway, I'm doing her up. Might sell her, might keep her. I've not yet decided.'

Polly loved the barge. 'I think we ought to christen the boat, don't you?' he said on that first visit.

'What, you've not named it?'

'Don't be so daft. *Christen* it…' And so they did. They christened it on the small caravan-like banquette, then across the table, giggling as Spike placed his hand over her mouth when a couple walked past up on the towpath.

'But why a boat?' she finally asked. 'Why, when you told me last night that you don't swim?'

Something which had come as a big surprise to Polly – who was a strong swimmer herself. She couldn't imagine how anyone in this day and age could not swim.

'So? I can't fly, either, but that doesn't stop me from getting on a plane.'

Spike liked to surprise Polly with romantic gestures – he'd leave little love notes around her bedroom for her to find after he'd left for work: *Missing you already – see you soon. S xxx* (discovered under her duvet when she threw her covers back); and *Thanks for a gorgeous sexy night – why not wear these frilly ones next time? S xxx* (hidden in her underwear drawer), and many others. It was a fun game, searching her room for little scraps of paper hidden – up the chimney, inside an empty packet of condoms, slotted in the corner of a picture frame. Once she'd woken to a Post-it note stuck to her forehead – *A kiss from me. S xxxxx.* One time, he even stuck a note under the windscreen wiper of her Citroën 2CV, parked in Clifton Village. Sometimes, in the quiet of early mornings, they'd congratulate themselves on how well they were doing, how liberating it was, being together with no expectations, how they could live in the moment, and risk loving – safe in the knowledge of when it would end. Snuggled up like two babes in the woods.

She loved their sleepovers on the barge – although Spike did stay at her house most of the nights they were together, because she wasn't that keen on the chemical toilet, and he liked to come and use her shower. Still, it was thrilling on board, as she loved the touch and creak of the barge's old weathered wood, the different sounds and smells, the way their lovemaking rolled with the elements, then waking up to moorhens messing about on the river, or swans majestically carving their way through the water like small white Viking ships; coming together in pairs, touching their beaks so that their heads and necks made the shape of a heart. Polly thought of, but didn't mention, how swans mate for life.

Once she saw a water vole. 'You sure it wasn't a rat, there, Poll?'

Often, when they were lying in their bunk at night, she'd fantasise about how they could slip their moorings and drift off to a land where the bong tree grows. ('Is that like a spliff, Poll?' he said sleepily. 'Shut up!' she said contentedly.) Sometimes she'd sing the song to him of how they'd dine on quince and slices of mince served up in a runcible spoon.

'Ah, you are daft there, Polly,' he said.

4
October, Low Tide

If there was such a thing as a weather god and he or she was a fair and just creature, then today would be overcast with a clap of thunder thrown in for good measure. Instead, as she drove up and over the Cumberland Basin flyover, the day was all picture-postcard sharp colours: bright blue sky, fluffy white clouds, and houses the colour of Neapolitan ice cream clambering up the hills of Clifton to where the majestic sweep of the suspension bridge spanned a glorious early morning.

So, it had finally arrived. The day circled in red, on her calendar hidden inside her broom cupboard. Hidden, so that Spike wouldn't guess that today was anything other than "no big deal".

She parked up and walked the short distance to her shop at a slow pace, wishing she didn't have to go into work today.

'How's Spike?' hailed one of the stall holders from the indoor market.

'Hmm? Oh, fine,' she answered, hurrying by so she wouldn't

have to stop and chat. It was scary how in a short space of time, Spike had become woven into the fabric of her life.

The phone was ringing as she opened the door to her shop. Her shop. It had taken her ages but finally she was here – and without the financial help that her mother, Suze, kept trying to foist on her; insisting that her tax accountant had suggested it. She wasn't fooling Polly; Suze's daughter could recognise mother guilt when she heard and saw it.

Hurrying through to the rear, she picked up her phone.

'Go on then, what are you cooking his lordship tonight?' said Mel on the other end.

Shoving her bag underneath the counter, Polly perched on her high fake-leopard-skin barstool.

'Steak and chips.'

'I see… Bit seventies, isn't it?'

'It's not *Come Dine with Me*.' Polly glanced at her clock. 10.00 am. Ten hours to go. 'Anyway,' she added. 'They're his favourite.' She emptied the float into her till. 'Even I can't go wrong with steaks.'

'You reckon? I'll bet you five squid you burn them.'

Polly slammed her till shut. 'Cheapskate. How about a tenner?'

'Tenner it is.'

Polly looked up as a customer entered the shop, struggling with a buggy. She smiled a welcome at her then turned back to whisper to Mel, 'You're on. Now push off, moron. Some of us have work to do.'

'Charming,' came the reply.

Dashing up the hill to Waitrose, she passed the tall gothic revivalist Wills Building – with its fripperies, gargoyles and fenestrations, all looking as if made out of butterscotch-coloured icing sugar – and dodged through and around the many students lounging about outside.

As she waited in line at the checkout, she remembered the last time she'd been in with Spike. When the girl at the till had turned to him and said, 'Bag for life?'

Quick as a flash, he'd answered, 'Thanks for the offer. But I'm not sure I'm ready to commit on so short an acquaintance,' which had given Polly a fit of the giggles.

Bit prophetic, though, wasn't it, she now thought, as she muttered her thanks and grabbed her shopping bags.

Outside, the sky was dark and angry-looking. She glanced up at the heavens. Oh great. Be careful what you wish for.

As Polly drove, her pathetic 2CV wipers did little more than smear rain across the windscreen, forcing her to lean forward and peer out; her heater doing its best to blast hot air onto her feet. The last of summer had duly arrived. Heralding autumn and the end of days packed full of evening drinks on the harbour, picnics on the Downs, boat trips around Bristol Docks. Oh, and wonderfully steamy sexy nights. Because… oh damn it… She shook her head. *Come on, get a grip. Of course you're going to miss him. Best to get it over with quickly – like ripping off a plaster.* She set her jaw and drove on.

Back home in her kitchen, she glanced at her clock. It was a little after five, and Spike wasn't due until eight.

Her mouth felt dry, and her stomach as jumpy as if a troupe of leprechauns were doing a performance of *Riverdance* in there. Better not start on the wine. Looking around for her small teapot, she recalled how it had been sent crashing to the ground that night when they couldn't wait to get upstairs, could hardly wait to get inside the door, and instead had wonderful urgent sex right there on her kitchen table. She grasped the kettle. Was everything conspiring to remind her?

Rubbing her forehead, she fetched her favourite cup from

The Trouble With Love

her dresser. The one Spike had bought on a day trip to Clevedon. (*Stop it!*) Turning to survey her kitchen, she leant back against the wooden worktop and gave a heartfelt sigh. She loved her house. It was chock-full of things. Bright shiny things she couldn't resist, and which she collected like a magpie. Her blue-painted dresser displaying an array of colourful plates and one-off pottery pieces from Mary Rose Young; its shelves decked in cheery patchwork bunting. Yes, she loved her house and her collection of stuff. Mel once asked if she was building some sort of nest. Maybe she had been. Okay, it might not be her dream house – but no one gets to live in their dream house, do they? Still, she loved her funny little home – with its leaks and creaks and draughts, like an old barely seaworthy vessel.

Opening her French doors onto her wooden verandah – painted pink and festooned with fairy lights – she stood on deck, forearms leaning on the balustrade, wild mermaid hair blowing all about her face, her eyes wet with salt tears. *Oh bugger.* With a sigh, she gazed out over a landscape thinned with rain.

*

And now her house phone was ringing. *Dear God, can they not all leave me alone?* Reluctantly, she headed back inside. 'Hello?'

'Polly.' Great – the last person she wanted to hear from – her mother. Sticking her oar in as per.

'What are you cooking? Sounds like you need a Hollandaise sauce,' Suze was saying down the phone.

More like Hellman's mayonnaise, Polly thought.

'You'll find the recipe in my book. You know, the one I gave you last Christmas?'

She glanced up at the top shelf of her dresser where her mother's cook books were lined up. Not one of them opened.

'Good idea, Mum,' she said, as in her head she shrieked, *Get off the phone, get off the phone.*

'I do hope you're going to do my own special thrice-cooked chips?'

'Yes. Of course.' She wasn't. She'd use oven chips.

'Suze, I'm sorry, but I really do have to go and get ready.'

'Well. Good luck, my darling. Make sure you make yourself gorgeous. Let him see what he'll be missing!'

Honestly, at times her mother could be so insensitive.

Replacing the receiver, Polly remembered how the only time she'd come close to having a row with Spike was on the subject of how she didn't like taking money from Suze, but how Suze found ways of giving it to her in any case.

'Maybe it's her clumsy way of showing you she loves you. Did you ever think of that, Poll? She seems like a grand woman. A right barrel of laughs.'

'Oh yes, she's a laugh, all right,' she had said, not bothering to keep the sarcasm out of her voice. 'Especially with a few drinks inside her.'

'Ah right.'

'You don't know the half of it.'

'So tell me,' he said.

And she did. She told him how her mother met her father. How she was an art student, and he, her lecturer. How they lived in a housing co-op in Brixton with a mixture of artists and layabout "trustafarians", and how Suze relished their carefree life but Jeff wanted to settle down. How her mother declared she was a "free spirit". How, when she got pregnant with Polly, she'd felt tied and housebound. How she would leave Polly the baby, Polly the toddler, and finally Polly the child, with Jeff as she went out and partied. How much Suze hated Bristol when Jeff took a job here and insisted they move. How she missed her London

The Trouble With Love

friends. How her parents would row and Suze would take off back up to London. And how one day she never came back.

Spike had listened and held her as she cried herself to sleep. Sometimes she thought he knew her better than even Mel did. Sometimes she'd found it hard to tell where he ended and she began. Often he brought out the best in her, especially when Suze was around… banging on about Virginia Woolf – for the nth time – and how every woman ought to have a room of her own. Hardly difficult for Suze these days, she thought, given the size of her houses.

Was funny how things had worked out for Suze. From a chaotic start, she'd turned her life around, gone into rehab, joined NA, become the famous TV chef Suze Chambers, with a regular slot on Sunday morning television, and now lived with long-term boyfriend Brian – a movie actor who'd cornered the market in East End thugs or Russian mafia bosses. They owned a large house in Hampstead, a weekend cottage (huge) on the banks of the Tamar Estuary, restaurants in London and Devon. Lucrative cookery book deals… What hadn't changed was Polly's blaming Suze for leaving her at such a young age.

It was no good Mel suggesting she "do therapy" as Polly claimed to be allergic to all therapists. Down to many years of her mother spouting feminist and self-help claptrap with her London friends. Once, on a visit to Suze's place in Brixton, she remembered how – during one of her mother's women's group meetings – Suze had encouraged a twelve-year-old Polly to "embrace her cunt", and invited her to peer up it with the use of a speculum and mirror.

'You can look at mine, if you want,' she'd said. Unsurprisingly, Polly hadn't, and instead ran upstairs to lock herself in the spare bedroom.

There were some good, if not brilliant, times too. Even though Polly had been very young, one particular memory stood out of that time in 1984 when a friend of a friend of Suze's – who'd been dating one of the Spandau Ballet boys – had invited them down to the recording studios where the Band Aid single was being recorded. Paula Yates had passed them by – like a little punk fairy – her tutu just brushing Polly's arm, and she'd spotted Polly, bent down, picked her up and spun her round and around. She often thought of that day, and of how Paula must have sprinkled her with some kind of fairy dust, as she'd stayed under her spell ever since. Often, when selecting dresses to buy for her shop, she would ask herself what Paula would think of this or that dress, and whether she would wear it.

Funny how moments stay with you, like the montage of a film: Polly, as a tot, dancing with fairy Paula; Polly crying as Suze left the house one foggy morning, clanging the gate behind her; Polly, aged ten, running through the fields at the back of their house in Bristol, hand in hand with her new best friend, Mel; Polly standing back to admire the signage of her shop, Cutie Pie; or that blustery day in April when Spike had barged into her shop. And now here she was. Cooking what was in effect going to be their very last meal before the credits rolled. *Oh, shut up*, she told herself. *You really are an idiot.*

She reached for her tin of emergency biscuits, the Jammie Dodgers kept for times of stress. Biting into the shortbread outer to its jam heart, she savoured the biscuit's sweet claggy feel in her mouth, before dunking it in her tea. Her mind went back to last week when Spike had bought her a packet of Love Hearts – 'Because we won't get to do Valentine's Day,' he'd said, causing her heart to contract. They took it in turns to select a round sherbet-flavoured sweet, read out loud the message written inside the outline of the heart, and pop them one at a time, into the other's mouth: Sweet Heart – pop – Be Mine – mmm chomp

– Love You – suck – Kiss Me – now… 'If only we had one that said Shag Me,' he'd joked. And they had anyway. Tenderly.

She shook her head to clear her mind. *This won't do.* For some reason which escaped her, and which would prove to mean nothing at all, she set about filling with water the ice cube tray from the freezer box in her fridge.

These last few days, Spike had been in London, to sort stuff for his trip, and to spend quality time with his godmother Elspeth, who was putting on a brave face at his imminent departure. She'd been his guardian since his own mother died of a stroke (freakily rare for a woman so young) when he himself was a small child, and then later his father (who'd never remarried) died of a heart attack when Spike was just sixteen. The teenage Spike had been despatched from Dublin to England to stay with Elspeth in Notting Hill, and had not surprisingly gone off the rails. Messing about doing this and that instead of staying on at school. But he'd always been good with his hands and had begun making his own chairs from upcycled pieces of wood and broken furniture, which sold well at Notting Hill markets, and his lively and witty way with words – which he successfully married with his love of live music – meant he was soon writing reviews for the local rag, and on occasion London's *Time Out* magazine.

Ring ring, ring ring. It was her mobile. Mel again.
    'How's it going?'
    Sigh. 'Fine.'
    'Liar! I can come over and give you a hug, if you like?'
    'I'm just about to make myself beautiful.'
    'You sure you got enough time for that?'
    'Oh ha ha.'
    'Seriously. Call me. Whenever. I'll be thinking of you.'

On the dot of eight, Spike arrived at Polly's house with a bunch of hand-tied peonies and freesias plus a packet of Jammie Dodgers. 'Budgen's finest,' he said. 'Just in case you run out.'

'As if.' She reached forward to gently unpeel a piece of tissue paper stuck to his face, where he'd clearly nicked himself shaving.

She busied herself arranging the flowers in a vase as he proceeded to stride about her kitchen, the pair of them acting like almost-strangers.

'Good time in London?' she asked.

'All right,' he said. 'Umm, Elspeth sends her love.'

'Hungry?'

'Bit peckish.'

Placing a tray of chips in the oven, she wished he'd sit down. He was making her dizzy; she already felt as if she might throw up.

'You okay there, Poll?' he said. 'Only you're lookin' a bit green about the gills.'

Gills? What an odd fishy expression, she thought, wiping her hands on the flowery vintage apron tied tightly about her neat hourglass waist. God, she felt weird.

'I'm fine. Just fine,' she lied. She was wearing that floaty tea dress he liked, plus stockings, suspenders, high heels, and her hair loosely teased into tumbling ringlets.

'You look gorgeous,' he said. 'Here.' He advanced on her with kitchen towel in hand. 'You've smudged your eye makeup.'

'Silly me.' She sidestepped him to move in front of the mirror, and to dab at her eyes. 'Must've been a blast of hot air from the oven, or something.'

He was half smiling in that amused way of his as she took in the way his hair – longer now than when they first met – flopped forward in soft waves. That strong lithe frame of his: those big hands, that tight body in jeans and checked shirt. God, he looked good.

'What?' Then, as if sensing her sadness, he added, 'Seriously, darlin'. Come here,' and he folded her in an embrace while she leant into him, breathing him in; he smelled like cinnamon and toast.

'Shall we crack open this bottle of wine?' He set about the task of opening and pouring while at the same time filling her in on his visit to his stepmother Elspeth's house, retelling some funny anecdote about an encounter on the tube train, and saying how much he hated London, with its grime and people with grumpy faces. On and on he prattled as she nodded and added 'Hmm,' in what she hoped were the appropriate places, all the while watching his strong hands turn the corkscrew round and round until it was home. His chest lifting as he pulled the cork out of the bottle.

Her mind could not quite fathom how this would be the last time they'd ever be in her kitchen together, with him pouring her a glass of wine like this, as if it was something they'd do together forever and ever.

Then the thought she'd been trying so hard to banish crept in – *What if you were to ask him to stay?*

But how could she? She knew how much he wanted to go to bloody Australia. It was his dream, and no way could she ask him to give up all that.

She went to stand by the window, staring out at the lights going on in rooms up and down the harbourside apartments. People coming home, getting ready to go out, having meals together. Normal everyday stuff.

'You all right there, Poll?'

'Yes, I'm fine.' And what if he were to stay? What if he decided to stay just for her? *Well, then he'd end up resenting you, wouldn't he?*

She drank a good glug of the red wine he'd held out for her. It tasted sour in her mouth, even though it was a good Shiraz. She gave him as much of a smile as she could muster.

'You're starting to worry me. Grinning away like that.'

'Oh. Sorry. Don't mind me.' She set her shoulders. 'Right,' she managed in a determinedly breezy voice, 'can you fetch me down that big bowl?'

She didn't say the one that they'd bought together during one of their many mooches around Bath's flea markets, but the knowledge hung between them.

'Here you go.'

'Thanks.' She tipped in the contents of a bought salad pack, and drizzled honey & mustard dressing – from a bottle – over the top of it.

'I see you're applying the full range of your culinary skills there, Poll,' he said, the beginnings of amusement in his voice. 'Spoiling me something rotten. What with your home cooking.'

'Very funny!' She plonked the salad in front of him, dodging away from his reach as he gave her an exaggerated disappointed look.

'Packing go all right, did it?' she said.

He pulled out his baccy tin. 'Umm, well, yes. Yes, it has, Polly.'

Her stomach was all over the place. Maybe she had a bug or something. She filled a glass from the tap and switched on a CD to ease the tension. Amy Winehouse began a plaintive song. Bad choice, she decided, and swapped it for a Roxy Music compilation. 'Virginia Plain' blasted out as Spike concentrated on rolling a cigarette; long eyelashes dusting his cheek. She couldn't stop herself. She began to think of his visits to her shop, when he'd pretended to be a shoplifter and would stuff a shirt or tie into his pocket with part of it hanging out, just to see if one of Polly's customers would notice and "shop" him to her. Or that time when she'd gone upstairs to change for a night out, only to come down and discover him – feet up on her sofa – eating her chocolates, his face plastered in her drying strawberry face pack, going, 'What?' His hands spread out as she threw a cushion at him. 'What?'

In her kitchen, he was now licking the gummed cigarette paper, and asking her if she wanted one.

'Sure, why not? Thanks.'

It would never have worked, she reminded herself. *Him and me.* He'd once told her how he couldn't bear to feel like he might be missing out on anything. 'It's a big world out there,' he'd said.

'Shall we take our drinks outside?' She felt the need for fresh air. 'It's stopped raining.'

He looked at her uncertainly. 'If you're sure? It might start up again.'

'Who cares?' She flung open her French doors in a more dramatic way than she'd intended – 'Here' – and handed him a soft red blanket while she wrapped another about her shoulders.

He shook his head. 'Not for me. I'm fine. Got me own internal central heating.' This snagged on Polly, as yes, she knew that. She loved to cuddle up to him, warming her cold feet on his legs.

Spike joined her on the balcony as a cold wind blew across, causing her to pull her blanket tighter around her. 'Careful you don't catch your death now,' he said, placing his arm about her shoulder and handing her the cigarette he'd rolled for her, then reaching up for his own, tucked behind his ear.

The two lovers leant on the rail, smoking their cigarettes as they gazed into an uncertain night, while at the bottom of the yard a seagull – otherworldly in its black and grey – flew across their line of vision like some ghost bird.

'I love it here,' Polly said, as she crushed her cigarette stub into the ashtray and half turned towards him. He continued to stare into the dark.

'I know you love it.'

'It's book club next week,' she began to prattle. 'Of course,

Mel's read the book, but I don't know… I just couldn't get into it. It was *The Time Traveler's Wife*. I should have watched the DVD instead.'

'What's it about?' He stood up straight.

'Oh, nothing much,' she said, not wanting to tell that it was about a couple whose love transcended time… 'We're pretty busy at the shop right now. You know, what with the run-up to Halloween. I got in tons of those little devil's horns and pitchforks, that kind of thing.'

'Yeah. Halloween parties,' he said distractedly.

Down below on the deck of a moored boat, all a-sparkle with its own multi-coloured fairy lights, a couple came together for a kiss. Polly wondered how they were doing. And now Spike was staring down at her, his eyes as round and dark as a moon in negative. Without a word, she rose to go inside, leaving him to follow behind.

'What's wrong, Polly? Will you not tell me what it is?'

She had no idea she was going to be angry until she faced him, eyes flashing so that he stepped back as if she were giving off sparks. 'Don't be so bloody dense. What's wrong is this! All this! Our last night together and all we can do is exchange small talk!'

'What would you have us talk about, Polly?'

She just stared, thinking how bloody unfair. She didn't trust herself to say anything. She'd already ruined their last evening with her outburst.

'I thought,' he was saying slowly and deliberately, 'that we could have a pleasant meal. Share some time together, and instead you're angry.'

Of course she was angry. But instead of letting rip again, she felt herself deflate like a punctured balloon. Eventually, her voice barely above a whisper, she said, 'I don't know how to deal with this. I hate goodbyes at the best of times.'

'Me too. I feel the same.'

Then before she could stop herself, she added, 'We don't have to say goodbye, not if we don't want to. Look. Hear me out. If I don't say this, I might regret it for the rest of my life.' She took a deep breath. 'You could stay. Seriously. You could not go to Australia.' She gabbled on before her thinking brain had time to catch up. 'I know I'm rubbish at relationships, but… if you stay… well… Spike, please don't go.'

She didn't know who was more surprised at her outburst, her or Spike. Talk about begging. Pathetic idiot. For one horrible moment, she thought she might throw herself on him; she had a full vision of herself holding onto his legs as he endeavoured to leave.

Instead, he had an amused look on his face. 'Truth is, Poll,' he was saying, 'I've been thinking about this myself. All day. No, longer than today, in fact. And I think I've come up with the perfect solution.' He took both her hands in his. 'Why don't you come away to Australia with me?'

'What?' She moved away from him, at a loss as to what to say, so she placed their steaks under the hot grill. It was all she could think of to do.

'Don't bother with that,' he said, coming up behind her. 'You've been fidgeting about all evening.'

'I must start cooking the steaks.' Suddenly that had become vitally important. 'The oven chips are nearly done.'

'Polly. Did you not hear what I just said to you?' He turned her to face him. 'I asked you to come away with me. To Australia?'

'What?'

'Will you stop saying What?' He was full-on grinning at her. 'Darling Polly,' he said, grabbing hold of her hands as if scared they might fly away, 'come away with me. Be spontaneous. You could pack a few bags, buy an airline ticket, and we could meet up in London. I'll be there a few days with Elspeth, that's all.

And then we could fly off to Australia, together. What do you say?'

She stared as if he'd asked her to chop her leg off. 'You have got to be kidding, Spike,' she finally said, removing her hands from his.

'But why? Life's for grabbing, Polly. Come with me? We could see how things go…'

'See how things go?' She moved to stand by the sink. 'Are you mad?'

He made no move towards her. 'No, I'm not mad. If anything, I just came to my senses. We get on grand now, don't we? I can't think of anyone else I'd rather go with, we could—'

'You want a travelling companion, is that it? And you couldn't find anyone else you get on better with? Is that what you're saying?'

'Don't be so daft. Of course that's not what I'm saying. You're getting this all wrong.'

But her colour was up – face red, hair dishevelled, like some warrior queen about to lead her troops into battle. 'Getting this wrong, am I? I'm sorry I made a fool of myself asking you to stay. After all, we only agreed on a bit of fun, didn't we? That was the deal. I see – of course I do – that you have to go. It was silly of me to think you might stay. But there's no reason on earth for you to feel obliged to ask me to come with you. As some sort of consolation prize!'

His voice was steady. 'I don't feel obliged, Polly. I want you to come.'

She felt queasy again, like her stomach had gone moonlighting on a big dipper. *Damn this bug.* She took a deep breath. 'Whether you do or not makes no odds to me. I can't possibly drop everything. Leave my friends, my house, my shop, and travel to the other side of the world… because… because of some pie-in-the-sky plan of yours! Much as I love you…'

'So you love me now, do ya?' Doing that half-grin of his – which was starting to wear rather thin now. The way he wheeled out his Irish charm, as if a touch of blarney could solve everything. 'Then why not come away with me? Don't you know, Poll,' his voice low and intense, 'you're imprinted on me like… like that little monkey fella with his furry mother substitute.'

'You're saying you want a mother, now? Is that it?'

'Don't be such an eejit.' He moved towards her. 'You're dead sexy when you're cross.'

But she was having none of it. *Good God*, she thought. *This can't be straightened out with a kiss and a cuddle.* She sidestepped him, determined not to be swayed.

'We're good together, Polly. You know that.'

'Spike… look… come on. We don't even know each other. Not really…'

'We could rectify that. Wouldn't it be great if you came along? Give ourselves more time to get to know each other. If you wanted to.' He paused. 'I know I do.'

She couldn't believe what she was hearing. 'That's not enough for me. It's not what I want. To go off gallivanting around the world!'

'What do you want, then? Marriage? Is that what this is all about?'

'Marriage? I wouldn't marry you. I don't want to marry anyone. That's just plain nuts!' She stopped, her heart pounding away.

When he next spoke, it was so quiet she was forced to lean in to hear him. 'You know I can't stay, Polly. It's too good a chance to miss.'

He was standing so close she was sure he must be able to hear her heart hammering away at her chest.

'I know.' There was nothing left to say.

'Ah,' he said, a half-smile dimpling his cheek, his gesture

open-handed. 'But aren't we a right pair of eejits?' He let his hands drop by his side. 'Our timing is all wrong, that's the top and bottom of it.'

'If I were to go with you, or you were to stay with me, then there'd be no hope for us...'

His eyes contained much sorrow, but she didn't notice and carried on regardless.

'...whichever way, one of us would end up resenting the other. Wouldn't we?'

'Yes,' he said, his voice devoid of its dancing laugh. 'We would at that. Aren't you the wise one.'

He collected his jacket from the back of the chair.

'You're not leaving now, are you?' She couldn't bear that he was going to leave. She grabbed hold of his arm. 'Tell me we can keep in touch, yeah? Skype, email, Facebook, carrier pigeon?' She attempted a smile, but his face was grim.

'I doubt that would be a good idea,' he said, shrugging on his jacket. 'I think it's probably best we make a clean break of things.'

'Can't we at least stay friends?' She thought she might vomit. Right there on the floor.

'Friends? I don't think so,' he said, with a finality that echoed around her kitchen and hallway. He was heading for the door when – to her later shame – she grabbed his arm once more.

'Please, Spike. It doesn't have to end like this.'

'I think I'd better leave right now,' was his answer.

She stared, appalled that he was leaving to the title of a Will Young song!

She rushed after him to the front door, where he planted a kiss on the top of her head. 'Bye, Polly.'

Helpless, she watched him go. *Spike!* she wanted to call out, but it got strangled in her throat. EEK EEK EEK EEK. Behind her the smoke alarm – from their now burning forgotten steaks – was screaming at them both.

*

That night, when she finally drifted off to sleep, she dreamt of a small Polly looking out of her bedroom window. There was a path leading away from her house to a green gate, which creaked back and forth on its hinges. Thick mist swirled in an early-morning light, before the sun had climbed high enough to burn it off. And there, just beyond the gate, someone turned to look up at Polly in her window. Someone turned and looked up. But Polly couldn't see their face.

5

At first, when Spike left for Australia, she would rush home from work to check whether he might have changed his mind and sent her a card, a message on her ansaphone, an email, anything. But as each day passed, there was nothing. Finally, she sent him a "Hi, how are you?" type of email – which bounced straight back with a message stating the address was no longer valid. She tried a text. Number discontinued. In the end, she called Elspeth. They had an awkward conversation where Elspeth informed her… that Yes, Spike had arrived safely in Australia, and that No, she couldn't give Polly his phone number, but she'd let him know that she'd called.

As weeks crawled by, she tried to stay chipper, even though she felt as if someone had shoved a large fist deep inside her solar plexus, grabbed a bloody handful, twisted, and then ripped it out. Like Magua from *The Last of the Mohicans*, she might have told someone. But didn't. So determined was she to appear chirpy and to hide her shame. She knew she wasn't fooling Mel, but at least Mel had the sense not to let on.

The Trouble With Love

When not at work, she'd mope around her house – watching reality television and writing poetry. Really bad poetry involving sea journeys. (*Why sea and not planes? Makes no sense.*) She read sad books; and developed a fascination for eels after reading about their plight online. She signed an online petition against the Severn Barrage Scheme – a proposed concrete monstrosity for harnessing the biggest tides in the UK, but which would have the detrimental effect of blocking the path of the returning eels. It made her cry; their determination to find their way home. She cried at soppy films on the telly. At animal rescue shows, and she couldn't bear to watch the news.

Neither Donna – her assistant at the shop – nor Mel had ever seen her like this. They each kept a watchful eye on her. 'Wanna come downtown with me and the girls tonight?' tried Donna.

'Fancy coming to the Watershed? Catch a movie? Cary Grant season's on,' tried Mel.

Then came the morning when a postcard finally arrived on her doormat; landing, as all postcards do, picture-side up. She bent to collect it, knowing with a miserable sixth sense just who it was from and what was to come. The picture displayed an impossibly blue sky over Sydney Harbour. Her heart flapped about like a newly landed fish as she turned it over and read:

Dear Polly, I'm sorry it had to end the way it did. At the risk of sounding like a right eejit – I want you to know that what we had was like a perfect painting. And you wouldn't want to keep returning to a perfect painting to give it a touch-up every now and then, would you? For fear you'd spoilt it. Do you see? What I need to say, and what I hope you will understand, is – please don't try and contact me again. It's for the best. Spike x

She tore the card in two. That was that then. A kiss-off postcard. Well, he'd made his position crystal clear and she was damned if she was going to cry. 'Fine,' she announced to herself. 'Fuck him.'

But deep down she didn't feel that way at all. Deep down in those secret places, she felt ripped. Cut. Cast adrift. And yes, abandoned, with a hurt she'd not felt since she'd realised her mother was no longer coming home. Not ever. It was all she could do to not drop to her knees and keen like the Cornish fisherwives of drowned men.

*

Polly was right off her food. She couldn't even stomach Jammie Dodgers. She would retch – even vomit – at the smell of coffee, strong perfume, or for no particular reason at all. At first, she put it down to Spike's leaving.

'Cheer up,' Mel said on the day when Polly finally realised she wasn't only nauseous from a broken heart.

Her friend had popped round for a girlie night in – just the two of them – and was emptying a whole bumper packet of Kettle crisps into a bowl. Polly had her gimlet eye on them, sure she was about to hurl any moment at their disgusting oily-crispy stench.

'With any luck, he's been kidnapped by Somali pirates,' Mel said.

Polly burst into tears. Big ploppy ones. In between the sobbing, the hiccupping and the nose-running, she nodded at Cap'n Jack, who now resided in her sitting room – all tall and handsome. 'You shouldn't d-diss pirates...' She reached forward for a handful of tissues from the box.

Mel came in for a hug, but she waved her away. 'I'm fine.'

'Honestly, I could kill him.' Mel flopped backwards on the sofa, regarding her friend as Polly's sobs calmed to sniffles.

'See? Better.' Polly lifted her head, eyes all blurry and mascara-smudged. Then, before she knew it, she was thrusting her hand in front of her mouth, up on her feet with a 'S'cuse me,' and dashing off to the kitchen where she vomited into the sink, bile burning the back of her throat.

'You being sick in there?' called Mel.

'It's all right. I'm fine. Put that DVD on, will you, and I'll be with you in a minute.' *Bloody bug.*

She leant on the draining board to catch her breath as she thought of how Christmas was fast approaching, and how she wished she could curl up into a ball and hibernate the winter away. But it was the busiest time of year for any shop owner. Christmas with all its jolliness and ho-ho-hos. Donna acting as skittish as if she were one of Santa's reindeer, prattling on about how she and Jase (her latest boyfriend) were going to go away – 'For a proper dirty weekend, mind. Four-poster bed, Christmas tree, the lot!' Polly had put on a brave face, pretending she was well and truly over Spike. 'Sorry,' Donna said, but she'd assured her all was fine and hunky-dory. Kidding no one, of course.

Normally she loved Christmas – but this year, it was doing her head in. She couldn't face Christmas Day at Suze and Brian's in Devon. Her dad had invited her over to his, as well. No way, José.

The only way out was for her to pretend to each that she was going to the other's (she wouldn't be found out as Suze and Jeff weren't on speaking terms), and then she could shut out the world. Just her, some ready-made meals and crap telly.

Polly wiped her mouth with a few sheets of kitchen roll and returned to the sitting room. Lately her stomach had become all bloated from some wheat allergy or something – lactose? Maybe she had irritable bowel syndrome. She'd stopped taking the pill (what was the point?) and her periods hadn't settled down yet – but that was to be expected. She'd had some spotting, that was all. And her boobs were sore – which must be down to changes in hormones. Hardly worth bothering the doctor with. He'd only say it was stress. Stress? She thought of the horrible humiliation of her friends asking whether she'd heard from Spike and how, in the end, they'd stopped asking altogether. She still wasn't sure which was worse: the asking or the stopping.

As she entered the room, her friend looked up from where she'd been fiddling with the television and DVD player. 'Polly? You're not – you know?'

'What?'

'All this throwing up.' Mel rose to her feet. 'Bloody hell, Poll. You don't think you're pregnant, do you?'

'Don't be stupid,' she answered. 'I can't be.' And they both stared at each other.

On the day that baby Rowan arrived, Polly at first thought her stomach cramps were caused by a bad curry, because she wasn't due for another three weeks. She'd been up and down all night, wondering whether or not to wake Mel and insist she call a doctor. Now, a little after 04.00 am, she'd taken two ibuprofen tablets, but, if anything, the pains were getting worse. Weird pains, coming in – whooooah – waves.

Slowly she entered her spare bedroom and shook her friend awake.

'What? What!' Mel sat bolt upright, rubbing her eyes. 'Where's the fire?'

'I think I need a doctor,' said Polly.

Five minutes later, a dressed Mel had joined her in the kitchen, where she was making a pot of tea. 'Bloody hell, Polly. You look dreadful.'

'Thanks.'

'Hadn't you better change out of your nightie?' (Giant T-shirt, more like!)

'After I've had a cuppa.'

Mel had stayed over following their girls' night in with wine (sparkling water for Polly), curry and a DVD of *Mamma Mia*. What a revelation Meryl Streep had been, thought Polly, who now loved her. Once Meryl did that mid-air split-jump in the middle of singing Abba's 'Dancing Queen', she was a converted fan. Priceless.

'So,' said Mel, as she stretched and yawned, rubbing at her forehead and dishevelling her short blonde hair. 'What's up?'

'It's just…' Polly gripped the side of the table. 'Oh no. Nnnnnnnuhhh.' She looked up at Mel. Scared. 'What the fuck did they put in that jalfrezi?'

'It can't be that. I had it too, remember? And I'm just fine.' She began to rub her friend's back, low down. 'Does that help?'

'Noooo. Nnnnnhhhhhhh. Oh bugger,' as another wave hit. She doubled over, one hand on the table, the other on her bent leg.

'You sure it's not the baby?' said Mel.

'No, it can't be. I'm only thirty-seven weeks. Nnnnnnnnnnnhhhhh. Oh shit!'

Followed by a Splat!

Then a 'What???'

And a Gush.

They both stared in disbelief at the big flop of fluid splattered on Polly's quarry tiles. From between her legs.

Polly stared. Bloody hell. 'What's that? Have I just weed myself?'

They both peered more closely at the watery fluid, which appeared to be tinged with something. Was that blood? It was definitely not wee, and it smelled sort of animal.

First, Polly looked at Mel, then Mel looked at Polly, then they both said, 'Oh fuck.'

'I'll get your overnight bag.' Mel sprang into action. 'Just as well I insisted you pack one early, wasn't it?'

Polly would have thrown her a yeah-no-shit Sherlock look, but right at that particular moment she was experiencing the urge to bear down.

*

'Blimey,' said Mel. 'She looks just like ET.'

Polly couldn't care less. As far as she was concerned, her baby was the most beautifullest baby in the whole wide world. Even at three weeks early, she was the wriggliest, squiggliest baby on the ward. But Polly didn't care. High on hormones and love.

'She's gorgeous,' cooed Daisy, Polly's friend and close neighbour.

'You think all babies are,' said Mel. 'Her face doesn't look so squished and angry today.'

'Honestly, Mel. All babies look like that. Now, give me the gory details,' said Daisy, who'd given birth to her own daughter Morwenna just twelve days before, and was at the eager-to-share stage.

'You should have seen it!' said Mel. 'Like a bloody horror movie!'

'Never mind all that,' said Suze, who'd claimed the chair by the side of Polly's hospital bed. Suze oozed elegance and glamour from her carefully coiffed-within-an-inch-of-its-life pixie-short hair to her painted toes in designer sandals. She was as thin as a whippet, and proud of it too. When Polly was young, one of her mother's favourite tricks was to breathe in hard so she could then reach both hands up and under her ribcage. Which just looked wrong, Polly thought, wondering why on earth she should be thinking of that now.

'What are you going to call her?' Suze was saying. 'How about Poppy? Poppy's a lovely name...'

'Poppy?' said Mel, turning to Suze with an exasperated look. 'Are you mental! You can't have a Polly and a Poppy.'

'I do wish I'd called Polly Poppy now. What do you think she should call the baby, Brian?'

'Is up to Poll, Suze. She's the one to decide.' He was leaning his arm on the back of Suze's chair, his bulk taking up more than his fair share of room.

'How about Blossom?' continued Suze.

'Blossom?'

But Polly had zoned out, as her nearest and dearest continued to squabble until the nurse came and shooed them away, leaving Polly exactly where she wanted to be, in her own little bubble of just her and the baby. Her baby. She'd done it all alone. Without Spike. 'See? We don't need men, do we, baby?' She kissed her daughter's tiny head, still with its cradle cap and faint animal smell. 'Rowan,' she whispered to her baby, who stared up into her face with big button eyes. 'Rowan. Welcome to the world, baby.'

Polly was chauffeured home in Brian's roomy car with the comfy leather seats, and ushered into her house, where a "Welcome Home Polly & Baby Rowan" banner adorned her kitchen, and where her friends and family were gathered around for much oohing and aahhing. Soon Polly made her way upstairs to where Brian or Suze had erected a cot in the spare room and a Moses basket on a stand next to Polly's bed. They'd also installed a changing cupboard, changing mat, bouncy chairs x two, mobiles, mounds of folded-up baby clothes, nappies; piles and piles of stuff. She was too tired to do anything other than go straight to bed.

But there were unforeseen complications. Polly haemorrhaged and was rushed back to hospital, taking Rowan with her as she'd mild jaundice and couldn't latch onto the breast properly so cried and cried.

Her mum took the opportunity to swoop in and buy Polly's house outright, as well as a shop in the arcade in Clifton Village, complete with a flat upstairs. All without consulting her. 'Better to have some of your inheritance now than when I'm dead and buried,' she'd insisted. 'You need financial security now you're a mum.' Polly had been too weak to resist.

Back home again, and she was sitting up in bed, like a miser protecting a bag of gold, as she held onto Rowan in an uncertain world, where all had changed and people tiptoed around her.

Her father, who'd arrived with wife Gillian in tow – much like the bad fairy to the ball – puffed himself up (how strange, she thought, how it had taken a baby to bring out the protective father in him) as he said, 'Don't you think you ought to tell Spike?'

For that one single moment, everything stopped, and then jumped on again as Suze demanded, 'Why? He was the one who buggered off.' She glanced across at her daughter. 'I know it's all rather scary. Being a Mum…' (*How would* you *know?* Polly could have quite easily said.) '…but, well, you're not alone, darling,' continued Suze. 'We're all here for you, aren't we?' as she turned to the gathering of Mel, Polly's dad, Gillian and Daisy, who were all grinning away and nodding their heads.

'I'm tired,' said Polly. 'So very tired.'

'C'mon, let's let her get some sleep,' said Daisy, passing her own peacefully slumbering baby, Morwenna, to Suze to hold. 'Here,' she said to Polly. 'Let me take Rowan for you so you can sleep.'

But on reaching out her arms, Polly insisted 'No!' with a fierceness that surprised them all, making them back off. 'I know you're trying to help, but baby stays with me.'

The Trouble With Love

And so they placed little Rowan in the Moses basket right next to Polly, said they'd pop back later and quietly closed the bedroom door behind them.

'Just you and me, kid,' said Polly, as she gazed down at her sleeping child, wondering if you could burst from love, as she took in each and every soft feature of her baby's face, bending across to smell her intoxicating baby smell and to marvel at how, even at this stage, she had the look of her father.

Satisfied that her child was sleeping, Polly closed her own eyes and was soon in a land where the bong tree grows, back on board a pea-green boat, where the rise and fall of tides rocked her to sleep in its arms.

PART TWO
Spring Tide

6

Three Years and Five Months After Spike Left...

They'd all had a pub lunch at the Severn Inn, and it was late afternoon. Overhead, the sun proved lukewarm, as if it was done with being high enough to shine down on the pub garden below, which stretched all the way down to the riverbank. The last few days had seen much rain, and the grass had sprung to life in its rich green emperor's clothes. It was still wet underfoot, even though it hadn't rained that day.

The river was swollen and brown with silt, and a particularly high spring tide was expected. All around its banks small groups gathered here and there, ready to watch the next batch of surfers catch the Severn Bore as it swept upriver from the Bristol Channel.

'Hurry up, slow coaches,' called Polly, as behind her came Mel and Rowan – Rowan haven shaken off Mel's hand to run full-toddler pelt down the small incline, her blonde ringlets streaming out behind her like an ad agency's dream casting –

cute, blonde and wearing a bright colourful Oilily dress bursting with flowers, rainbows and butterflies. Polly watched as if in slow motion as her little chubby legs did not quite keep up with her body, and she took a tumble forward. Whoops. Mel, charging up behind the little girl, scooped her into her arms. And Rowan was giggling away by the time they reached Polly's side.

'Cheeky little monkey, this one,' laughed Mel, as she handed her charge over to Polly, who hugged and then lowered her daughter to the ground.

'Blimey, what have you been feeding her on? Concrete sandwiches?' said Mel. 'She weighs a ton!' Mel's short blonde-streaked hair glinted away in the April sun, and Polly noticed how these days her friend seemed softer, a little rounder, and even had on a cheap jumper with a big red heart right smack-bang in the middle (although her cropped jeans were obviously expensive).

'Bamma!' said Rowan, pointing in the direction of Suze, who was striding away from the riverside to stand next to Brian, who was scanning the river, watching for the Bore. Brian was wearing a wetsuit, and for the life of her, Polly couldn't stop thinking that he looked like a giant black pudding on legs.

'Suze!' she called out to her mother. 'Hang on a tick!' But her mother just waved, her attention being on peering over the hedge into an adjoining field. 'We'd better go join them,' said Polly. Mel didn't hear as she was too busy waving back up towards the pub, back to where her loved one was strolling down to greet them. Fen. Good-looking in a Sharleen Spiteri rock chick kind of way, dressed in black from top to toe. Black leather biker jacket, black T-shirt, black skinny jeans, black R. Soles snakeskin boots and jet-black dyed hair. Fen, the love of Mel's life, so she'd told Polly. Fen, a thirty-one-year-old woman. Because sometime last year (when exactly, Polly couldn't quite remember), Mel had fallen in love and gone to bat for the other side, or – as Polly had so charmingly put it – 'Actually turned lezzer!' Not that Polly was altogether surprised, when she had time to gather her thoughts and think about it.

Fen arrived, delivering her trademark smile, which resembled a snarl. 'Where's this Severn Bore, then?' She slung a proprietorial arm around Mel's shoulder.

'Just here,' said Mel, indicating to Polly.

'Oh ha bloody ha,' said Polly, trying not to mind a joke which at one time Mel would have made, with her, about somebody else.

Rowan tugged at her mother's hand, trying to pull her along. 'Bamma! Bian!' she was shouting, and Polly allowed herself to be toddler-dragged along the bank to stand next to where Suze and Brian were on tiptoe, trying to see into the adjoining field. Mel and Fen followed at a more sedate pace, still entwined in each other.

'What *are* you looking at?' Polly said to her mother.

'Shh. They're about to start filming.' Suze gestured towards a gap in the hedge, through which they could see that there on the grassy riverbank a cooking station had been set up, comprising a table, burner and wok. A small film crew gathered around a man dressed in expensive casual gear – Barbour jacket, cord trousers, brown brogues and a Jack Wills-type shirt. Polly recognised him.

So did Fen. 'Isn't that Rory McCloud? That Scottish chef who thinks he's the new Keith Floyd?' she whispered loudly to Mel.

'Ha! He wishes – in his dreams!' said Suze. 'I used to know Keith – back in the day. And he was pure genius. A total one-off. But, shh, if you hang on here, I'll see if we can get a closer look.'

She walked over to have a word with the crew, and with Rory. There was some nodding and pointing and eventually she beckoned them over. *Just in time*, thought Polly, who was feeling rather uncomfortable and not quite knowing where to look. Because Brian stood hands on hips, proud in his black wetsuit that clearly showed how well endowed he was. Hard to miss, or the fact that it looked like he had a stuffed rugby sock down there.

He grinned at her as she blushed. 'Oi. You checkin' aht my lunch box, cheeky?'

'Sorry, sorry,' she mumbled.

'Honestly, darling,' said Suze, returning to Brian's side. 'Stop acting like you've never seen a big cock before.' She snuggled up to Brian in that kittenish way of hers.

'Mind yerself, Suze. You're embarrassing the girl.'

'Stuff and nonsense. Come along, darling.'

And they wandered off, Brian grinning away like the Honey Monster.

'There's big, and there's plain showing off,' Mel whispered delightedly in Polly's ear.

'She always like that?' said Fen, nodding Suze's way. 'Your mother?'

''Fraid so,' said Mel.

But Polly said nothing, because it was one thing to mildly slag off her mother to Mel, but quite another to have Fen join in, and quite frankly, she didn't much care for it.

As ever, Suze was dressed in stylish casual gear with her honey blonde hair cut in a Victoria Beckham sharp cut. It suited her. (She even wore some of VB's creations every now and then.)

'Hang on a minute, Mum, wait for me and Rowan.'

Suze turned, seeming both pleased and surprised as she waited for daughter and granddaughter to catch them up.

'Tell you what,' said Suze, giving everyone a most impish look, 'let's see what they're up to further up the field, shall we?'

'Suze?' warned Brian.

'I don't know what you mean,' she said. 'Besides, it'll be good for me to check out the competition. Right, we'd better get a move on… it's all about to kick off.'

The Trouble With Love

Which, at the time, Polly thought a strange thing to say – and later she'd wonder if Suze had been given the nod by someone who knew what was to happen.

'His cooking's not a patch on yours, babe,' said Brian.

They filed into the field, taking their positions close enough so they could see the cooking action, but not so close that they interfered with filming. Brian lowered his voice. 'That Rory geezer's a right ponce.'

Polly could swear the cameraman smiled at this. And a very cute cameraman too, she noticed. Nice and tall – blond hair. (She didn't normally go for blonds but could make an exception in his case.) Then she noticed that he seemed to have his camera fixed on her. Checking behind to see if he was filming someone else – which he wasn't – she blushed. (*Idiot.*) Lowering his camera, he gave her the mildest of smirks before turning away, leaving her unsure whether or not he'd been checking her out.

'Sorry, mate,' said Brian, as he shifted out of the way to allow a man sporting anorak and large Wellington boots to stride past and hand a bucket to Rory McCloud. The chef promptly peered inside, gave the thumbs-up then proceeded to plonk a pan on the hob, before whacking up the heat. Clearly, he was about to cook something – that something being whatever was in the bucket.

Next to Polly, little Rowan was on tippy toes straining to get a better look, so Brian reached down to lift her up onto his shoulders, and was rewarded by her slapping him about the side of his face, much to his delight.

'Careful,' Polly said to her daughter. 'Don't hurt Brian.'

'Bian!' she declared, now bumping him on the top of his bald head.

'Dontcha worry, sweetheart,' he said, beaming with delight. 'I got a tight hold of our little twinkle here.'

One of the filming crew called out, 'And action!' and Rory began his spiel.

'Here we are on the banks of the glorious River Severn... blah blah blah... wee local delicacy... blah blah... time-honoured tradition... blah blah... what better way to cook them than here outdoors... blah blah... Severn Bore... blah blah.'

Polly wasn't paying much attention when, out of the corner of her eye, she spotted a small group break away from those lining the riverbank and begin to edge their way across to Rory's cooking station.

She turned her attention back to the chef. 'You have to be quick... make sure the oil is hot. Sizzling hot...' He bent down to scoop a handful of whatever was in the bucket. 'Cost a fortune on the Japanese market...' and next threw the whatevers into the hot pan, where they hissed and jumped about.

'Look! Dancing bibbons! Dancing bibbons!' Rowan was shouting. At first, Polly thought she was shouting Dancing gibbons – but it was dancing ribbons! Then all hell broke loose as three women tore screeching across like banshees, one wielding a placard – "Save the Eels" – while their ringleader dashed the pan off the hob. Then, before Rory or any of the crew could stop her, she chucked it into the river, from where squabbling seagulls swooped to claim their half-cooked prize.

'Wahay! Yay!' They cheered and danced.

'You stupid fuckin' women!' Rory McCloud screamed. He'd gone puce and Polly hoped for his sake this wouldn't make its way onto YouTube. (Fat chance of that not happening, as members of the public were gathered around, mobile phones aloft.) 'Those fuckin' elvers cost me a fuckin' fortune! Yah feckin' cunts!' Rory was apoplectic.

'Murderer!' one woman screamed, as she was being manhandled away.

'Cooking them alive! Disgusting brute!' shouted another.

The Trouble With Love

Only then did it dawn on Polly that McCloud hadn't been frying a new kind of ribboned pasta but instead frying baby eels, which were still alive. And that was why the poor things had been jumping around like mad – they'd been slung *alive* into boiling hot fat! Ugh. Alive! What an appalling bastard! She felt like walloping him herself. And applauding the ringleader who'd managed to sidestep Rory's minders and, brandishing her placard at him, catch him in the corner of his eye, causing him to bellow with pain, shouting that he'd fuckin' kill her!

'Who knew cooking could be such fun!' said Fen.

'Serves him right!' said Suze, unable to hide that big smirk on her face. 'That'll not be good for Rory McCloud's reputation, will it?'

'Oh, you are wicked, Suze,' said Mel. 'You knew all along, didn't you?'

There came a shout from the side of the river with a 'Here it comes!' – and attention switched to downstream where, in the distance, and coming along at quite a lick, could be seen a large wash swooshing out and up over the land as it swept towards the sea. The Severn Bore was coming!

'Here, take little twinkle!' Brian handed Rowan to Polly, gave Suze a swift kiss on the lips then hurried down to the river's edge where surfers were already in the water, jostling for position, trying to secure the best place in the river to catch the large swell.

'Looks like I'm on!' Brian called back over his shoulder as he waded out with his surfboard, just in time to catch the wave.

'Go, Brian!' They cheered as he managed to clamber to his feet, Rowan jumping up and down on the spot, clapping away and enjoying the excitement, even though she had no idea what was going on. Polly watched Suze proudly cheer on Brian then turned to her left to say something to Mel… and stopped. Her friend had her head resting on Fen's shoulder, very much the couple. *Great. Everybody coupled up but me.*

She sensed someone's eyes on her and, looking up, saw that the camera guy was watching her and not the Bore. He gave her a slow and deliberate smile, before someone from his crew called out to him and, giving a shrug as if in apology, he moved off. But not before she felt a flutter, deep down in her tummy. *Ah hello*, she thought, *mojo not totally dormant, then*. The others began to walk a way up the river, following Brian's progress. She made to join them, a decided spring in her step.

Much later, back at Polly's house, all the others were ganging up on her. 'Isn't it about time you started dating again?' said Suze.

'Whatcha waiting for?' said Brian.

'Three years is long enough,' said Suze.

'I agree,' declared Mel. 'And I know just the thing for it. You leave this to me.'

'What?'

Polly knew when she'd been done up like a kipper.

7

The upside of having your best friend to stay is that she can provide you with an extra pair of hands. The downside is that she is on hand to talk you into doing something you might otherwise not want to do. Like speed dating. This being "the thing" that Mel had arranged for Polly. That and the small thing of being filmed by Daisy's friend Vanessa – and she wasn't exactly thrilled. Ah well, nothing ventured…

'Mel? Mel! Have you seen my other shoe?' Polly dashed into the kitchen, waving aloft a *single* black strappy sandal and trying to do up the back of a green silk dress which clashed beautifully with the kind of red hair any pre-Raphaelite artist's model – posing for a painting of, say, *The Lady of Shalott* – might well have been proud of.

'Hang on, let me give you a hand,' said Mel, zipping her up.

'I could just not go,' Polly said, as she plonked herself on a chair in front of Mel, who'd returned to coaxing Rowan into eating an eggy soldier. But she was having none of it. Instead, she beamed at her mother – egg solidifying on her chin. Hard to resist! 'Hey, Ro Ro.' Polly set about tickling the tot under her arms.

'Oh great,' said Mel, putting down the spoon – as Rowan giggled and wriggled. 'You're like a wriggly worm. A wriggly, squiggly, giggly worm.'

'Not a burm, Mummy. Ha hahaha eeeee.' As Rowan squirmed, Polly continued to tickle away. Just look at her. Ro Ro was as cute as cute could be. What with that little button nose and those strawberry blonde curls – a colour that Polly and Mel called blorange (it being somewhere between blonde and orange).

'Tears before bedtime,' warned Mel. 'You'll make her sick with all that tickling.' To which Rowan promptly obliged by coughing up Ribena all over her mother's arm.

'Whoopsie!'

'See?'

'All right, all right – know-all!' Polly wiped first her arm and then her child's face with a tea towel, then turned to Mel. 'Oh no,' she said, making a show of feeling Rowan's forehead. 'You don't think she's coming down with something, do you? Because if that's the case then I'd better not go...'

'Nice try,' said Mel, 'but you're going to this speed dating and that's final.' She gave Polly the kind of stare which brooked no argument, as she stood behind her friend, placing her hands on her shoulders. 'Besides, we promised Daisy's friend—'

'We? *You* promised her, more like!'

'Whatevs. Daisy has agreed, on your behalf, that you'll take part in this short film Vanessa Whassername is making about singles and dating. You never know, you might even have fun. Remember what that was? Fun?'

'I'm a responsible single mother, now...'

'If you say so.'

'I'm still not sure this is a good idea. Imagine the

embarrassment if I go and do something stupid – it'll all be on film.'

'Remember what your mother says? Any publicity is good publicity – for the shop! Not you – unless you're planning on selling yourself…'

'Ha ha.'

'And it's free publicity, Poll, right? Free. Not to be sniffed at.'

'Okay, okay. Just so long as I don't come across as a right saddo… I mean – speed dating!'

Polly lifted her daughter out of her highchair, breathing in her freshly bathed baby smell. Rowan radiated that post-bubble-bath thermal glow they get, right from the top of her head, all the way down her cute pyjamas – populated with Tigger, Piglet and Pooh Bear – and on to those fluffy Winnie the Pooh slippers of hers, Rowan being Number One fan of the inhabitants of Hundred Acre Wood.

'You still haven't said how I look?'

Her friend gave her an appraising stare. 'Very nice. Hmm… Except…' and she pointed down at Polly's feet. '…you might want to rethink those Ugg boots.' All three stared at Polly's sheepskin boots – worn down at the heels and with a hole in the right toe, through which poked a tuft of white fleece. 'Unless you're going for the look of some C-list celebrity off to the corner shop for milk and a wrap of cocaine.'

'I'll never be girl-about-town again.'

Mel gave her a – were you ever? – look, which she chose to ignore.

'Help me! I've looked everywhere.' She picked up the single sandal she'd brought into the kitchen with her. 'But I can't find the other soddin' shoe anywhere!'

'Tsk. Swearing.'

'Don't suppose you've seen it, have you?' She stared expectantly at her friend. For Mel was a finder of things. The sort of organised person who had all her CDs and books carefully catalogued in alphabetical –and sometimes subject – order. Mel's idea of fun was to clean out her kitchen cupboards. And who knew at all times where everything was. Whereas Polly was the sort who was forever losing things: keys, handbags, umbrellas, gloves – she lived in fear of leaving Rowan on the bus or outside a shop.

Mel was staying in Polly's spare room – an occurrence so frequent it was dubbed "Mel's Room". (And why not? She was more family than Polly's own.) Right now, she needed a bolthole/stayover place while a leak in her bathroom was being repaired. An event which Polly found hilarious seeing as Mel had discovered said leak on her return from a weekend's course on dousing – for hidden springs – in Glastonbury. (She'd been dabbling in alternative therapies since hooking up with girlfriend Fen, who was a fan.) 'Darling, it'll only be for a couple of weeks,' she'd assured Polly.

'I thought you'd move in with Fen.'

'Best not. Fen might take it as a sign that I'm ready for this whole "urge to merge" lesbian thing, if I do.'

It's a different world, thought Polly.

Her best friend's arrival had cheered Polly up no end. She'd been on a bit of a downer, weary of coping alone with work and a toddler. And the housework had been getting on top of her. Now, her home had never been so clean and marshalled into order since Mel arrived. She half expected her objects to jump to attention the second Mel entered a room.

Mel was now giving Rowan a wink, as if they were co-conspirators. 'Silly Mummy would forget her head if it wasn't screwed on, wouldn't she?'

'Mel? Shoe?'

'Silly Mummy,' said Rowan, clapping her hands.

'Okay.' Mel bent down to a level with hard-of-hearing

Rowan. 'Shall your fairy godmother wave her magic wand and find your Cinderella-mummy's glass slipper?'

Rowan's eyes grew big and round with expectation.

'Stop filling her head with ideas,' said Polly. 'Fairy godmother, indeed. Please, please tell me. Have you seen my shoe or not?'

'Here goes. Ta da!' Mel gestured as if waving a fairy wand. 'Your other sandal is over there, by the dresser.'

'Thanks, Mel. You are a real lifesaver!'

'You shall go to the ball, Cinders!' Bending down again to the little girl's height. 'Did you see my magic wand, Ro Ro?' She nodded enthusiastically.

'You really shouldn't fill her head with such stuff...' said Polly, kicking off her Uggs and hopping first on one leg then the other as she strapped on her sandals. 'I'm trying hard not to expose her to that whole Disney happy-ever-after world.'

'Oh, spoilsport. Couldn't we all do with a bit of romance and magic in our lives?'

Polly looked around. 'You've not seen my handbag as well, I suppose?'

Mel retrieved the bag from beneath the table. 'You should pay me, you know.'

'Ah, but crass payment would ruin the magic, wouldn't it? Because everyone knows that fairy godmothers perform spells out of the goodness of their hearts.'

'I should join a union.'

When Polly met Mel, it was love at first sight. Best Friends Forever. They'd clicked straight away.

'Wanna come round mine and watch *Doctor Who* videos?' was practically the first thing Mel said to Polly when she sat next to her on Polly's first day at Bishopston High School. Polly, being a big fan of *Doctor Who*, thought Mel was brilliant.

'Yeah, great,' she'd said.

'Jammie Dodger?'

Even better: 'Cool.'

'You're not a lezzer, are you?'

'No. Naff off.'

Which was funny, when you consider how things had turned out: what with Mel bumping into Fen in a pub on that fateful night of the Gay Pride march last year. Mel, caught up in the crowd on her way home from work, had ducked into the first likely place, where Fen – who'd popped in to use the loo – had approached her, chatted her up and – 'It was lust at first sight,' Mel had told her.

Polly was still trying to adjust. If she was totally honest with herself – which she did try to be – then she was a teensy bit jealous of Fen. Jealous that Fen was now – more often than not – Mel's first go-to person. And that used to be Polly's job. Everything changes when your best friend in the world takes up with a female instead of a male lover. No more girls against men. Polly hadn't quite got her head around the sexual politics of it, let alone how she felt inside. She didn't like not being wholly happy for Mel, and she was going to give it her best shot. Even though she didn't much care for Fen. There was something about her. Or perhaps she saw her through green-eyed monster spectacles. It was a right old muddle.

Now Rowan was jiggling enthusiastically up and down on the spot, executing her Tigger bounce and shouting, 'Rain has gone! Rain has gone!'

'Hang on a tick.' Polly smiled at Mel then, gathering her daughter into her arms, pressed Play on the CD player, and out loud came their favourite song: Johnny Nash singing his sunshine Caribbean lyrics.

'Bance, Mummy. Bance!' shouted Rowan, as Polly lowered her daughter to the ground from where she busted her little moves in the middle of their bright yellow kitchen, with Mel joining in. Rowan, the child that Polly and Spike had made. Not like made from Plasticine or anything. No. Made by accident, and much loved and wanted by Polly. Her beautiful Rowan, with the same smile and dimples as her father, making Polly's heart skip a beat each time she turned it on.

'Bance, Mummy. Bance.' And Polly joined in, with Rowan clapping her chubby hands, then holding on first to Mel, then onto Polly as she danced and twirled and delighted them both by singing how it was going to be a bright, sunny day.

As the song ended, Polly glanced up at the clock. 'Right. I need to pop to the loo after all that dancing.'

'You should have kept up those pelvic floor exercises,' Mel said. 'Hope you remembered to pack your Tena Lady pads.'

'Oh, ha bloody ha.'

'Okay. Now, are you sure I look okay?' Polly asked her friend.
'Yes!'

Bending down to give her daughter a goodnight kiss, Polly knew Mel was right and that moping around the house like a wet weekend was pathetic. Spike was never coming back. (Secretly, Polly was rather touched that her friends had arranged this night. Even though it was hardly dignified that she, Polly Park – queen of cool children's clothes – was going speed dating!)

'And you are absolutely sure that I should wear this dress? Or… I could try another one?'

'How many more times? You look fabulous. Don't you think so, Roly?' Mel gave the toddler a small nudge. 'Shall we send your mummy off to meet her Prince Charming?'

Polly forced a smile at them both. She could hardly bear to leave her daughter. Because the first time she set eyes on her Rowan, not only was it love at first sight, but everything changed forever and Polly's life became one full of sunshine, with just the merest light dabblings of rain.

8

As Polly arrived outside the entrance of Marco's, there was quite a kerfuffle, as a cluster of men and women stood on the harbourside chattering away in a most excited fashion. 'I wouldn't have come if I'd known – would you?' 'We're going to be filmed?' 'Oh, I don't think that's for me.' 'Filmed, you say? I'm off.' 'Me too.'

Polly wrapped her thin velvet coat tighter about her, the distinct chill in the air serving as a reminder that winter was not done with them yet. Casting about her, she realised she didn't have the foggiest idea what Vanessa even looked like.

'Ah, Polly. There you are,' announced a woman, disentangling herself from the throng.

Mid-forties – Polly guessed – dressed in jeans and denim jacket. (Ooh. Double denim, she thought, mentally sucking in her teeth. So not a good look.)

'I'm Vanessa, and this is Sam. Tonight's organiser.' She proceeded to pull forward a woman in a smart navy suit and polka dot blouse, complete with pussy bow tie.

Very Margaret Thatcher.

Sam shook Polly's hand, muttering a brief 'Hi' before returning to her chivvying up of the punters.

'You don't remember me, do you?' Vanessa said, giving Polly one of those apologetic grins so beloved of passive-aggressives everywhere. 'I met you once with Mel, at the Watershed.' Weird grin again. 'Yeah? No? You probably don't remember.'

Polly didn't. 'Sorry.' Because since becoming a mother, she was terribly forgetful and awful with names.

*

Once inside, Polly observed the combined powers of Vanessa and Sam as they managed to persuade roughly half of the potential speed daters to stay and sign a waiver. Some plain refused and scarpered. 'Probably married,' Vanessa stage whispered to Polly.

'We carefully vet our clients, I'll have you know…' Sam started, but Vanessa had taken charge, proceeding to herd people inside.

Polly felt trapped. *A whole chuffin' evening of this*, she thought, as she cast her eye over the upstairs bar of Marco's, and then remembered. She'd been here before – when it had a different name – to open mic nights of poetry readings and music. Sometimes a group of them, or just Polly and Mel, would come along for live gigs of local bands. She hadn't performed poetry for ages. If truth be told, she'd only dabbled in the first place. Still, it'd been fun while it lasted.

Looking about her, she took in the mocha-coloured walls of this new Marco's, with its art photographs of harbour scenes, and its small wooden tables. She wasn't convinced this revamp was an improvement on its dingy former life when being a bit of a dive had held its own charm. Still. Here she was. Changed venue, changed Polly. Speed dating. What would her friends have her do next? Cruise the internet?

Of course, she'd been here with Spike too. Back when. She sighed. Remembering the past didn't hurt quite as much as it once had... *C'mon, Poll. Enough already. Truly enough.* Determined to put a brave face on things, she pulled herself up to her full five feet seven and tried to mentally prepare for an evening of getting back in the saddle (as Suze had so charmingly put it).

'Come on, it's time to move on,' she'd said. 'All this moping about is plain ridiculous.'

She made her way over to the bar. Tonight would be a good night, and this speed dating malarkey was a positive choice for any single mum trying to find a date... Smiling away (as smiling is supposed to put you in a good mood – or so she'd heard), she told herself she must put her best foot forward, chin up, and spit spot. (Although why she was channelling Mary Poppins...)

She wandered idly over to stand by the window and wait for Vanessa to finish whatever arrangements she was making with Sam. With no particular thoughts, she gazed out of the window, her attention snagged by a swan, majestic on water slick black in the darkness. She watched its progress as it glided past an assortment of moored boats and cruisers, as if a toy pulled along by a piece of string. *I shall do my level best to be open*, she thought, as she turned back to face the room. *Who knows? I could meet someone, couldn't I? Stranger things happen at sea.*

Taking out her compact, she applied a dash of her new Starlet Red lipstick and then scooped up a glass of wine from the tray of a passing waiter. *Best stick to red*, she thought, as she fixed what she hoped was a welcoming smile on her face. *But – wait! Oh God, no. Is that...?* She ducked behind a pillar, because over there, next to Vanessa and looking far too hunky for his own good, was him... thingy... Dressed in tight jeans and white shirt combo, standing nonchalantly (as far as it was possible to be nonchalant with something as heavy as the camera he was carrying), was that good-looking blond cameraman from the Severn Bore shoot.

Okay, it's okay. Deep breaths.

She risked another peek around the pillar, but – drats – he'd seen her. And now he was coming across with Vanessa. Polly tried to check her reflection in the window, but it was useless. Giving her hair a quick zhuzh with her hands, she turned with what she hoped was a welcoming face, conveying just the right mix of cool but friendly. 'Hi,' she managed.

Cameraman pointed to his front teeth while Polly just stared in return. He tried again. What was he playing at?

'Lipstick,' he said. 'Front teeth.'

The penny dropped. 'Oh, oh.' Fumbling for her compact, she scrubbed her teeth with a tissue.

'Never mind all that,' said Vanessa, as she grabbed her arm. 'We have to get a move on before we get thrown out.' She lowered her voice. 'That Sam woman isn't happy about the recording.' She looked out over people's heads. 'Ah. I see that your seat's over there. Max?' Turning to camera guy. 'Can you manage with this lighting, or do we need to rig up more lights?'

'Sure, it'll be fine,' he said, grinning away at Polly with a look she considered hardly professional.

'What are you doing here?' she hissed at him as they moved off.

'My job,' he said, again with the amused face. 'Wouldn't have said you were the type to go for speed dating.'

'Ah. No, no, of course I'm not... but...'

'Oh, do hurry up, you two,' Vanessa frantically beckoning to Max.

'God, she's bossy,' whispered Polly. 'Who is she? Your mother?'

'Well, actually...'

'Oh God. No. She isn't, is she?'

He laughed – a good strong laugh. 'No, she's not... I couldn't resist teasing you. And your face! Whoops – watch out, here she comes. Best behaviour.' Giving her a "behave yourself" smirk.

Polly decided she might yet enjoy herself. She hadn't flirted this outrageously since – well, she wasn't going to think of since when.

Okey-dokey – here goes nothing, she thought, downing the rest of her red wine, to skip along behind Max, already feeling decidedly squiffy. (Not her fault. She couldn't help being a lightweight – she hardly ever went out for a good sesh, these days.)

Vanessa flapped around, ushering Polly into a seat at the table allocated to her, then informed her that Sam felt uncomfortable about Polly staying for the whole evening. 'So we're going to round up at least two men to film, okay? Before the going gets tough.' (A blast of the lyrics from "When the Going Gets Tough" played in her head.)

Great, she thought. *Next they'll be paying men to sit opposite me. Not terribly great for one's confidence.*

'It'll be fun, you'll see,' assured Vanessa. 'Don't you go worrying yourself. We'll do our level best to pick out some nice ones for you.'

'Gee, thanks.' But Polly's sarcasm was lost on Vanessa.

At their own individual tables sat well-turned-out women, all about Polly's age, while the men milled around before choosing who to sit with. It appeared to be with anyone but Polly. Oh dear. She wasn't terribly hopeful this was going to turn out okay. None of them appeared to be her type, being a motley crew of David Brents, spotty youths and spray-it-on-all-over-Lynx wearers. (*Don't be such a snob, Polly.*) She tried to sit straighter and appear inviting. Proceedings were about to start.

Organiser Sam took to the handkerchief-sized stage from where she delivered her welcome spiel. On and on she droned... 'Blah blah blah blah...' Polly sipped her wine – *Ugh*. She winced. *Could strip paint with this bilge.* Gamely she ventured another sip. *Mmm, tastes better the more you have?*

'...and so, after your allotted three minutes, the ladies will remain seated, I shall blow my whistle, and you men will move on to the next lovely lady. Yes?' The microphone gave out an ear-splitting squawk, so she tapped it. 'Testing, testing – one, two three... Good. Now, don't forget to fill in your scorecards at the end of each date.' Polly examined the card they'd been given; it had columns to enter each guy's name and then rate him: Date/ Maybe/ No Way. *Charming.* Inwardly she groaned.

'All of you, please take your seats.' Sam checked they had. 'Good. Off we go, then, and remember to have fun!'

Vanessa brought to Polly's table what appeared to be an old rocker, sporting grey pony tail, faded jeans with ironed-on-crease-down-the-middle, plus rhinestone-studded Rockabilly shirt straining over his beer belly. Camera guy started filming while Vanessa tried but failed to keep a discreet distance. Rocker guy – name of Wayne – was lapping up the chance to be filmed, while Vanessa raised her eyebrows at Polly as if to say *See? I got you a media type.* But Wayne showed no interest in Polly and offered her no chance to mention her performance poetry (which Vanessa had instructed her to do). Instead, he held forth on his band – The Fat Slappers – making a point of doing so directly to camera, as he announced that they did weddings and the odd '70s night at Minehead's Butlin's. 'Played with the Bay City Rollers last year,' he said. She feigned interest, trying to imagine how different it would be if, say, Damon Albarn had been sitting opposite her.

He liked poetry, didn't he?

Yes, she decided, they'd get on like a house on fire. She would tell him tales which he'd find oh so amusing. He'd give her the inside story of the whole Blur vs Oasis feud, and then he'd hold her gaze and say, *You're a performance poet, are you? How wonderful. You should keep it up, love.*

'Hello? Are you even listening to me?' said Wayne, while off to the side. Vanessa stared daggers at her.

'Hmm?'

'Brrillll!' went the whistle; signalling time was up. At which Wayne leant across to plant a kiss on her lips. She wasn't expecting that! Bloody nerve!

'Sorry,' he said, spreading his hands wide. 'But how could I resist?' He pointed at her as he backed away. 'You're one gorgeous chick. Hope we hook up later, babe.'

She gave him a polite yet (hopefully) non-committal smile, just in time to catch Max cameraman bestowing another of his amused smirks. *What? Oh no. I hope he doesn't think I encouraged that kiss!*

'This is your final swap, ladies and gents,' called out Sam. 'Better make it a good one.'

'Max, do be a darling and come in closer this time,' Vanessa said. 'It'd be good to get a few clean headshots.'

Polly couldn't help admiring those lovely big hands of his as they manipulated the camera… Mmm… But Vanessa cut across her reverie before it had the chance to get going. 'Okay, okay. This time, Polly, can we please get in that you're a performance poet – yeah?'

Her head was thumping. Paracetamol. A quick rummage in her handbag – et voilà! Reaching for a glass of water, she caught the eye of the woman at the next table. She was attractive in a

The Trouble With Love

Sarah Parish from Mistresses kind of way. 'Bit grim' the woman part mouthed, part whispered, and Polly nodded in agreement.

Her eye was then caught by a group of four or five who'd escaped outside to the small roof terrace for a fag break. Huddled against the cold, they were throwing their heads back and blowing smoke into the night. A woman laughed. Oh, how I wish I still smoked, thought Polly, as a new speed date approached.

'May I?' he asked. Vanessa gave the thumbs-up and mouthed 'Poetry!' at her.

Turning to the man, Polly gave what she hoped was her best open smile, even though he had the most alarming sprouty eyebrows she'd ever seen. They vied for attention above thick, bushy nostril hair. She tried not to openly stare at such non-hair-trimming – but honestly – when he splayed his large hands on top of the table, and she saw that he'd hair on his knuckles and hair poking out beneath his shirt cuffs too, she found it hard to resist spouting the old joke – I used to be a werewolf but I'm all right now – ow-ow-ow – at him, and just stopped asking if there was a full moon tonight! Oh God, I'm in danger of getting the giggles. Lightweight.

She reached to take a sip from her dwindling wine.

'What is it you do, then?' he asked.

And Polly, remembering Vanessa's prompt about poetry, wished fervently that she was at home right now, feet up on the sofa, snuggled in a Slanket (not that she had one, but she might get one now), munching Maltesers as she merrily watched several country stereotypes come to a sticky end in Midsomer Murders. Instead, she took a deep breath – 'I'm a performance poet,' she said, and smiled pointedly at Vanessa, who was busy eavesdropping, alongside the sound man and Max.

'Really?' the werewolf was saying. 'And do you make a living from that? Hmm?'

Giving him a steady look as she thought, Here goes nothin', 'Yes, I do,' she began. 'Plus, I've had my first novel published in hardback after a fierce bidding war, sold the film rights to Steven Spielberg, am about to embark on a one-woman show called Fabulous Women, No Men, which will tour all major cities in the UK, and I teach snake charming at Bristol University.'

'That's nice,' he said, in a flat yet ingratiating manner, all the while peering down her cleavage.

'Yes, it is nice,' she continued. 'Why, just last month I was featured on the front cover of Gossip magazine snogging Peter Andre on our way to the Brit Awards.'

'Cut! Cut!' called Vanessa, who didn't look best pleased. 'That's all very lovely and fantastic.' Behind her, Max, his handheld camera perched on his shoulder, was clearly trying not to laugh. Next to him, sound guy took off his headphones and lowered his sound boom – covered in some kind of fun fur.

'You want to get a glass of milk for that,' she quipped to soundman, who pretended to ignore her, his eyes fixed on Vanessa, who shoved her microphone in between Polly and Mr Werewolf.

'Can you say all that again, please?' She looked from Polly to wolfman. 'About being a performance poet. For the camera, yeah? Only...' and here she leant closer to Polly '...this time without quite so much embellishment. There's a love.'

And it was almost over – the evening was meant to finish with some sort of disco, but Polly was let off the hook as speed dating hostess Samantha had a word with Vanessa, saying wasn't it time for them to leave?

Polly watched Max head for the bar, holding his camera up and away from him like he was hefting some large firearm. *Ooh. He's swaggering*, she thought. *Yes, that's definitely a swagger.* She took a moment to admire the shape of his bum, his muscled arms and how fine his legs looked in those khaki chinos. And now he was ordering from the barman who – *Oh no* – was looking across at Polly! Too late, she realised the barman had thought she was eyeing *him* up, as he gestured, 'You and me, huh?'

'No, no.' She was shaking her head just as Max turned, caught the exchange and gave her an amused smile. *Oh great. Now Max will think I can only pull some greasy middle-aged barman. Fantastic end to the evening!*

But Max was now beckoning her over. 'Drink?' he asked.

'Oh, yes please,' she said, her heart skipping around as she said a silent thank-you to the fates, for the return of her mojo.

*

'You see,' Polly was saying, slightly slurred to camera as they recorded the final section of that night's filming on the steps outside the restaurant. 'Don't get me wrong. I love a bit of romance, me. It's lovely, isn't it? But this whole wanting to find "The One". That's rubbish, isn't it? Don't you think? I mean…' and here she swayed a little. 'Look at me. I've got my own house, my own business, my own child and brilliant friends. This is the twenty-first century, after all. And you know what? I am a Renaissance Woman,' she announced, waving her glass of wine in the air, narrowly missing the woman who'd earlier been sitting at the next table. *Wendy was her name, wasn't it? That's right. Wendy. And there she goes – wending her way off into the night.*

'G'night,' Polly called after her.

'Night,' Wendy waved back.

'Now, where was I? Oh yes. Like I said. Renaissance Woman.' She reckoned she was definitely having a lightbulb moment. 'Us women, we have choices, right? We can be single. We can have lovers. Whatever. That's the trouble with this love stuff, innit?

Slipperier than an eel coated with extra-slippery eel stuff. And – here's the thing, right? People expect too much, don't they? Too much of the other person. Too much of love – but not me – oh no.' Polly was aware she was babbling but was unable to stop. 'From now on, I shall only need men for romance, passion and sex.' She emphatically nodded her head.

'So, for the camera now, Polly,' said Vanessa. 'Any potentials here tonight?'

'God, no. Get me back among my own people.'

9

Polly quietly closed her front door so as not to wake Rowan and placed her bag on the dresser in her kitchen… her uncluttered kitchen, which was normally covered in books, newspapers, spilt Ribena, Cheerios cemented to surfaces, with her sink chock-a-block with dishes, cups, pans all waiting for the washing-up fairy to appear. Now her table appeared clean! Her worktop free of gunk, the sink clear – pots and pans nowhere to be seen – and as for the floor! It shone a lighter and brighter colour than Polly ever remembered. And instead of stale aromas – she sniffed the air – the whole room smelled fresh and airy.

Clearly Mel had been cleaning. She liked to clean. Found it therapeutic.

'In here,' called Mel's voice from the sitting room.

'Shh,' said Polly as she entered the room, where Mel was sitting on the sofa alongside Daisy (who lived a couple of doors down), a DVD of *Salmon Fishing in the Yemen* – by the looks of it – playing in the corner. Both turned to greet her. 'What you doing here?' Polly asked Daisy, who got to her feet to give her a hug.

'Came to see how it went with the speed dating. Phil's been looking after Morwenna, Tiggy's round her boyfriend's and Zak's at band practice, so I snuck round to join Mel. Gosh, is that the time?' (Tiggy was the nickname for Daisy and Phil's fifteen-year-old daughter, Imogen, their son Zak was two years older, and Morwenna was Rowan's best friend.)

Daisy indicated Polly sit alongside Mel on the sofa while she took the easy chair.

''Lo, Mel – how's Ro Ro been?' Polly managed.

'Good as gold.' She pointed the remote to freeze the movie. 'Read her a story and she went to sleep, no problem. See? Didn't even notice you weren't there.'

'Awww. You did remember to leave her nightlight on, didn't you?'

'Duh. Of course.' Mel gave Polly an expectant look. 'So c'mon, spill the beans. How was it?'

'A disaster.' Polly pushed herself back onto her feet. 'I'll tell you all about it in a minute, I promise. First, I want to check on Ro.'

'Fine, but make sure you don't breathe those wine fumes all over her.'

Polly didn't think she'd ever get over the sense of wonder that filled her whenever she stood like this, in the doorway of her daughter's tiny bedroom, and watched her breathe. In. And out.

Not so long ago, when Rowan was a wee baby, Polly would creep into her nursery at the dead of night to sit quietly next to her cot. Just to watch her breathing. At first, it was to check she was still alive, and then simply because she loved it. Loved to sit there and watch her daughter's plump little face with its flush high on her cheeks, her thick eyelashes fluttering as she slept, mouth slightly open revealing bright pink gums and baby white teeth. Sometimes a small bubble would blow in and out as she breathed. In. And out. Sometimes she would bend over her child, placing her mouth close to hers, just so she could breathe in her little baby out-breaths. Inhale her sweet fresh baby smell and then tiptoe out. A thief of her own child's sleeping. She couldn't help herself. Rowan was so perfect, so plump, and so beautifully full of promise and life.

She moved across to kiss Ro's cheek, leaving her to her dreams, and then stood outside on the landing, fingering the card nestled in the pocket of her velvet coat. The card that Max had given her. 'Ring me,' he'd said, as she was about to make her walk home. She was so surprised that she'd not said anything back, but on her way home, underneath a streetlamp, she'd pulled it out and read *Max Somerton.* (*Hmm, summer town. Nice name. Polly Summertown – stop it!*) His mobile number could remain there nestled in the pocket of her coat, together with his address in Clifton Wood. Would she keep it to herself, like some delicious secret, or spill the beans to her friends waiting downstairs for the lowdown?

Well – she'd never been able to keep anything from Mel.

'So?' Mel said, after she'd shown her the card. 'When are you going to ring him?'

Daisy perked up. 'Max?' she said. 'I'm a bit lost now. Who is Max?'

'You'd better tell us both everything. From the top,' said Mel.

'Oh, okay.' She didn't need much persuading. 'It was like this,' she began, as she set about regaling them with tales of television people, the programme, the speed dating, the men from IT, how Vanessa had the brainwave to commission Polly to pen a poem for performing at an open mic night. 'How much will you get for writing that? She is paying you, isn't she?'

'Fifty quid.'

'Fifty quid, is that all?'

'Don't knock it – money's money.' She retold the whole kit and caboodle, with a few embellishments for extra laughs.

'And now my head hurts,' she said. 'Anyone got any paracetamol?'

'Here, take mine,' said Daisy, as she produced some from the depths of her voluminous designer handbag. Polly wouldn't be surprised if she had a piano in there too. God, she really couldn't handle a few glasses of wine. *What a lightweight.*

'Whatever you do,' Daisy was saying, as she handed over the tablets, plus a glass of water, 'you must not email or text him straight away. It never pays to appear keen.'

'Daisy the relationship guru!' said Mel. 'You've only had three boyfriends in your entire life, and you married two of them.'

'That's beside the point. In any case, I get to hear all about dating etiquette from Tiggy. She keeps me up to date on things.'

Her eldest daughter from her first marriage was Tiggy: fifteen, tall with long legs, body to die for, including perfect breasts. She was currently dating a boy called Fin – short for Dolphin. His parents were hippies who lived in Montpelier. Polly guessed it could have been worse. They might have named him Whale. She squinted at Daisy and then gave her a large smile as somehow Daisy had now materialised with a nice cup of tea for them all.

'Apparently kids these days never ring each other. They only text – or sometimes message on Facebook. Oh, and what is it she says? I know – if you're hanging out with a boy then you're having sex but not dating...'

'That's terrible.'

'Seems it's the thing these days. And you're not dating until you've been hanging for a while and he decides that you are. Or something like that – honestly, it's like feminism never existed. Still, you must not text him. Else you'll come across as needy – or desperate, even.'

Mel looked most agitated. 'Typical patriarchy,' she said.

Oh no, here we go, thought Polly.

'All goes in the boys' favour. As usual. Tell you what, Poll. You go for whatever feels right for you. That's what we do in the LGBT community.'

'Isn't that a book by Roald Dahl?'

'That's *The BFG*, you dearheart!' said Mel, giving her a pitying look.

Polly giggled, allowing herself to flop back in the red Chesterfield she'd bought for a song on Stokes Croft. It had seen better days but retained much of its charm. *Bit like me*, she thought, and giggled – again.

Mel peered at her. 'You all right, there?'

Polly decided she really loved Mel. 'I really love you, Mel.'

'Quick, someone get a bowl.'

'Ah, too late.'

And her nearest and dearest dashed about getting paper towels, wet cloths and bowls of water, while Polly stared at the card in her hands.

After Daisy had left and Mel was in bed, Polly woke with a tongue as dry as sandpaper. She decided the best remedy was to go fetch a glass of water. *God*, she thought, as she shuffled down the stairs to her kitchen for a glass of water, *did I really only have a couple of glasses of wine? It's not much, is it?* But then she remembered that she'd actually drunk almost a whole bottle – on her own.

In the kitchen and drinking a half-pint glassful of water down in one go, she burped, said, ''Scuse me,' and then reached for the Jammie Dodgers on the top of her cupboard. She had the munchies. Nom, nom, nom.

Taking a further glass of water, plus the biscuits, into the sitting room, she spotted her laptop on the table where she'd left it, still plugged into the internet. *Might as well check my emails –*

because you never know. Stranger things happen at sea.

She waited for her inbox to come up. Two new emails. Nothing from Max. Just the usual mailings, and a reminder of an invitation to the acoustic night at Angel Café next week. She had that poem to write for Vanessa – and a couple of new ones in the pipeline. Maybe she ought to suggest the Angel to Vanessa for the filming of her performing poetry? She stared at the screen. Should she ignore Daisy's advice and not wait two – no, hang on, didn't she say three days to contact Max?

She could see him now as he had been earlier, standing on the step outside Marco's, waving the piece of paper on which she'd scrawled her mobile no. and email address after he'd handed her his business card. 'I'll be in touch,' he'd said. 'Or you could email – or text – me?' And she'd felt a thrill go up and down her spine.

He'd more or less asked her to contact him, then, hadn't he? So why shouldn't she? *It's nice for someone to show an interest in me.* (She rubbed her head.) *Even if it does come to nothing*, she thought as she fiddled with his card. *All I seem to be known as these days is "Rowan's Mum"*. She sighed. *It's been a long time since Spike... No, I will not think about Spike.* But the faintest shadow of his face and smell of his jumper passed over her like a ghost. Even as she closed her eyes, she knew it wouldn't take much to recall his touch, his laughing smile, that devil-may-care accent and eyes so dark as he moved towards her... *No, no, no. Now stop it.*

She'd check once more so clicked on her email receive button, just to make absolutely sure that Max had not sent her a message in the last couple of minutes. Nope. Nothing. Nada.

You're being stupid expecting something from him now. Not everyone's up at this time of night, are they? Just what time is it? She peered at her computer. *Ye gods! Nearly 03.00 am. Better go back to bed.* She stared at the screen. *Pah. Who decided on these dating rules, hmm? I hate dating rules. Who made them up anyway?*

'No,' she declared out loud. 'I am *not* going to abide by some twenty-first-century dating etiquette. Even Jane Austen knew that was rubbish. Pah! Not email him? Not email? Says who?' And before she could think better of it, she began to type.

Re: Tonight
_____

Hi Max, Thanks for coming along and filming me

(Oh, he had to anyway, she remembered. She hit the delete button several times.)

Max, was good to meet you. I think you're cute. Is that allowed?

(Why not? she thought, moving into defiant mode.)

Be lovely to hear from you.

With a flourish, she clicked Send.

Then sat, staring at the screen. *Oh shit. Maybe the cute bit was coming on too strong. Damn emails. They're way too easy, aren't they? If that was a letter then I'd have to wait until tomorrow, buy a stamp, walk to the letterbox, and finally post it. Plenty of time for second thoughts. Or...*

I could phone him. Or rather text him. Yes, good idea. Now, phone, phone, where's my phone?

She rooted in her bag for her mobile. Yes, a text message would set things straight.

Max, soz bout email. Am a bit drund

Oops, better click on Clear to delete d and put in k so that reads *"drunk"* – *oh crap!* She'd clicked on the wrong button – and it was sent.

Staring at her mobile as if it was a traitor, she muttered, 'Bloody treacherous things. And they say they're inanimate!'

Resisting an urge to fling her phone to the ground and stomp up and down on it until it smashed to smithereens, she decided she'd best send another text to rectify matters – quick.

Max, dont know wot happend there. Its l8 & I'm an idiot. Txt or eml me.

Press Send. Ah damn, I forgot to sign it. He won't know who it's from. Send another.

This is Polly. luv Polly ☺ x

After smashing her forehead with her hand several times, she sat staring at her screen and then at her mobile. *Idiot!* She padded through to the kitchen to fetch yet another glass of water, hoping against hope that by tomorrow this would all have been a dream.

Standing at her sink and gazing out of her window, she could see an animal moving at the bottom of the garden. About the size of a cat, it slinked – in a different, not feline, way. More sinewy. She realised it was a fox, although its outline was long and low, its head, body and tail all on a line, more like a large stoat than her picture-book idea of a fox. *It must be a youngster*, she thought, then spotted that in its mouth was a plump child's guinea pig, snatched from a garden hutch. The pet animal half-heartedly kicked its short legs, seeming more or less resigned to its fate, when the fox turned its head to turn its glass-bead eyes on Polly. Next it was gone, disappeared into next door's garden from where it was an easy lope down to the dark riverbank.

She could imagine Mr Fox quickly merging into the deep

shadows that lined the river's sides, on down to the smooth dark of the water where lurked city rats and cross-not-friendly badgers in their urban version of *Wind in the Willows*, a place where guinea pigs with fat, stumpy legs were soon gobbled up.

10

Polly sat with Rowan perched uncomfortably on her lap, in front of the doctor, who'd just finished peering down Rowan's ear with his ear-peering thingamajig.

'How are things since Rowan had grommets put in?' he asked.

'There has been an improvement,' she said, 'but she still misses things – not only conversations but also background noise, like traffic. I have to hold tightly onto her hand or she might rush out into the road. It's dangerous when she doesn't hear traffic.'

'Yes, of course.' The doctor – whose name she couldn't remember (God, she was still so forgetful!) – went over to the sink to wash his hands. 'Have you considered whether it might be selective hearing?'

'What do you mean?' She was insulted on Rowan's behalf. Was he really suggesting that her daughter would choose to be deaf?

'What I mean is that because she's been so used to *not*

hearing, she may be tuning out more easily. How's her speech coming along?'

Polly pulled Rowan more upright, but Rowan wriggled in protest. 'She tends to miss words, and she mispronounces them often. Someone told me that's normal at her age?'

He glanced at the computer screen. 'Hmm. Try not to listen to well-meaning people. You know your own child, and I'm sure you're right. Also, it is not wholly normal, Mrs Park.'

Polly couldn't be bothered to correct him and say *It's Ms Park, thank you very much.*

'We ought to keep an eye on things. She might well need speech therapy further down the line. But why don't we see how things go.'

He clapped his hands to the right of Rowan, and she smiled up at him from where she'd been engrossed in her cardboard book. 'That's good. Most promising,' he said.

'Will it be permanent? I mean, will there be any hearing loss?' asked Polly.

'It's a possibility but like I said, a bit early to be sure. Why don't we refer Rowan to audiology, shall we? Ah, I see from her notes that she's been before. How did she do?'

He was glancing at his screen again.

'Better than I expected,' Polly said. 'Although I did wonder whether it was more of the case that she *guesses* when she's meant to hear those bleeps. All I know is that she misses a lot of background chatter and noise at home, and I've noticed it's even worse when we're out and about.'

'Well, she's clearly a bright little thing, aren't you, Rowan?' But Rowan didn't look up. He lifted her chin and tried again. 'You're a bright girl, aren't you?'

Rowan nodded and smiled and returned to her book.

'Whatever the cause and whether she'll grow out of it or not will depend to some extent on what you do at home.' He leant back in his chair. 'At present she's getting a lot of her cues from whoever's talking to her. Even at this age she can read lips.' He stopped and steepled his fingers. 'I don't think we'll introduce Baby Signing, because that might well delay her speech further.'

'Well yes,' said Polly grudgingly, as she wasn't used to liking the doctors or their opinions, but this new one was better than the older one she'd seen in the past. 'That's what I thought too. About the signing, I mean.'

'Make sure she can see your face when you speak to her. It's like – well, it's like she's hearing words underwater...' he put his hand over his mouth '...like this,' he said, smothering the last words.

Polly sighed. She knew this already but thought it rude to say so.

'Come back and see me after she's been to audiology,' he said, not unkindly, 'I'd like to monitor her progress.' He regarded Polly with a warm smile. 'And try not to worry so much, Mum.'

Cheek – he's old enough to be my father!

'Your little girl is clearly coping very well so far. You say she goes to a childminder?'

'Yes, and she attends Montessori playschool.'

'Good. Good. The more socialising she does at this stage, the better.' He leant back in his chair. 'Thank you for coming. We'll make an appointment and then arrange to see you—'

'Once I've been to audiology,' said Polly, not meaning to be rude. Getting to her feet, she took Rowan by the hand and then tapped her on the shoulder. 'Say bye bye, Doctor.'

'Bye bye, Boctor,' Rowan obliged.

Her car was in the garage, so after dropping Rowan off with Trudy, the childminder, she set off on foot, up the hill, taking a short cut through Canynge Crescent – her favourite street in

Clifton. A man with a clipboard and headphones held up his hand, barring her way.

'Hold up,' he said. 'You'll have to wait. We're about to film a scene. Won't be long, love.'

Polly cast anxiously about her for Max. *Please, God, don't let him be filming here.*

That would be too embarrassing. Up ahead were a couple of large equipment vans, lighting, people milling about with cameras and sound booms, and in the middle of it all, a milk float under which was pinned a man having red substance applied to his wounds.

'More blood. C'mon, c'mon. We need more blood on this!' shouted clipboard man, who was now doing much pointing and pacing about.

'Hurry up! While we still have this light.'

'Sorry,' a woman with headphones and a large mug of coffee said to Polly. 'Not much longer now.'

'Okay, Sarah,' another man was calling. 'Sarah, over here, darling.'

Polly watched as an actor dressed in the green uniform of a paramedic leapt out of the ambulance parked at an angle across the road then rushed to the man bleeding underneath the vehicle.

'Quick. He's tachycardic,' Sarah called over her shoulder to the other actor, who Polly recognised as the fanciable black actor who won last year's Comic Relief Let's Dance. (According to Mel, she watched far too much telly. But, that's what you do when you have a kid and no life, don't you?)

An old lady dressed in tweed strode past the film crew as clipboard man screamed – 'Ah fuck!' Polly recognised the old lady as the owner of Polly's very own dream house.

'Cut! Cut! Silly old cow!'

Polly's dream house was at the end of the long curving

row of four-storey Georgian townhouses, and this was the one she'd decided she would absolutely definitely buy if she won the lottery. (Okay, she didn't do the lottery, but if she did!) It featured in many of Polly's night- and day-time dreams, did this house. Once, a couple of years ago, Polly had been invited to one of the flats in another building in the same crescent, and so she knew first-hand that at the back was a huge communal garden with sweeping lawns and its very own wood. *How cool is that?* She'd been utterly enchanted.

It had been Bonfire Night, and the residents were having a communal party. A magical night with towering bonfire, a proper Guys Fawkes on top – 'Just hope they haven't got Edward Woodward inside,' Mel had joked – and the whole feel was that of a country village fete instead of a shared back garden. The children were dressed in woodland gear, and some of the parents came as Morris dancers. There was even a mummers' play, complete with kids and adults in medieval folk garb. It told of an old eel-catcher of Gloucestershire and finished with the children forming a procession underneath a willow and papier-mâché frame, much like a Chinese dragon, but in this case in the shape of a giant eel. There'd been fireworks, potatoes baked in the embers of the bonfire, chestnuts roasted in a brazier, barbecues manned by the men in aprons – wielding their instruments of tong and spatula – as they charred sausages and undercooked chicken drumsticks.

Polly had loved it. It was eccentric, it was twee, and it was very Clifton.

As the stars had dotted a cloudless sky, the adults had sat on the terrace running the whole length of the crescent, sipping their mulled wine and champagne as their children settled down for the night in tents pegged out on the lawn. *To think*, Polly had thought then, and since, *this kind of thing is commonplace for these lucky, lucky residents.* The night air full of magic as they sat at the top of their high hill, overlooking other terraces and crescents that strode down to the river and the docks below, while overhead a meteor shower of shooting stars had whizzed by. *I kid you not*, thought Polly now, as she smiled at the memory.

Of course, her dream house – which was ice cream-blue in colour – would still have its original features (she imagined). There'd be plaster mouldings and large ceiling roses, marble fireplaces, and dark stained wooden floorboards which would bounce beneath running feet and creak at night while the house settled to sleep.

She'd already allocated the rooms. On the first floor, next to her own bedroom, she'd have a workroom-cum-study, where she could work on clothes designs for children. Because Polly was full of ideas and liked to while away spare time in the shop sketching and collecting swatches of material – if and when she had the time.

Her large kitchen – the heart of her home – would open out onto their own private courtyard, which would have a garden door – much like the one in that children's book *The Secret Garden* – all covered in ivy and so weather-beaten that it needed a good push. Maybe she'd have a rocking chair in the corner next to the Aga (of course there would be an Aga – a cream-coloured one), and there would definitely be a Labrador, or a Springer Spaniel, to take on long walks and to tut over when it waffled down food left unattended on the side, or had rolled in fox's poo so that it was down to the courtyard to be washed off with a garden hose and Bob Martin Deodorant Dog Shampoo.

'Oi you! That's right – you! Dolly Daydream! Get a move on, will ya. We've finished filming for the day, so you can go on through now.'

'Right, sorry, sorry.' She hastened past clipboard man, who watched her go with an I-don't-know look on his face.

'Dozy mare,' she heard him mutter.

Yeah, one day I'll have my dream house, she thought. Although it was strange how whenever she had this dream, there'd be her, Rowan and another child – oh, and a soft-eared liver and white Springer Spaniel, and – nope – nobody else. No body. *Must be a sign*, she thought now as she headed for her shop.

*

Polly stood at her counter, surveying her shop. She knew she'd never make enough money to buy a house – or a flat even – on Canynge Crescent. But a girl can dream, can't she?

Running her fingers along a rack of girls' clothing, she wished she could shrink herself to Rowan's size. *Children's clothing can be so much more exciting. Just look at this* – from the rail she pulled a gorgeous little dress with exotic flowers and birds embroidered onto an orange background. *What I wouldn't give to have that in my size. And wouldn't it look adorable teamed with this purple faux-poodle fur gillet.*

Sometimes she'd splash out on the Oilily adult line, but there was no mistaking it was no match for their kids' range. She owned many of their bags, with their trademark flowers, polka dots, birds, tassels, appliqué – *think of anything that shrieks fun yet cool and they've got it.* She began to stroke the felt grey owl bag when the landline rang.

Suze. 'Yes, Mum, what is it? Only I'm very busy and have promised to take Rowan swimming before she has her tea.' Polly made an it's-my-mum face at Donna, who rolled her eyes in sympathy.

'I'm coming up to Bristol on Friday and thought we could do elevenses at the Avon Gorge. My treat.'

'Umm. Yes, right. Okay, Mum. I can't promise, but I'll see what I can do. Now I must go.'

The Trouble With Love

'Ciao,' said Suze.

Polly replaced the receiver. 'Grrr, I do wish she wouldn't say "Ciao". It's sooo blinkin' pretentious.'

'Your muh, right,' said Donna. 'She gonna do summat about my boiler in the flat, yeah? Only it's bin on the blink forever, mind.'

*

Polly held Rowan's hand as they stood at the counter of the swimming baths, waiting for their tickets.

The first time she'd taken Rowan swimming, the little girl had managed to wriggle free before she had time to slip any armbands on her. Once free of her mother's grasp, Rowan had run full pelt – and much quicker than Polly knew she could – to the side of the pool where, without hesitation, she had jumped straight in! Polly had dived in after her, locating Rowan swimming underwater like the baby on Nirvana's iconic record sleeve; she was smiling away, her blonde wispy hair billowing about her as she moved perfectly calmly through the blue while perfectly holding her breath.

Once back safely on the side of the pool, Polly caught hold of both of Rowan's arms. 'Don't you ever do that again!' she said loudly into her daughter's face, causing the other parents to turn and tut at her.

But Rowan just chortled, and Polly hugged her tight.

'Not without Mummy. Okay?'

'Kay.'

'My little mermaid,' Polly had said, shaking her head.

Now, Polly bent down and – making sure her daughter could see her lips – she said, 'Now, don't forget. No running off. And what do we wear?'

Rowan frowned at her mother. 'Nop *we*, Mummy – is silly. Just me. Me wear ambans,' she said gravely, nodding her head emphatically.

'Well done, that's right.' Polly got to her feet, still holding her daughter's hand, because these days she liked to keep a tight hold of her.

11

The next morning, Polly was working alone – Donna having taken time off. Taking a large pair of scissors to one of the boxes just delivered, she pulled out a bright and wacky range of spring/summer girls' clothing. This was the part of her job that she enjoyed the most, because it was like opening Christmas presents. As she lifted each item out, she gave it a shake to loosen any wrinkles. Gorgeous. And they smelled so beautifully clean and fresh. Next she'd get them onto hangers and run the steam iron over those still creased. *Right, better get a move on before the mid-morning rush.* Sitting back on her heels, she admired her pile of new clothes, knowing she'd have to juggle the stock to make room.

Even though Polly sold to the well-heeled in Clifton, she also catered for the strapped-for-cash and struggling mothers who liked their children to look good too. For them, she kept a rail of secondhand clothes near the back of the shop so customers could come and sell back clothes outgrown, and that way those on smaller incomes could still kit their kids out in colourful designer gear. She bought and sold many of Rowan's clothes this way, somehow making up for the wealth that her mother tried to foist on her.

Wonder what Suze will have to say at elevenses on Friday, she thought as she whistled away, ironing those clothes which needed it.

On occasion Polly would carry out small alterations, or customise clothes for Rowan and a few select customers. Donna – who now lived in the flat above – did most afternoons, and was often handy for other times as well, being prepared to be accommodating, in exchange for which Suze charged her less-than-Clifton rents. Polly's spirits were high as she once more thought how lucky she was to work with such beautiful things. In between sorting, custom was brisk, and even Jazz from local band Jango popped by to see how she was doing with her turning his jacket punk with zips, appliquéd slogans and carefully designed tears. 'Cool,' he said, as she showed him her progress, trying it on as she worked on pinning alterations.

'It'll be ready for your gig next week,' she assured him, pins clasped between her teeth like tiny pirate swords.

'Thanks, man,' came his cheerful response.

In no time at all, Donna had arrived for her shift, breezing in through the door.

'Hey, babes,' she said.

'Hey.'

Polly thought Donna was rather scrumptious, what with her plump curves, red lipstick and black beautifully cropped hair. But Donna kept referring to herself as "a fat cow".

'Donna, you're not!'

'Am too.'

She had a string of boyfriends she acquired like pets, from The Hatchet or The Invisible Circus nights (when she liked to dress up in saucy burlesque gear). For her day job, she wore tight '50s-inspired vintage dresses or flouncy numbers from their adult range. Today, she was a vision of brightness in a dress with large sunflowers, matching her sunny disposition. Polly would have loved to stop and chat, but she was meeting Vanessa in the Honey Pot Café in about five minutes.

'How'd it go?'

Polly looked blank.

'You know,' Donna gave her a conspiratorial nod. 'with this Max fella? That good, eh? You're blushin'. You heard anything from him, like? Are you gonna see him or what? Get a move on, girl, or he'll get snapped up. YOLO, Poll. YOLO.'

'I didn't tell you about him. How did you even know about Max?'

'Not from you, that's for sure. Talk about keeping it to yourself! Innit 'bout time you got back out there? Honestly, I'd never know nuffin' if it weren't for bumping into your mate Mel down at the Fini.'

Blabber mouth Mel.

'Oh, so she told you, did she…? She had no right to. Oh, look, I've no time to tell you about it now. I'll fill you in tomorrow. Will that do?'

'You better had. 'Cos I ain't letting you off the hook that easy, mind.' Donna had her hands on her hips. 'But – hang on – you can quickly tell me this. Are you or are you not gonna see him?'

Polly gave her an enigmatic smile. 'Gotta dash, Don.'

'Poll? Did you ring him? Did he ring you? Text? What? C'mon, I'm dying for the lowdown.'

'S'laters.' Polly collected her bag and stopped at the door. 'Oh, and…' she waved her arm in the general direction of the rails '…be a doll. New girls' dresses, over there, and if you look hard, you'll find a couple of women's in your size, too.'

'Goodee.'

'So please finish pricing them up, for me, yeah?'

Polly opened the door.

'Oi. Full lowdown when you gets back, mind, innit.'

Polly blew her a kiss as she closed the door behind her.

Vanessa was sitting in the window nursing a cappuccino when Polly arrived, slightly out of breath. 'Sorry,' she said. It was then that Polly recognised the man standing at the counter waiting to be served. *Max. It's Max. What's he doing here?* She felt an urge to turn tail and run, but, 'What would you like to drink?' Vanessa was saying.

'Umm...' Polly was still transfixed by the sight of Max. She had not expected him to be here, especially after last night. God, what must he have thought about her emails – and then text messages? She blushed just thinking about it. 'Latte, thanks,' she said in an almost squeak.

'And a latte for Polly here,' called Vanessa. Max turned, making Polly's heart do a lurch – because – oh, there were no two ways about it – she absolutely did fancy him. But what must he be thinking after her stupid messages?

'Right you are,' he said, not particularly looking at her but not ignoring her, either. *Oh gawd.*

The café door creaked open as that actress/paramedic from earlier entered, squeezing past a couple of women waiting to be served. Spotting Vanessa, she sashayed over.

'Ah, Sarah,' Vanessa said in greeting. 'This is Polly. You two haven't met, but you remember I told you all about her?'

She did? Flustered, Polly could only stare blankly at both women.

'Hi,' said Sarah, who then also called to Max, 'make mine a tea. There's a love.'

He nodded as she took her seat, removing her coat to reveal

that she was still wearing her paramedic's uniform underneath. They must be filming today as well.

Even though Sarah's brown hair was tied in bunches, she managed to exude matter-of-factness with a touch of cute. She'd unzipped her overall just enough to show the curve of fantastic breasts, which Polly couldn't help staring at, wondering if they were real. Luckily Sarah didn't notice Polly's peering. Or perhaps she was so used to people admiring her boobs that she didn't react anymore. She gave Polly a slow smile.

'Been filming,' she said to one and all.

'Ah. I thought so,' said Polly. 'Only I saw you yesterday, you know...' Sarah looked puzzled. 'Filming in Canynge Crescent?'

'Of course.' Sarah gave Polly what could only be described as a once-over.

Quickly, Polly added, 'You can't move in Clifton for film crews, can you, Vanessa? Everywhere.'

'Right. I guess not.' Sarah turned to Vanessa, giving her a peck on the cheek. 'How's tricks?'

'Good, good, all good,' she answered. 'Thanks for agreeing to take part in our little film, lovey. So good of you.'

Sarah flourished off a blue polka dot scarf. 'That's what mates are for, aren't they?'

'Sarah and I go way back,' Vanessa explained to Polly. 'Max too. Don't we, Max?' as he joined them, squeezing into the seat next to Polly, who soon became acutely aware of his knee just touching hers.

Every single hair on her arms must be standing to attention, she reckoned.

'Yes, we three know each other very well,' he said, handing out the drinks from the tray.

'Sugar?' he asked Polly, who immediately reddened, inwardly cursing her Scottish genes.

'No. Thanks,' she answered, turning her attention back to Vanessa, who'd been watching their exchange with a positive smirk on her face. *Oh no, he's not told her about my messages from last night, has he?*

'Well, Polly, Sarah here – is single too – although I can't think why she hasn't been snapped up...'

Polly shot Vanessa a look. *Is she implying it's no wonder I'm on my own?*

'It does to keep one's options open,' said Sarah, giving Max a wink.

'If you say so.'

Polly saw Max start, and thought she noticed Sarah move as if she'd kicked him under the table. They exchanged a glance, which Polly couldn't quite fathom.

'So, what's going to happen is that we're going to film Sarah doing a spot at an open-mic comedy night... A little bird tells me you do comedy too, Polly.'

'Uh?' *Who on earth told her that?* Not on your nelly! Not after the one and only time when she'd somehow thought she'd be good at it but hadn't been and, to the delight of the audience and the annoyance of the host, had thrown up on her shoes. 'I do the odd poetry slam rather than stand-up, Vanessa.'

'Well, well, they're practically the same thing, aren't they?' she said, waving her hand about as if a mere trifle. 'Only I thought we could get you two girls to perform at one of those student comedy nights and, you know, film the audience clapping away. Show that you're sparky up-for-it girls, etcetera.'

'I'm sorry, Vanessa, but I will absolutely *not* perform in front of students. Those days in back rooms of pubs are long gone. And, in any case, I've moved on from all that,' said Sarah.

Polly hoped her stomach wasn't going to start rumbling. Where was the lunch she'd been promised? Ooh. And there was Max's knee again. She began to feel all hot and bothered and wouldn't have been at all surprised to see smoke rising up from beneath the table.

'Sweetie,' Sarah continued in a more conciliatory tone, 'I don't mind being interviewed, and I'm sure you could show some behind-the-scenes filming of *Emergency*, but no stand-up.' She placed her herbal teabag in the saucer and took a sip from the cup.

'That's a shame,' said Vanessa, giving Sarah a sideways look. 'Hmm. Okay, well, never mind. We'll do you instead, Polly.'

'I really only do the occasional poetry slam or open-mic night. Not comedy,' said Polly, glad that Sarah had given her an out.

'Poetry it is then.' Vanessa sat back with a job done air. 'Although it isn't very rock 'n' roll. Still, I guess it will have to do.'

Polly was so distracted by the presence of Max that she found herself saying *Yes, that would be fine*. If she could have kicked herself, she would have.

Finally they got around to ordering food, and a night for the filming was agreed upon. Vanessa and Sarah chatted about various people they knew in the industry, and just as the food arrived, Max rose to his feet.

'Gotta shoot,' he said and then, turning to Polly, added, 'Bye,' and gave her a big fat grin.

Once he'd departed and Vanessa had popped to the loo, Sarah leant forward and said, 'He so fancies you.'

'No. He doesn't, does he? Do you really think he does?'

'Christ yeah. My advice is to go for it. He's a right sex machine, that one,' she said. 'Hung like a donkey too, darling!' And she burst out laughing.

Polly walked back up The Arcade to her shop. She had to collect her things before going home. *But he only said Bye, didn't he? Nothing else. What did that mean? Bye. Was that Bye, I'll never speak to you again? Or Bye, I'll be in touch soon?*

What did Sarah mean? Does Max really fancy me, or was Sarah kidding? How does Sarah know he's a sex machine? Hearsay? Or is there history there? God, and talk about direct! That Sarah's a right one.

Donna must have popped out for a sandwich as the "Back in Ten Minutes" sign was on the door. She unlocked her shop only to be followed in by a woman with a recycled orange basket over her arm. *Maybe it was just a general Bye and he didn't even get my text and email. Don't be daft, of course he did.*

'How much is this cute nightlight?' asked the woman, holding a lamp which projected dancing wood nymphs onto a wall.

He might not have received the emails yet. But surely he would have received the text messages?

'The nightlight…?' said the woman.

'What do you think?' said Polly, not fully aware she asked her question out loud.

'Shouldn't you know the price? The ones over there are £24.99,' the woman said, clearly trying to be helpful.

'Oh, sorry.' Polly focused on her customer. 'Can I ask you a question?'

'Hmm? Oh. Yes, of course. All ears.'

'What would you think if you bumped into a man, a man who you thought you might like… might fancy even… and he doesn't say anything to you except Bye. Complete with a knowing kind of smile. What would you think?' She peered at the woman.

'I don't know, dear. But if it's all the same to you, I'll just have the nightlight.'

'Yes, of course. Sorry. That'll be £24.99.'

She rang up the money and gave the woman her change. As she was leaving the shop, the woman turned and said, 'It sounds to me like he's interested.'

Polly looked up from writing down the sale in her book. 'Do you really think so?'

'I do.' The woman smiled at her. 'Good luck.'

I think I'm going to need it after last night.

12

Max rang the following day, just when she was in the middle of a delivery at the shop.

'Max – oh, umm, hang on a minute,' she said, placing the receiver on the counter. Deep breaths.

'Where d'you wan' it?' said delivery man – tower of boxes in his arms.

She picked up the receiver again. 'Won't be a sec.' Then, 'At the back!' she gestured to the man. 'No, not you,' into the receiver. She called out, 'Donna! Donna, you there?'

Donna emerged from the back. 'Where's the fire?' she said, cup of tea in hand.

Polly mouthed *Max on phone*, then with elaborate head nods said, 'Sort – boxes – delivery.' She seemed to have lost the power of speech. Donna rolled her eyes.

'Hello? Ah, Max.'

'Yes, I'm still here.'

'Oh, speaking to Max on the phone, are we?' said Donna, as she ushered the man through to the back with as much skill as a

New York traffic cop.

Shut up, Polly mouthed.

She checked her reflection in the small mirror on the wall by the till. (*Why?* She had no idea… *Phone…?*)

'Did I call at a bad time?' Max was saying, his voice all smiley and playful.

'No… I mean, yes… No… of course not. Just typical, eh? – Delivery man arriving. Hah.' (*Idiot. Be cool.*)

'So I was wondering,' he was saying, 'whether you fancied dinner tonight? My treat, of course?'

'Umm…' Her mind was now going nineteen to the dozen – Mel, not home, off out with Fen… too late to get Tiggy for babysitting… Donna… no…

Just at that moment, Donna poked her head round the curtains. 'Well?' she hissed.

'Hang on, just one moment,' Polly said to Max then placed her hand over the receiver. 'Can you babysit tonight?' she asked Donna.

'No can do, babs,' she answered, beating a hasty retreat back to delivery man. 'Want another cuppa?' Polly could hear her saying to him.

Before she could stop herself, Polly said, 'Why don't you come round to mine? Eight o'clock, suit? I'll cook.'

'Can't wait,' Max replied, in a voice much like a young Leslie Phillips.

Polly replaced the receiver. She'd done it. She'd only gone and done it. A real live date with an actual man.

Donna, seeing delivery man out the door, patted Polly on the shoulder. 'Never mind,' she said. 'Doubt he's coming round for the food, babs. Just as well, too, seein' as you can't cook.' Polly chose to ignore her.

Time to phone Mel.

'You've got Max coming round?' said Mel. 'For a meal?'

'Yes.'

'Are you mental?'

Because Polly's inability to cook edible food was legendary.

*

Things had been conspiring against Polly all day:

Trying to leave early, she was buttonholed by the chair of the Clifton Arcade Shopkeepers' Association. And no amount of You Go On from Donna or I'm Running Late from Polly would put him off.

The moment Polly got home, her daughter decided to tearfully latch onto her, ignoring Mel's ministrations and promises of chocolate fingers if she'd let her bathe her – 'Nooo!' she'd screamed. 'Mummeeee!' Thereby proving Polly's theory that toddlers, like dogs, know when you're going out, or – in this case – have someone coming round.

In among the screaming and cajoling and the final getting into bath of Rowan by Mel, Polly's mother phoned.

'Suze, not now,' she muttered. But Suze didn't get where she was by not being tenacious – and selectively deaf. Reluctantly Polly answered her mother's call, and listened – occasionally trying to get a word in edgeways – as Suze ploughed on through Polly's protestations and pleas. On and on she went about how she thought Rowan ought to go to Clifton High School for Girls and not the Steiner School, which Polly proposed.

'Bit rich, coming from you, Mum. Whatever happened to Anarchy in the UK?'

'Smash the establishment? We all grow up and learn that's not how the world works. Take me.' (*I wish someone would*, thought Polly.) 'I now know the value of a good private education, and I don't want Rowan to miss out. I could buy you both a house, darling. Just consider it. A lovely house in the country, where Rowan could have a pony.'

No, no and no, she tried to say, but Suze was not listening, and Polly was close to slamming the phone down on her. Overhead, she could hear a commotion. (Good excuse.) 'Gotta go, Mum. Rowan is drowning Mel in the bath.'

'Well, think on,' was Suze's final salvo. 'Oh, and I can't do lunch on Friday. Ciao.'

Ciao? Polly thought as she hung up. *I mean, who in their right mind says Ciao?*

Mel walked into the kitchen: hair sticking up, the front of her shirt soaked.

'I should get danger money. Or at the very least, a snorkel.'

'She okay now?' asked Polly.

'Yeah, fine. Burbling away to herself in bed. I told her you'd be up in a min. I'd better show you what you're going to cook tonight, then, I suppose.'

'Mel. You are a lifesaver.'

'I know.' Mel proceeded to produce items from a carrier bag with all the aplomb of a magician pulling a rabbit from… well, you get the picture… 'Here we are,' she said. 'Angel hair spaghetti and clam sauce from the pasta shop on Gloucester Road.' She gave Polly a look. 'Even you can't mess that lot up, Missy. Simmer pasta for two minutes and reheat the sauce.' Another flourish from out of her bag. 'Ta da! Garlic bread from Tesco. Pop in the oven.' Plonk on table. 'Bag of salad.' Plonk. And finally…' opening the fridge door '…voilà! A bottle of Tesco's finest Prosecco!'

'Oh, thank God,' said Polly, giving her best friend in the whole world a hug. 'This is all great and foolproof. What would I do without you!'

'Probably never have sex again,' said Mel, grinning fit to

bust. 'But seriously, hon, if you manage to not burn any of this food, then your luck might well be in tonight.'

'Shut up!'

'Okay – backup plan – you could get him drunk if it does go wrong.'

Polly shot a look at her clock. 'Will you look at the time, Mel. Oh heck. Should I phone and cancel?'

'Don't you dare! Now, so long as you don't panic then everything will be fine. I'll tidy up downstairs while you go have a nice bath. Oh, and think about what you're going to wear.'

'What to wear? Oh crikey. What to wear? What on earth should I wear?'

Mel guided Polly out of the kitchen to the stairs. 'You're starting to panic. Take deep breaths. You have a whole wardrobe bulging with clothes, the food's bought, and it will practically cook itself. Now go!'

Polly gave her a smile. 'You're right. Of course you're right. Is simples, yeah? I'm a little rusty, that's all. What can possibly go wrong?'

Mel had left for Fen's for the night, Polly had finished her bath and now had Rowan's Little Mermaid towel wrapped around her middle, and a pink towel in a turban about her hair. As soon as Polly entered her daughter's bedroom, the little girl stopped whacking Cookie Monster on her bed and held out her arms. 'Hug, Mummy! Hug!'

She sat on her daughter's bed and happily obliged. 'Ook,' demanded Rowan with that stubborn look Polly knew meant business. There'd be no bargaining with her tonight, and so the sooner she read her a book, the sooner Rowan would be asleep, and the sooner Polly could finish getting ready.

'Okay. But one book only, yes? Which one shall we read?'

Rowan produced a *Meg and Mog* book from underneath

the covers of her new bed. She was proud to be in a big bed, which Polly had set against the wall to stop her from falling out. She liked to fill her bed with Poohs, Piglets, My Little Ponies, Tellytubbies, Ernie and Cookie Monster from *Sesame Street*, picture books, her beaker with water in, and – *ah yes*, thought Polly, retrieving a half-eaten digestive biscuit from underneath a pillow – snacks, and anything else she could horde. It was as if she were constructing her own little fortress against the world. A plug-in nightlight kept monsters to the corners of her room, or behind the wardrobe. Rowan was fine so long as her light stayed on. But switch it off?

'Right,' Polly said, as she reached across to turn on the small reading lamp. 'Just the one story, madam.' Stretching out alongside Rowan on the small bed, she propped herself up with a spare pillow...

...and awoke with a start. The doorbell ding-donging. No! It couldn't be! She glanced at Rowan's *Alice in Wonderland* clock, where the white rabbit was clearly pointing out that she was indeed late. 8.30 pm!

Oh shit. Ding dong. *Max. It must be Max.* Quietly she slipped out of Rowan's room – oh shit – and caught sight of herself in the mirror, red sleep creases down the left-hand side of her face; Little Mermaid bath towel only just covering her nether regions; hair limply damp and plastered to her head. 'Ah fuck,' she muttered.

'Hang on, I'm just coming,' she called downstairs – then dashed to the bathroom – *Where the hell's my bathrobe?* – gave up, swapped her towel for a new big fluffy one, wrapped a matching towel around her head and splashed cold water onto her face.

As she flung open the front door, Max stepped back, nearly falling down the small flight of steps. 'Am I too early?'

'No, no,' she said, not letting him in. 'It's just… it's just…' She glanced behind her. 'It's just that I'm running late. Yes, that's it. And… everything's gone bonkers. Kid. Bedtime. Mental.'

He stared as if she were indeed mad. 'Ah,' he said, as he now took a slight step forward with his bottle of red in one hand and flowers (definitely not garage-bought ones) in the other.

'There's a pub… a pub… just along the road,' she said, waving her pointing finger at him and down the road.

'A pub?' He looked uncertain.

'Yes. A pub. What a good idea. You pop along to the pub, and I'll be ready in – ooh – shall we say half an hour?'

'Half an hour?'

'Good, that's settled.' And with that, she closed the door.

'That's the first time I've been chucked out before I've even had a meal,' Max was saying, as he leant on the back of a kitchen chair.

'I am so, so sorry.'

'Don't apologise.' He smiled at her. 'It was hilarious.'

'I'm afraid I'm not very good at cooking,' she said, plopping the shop-bought homemade pasta into boiling water.

'Polly,' he said, giving her a slow appraising look, 'I didn't come here for the food.'

'Oh,' she said, feeling flustered.

'May I say how gorgeous you look,' he said, moving in for a kiss on her cheek. 'Hmm. Something smells good.' He lingered a while before straightening up.

She was just grateful he'd not witnessed the last half-hour when she'd been dashing about, as if fast-forwarding a silent movie, throwing things here, brushing hair there, applying makeup while hopping on one foot trying to find her other elusive sandal, flicking hair off face, spritzing herself with perfume, wriggling into silk underwear, pinning up curls, squeezing into dress and finally taking a swig of pre-date wine, casting a quick that'll-do glance at the mirror before opening the door on his ring.

She was happy with the result his delay had afforded her: her '50s-inspired dress – turquoise, covered with little kissing love birds – giving her a fantastic cleavage and the illusion of a tiny waist. Max was looking not so bad himself. Fine long legs in skinny blue jeans; soft grey flannel shirt, unbuttoned just enough. Hmm. Not bad at all.

'Take a seat,' she said, then glanced the cooker's way. *Oh shit.* She'd forgotten to time the pasta. *No!* It was only supposed to simmer for two minutes, wasn't it? Now once she'd drained the pasta, she could see the horrible truth. It had welded itself into one glutinous mass.

And the sauce was burnt.

Cutting the pasta lump in half, she dumped one into each of the bowls.

'Ah,' he said, on her presenting his before him.

'Hang on.' Fetching the smaller saucepan, she poured (or more like plopped) the brown (okay, burned) sauce on top.

'Mmm,' he said (rather pluckily), as he leant forward to peer at what was meant to pass for food. 'What's the sauce when it's at home?'

'It's meant to be clam.' She stood back, tucked a stray strand of hair behind her ears and blew her fringe from her eyes.

'And these shrivelled-up black bits?' he asked, poking at them with his fork. 'Are these the clams?'

'Umm… well…' She bent over his dish then glanced at him sideways. Both burst out laughing.

'Oh God,' she managed, in between guffaws. 'I'm totally rubbish, aren't I? I'm just not used to all this – you know – cooking for adults. Dating. I'm a dab hand at fish fingers or oven chips, though.'

'Seriously, Polly,' he said, wiping his hands with a paper towel (she hadn't been able to locate the napkins). 'Dating – as you so quaintly put it – is like riding a bike. Oh.' He held up his hand. 'Not that I'm suggesting you are, or indeed were, in any sense – a bike.' She tried to clear his plate and he grabbed hold of her, pulling her towards him, so that her breasts were in line with his face. She thought for one moment he was going to nuzzle them, but instead, he smiled up at her.

He really does have very nice teeth, she thought.

'I've not finished yet,' he said, as he signalled for her to leave his plate. He manfully (so she thought) cut a chunk of the glooped mess and popped it into his mouth. 'Mmm, lovely,' he mumbled, as if his mouth was full of marbles – hardly surprising when the whole pasta dish proved solid as a brick. She tried to cut into hers with her spoon, but it bent. He swigged his down with wine.

'Look at it this way,' he said, when he finally managed to stop swallowing. 'At least we won't get food poisoning. Because you've pretty well nuked any bugs which may have been in there.' He was now grinning from ear to ear.

'Don't laugh,' she said. 'It's a disaster.' She prodded at her own pasta. 'You'd need a bloody chisel for this.'

'Hey, never mind. Let's make do with the wine instead,' he said, as he topped up her glass. 'If we get peckish later,' he added, with an emphasis on "later", 'then I'm more than happy with toast. After all, it's you I came to see.'

'Did you?' she said, blushing to the roots of her newly hennaed hair.

'Of course, you idiot,' he said. 'Hang on. Hold still.' He leant forward to swat at her head.

'Ouch!'

'You had a fly, crawling…' He put his hand out to straighten her hair, then began moving in closer and closer… until… *This is it*, she thought, closing her eyes and lifting her head. But instead of the expected kiss there was a loud ding dong, and her eyes pinged open. Mobile. Whose mobile phone? Hers or… ah, clearly his, as he was retrieving it from inside his jacket pocket.

'Sorry,' he said, moving away from her. 'Text message.' She waited while he read it. 'I'm afraid,' he said, 'that I have to call somebody back. Excuse me for a minute.'

Heading for her open French doors, he stepped out onto her verandah. From inside, she could make out part of his conversation.

'…blah blah… he what? Right. Right. No… blah blah…' as he paced up and down. 'Yes – bloody hell – all right, all right… yes, straight away.'

Polly cleared the rest of the dishes, keeping half an eye on Max staring into the middle distance and then snapping his phone shut. Clearly not good news. He returned.

'Looks like it's my turn to ruin the evening,' he said, giving her an apologetic look, then clearly realising what he'd just said. 'Oh, I didn't mean…'

'No, no, it's fine.' She touched him on the arm. 'It sounds like you have to go. Is that right?'

Running his fingers through his short already sticking-up hair, he said, 'It's complicated.' She waited for him to say more.

'Okay,' he added, looking her straight in the face. 'This isn't great timing… and… I was going to explain all this properly… Tonight, in fact.' He gave her an uncertain smile. 'You see… you're not the only one with a kid.'

'I see.' Although she didn't but wasn't sure what else to say.

'Yes. I have a child. A boy. His name is Ben. I had him with someone called Claire. She lives in Clifton. On her own. Or rather, she lives with Ben, of course, but she doesn't have a partner or boyfriend or anything. Sometimes she can't cope, and when she can't cope she rings me up. Which at times… can be a right pain.'

He pulled his jacket from the back of the chair. 'I do have to go. It seems that something's happened to Ben. Apparently he's had some sort of accident.' He gave her a half-shrug. 'I have to get over there.' He turned to go then turned back. 'So, you see, I do sympathise. You know. With you. About having a kid an' all. It sort of complicates things, doesn't it?'

'Umm, so this Claire,' Polly couldn't stop herself asking, 'were you married? Or living together?'

He checked his pockets. 'God no,' he said, jingling his found car keys. 'We were going out. Y'know. Dating. Then she… Well, there's no easy way to say this. She tricked me into getting her pregnant by telling me she was on the pill when she wasn't. Polly, look. I really must go. Claire's going mental. Says he's got a huge bump where he fell off the chair, and she's convinced herself that he has to go to hospital.' He made a move to leave. 'I'm so sorry, but I could hear Ben screaming in the background. You see how it is.'

'Yes, of course I do. You must go.' She started to lead the way to her front door, her mind racing. *He's got a kid. That's good, isn't it? Still. What did he mean? Tricked into it? Oh, give him the benefit of the doubt. You've not heard his side, have you? All the same…*

They reached the door and, before she knew it, he was kissing her. A sweet deep kiss – one of those you can fall right into. Down and down into a rabbit hole. He smelt good, tasted good… and too soon it was over.

Kissing the top of her head, and then lifting her face to his, he said, 'Your face.'

'What's wrong with it?'

'Nothing,' he said. 'Nothing at all.'

'Shut up!' She gave him a little shove but couldn't help smiling.

'Be best if I ring you, don't you think? Because you're not safe to text or email, now, are you?' He gave her a wink.

The Trouble With Love

'Oh God,' she said, covering her eyes. 'Don't remind me.'

'Hey, it's fine,' he said. 'In fact, was kind of cute.' And he headed off down her steps.

Back in the kitchen, Polly topped up her glass of wine, kicked off her heels, slipped into her Ugg boots and wandered outside. What a night! First her mum being weird and then discovering Max had a child. She flopped onto her chair, wrapping her blanket about her. *So this Claire? Just how well do they get on? Are they still in a relationship?* She sighed and gazed up at the night sky. A star, which might have been the planet Venus, twinkled down at her. She stretched her legs until her feet were resting on the wooden struts of her balcony. Draining her glass, she toasted the night then headed back inside to her dining room to turn off her laptop. *Might as well check my emails while I'm about it,* she thought. *Could check Facebook too. See what people think of the new range of dresses.*

Logging onto Facebook, she saw she had a new Friend request. Clicking on it, she nearly had a heart attack. Spike! It was Spike! Quickly, she clicked *Ignore!*

Later in bed, she couldn't get to sleep. Unable to get out of her mind that image of Spike's face grinning at her from his Facebook page. Why? Why would he want them to be Facebook friends? After all this time?

In the wee hours of the morning, she padded back downstairs, fired up her laptop and spent the next hour or so rummaging around in Spike's online photos. He looked the same, and different. She'd never seen him that tanned, for a start. Had never known him to smile that Say-Cheese-smile for the camera. He hated swimming, yet there he was on the beach, carrying a surfboard, laughing, smiling, and nearly always with the same Aussie beach babe. *Why torture yourself?* she thought, taking yet another peek before breakfast – like some woebegone addict. It might have been the early hour – Christ, was it only 05.30 am? – or it might have been the wind woo-woo-ing outside her windowpane, but Polly could sense something stirring, and it wasn't her tummy rumbling, either. More like the bottom of a tall ship sailing too close to shore, churning up what was best left undisturbed.

13

Up on the Sea Walls that edge Clifton Downs at the top of Avon Gorge, she stood looking down to where the river meets the sea, just able to make out three working cranes standing sentinel on the docks at the mouth of the River Avon. Her gaze now rested below, on a pleasure boat ploughing through brown-green water, chevron-shaped ripples fanning out behind, in its wake.

She loved this view and liked to stop here to enjoy a break. Taking a bite from her scone, she next sipped at her takeaway latte from the local deli. Just in front of her, two jackdaws perched on the bald branches of a tree which clung for life onto the top of the cliffs; railings guarding a two-hundred-foot drop. And looking out and across the gorge she could see a peregrine falcon shoot across, skimming the chasm to land somewhere in the opposite woodland.

A jackdaw's caw caught her attention. 'Okay. Here you are, birdy,' she said, as she scattered the last of her scone on the ground. One jackdaw nonchalantly cruised in to land, its claws outstretched, then strutted about, pecking at crumbs with all the sense of entitlement as its dinosaur ancestors. Funny how we used to think they were all lizards, she thought, when clearly they were birds.

Her attention returned once more to the beauty of the opposite side of the gorge, where there stood – between clumps and clusters of trees – a cliffside of granite and sandstone layered in humbug stripes of grey and orangey-gold.

She shivered as a haze and chill arrived on the air. Time to go. Pulling her jacket around her, she allowed herself one last inhale of an incoming sea breeze, before leaving incoming tides to do their thing.

'This had better be good.' Mel sounded groggy down the phone. 'Fen's left for work and I was planning on having a lie-in. So what is it? What's up? You didn't give Max food poisoning, did you? He still there tucked up in your bed, is he?'

'No and no. And not in front of Rowan,' Polly hissed, as she handed her daughter a beaker of Ribena to be getting on with. 'Look, can we meet up? Please, Mel. It's an emergency.'

'It had better be.'

Polly waited as Mel had a think down the line.

'Okay – meet me at the M Shed. Half an hour.'

Polly strode along the harbourside pushing a suitably wrapped-up Rowan in the buggy. A fresh river breeze caught her hair in blowing-cobwebs-away mode. She thought of how things had subtly changed since Mel had "gone lezzer". Although they joked and, on the surface, things were the same – Mel continuing to tease her mercilessly, and Polly to josh that she was a bossy cow – still, Polly was all too aware that while she felt free to chat to Mel about her sex life (or lack of it, more like), there existed some kind of agreed embargo on discussing Mel's girl-on-girl action. *Maybe we both need time to adjust*, she thought, as she lengthened her stride to pass a crocodile of schoolchildren heading for SS *Great Britain*.

There was that moment, soon after Mel come out, when Polly couldn't stop herself asking Mel if she'd ever fancied her.

'What? You? Do me a favour! Ugh!' was what she'd said.

'Why not? What's wrong with me?' Polly had felt a little put out, if she was honest.

But Mel had placed her arm firmly through hers, chuckled softly and said, 'Don't be daft. You know I think you're gorgeous. But, come on. We're like sisters, you and me – and fancying you would be pervy!'

And that was that. But she remained unsure about what *was* the social etiquette when your best girlfriend turned lesbian.

'Ro, come along. Mel's waiting.' She looked down at her daughter, whose cheeks were pink from the cold. Next thing, Rowan had somehow managed to get her feet tangled up and fallen headlong.

There was a gap as, shocked by her fall, Rowan held her breath and then, 'Whaaaaaaa!' let rip with a full-on toddler it's-not-fair-why-me cry. Bending down, Polly picked her up to plonk her back on her feet, then set about brushing dust from her child's duffle coat.

Rowan, sobbing away, pointed a chubby finger at her chin. 'Hurt chicken,' she blubbed in between sobs. 'H-h-hurt ch-chicken.'

'Oh dear,' said Polly.

'Oh-oh-d-d-dear,' responded Rowan.

Polly tried not to laugh at her daughter getting the word for "chin" wrong. Mishearing it for chicken. It did make her amused, though.

'Is it better now, Ro?' she asked, putting on her concerned face.

'Yuh-uh-uh-ess.' Her chin now had an angry-looking graze on it.

Polly got down so she was face to face with her daughter. 'Ro

Ro? Shall Mummy kiss it better?'

Nothing.

'Ro, darling?' Making doubly sure Rowan could see her lips.

'Ro? Say something.'

'Nuffink.'

'What's nothing, darling?'

'Nuffink means no,' pronounced Rowan.

'Sorry?'

'Nuffink means no,' she insisted.

Scooping her up into her arms, she kissed her all over her face and chin. 'Ah, Ro, you are so funny.' And Rowan, now happy as Larry, slapped Polly on both sides of her face – like a little Eric Morecambe to Poll's Ernie Wise. God love her. Chickens for chins. Nothing means no. She felt blessed to share her daughter's faltering starts at making sense of her world.

'C'mon. Spit spot.'

'Pit pot!'

'Up you get! Your carriage awaits!' She strapped her back into her buggy and set off once more. Wouldn't pay to be late for Mel. Overhead, a seagull hung suspended above the river like a mobile over a child's cot. *Am off for a rendezvous with Mel. Rendezvous. That's a good word, isn't it?*

Across the water, in the amphitheatre-type space in front of the Lloyds TSB building, skateboarders zoomed from one side to the other. Up a ramp, up up into the air, pause, turn mid-flight and down, while above them, black-headed gulls rightly showed off their own prowess; soaring, tilting and perfectly judging the thermals. Further along, two idiots – with beer in hand – were trying to rock a wooden jetty, where a squadron of gulls rested. As the youths ran at them, the birds nonchalantly took to the air, squawk-shouting – what very much sounded like – *Tossers!* at the yobs below.

The Trouble With Love

Mel had arrived at the café ahead of them and was well through a latte.

'Sorry we're late,' said Polly even though they weren't. She unfastened Rowan then wrestled her into a highchair. 'I think an emergency chocolate brownie might be in order.' She pointed at Rowan's chin. 'Accident.'

'How's my gorgeous Ro Ro?' Mel asked, and was rewarded with a cherubic grin. She summoned a waiter to give their order.

'Show Mel your chin.'

But Rowan was giving all a stare worthy of Queen Elizabeth I showing disdain to her courtiers. 'She hurt it,' murmured Polly.

'Chicken,' said Rowan, and nodded at Mel. 'Chicken.'

Mel gave the little girl's tubby thick woolly tights-clad legs a sympathetic waggle.

'Oh no,' she said – which appeared to appease Rowan. The drinks and brownie order duly arrived, and Mel – once the waiter was safely out of earshot – said, 'Come on, spill the beans. Is it true, or not?' She glanced at Rowan, but there was no need to worry about little ears overhearing, because squeezing the life out of her cake – ahead of shoving it into her mouth – was taking all of Rowan's attention.

'I'm dying to know – you have to tell me,' she said, lowering her voice a little, just in case. 'Now.'

'Is what true?'

'Does he have a big… you know…' She glanced over her shoulder. 'Does Max have a big –' *knob?* she mouthed.

'God's sake!' hissed Polly, jerking her head towards her daughter. 'Rowan…'

Mel raised her eyes at her. 'I've heard he's a –' *sex machine*, she mouthed again.

Polly glanced around the café, checking no one was paying attention to them. She needn't have worried; there was a group of what looked like foreign students, complete with backpacks, anoraks and guidebooks at the next table, and that was about it.

'Shh. I didn't find out. Okay?' She glanced around again. 'In any case, that's not why we're here.'

'It isn't?' She sat back. 'That's a shame.'

'No. Look. I'll give you the lowdown on Max later. I promise.'

'The lowdown? Or was it the down-low? You filthy cow!'

'Shut up.'

A waiter began to clear away their things, but not before he'd given Rowan a little chuck under the chin, which caused her to give him a grumpy look. 'Sorry,' explained Polly. 'She fell and hurt her chin earlier.'

'Hang on a tick, I have just the thing,' he said, as he headed off to return with a colouring book and pens. 'There you go, young lady.' Polly mouthed her thanks.

'So, if it's not Max and his gigantic wanger,' Mel said, once the waiter had left, 'just what is this big emergency you dragged me down here for?'

Polly made sure Rowan was busy scribbling in the book. 'Right,' she began, leaning in towards her friend. 'You'll never guess who poked me on Facebook last night?'

'Umm... Johnny Depp? David Dimbleby asking you to be on *Question Time*!'

'Be serious.'

'Oh, all right. I dunno. Who?'

Polly spelt out Spike's name because Rowan was in earshot.

'No! You *are* joking.' Mel slapped the table, causing Rowan to jump a little.

'Shh,' said Polly, looking pointedly at Rowan, who was now trying to feed part of her brownie into the opening of her beaker.

'What? He poked you? Just like that? Christ. That's a turn-up for the books.' Mel fixed her with a steely look. 'So what are you going to do about it?'

'I don't know. What do you think?' Polly sat back, casting around the café as if for inspiration. It had soothing stripped wooden tables and chairs, with waiting staff dressed in smart black. People milled about outside, walking past the floor-to-ceiling windows, dashing to work appointments, or strolling hand in hand, or skateboarding past…

'Maybe,' said Mel, bringing Polly back to the discussion, 'this could be a golden opportunity for you to build bridges with Spike. Perhaps *now* is the time to let him know that he has a beautiful daughter.'

'Is it? Is it the right time, though? What good can it do when he lives on the other side of the world? In Australia? It's not like he can play an active part in our lives, is it? In any case – *he* was the one who told me not to get in touch. Remember?'

'But clearly he's changed his mind and is reaching out to you. And what about Ro?' she said, lowering her voice once more. 'Is it fair on Ro to deny—'

'Shh.' Polly nodded across at Rowan. 'Little girls have big ears.'

Rowan stopped mid-grasping her cake like a wildlife expert might strangle a venomous snake. 'Have I got big ears, Mummy?'

'Of course you haven't,' she said, reaching across to wipe Rowan's face and hands with wet wipes. 'I meant other little girls. Your ears aren't big. They're like shells.'

'Like smells?'

'No, darling.' Polly smiled at her daughter. 'Your ears are lovely, aren't they, Mel?'

'Sure are. They're the best ears in the whole wide world.'

Suitably pacified, Rowan set about sucking the remainder of her apple juice from her beaker.

'I'll walk back to the house with you,' said Mel, as she picked up her mobile to text Fen. 'I've just got to see those pictures. And – you don't mind, do you, but I thought I might as well shower and change while I'm there. Only I'm a bit whiffy.'

'Charming. Oh, and Mel… I'm really sorry if I've not always listened about Fen. I hope you know that if you do ever want to discuss anything – anything at all – with me… then feel free. That's what best friends are for, yeah?'

'I do love you, ya muppet.'

A dockside steam engine trundled past the trio on its way to Ashton Court Estate – tooting its whistle – which was all very exciting for Rowan. Mel whipped her excitement up further by woo-woo-ing, while Polly thought of her Scottish explorer ancestor – Mungo Park. Once, she'd seen a copy of a painting of Mungo, and he'd owned the same determined chin, the same hair and the same blue eyes as Rowan. The story was that somehow Mungo had managed to fall out of his canoe and drown in the River Niger; which Polly, as a child, had thought hilarious. Up the creek without a paddle.

Toot toot. Hurrying up the path to her road, she could smell the cinders and burnt iron in the air – conjuring up memories of iron filings and school lab experiments on magnetism. Unseen forces, she thought, as she gave Rowan a final push to the top.

Back at her house, she put Rowan down for a nap, while in the kitchen Mel had made them both a hot chocolate.

'Ooh, lovely,' Polly said, as she cupped hers in her cold hands.

'Rowan is so adorable,' Mel said. 'You're lucky to have her. You do know that, don't you?'

'Yes, Mel. I do. Thanks. Still, it's good to be reminded, now and then, because when you're in the daily grind it's easy to lose sight of things. And,' she said, giving her friend a quick hug, 'this is exactly why you are such a good godmother.'

Mel gave her a look that she couldn't quite work out… Before she could ask her, Mel clapped her hands together. 'Right then. You might as well tell me *everything* about Max. And I mean everything. Plus the whole SP on Spike too. I mean, honestly, I leave you for one day and look at the fine mess you get yourself into.'

'Yes, Olly,' said Polly in her best Stan Laurel voice, causing Mel to flick her with a tea towel.

'All right. All right.' Polly began to fill her in about Max when Rowan called from upstairs for a drink of water.

'Sorry, Mel – hold that thought. I won't be long…'

'No worries, you go ahead,' said Mel, as she turned to stare out of the window.

Once Polly had attended to her daughter and returned, it was to find Mel furiously attacking the kitchen work surfaces with Cillit Bang. Rub rub rub rub, as if she'd been hired to clean up after a murder crime scene.

'Everything okay, Mel?'

'Yes.' Then turning to face her friend, cloth in hand. 'Sort of.' She flung the cloth into the sink and pulled off the Marigolds. 'That's not quite true. I'm not really all right, because the thing is, Polly. And – this is so exciting…'

'Yes? Go on, what is it?'

'I don't know where to start. I've been dying to tell you for ages, but Fen said I should wait, but I can't. We were discussing it into the wee hours last night.'

'You were?' Polly had not seen Mel this excited since she managed to land Tony Wolf, the best-looking boy in Bristol.

'Okay – now don't be shocked. Here goes. Fen and I are

planning on having a baby. There. I said it. So, what do you think?'

Polly gawped. 'A baby? But how? I don't understand. You and Fen? A baby?' Nope; it still made no sense when she said it out loud.

Then she saw – really saw – her friend's face. Saw how radiant she looked as she explained to Polly how her biological clock was tick-tocking away; how she admired Polly and adored Rowan; and how these days you didn't have to deny yourself the right to a child just because you happened to be gay. Hadn't she seen that film where those two lesbians use an anonymous donor? And how there were plenty of clinics around offering sperm donors, and that her and Fen had decided to go for it. And no, last night wasn't the first time they'd discussed it, and yes, they were sure.

'You know how much I love Ro. If I could have a child half as gorgeous as she is…'

'Yeah, well, being a mother's not all that easy,' Polly felt obliged to mutter. Because it wasn't/isn't.

'I'm sure if you managed it, then I can,' said Mel, giving her a determined look.

But Polly was thinking of how Mel didn't know the half of it. How she'd not witnessed those horrendous ear infections when Rowan had screamed far into the night. How she didn't know the toll that being dog-tired can take on you. How you can't think straight. How your boobs go west; not to mention the stretch marks, haemorrhoids, the loss of libido, and the wondering where on earth *you* went.

'Be happy for me. Can you at least be happy for me?'

'Oh sorry, babe.' She took her friend's hand and gave it a squeeze. 'I was just considering it all. I mean, it's a big decision. And yes, of course I'm happy for you.' Polly dunked a Jammie Dodger in her hot chocolate. 'Just getting my head around it, that's all.'

'I've been doing some thinking myself,' continued Mel. 'I'm thinking how it's a shame Spike's not here in Bristol, instead of poking you on Facebook.'

'Eh?' Polly shot Mel a look – she was in dead earnest.

'Now hear me out,' Mel said, as she twiddled one of Rowan's hair ties. 'It could have been perfect – if he was here. No, listen...' (But Polly was way ahead of her by now, her mind boggling away.) 'If Spike could... or more like if he would... somehow... you know.' Mel spread her hands out wide like some Yiddish Mama. 'Spike could be my sperm donor!'

What? What? Even though she knew what she was going to say, it was still mad. Stark raving mad. Did she seriously want Spike as her sperm donor?

'That way,' Mel was continuing, clearly getting up a full head of steam, 'my child – that is mine and Fen's child – would be Rowan's half-brother or -sister. We could all be a proper family. It fits, yeah? Spike's obviously got good genes, and you know how much I adore Rowan. So what do you think? Fab idea, or what?'

Fab? It's the blinkin' opposite of fab. But Mel looked so chuffed about the whole thing. She turned away and gazed out to where the garden met the incoming tide. *It's academic anyway, isn't it? He's halfway across the world in Australia, so it wouldn't happen in any case.*

'Well,' she began, 'I can – umm – see some merits in your argument...' (If this was an alternative universe where getting pregnant by your best friend's ex-boyfriend didn't mean anything at all!) She coughed and tried again. 'And, of course, Rowan's the best little girl in the whole wide world.'

'See? I told you it would be perfect.'

Polly couldn't help but see the desperation on her friend's face.

What harm would it do if she gave her approval? *It's not like*

Spike could FedEx over a load of fresh sperm from Melbourne, now, is it?

'I guess,' she eventually said, 'that it does make some kind of sense. In principle.' She gave her friend a half-smile – not feeling up to a full one.

'Yeah. Well.' Mel's shoulders dropped. 'It's neither here nor there, is it? In the absence of Spike.' She grabbed a Jammie Dodger. 'Looks like it'll have to be a trip to the old anonymous donor clinic.'

'I hear they're pretty good these days. So,' said Polly, keen to move on, 'have you decided who's going to be Mother?'

'Me. Definitely me. If only because… and it's just a niggling feeling, I mean, I could be wrong – but Fen isn't quite as keen as I am.'

'But you said you'd discussed it all last night.'

'Yes… but… Oh, never mind.' She got to her feet to place her empty cup in the washing-up bowl. 'Dare say I'm imagining it. She came round in the end.'

Polly grabbed hold of her friend by the shoulders. 'Now listen up. If you do ever end up doing this solo then you've always got me. We can be single parents together. I know, let's make a pact right now that we'll set up house together. If need be. But not in a lezzer way, obviously.'

'How many more times?' joked Mel. 'You are so not my type. Ugh.'

'Charming.' Polly rested her forehead on her friend's. 'Seriously, babe. We could get a house, share childcare, housing costs, the whole kit and caboodle.'

Not that Polly was keen on communes, having witnessed them first-hand as a child with Suze. All lentil stews and rows over who's-eaten-whose-food; plus passive aggression, house meetings, heated discussions on sexual politics, in-fighting and on-the-surface-but-not-really-tolerated infidelities. But this was

Mel, and they were family, whatever happened.

'So, do tell,' said Mel, moving away and putting back on her I-can-handle-anything attitude. 'Have you Facebooked Spike's Profile yet? Who'm I kidding? Of course you have!'

14

It was the day of the filming of the open mic night. Mel was unable to babysit, as Fen had announced she was going to sing. (Apparently she had the voice of Marianne Faithfull – who knew? Certainly not Polly.)

In her bedroom, she attacked her hair with a hairbrush. Polly couldn't help it, but she wished Fen wasn't going to be there. She was nervous enough as it was; God knew she'd be more on edge with Fen there – being all silently judgy, because it didn't take an agony aunt to spot that Fen was jealous of Polly's relationship with Mel. And Mel herself had hinted this, on several occasions.

She considered she'd made an effort to put Fen at her ease, but Fen would have none of it. She'd feign headaches if invited to dinner, sulk her way through movies, hog Mel's attention at every opportunity, and in the end, Polly had stopped inviting her to things. *So don't say I haven't tried... Ouch...* Her tangles were proving particularly wayward tonight, as if they knew she expected them to be on their best behaviour. Getting out the de-frizz stuff, she sprayed her hair. *There, that'll teach it.*

Of course, now that Mel and Fen were to be parents, she'd have to try harder with Fen. Clearly their relationship was stronger and more long-term than Polly had thought. Which was a first for Mel.

Polly could see her now, adopting a defiant stance as she fixed Polly with a stare when she first told her about Fen.

'Don't laugh,' she'd started.

'What?'

'I've met someone.'

'That's great.'

'A woman. Her name is Fen.'

'What?'

'I'm gay.'

Polly had burst out laughing – not because she thought it funny, even though she did wonder at the time if there was a punchline coming up, but more from nerves. One look at Mel, though, and she could see that her best friend in the whole world was deadly serious and anxious for her approval.

Since then, there had been times when she'd wondered if Mel's love affair with Fen might prove to be a passing phase, but Mel assured her it was the real thing, and Polly had to respect that.

Still. The two of them – Polly and Mel – had shared pretty much every rite of passage – first drink, first cigarette, first hangover, first shag – and so when Mel did come out, they'd sat and discussed it at length over more than one bottle of Lidl's finest wine; Mel insisting that when she met Fen, she realised how part of her had always known she was gay. 'Really, Polly, it feels so right. It does! I never did totally like sex with men,' she added.

Well, you could have fooled me, Polly had thought, but didn't say.

Remembering times gone by brought back memories of her

mother, Suze. How she'd turned up one day at Polly's home in Bristol, with her arm draped across the shoulder of a woman with a skinhead haircut, bovver boots and Levi 501s. 'This is Ajax,' she'd announced. 'My lover.' Causing Polly's dad to merely shrug his shoulders and hand his daughter over for her weekend access visit.

'Lovely,' her stepmother, Gillian, had said, not terribly convincingly.

*

'Being lesbian is a natural progression of radical feminism,' Suze had announced over a largely indigestible lentil burger. 'We reject male hegemony and penile penetration. It's a violent manifestation of the patriarchal domination of women,' she was saying, loud enough so that people in the vegan café feigned sudden and intense interest in their plates. Polly had stared at the alfalfa sprouts and mung beans that accompanied her lentil burger as Ajax gave Suze a full-on wet snog, and Polly wished she was anywhere else. Even Gillian's homemade cake stall at the local WI would have been preferable to this, she'd thought at the time.

Looking back on those days with Suze and her women friends, Polly could now find it funny, even giving herself a wry smile in her dressing-table mirror as she recalled the time when her mother had taken her to a women's group where they were all to "embrace the cunt". Polly had been invited to inspect hers with a torch and a large mirror. 'If you're too shy, you can look at mine,' Suze had offered, oblivious to her daughter's obvious-to-anyone-else-with-half-an-eye embarrassment.

'No, thanks,' she'd muttered, and left the room to make the teas.

What Suze now referred to as her "lesbian phase" had lasted

about twelve years, before she dabbled a little with men (as she called it) and then met Brian. 'Does this mean you're definitely not lesbian anymore?' Polly had asked.

'Oh, I don't hold with labels,' Suze said, waving her question away. 'We're all on a spectrum of sexuality, aren't we, darling?'

Suze's most famous partnering had been with celebrated chef Petronella Dawson. Although Suze would have none of it, her high-profile relationship with Petronella had helped her career no end. Their messy break-up, chronicled in red tops and celeb mags, had merely increased Suze's celebrity status, until here she was: a television chef with her own popular show *Keep Calm and Bake On;* a couple of high-end restaurants specialising in vintage make-do-and-cook, staffed by waitresses in vintage hairstyles and clothes; and of course her especially-popular-at-Christmas cookery books, complete with enclosed prints of her specially hand-painted winter-wonderland-scene Christmas cards. (She didn't go to art school for nothing!) Sometimes Suze's latter-day high-achieving left Polly exhausted.

Polly placed the brush back on her dressing table, pinned her hair into an up-do and then appraised herself in her long wardrobe mirror: tight black capri pants, Vivienne Westwood-style peplum top, accentuating enough – but not too much – of her impressive embonpoint. Her boobs had not shrunk after breastfeeding – much to Daisy's supposed annoyance (Daisy was much too equanimous to be annoyed). 'Like a couple of half-empty plastic bags, mine are,' she'd confessed. 'I'm saving up for a boob job. But shh. Don't tell Phil.' (Wink.)

Face finished, Polly slicked on bright red lipstick, blotted her mouth with tissue paper, and then – with one last check in the mirror – hurried downstairs to where Mel was waiting with Rowan.

'I'm not sure about this. Rowan should be having her bath now. Getting ready for bed ' Polly told Mel.

'Earth to Polly!' Mel was saying, as she pulled Rowan's little hand through the sleeve of her Oilily orange and flower-patterned parka jacket.

'Hmm?'

'It'll be an adventure,' said Mel, giving Rowan's face one last wipe with the flannel. 'Won't it, Rowan? Be fun seeing Mummy perform poetry. Yes?'

The little girl, clearly not hearing but sensing something different was indeed about to happen, presented a picture of wonderment and growing excitement as she smiled uncertainly up into her mother's face.

'But what will people think? What will they say?' Polly asked, as she crossed first one ankle in front of the other and then changed legs. (She had a tendency to fidget when anxious.) 'I can see the *Bristol Post* headline now: "Single mother takes two-year-old daughter to a bar—"'

'Don't exaggerate.' Mel zipped up Rowan's coat.

'Café/bar then. What if someone calls social services? I couldn't bear it.'

'Now you're being ridiculous. No one bats an eyelid on the Continent, do they? They all take their babies and toddlers everywhere, don't they? Just bung her in the buggy and she'll be fine. There's no reason why being a single mum should stop you from doing *everything*.' Mel stood back to admire her handiwork. 'You'll do,' she announced, and Polly wasn't sure if she meant Rowan or herself.

'Will Max be there?' Mel gave Polly a suggestive look.

'Yes. Now shut up. We've got to go.'

Polly had not seen Max since their failed date. They'd texted, and she was pleased to hear that Ben was fine and had just had a bit of a scare. Max reckoned Claire had overreacted, and Polly let it slide because she knew that if it was Rowan who'd fallen off a chair and hit her head on a stone-flagged floor she'd have been in a right state, too. *Ah well*, she thought, now shrugging on her jacket and switching off the kitchen light. Hopefully tonight they'd finally get together, have a chat – who knows? Maybe more? She felt a thrill zing through her, which had more to do with seeing Max than nerves about performing.

*

'You all right, Polly?' asked Leo, who worked on the door of the *Chill Out* café's back room. 'This your babby? Aww. Beautiful, ent she? Not sure you can bring her in here, mind.'

'Oh, for Chrissake, just let her in,' said Mel, barging forward and indicating that Leo ought to go ahead and stamp Polly's hand. 'Polly's here for the filming. She'll only be half an hour, tops. We'll be in and out before Mike even gets here.'

'Well, I s'pose...'

'Good. Good.' Mel craned her neck to see into the room. 'Only we're on a tight schedule,' she said, back at Leo. 'Have to get this young lady' – referring to Rowan – 'home in time for beddy-byes.'

Just then, Vanessa arrived. 'Polly?' She peered askance at Rowan then bent down to her level. 'This must be your beautiful daughter.' Rowan stared back: Pooh Bear clutched in one hand, beaker of juice in the other.

'Umm yes. Sorry. Babysitting problems.'

Placing her hands on both thighs, Vanessa stood back up. 'Can't be helped, I suppose,' she said, bestowing on Polly a false smile. 'Still...' and here she gave Polly a most pointed look '...I could have made *alternative* arrangements, had I known...'

Leo stamped Mel's and Polly's hands. On impulse, Polly gave her a quick hug. 'We'll be quick, I promise,' she whispered.

'You better be,' said Leo. 'Only, his nibs will be in later and you'd best be gone by then, what with the babby an' all. He's iffy as fuck about having poetry nights in here. He hates poetry.'

Polly was about to go through to the back room when she remembered that Leo was renting Spike's houseboat. 'How's the boat?'

'Oh, didn't you know? I'm moving out, and—'

'No time to hang around chatting. We'd best get a move on,' said Mel, giving her a shove before she could ask Leo whether or not she'd heard from Spike. Darn.

The lights were up. Polly didn't think she'd ever seen the space with its lights on before. It looked better than expected. Gone were the sticky beer-stained carpets, to be replaced by stripped wooden floorboards. The new tables even had small glass vases with little posies in them.

Max emerged from the door to the toilets, at the side – causing Polly's heart to do skippity-skip little bunny hops. He hurried over and gave Polly a kiss full on the mouth – which made her blush. Stepping back, he raised an eyebrow at Rowan. 'Don't ask,' whispered Polly. 'Couldn't get a babysitter.' *Might as well be wearing a badge saying* Really Bad Mother.

'Won't be long now,' said Vanessa, squeezing past the two of them only pausing to ruffle Rowan's hair. 'We want to get this young lady back to bed, as soon as.' Hands on hips. 'Sound guy here? Has somebody checked the lighting? PA? Chop chop!'

'Who does she think she is? Attila the Hen?' Mel stage whispered, but Polly was hoping Max didn't feel badly about her. He moved off with Vanessa, to do her bidding, while Polly couldn't resist watching his retreating bum, and then blushing when he turned and caught her.

'Busted!' said Mel, who never missed a thing.

'Oh, shut up.' Polly gave her a small shove then turned her attention to Rowan, who'd started to grizzle. 'Here you are,' she said, giving her a packet of raisins and hoping that the parenting gods weren't gazing down and judging her.

I just don't feel comfortable, she thought, taking her seat at the table as Rowan clutched the packet to her chest, like a miser with a purse full of gold coins.

The club began to fill up, with people stopping by Rowan's buggy, as if courtiers paying homage to a queen, as the child smiled and waved, accepting all as her due.

'She's beautiful, Poll.'

'What's her name?'

'Gorgeous kiddie.'

'I want one of those.'

Mel whispered, 'Don't you go worrying what that Max might think. I'll bet he's cool with your bringing Ro Ro. Now, have you got your poem all ready?'

Polly had been practising it all day and was now pretty sure she was word-perfect. Even Rowan could read along to snatches of it. Vanessa said that if it came out well, they might feature it in the titles and pay her an extra fee. Which would be nice.

'I'll go get us a drink,' said Mel. 'What'll you have?'

'Diet Coke, ta.'

'How about Walkers crisps for madam here?'

'Oh all right… go on then. But make it plain – if they have them. And if not – cheese and onion.'

Rowan perked up at the mention of yet another treat. 'Cisp,' she said, unable to pronounce the "r" and extra "s" in crisps. Polly set about her child's face and hands with a wet wipe, as Rowan wriggled and squirmed in her buggy, unable to escape her mother's ministrations.

'Here we are.' Flopping down on her seat, Mel had returned

with drinks and crisps, which she duly opened before handing to Rowan. 'I'm so excited about Fen singing.' She picked at a beer mat. 'And – I am of course excited to be giving my bestest friend in the whole world lots of encouragement and support.' She grinned. 'See? All turned out okay in the end.'

Polly wasn't quite sure what the "all" might be, but Mel had spotted Fen, and was now standing and waving. 'Fen! Fen! Over here!' Fen dashed, if not ran, to greet them.

'Hi, Poll,' she said, then – draping an arm around Mel's shoulder – 'Hey, babes. You look divine.' The two of them beamed at each other: so happy. It threw Polly, somewhat.

'Hey, Poll. Look. See that guy over there?' said Fen.

'Where?'

'By the bar.'

Ah yes, she could see him now. Random-yet-good-looking-guy-by-the-bar. He lifted his drink in salutation to them.

'He's been chatting me up like crazy. Watch this.' Fen grasped Mel's face between her two hands and gave her a full-on passionate snog – tongues an' all.

The man turned away, feigning an acute fascination with his pint.

Poor bloke.

'Honestly, Fen,' said Mel. 'You are such a prick tease.'

'Who cares, he deserved it. Bet it gave him a cheap thrill. Blokes and their lesbian fantasies.' Fen grinned at Mel, who grinned back like a – well, like a lovesick moron, Polly thought. She also thought Fen was being a right cow.

'How's the book going?' Mel asked, as her girlfriend pulled up a chair, so close that it seemed as if she was attempting to merge with Mel.

'Oh, the book? You know. Knocked out another dashing-doctor/dopey-nurse romance,' she said, leaning back and crossing one black-jeaned leg over the other. Polly couldn't quite square the fact that the oh-so-goth and on-the-surface-feminist-and-into-sexual-politics Fen supplemented her salary as a high-flying corporate something-or-other by bashing out Mills & Boon hospital romantic fiction. She insisted they were dead easy if you could pen them without taking the piss, and that when writing, she'd imagine herself as frustrated housewife Lois – clearly modelled on Doris Day. Fen was fond of Lois. According to Mel, she liked to rummage around vintage shops buying 1950s aprons for Lois to wear.

'How's Lois?' Mel would ask.

'Earned two grand pin money last month,' Fen would say.

'Way to go, Lois.'

As Mel and Fen got stuck into an intimate conversation, Daisy arrived and took in the situation. 'Good grief. What's Rowan doing here?'

Polly couldn't face explaining it all over again and luckily Mel came to her rescue. 'Cut her some slack, Daise. It's a long story… Polly didn't want to but… well… let's have some female solidarity here, yeah?'

'Okay, point taken. Was only asking.' She turned to Polly. 'It's a shame Tiggy's ill and couldn't babysit. Right!' She slapped her thighs in that jolly-hockey-sticks way of hers. 'Shall we start afresh, then… Hello, Polly, good to see you,' and she bent to kiss first her friend on the cheek, and then Rowan. 'How are you, young lady? Are you okay?'

'K,' Rowan duly answered, before stuffing as many crisps as she possibly could into her mouth.

'Now, ladies, budge up,' said Daisy, as she squeezed into a space.

'How's Tiggy feeling now?'

'Still rough. Throwing up. The works. I've left Phil behind looking after her. I could have stayed but then I thought – fuck 'em. It's about time I had a night off – for good behaviour, if nothing else.'

'Good for you,' said Polly, while Mel and Fen grinned their agreement.

Polly was glad to have her friends around her. In the past, they'd made it crystal clear they only attended poetry nights on sufferance, to support her. Full stop. The fact that they sometimes enjoyed themselves being beside the point, and soon forgotten as they declared that they hated poetry, full stop.

Of course, the fact that Fen is doing a solo spot later on tonight means that wild horses and smelly poets couldn't keep Mel away. Polly contemplated the two of them. *They do seem happy, don't they? But a baby? Together? Isn't it too soon?*

'We're ready for you now, Polly,' called Vanessa – cutting through her reverie, as she waved at her from the stage, where she was fiddling about with the microphone stand. Mel gave Polly a go-get-'em double thumbs-up as she rose, pulled herself upright and walked to the small stage; fingers mentally crossed that she wouldn't fluff her lines.

Okay, now don't forget to breathe, she told herself, as she took three small steps up to the wooden boards. *Remember – it's not how you're doing, but what you're doing* – this being her confidence-boosting mantra. The one she'd learnt from another poet, meant to stop those butt-clenching moments when you're convinced that it's all gone to pot, that the audience hate you and that every single person in the audience wants you *off*.

As she scanned the room, she estimated there must be ten, fifteen people, tops. She waited as Vanessa herded the punters into a group near the front. Next she got them all geed up, by making them practise their clapping and cheering. Then – 'Off you go, Polly,' she said, taking her place at the side and giving the audience a *C'mon-clap-and-cheer* signal, and – '*Woop woop*' – they obliged.

First clenching then unclenching her fists, she told herself to *Relax*. From her spot in front of the mic, she took a deep breath.

The Trouble With Love

Own the stage, Polly. Own the stage. And breathe. Lifting her head, she took the mic off its stand, glanced across to the sound technician, who gave her the nod, and she was off – starting with her poem about singles and dating (with an especial nod to her own disastrous speed dating night).

"'At the lonely hearts disco, ladies dressed for the night
Are expectant and willing to find Mr Right…'"

*

Poem finished to wild (Vanessa-generated) applause as she hopped off the stage. 'Well done. That was super,' said Vanessa.

The regular compère, a rotund man in his thirties, red-faced and out of puff, asked if they were finished and then gave Polly a pat on the shoulder. 'Do come along to another open mic night,' he said, with a wink, and turned to have a conflab with the sound guy, who'd magicked another couple of mics to rearrange for the rest of the open mic night.

As Polly moved offstage, Max appeared beside her. 'Can you hang on?' he asked, as he bent to pack up his own kit into a series of bags.

'Not really,' she said, looking towards her daughter. 'Only I've got to get Rowan back home. You know how it is.'

He stood up. 'That's me done,' he announced, hauling the larger bag over his shoulder. 'If you're ready for the off, I'll walk you to your car.'

As Polly returned to her table, she caught a pungent whiff of skunk. A group of students were giggling in the corner. One of them had rolled a spliff, seemingly not bothered if anyone saw. Definitely time to go. Making sure her daughter was securely strapped in her buggy, she collected the rest of her stuff and was kissing her friends goodbye, when a scuffle broke out at the students' table.

'Oi! You there! That's right. You fuckin' students!' Mike – big and burly Mike, owner of the café – had a student by the scruff of his skater jacket. 'Can't you bleedin' read, you ponce?' he shouted, and pointed to the "No Smoking" sign. 'None of that wacky baccy in 'ere, ya lummox!' Mike proceeded to drag the guilty student towards the door. 'I'll have no fuckin' hip-hop students in here!' he bellowed, giving the student one last shove. The students all scuttled for the exit. Then Mike spotted Rowan, and Polly froze. 'Ah look, a little kiddie,' he said, his face all soft. 'Ain't she a sweetheart.' Back to students. 'Now fuck off out of here.' To Polly. 'Excuse my French.'

*

Outside, Polly was backing out of the doorway, dragging the buggy with her, Max and Mel close behind, all smiles, when somebody held the door open. She turned to say thanks and came eyeball to eyeball with the impossible.

Spike! What? Spike? Here? She had to blink. Look again. Make sure she hadn't conjured him up out of thin air. Brain desperately trying to compute. It was Spike all right. For one mad nanosecond she wondered whether all that checking of his Facebook page had somehow caused some kind of electronic voodoo, conjuring him out of thin air. But no. There he was. The whole flesh and bone and length and hair and smile of him. She had no idea what to say. Her brain had clearly gone *nah, too tricky* – and snuck off for a bit of a lie-down.

'Wha…?' was all she finally managed.

'Polly?' Clearly he was as surprised as her.

'You're in Bristol!'

'You don't say!' He smiled an amused smile at her. That amused smile she knew oh so well. 'I did try to Facebook yeh, but I got no response.'

'Wha…?'

'Fuck me,' said Mel, who'd followed Polly out the door. Spike gave her a nod in greeting. Max moved next to Polly.

'You all right?' Max said, placing a proprietorial arm around her waist in a gesture not lost on Spike.

'Spike?' came a voice, and as one they turned to see a vision of sun-kissed loveliness emerge from the late-night shop next door. 'Spike, wait for me, hun,' she called. Polly recognised at once that she was the tall blonde from Spike's Facebook pictures. 'You gonna introduce me?' the vision asked, as she joined them and threaded her arm firmly through Spike's.

'Sure.' He patted her hand. 'This is Bam…'

Bam? What sort of frickin' name is that? Polly thought.

'Pleased to meet you. I'm Spike's girlfriend,' Bam said, in perfect RP, and not the Aussie-from-*Neighbours*-accent that Polly had expected. Clearly this was a night where expectations were confounded at each turn, as if the Lord of Misrule was out and about, turning all topsy-turvy with his mischief-making-bell-and-ribbon-bejazzled-stick. Polly shook her head – Nope, she wasn't imagining this. Spike and Bam were still there.

'This is all rather weird,' said Spike, his steady gaze not leaving Polly's face, making her feel as if their eyes were locked in some kind of ship-to-ship trajectory beam from an old episode of *Star Trek*. She couldn't look away. She physically couldn't pull her eyes away from his.

Max held his hand out to Spike. 'Max,' he said. 'Polly's boyfriend.' That broke the spell, as she gawped at him, thinking how presumptuous. They hadn't even slept together! Well, not yet… but, 'Pleased to meet you,' Spike was saying as he shook his hand, all perfectly polite and gentlemanly.

'Are you not going to say anything?' Mel stage whispered to Polly as she gave her a little nudge. But Polly was too busy staring at Spike, then Max, then back at Mel, then back again to Spike, who was doing that quizzical smile of his. The one she used to find so sexy. Who was she trying to kid? Used to?

'So, who's this little one here, then?' Spike bent his knees, getting a closer look at Rowan.

'Rowan,' said Mel.

Spike looked up at her. 'She yours?' he said.

'No. She's yours,' came Mel's reply.

Polly carried her child – more her child, she was reminding herself, than hers and Spike's – from the car into the house.

'My child...' Spike had said outside the bar, and then he'd repeated it, as if to root it all in reality. 'My child. Why didn't you tell me, Poll?'

And now she was just closing the door with her foot when a hand reached round from outside to stop her. Was it Spike? Had Spike followed her home? Standing, with mouth agape and Rowan in her arms, she watched as the front door swung open to reveal – Max.

'Max?'

'Have you forgotten that I was coming round after the filming?' he said, with an uncertain look on his face.

Yes, she had forgotten, but answered – 'No. No, of course I haven't forgotten – as if. Come on in.' She gave him a weak smile. 'It's been a funny old night. Look, make yourself at home while I put Rowan to bed first, okay?'

Rowan didn't stir as Polly placed her on top of the bed and gently manoeuvred her into a pair of pyjamas, all the while fast asleep like a big floppy doll. Even the momentous occasion of meeting her errant father, Spike, hadn't been enough to keep her awake. Spike. Had he really returned to Bristol? It hadn't been a dream, then, because there he'd been, large as life and taking her breath away. She wasn't sure if that feeling of breathlessness

– as if someone had pulled the plug on all the oxygen in the night air of that particular north Bristol street – was from the shock of seeing him, or whether her hormones had gone into overdrive from some sort of Pavlovian response. Did she after all still feel… what? *Don't be stupid. Anyway, best not to think about any of that right now. It was shock, that's all. Just shock.*

She tucked Rowan beneath her Winnie the Pooh duvet, placed a kiss on her forehead and closed the bedroom door softly behind her.

Downstairs, Max stood leaning against her kitchen sink, waiting for her. 'I'm sorry, Polly. I can tell you've had some sort of shock at bumping into your old boyfriend, but I've got to ask – is he Rowan's father? Only, I thought he was in Australia.'

'You and me both.' She moved past him to fill up the kettle.

'So, am I right in thinking that he didn't know? About having a kid?'

'It's not what it seems,' she said, distractedly, because all she could picture was Spike when Mel had dropped her bombshell – him standing on the pavement, gob well and truly smacked as he grappled with the whys, hows and wherefores. And she – not wanting to cause a scene (especially with Rowan present) – had left, muttering something about him giving her a call the next day – tomorrow; same number. Convincing herself that this was the sensible thing to do and not the coward's way out (which she now felt it might have been). The truth? She'd needed time – still needed time – to get her head around it all. To reshift her own thinking. It was all very well her dishing out the whole "abandoned pregnant girlfriend left to do single motherhood alone" routine to all and sundry when Spike was not around. But now he was back, and he'd be wanting answers.

'I'm sure you had your reasons,' Max was saying, bringing her very much back to the present. 'For not telling this guy – Spike, isn't it? – that he has a child. But it's hard for me to imagine what those reasons might be, given I'm a single dad myself.'

With no warning, her eyes began to fill with tears. *Trust Spike to turn up.* 'It's complicated,' she said, so quietly that Max had to take a step closer to hear what she was saying.

'Ah yes, complications. I guess I know all about those.' He held out his hand. 'Come here,' he said, his voice softer now as he pulled her close and she cried big floppy tears onto his shoulder. 'Look, we don't have to talk about it now, not if you don't want to,' he said. 'Shh.' He kissed the top of her head and then lifted her face up to meet his, her salt tears mingling with their kiss. His lips solid and soft. Her body responding – and she wanted to respond, wanted to lose herself in him, to wipe out the image of Spike standing on the pavement, the hurt in his eyes.

Max found the waistband of her jeans and slid his hand inside, feeling the roundness of her bottom, as she moaned, moving into him. She was thinking how sexy he was, what a good kisser, when before she knew it she was comparing him to Spike! *Oh, for Chrissake, Polly. Here you have a gorgeous, sexy man, turning you on like mad and all you can do is… Now stop it. Stop thinking about Spike!*

But there he was, in her head. And now she couldn't block an image of Spike with Bam. Spike peeling off Bam's clothes, dropping them to the floor as she stepped out of them with those long colt-like legs of hers. Spike smiling at Bam, not Polly, as Bam tossed her hair and climbed on top of him…

It was no good… She pulled away from Max, her hair all mussed up like a bird's nest, her focus all fuzzy. 'I'm sorry. I can't,' she said, Max's erection plain to see as it strained against the hard material of his jeans.

'Sorry… sorry…' On the wall, her kitchen clock – yes, the one she'd bought with Spike – ticked its loud tocks. 'I really am all over the place.'

'Oh, Polly,' murmured Max, his voice full of regret as he gently smoothed her hair. 'That is such a shame… because you are an incredibly sexy woman, and you're turning me on like crazy.'

'Then fuck me,' she said, reaching for his erection and stroking it from the outside of his jeans. 'Let's do it now – on the sofa,' she whispered, as she tried to manoeuvre him towards the sitting room. But instead of taking her up on her offer, he stood his ground.

'No, Polly, no,' he said. 'Because, as much as I'd clearly love to, and Christ knows I can't believe I'm going to say this… I'll be hobbling all the way home with this whacking big stiffy… but I honestly do think it's for the best if we wait.'

'Right,' she said, turning away from him. 'I see.' How could she have got it so wrong? Again?

'Only until tomorrow,' he added. 'That's if you're free? Are you free tomorrow?'

'I could be,' she said.

'Good.' He smiled a broad confident smile as he collected his jacket from the back of the chair. 'How about I come over after little Rowan's in bed? Say half past eight? You'll have had a chance to clear your head by then, and we can have a good talk. I know, I'll get us a takeaway, shall I?' He stroked her face. 'Because I know how rubbish you are at cooking…'

'Cheeky,' she said.

'We can pick things up from there,' he said as he placed a quick kiss on her lips. 'Because, sexy Polly, I want to be one hundred per cent certain that it's me you're having sex with – or fucking, as you so politely put it. I don't want any part of you thinking or worrying about your ex. Okay?'

'Okay,' she said quietly.

'Good girl.'

From the top of her front steps, Polly watched Max stride down the city road and then turn in a pool of light from a streetlamp, to give her a wave that was more like a salute. He carried on his way, his footsteps echoing as he passed a derelict warehouse on top of which the head of a buddleia nodded as a car swooshed by.

There was a full moon, so close that she could see its dips and colorations, giving it the appearance of a big flat pepperoni pizza with all its toppings picked off. The way Rowan liked to eat hers. Polly stood for a moment, breathing in the night air. Across the road, the tide had turned, the River Frome pulled back so far by the moon that the river was little more than a deep gully flanked by mudbanks. In days gone by, wooden ships – laden with their cargo – would have stuck fast, forced to wait for the next high tide to lift them free. She closed her door and went through to the living room to turn out the lights – not before giving her pirate figure a pat on his shoulder – then she climbed the stairs to bed, where soon she was dreaming of a chestnut-coloured galleon tossed on seas with waves so high they transformed into white stallions. On deck, Spike and Max were brandishing swords in a swashbuckling kind of way, clad in floppy white shirts, accompanied by shouts of 'Ar haar,' while Polly stood, hands on hips, clad in buxom wench outfit, when Rowan, white embroidered dress flowing behind her, ran past, chuckling out loud before launching herself into a flying leap, out and over and into the blue sea before Polly could reach her.

She woke in a sweat, unsure at first just where she was. Then, pulling back her bed covers and sliding her feet into her slippers, she rose from her bed to go and check on her sleeping baby Rowan. Satisfied all was well, she padded downstairs to fetch herself a glass of cool water.

15

All the next day, Polly was on tenterhooks waiting for Spike to ring or at the very least turn up at her shop. She kept herself as busy as she could, tidying up the stock and making alterations to a mother-of-the-bride's jacket, which had been bought off eBay and was too large. Each and every time the door pinged open, she more than half expected Spike to be standing there – dark and scowling – as he'd been last night. She couldn't tell if she was excited or scared about seeing him again – all she knew was that there was a growing knot in her stomach, making her too jittery to concentrate on much else.

Around lunchtime the phone rang, making her jump. It was Mel. 'Christ Almighty,' she said, after asking Polly if Spike had phoned yet. 'I nearly had a heart attack when he turned up last night.'

'You and me both. It's not every day your ex arrives from foreign lands only to be told by your best friend that he has a child. A child he didn't know about.'

Polly had two customers in the shop; a couple of women

browsing the toddler section, doing so very slowly.

'Yeah, well,' Mel was saying, 'I'm sorry I dropped you in it. Totally unintentional, babes. It just kind of slipped out.'

'You and your big mouth. So go on then, what did he say after I left?'

'I won't lie, Poll. He was pretty cross about your taking Rowan to a bar…'

She could scarcely believe her ears. 'But it was you who insisted I take her to a bar – if you remember. In any case, it's not a bar, it's a café…'

'Luckily I explained how you were forced to bring her along,' said Mel.

'And did you also tell him that it was *your* idea?'

'Was it? Never mind about all that. He had loads of questions, but I said he should wait until he's had the chance to talk to you… And you know what? I've been thinking about it, and it's probably *good* that he's come back.'

Polly made a spluttering sound.

'Don't you see? This will give you a golden opportunity to lay his ghost to rest once and for all. And then you can move on, perhaps even stop being scared of commitment – even have a proper go at a relationship with Max.'

'Oh, I don't—'

'Why not? He's here, he's available, and even I wouldn't kick him out of bed. And he has a big dick!' She roared with laughter down the phone. 'Not that I'm interested in that sort of thing anymore.'

Polly turned her back on the two ladies, who were doing a rubbish job of pretending not to listen. 'I can't really talk now,' she half whispered down the phone, then turned to her customers to say, 'Are you both all right there? Only I won't be much longer… Buyer…' she said, making a face and indicating to the phone.

The Trouble With Love

The women shook their heads. 'We're fine, dear. Take all the time you need.'

'Anyway,' Mel was saying, as Polly returned to her call, 'you haven't said if anything actually *happened* – you know – with you and Max.'

'No, I didn't have sex with Max last night, if that's what you're asking,' she hissed down the phone. 'And I am *not* scared of commitment. Look, I'll speak to you later when I don't have customers!' She gave the women a feeble smile and was saved by the *Ding!* of the shop doorbell announcing the return of Donna from lunch.

'You 'eard from lover boy, then?' she said, and Polly genuinely wasn't sure which one she meant – Max or…

'Spike. Duh,' said Donna, smiling at the two ladies. 'He called or anyfin'? No? Why don't you shoot off home, then? It's quiet and if 'ee phones here I'll let 'im know where you are. Yeah? Go on. You know it makes sense.' Tutting and shaking her head, she shooed Polly out of the shop.

*

Polly and Rowan were making the most of the warm afternoon in their backyard. She'd left the back door open so she could hear her landline ring, and her mobile – which she kept on checking – was nestled in her pocket. But there was still no word from Spike. As Rowan happily pushed her dolly in a Tonka toy truck, Polly half-heartedly snipped at a rambling rose scrambling up her back wall. Stopping to lean on the top, she gazed out over the water below. She loved her view, perched above the harbourside, where ferry boats chugged their zig-zag routes up and down the river as waterfowl pootled about, and where on high days and holidays tall-masted sailing ships might join the replica of John Cabot's *Matthew*, to stately sail under the span of Clifton's suspension bridge. You could never get bored, she thought, there's never a dull moment.

When she got the chance – which, let's face it, wasn't often these days, what with a child plus work – she liked to sit on her verandah and watch the changes in the river, reflecting the weather. Some days it was brown, some almost green, while other times it was grey, or shiny pewter if the sun bounced off it at a certain angle.

She could never imagine living inland; she would have to be near the sea. There was something about living on the edge of land which held the tension and promise of that possibility of launching oneself off to new adventures, or new worlds to be explored. Polly squinted at the sun, which now hung low in the sky, lifting her arm to shield her eyes.

D'you know what? It's nice enough for an ice lolly, that's what it is.

Ducking underneath her wooden verandah to get to the freezer kept in her basement, she lifted its lid to pull out two Fab ice lollies. Rowan – with the unerring instinct of a dog sensing food – had followed her in.

'Mmm. Lolly.'

'Here you are then, trouble. Just be careful you don't drop it.'

Gripping it tightly, Rowan dashed back outside to retrieve her dolly from the truck she'd crashed into their cherry tree.

Sitting cross-legged on the floor, acting as if she were a paramedic from Ice Lolly Land, she shoved the Fab into her doll's face 'Here y'are,' she said. 'Soon hab you bettah.'

Polly, returning to the leaning of forearms on her back wall, mused again on her view. Glorious. It was that kind of late spring afternoon when a warm day cooled with a chill served to remind you that it could, if it so chose to, still throw up a frost. But today, no – it was glorious. Hmm.

Feeling inspired, she rooted inside her bag for her notebook and pen then returned to observing the water, taking note of how the afternoon sun, as it peeped in and out of cloud, refracted and reflected its light on and off the water's surface. She jotted down her thoughts and ideas for poems: about the colours, about the cycles of the earth and the seas, about the strong pull of the tides. This year's spring tides were exceptionally high. Polly knew they heralded the arrival of elvers migrating upstream. *Elvers wriggling like sperm*, she wrote. A riverman had told her once how an elver fisherman had gone missing – feared murdered – somewhere along the River Peret. 'Them worth a fortune, them elvers, mind. Places like Japan,' he said. 'Dirty deeds afoot, I reckons.' She jotted more notes about the story, then paused, looking to the sky as if for inspiration when an overhead gull plopped bird poo, narrowly missing her. Charming.

Thoughts of Spike snuck in. Once, any thoughts of him had caused pain and she'd worked hard to shut them out; then he'd become a shadowy figure in the background, occasionally glimpsed in a memory here, a snatch of a song there, or in the features and facial expressions of her child, and now – well, now he'd become real again. Threatening to upset the safe world she'd constructed around herself and her child. If only Mel was still staying with her then they could have sat down over a cup of tea (or a bottle of wine, more like) and talked through the whole Spike-turning-up thing; formulate a plan as to what she should do next.

She couldn't imagine how she'd have coped with a small baby on her own – without Mel. In many ways, her friend had become more like a father to Rowan… She gave a half-smile at this – thinking how she must remember to tell Mel, when they next spoke. She'd think that funny. Or would she? Things had changed since Mel had become part of a couple with Fen, setting up home together. She could feel more of a sea change coming now that the two of them were planning their own child. Yes, she could definitely smell change in the air, she thought, lifting her face into the wind.

Turning away and leaning with her back to the wall, she thought of how she'd best get used to the fact that she'd lost her best friend. No more cosy evenings in together, no more someone to cook meals with, someone to chat to about their respective days; having a laugh; the whole having someone as backup. She glanced over to where Rowan was busy telling her dolly and a purple dinosaur that they must play nicely.

Never mind single parent, it should be double parent, she thought, and not for the first time – *because when you're single, it's double the work, isn't it?*

She returned her notebook to her bag then set about brushing dead leaves off the garden chair; it was more knackered than weathered, due to her forgetting to bring it indoors. Lowering herself gingerly onto its seat, she absent-mindedly watched her child potter about the garden. *I dunno,* she thought. *Maybe Mel is right, and I am scared of commitment. Maybe I did choose to fall in love with Spike precisely because he was due to emigrate. Maybe Mel's right and I ought to give a grown-up relationship a go. With someone who's actually going to stick around. Like Max. Because on paper Max seems a good bet, doesn't he? Good-looking, great company, single dad... gold-star kisser... Right,* she thought, *I'll show Mel she's not the only one who can do a "proper relationship". And that I am well and truly over Spike. Because why put myself through all that turmoil again? Still,* she thought, softening and glancing at her daughter, *what can I do? I can't deny Rowan access to her father... Okay. But this time my feelings are not going to ambush me. This time I'll be ready.*

'You daydreamin' there, Polly?'

You know what it's like when time slows down and two lovers move together for a clinch in glorious technicolour slow motion? Well, it wasn't like that. More like a Monty-Pythonslap-around-the-face-with-a-wet-fish moment, as she part leapt, part struggled to get out of her chair, nearly falling over in the process. 'You frightened the life out of me!'

'So how are ya, Polly?' Spike asked, standing there looking fit, amused and teasing.

She stared. How was she? For a nanosecond it felt like an existential question, and her mind boggled. Snapping out of it, she moved to greet him. A kiss? Or shake hands. She went for a handshake and he gave her his quizzical look. *Oh bugger, he's more handsome in the daylight than he was in the dark of last night.* Her heart bounded about like a Labrador puppy as she experienced a sudden longing to rest her head on his chest.

'Will ya close yer mouth and stop yer gawping, Polly. I thought you wouldn't mind as your back gate was on the latch.' He gave her that steady and unsettling stare of his. 'Some things never change, I see.'

'I think you'll find,' she said, finally pulling her wits together and brushing imaginary dust from her skirt, 'that things do and have changed.' She stood her ground, even though she wanted to step right into his arms. Which was ridiculous. *I'll bet it's some sort of muscle memory response. That, combined with being caught off guard.*

'So,' he said. 'Bit of a shocker last night.' Then without waiting for her to respond, he added, 'Are you not going to introduce me to your lovely daughter here?' He broke into a broad smile, nodding over to where Rowan was stopped – toy spade in hand – as if someone had pressed her Pause button, mid-burying her dolly in a hole she'd been digging in the flower border.

And so began a surreal, annoying and heartstring-tugging hour or so.

16

Spike broke the news that Elspeth had died, leaving him the house – this being the main reason why he'd returned from Australia.

'I've been up in London, putting her house on the market. Jeez, I had no idea houses in London were worth so much.'

Polly couldn't stop the begrudging voice in her head going: *That's because unlike me, you didn't spend time with a very small baby watching daytime shows like* Escape to the Country. 'I'm so sorry about Elspeth,' she said, out loud. 'I liked her.' (*Even though she wouldn't give me your number that time*, she thought but didn't say.)

'She died very suddenly, so there's no need to look sad. These things happen.'

A momentary shadow seemed to pass over his face, and she ached for him. *Already an orphan, and now he's lost his godmother too.*

'Still,' he said, stirring his tea with a teaspoon, even though he didn't take sugar, 'Bam – my girlfriend…' he added (as if she needed reminding) '...her family live here in England, so it made sense for us both to visit the UK. And then there's the boat... So. Here we are.' She was about to say something, but he held up his hand. 'Polly, look, I know I was cross last night – what with the whole not-knowing thing.' He glanced across at where Rowan was engrossed in a jigsaw. 'But once I'd had the chance to talk things over with Bam...'

Polly winced inside at the mention of her name. (*Stop it*, she told herself. *Stop being so stupid.*)

'...I could see how difficult it must have been for you, and how you might have thought it was for the best. And then I remembered how you did try and contact me. You phoned Elspeth, isn't that right?'

Polly nodded her assent – *ah, so she did tell him.*

He sighed and leant back in his chair. 'Turns out I was a right eejit. Handled it all badly.'

'You weren't to know,' she said, feeling conciliatory in the face of his almost apology. 'And I could have tried harder to contact you.' She attempted a smile. 'It's all water under the bridge now.' She took a sip of her tea – but she'd forgotten to take the teabag out and her teeth practically shrivelled from the strength of the brew. 'Anyway,' she looked up at him. 'What on earth were you doing outside...'

'...the café?'

She smiled. 'Well, yes.' Acutely aware of how – back in the day – he would finish her sentences. She cast him a coy glance, wondering if he remembered too.

Meeting her gaze, he said, 'Leo's been renting my boat,' and then looked away. 'I didn't sell it in the end.' It crossed her mind that he might have kept the boat in Bristol so that he'd have a reason to return. (*There you go with your wishful thinking again.*)

She offered him a plate with Jammie Dodgers. 'Ah, my favourites,' he said, taking one and dunking it in his tea.

'So when are you planning...'

'...on returning to Australia?'

'Stop that,' she said, giving his arm a playful punch. 'Stop finishing my sentences, you rotter.'

They both appeared to physically relax. 'It's a rotter I am now, is it?' he said, full-on grinning at her. Polly blushed as once this sort of behaviour would have led to play-fighting, tickling, and then ending up in a wrestling match – which would lead to...

She swallowed hard.

'If all goes to plan,' he continued, 'then we should be returning to Oz round about...'

October, she thought in her head.

'...October,' he said out loud, and then fell silent. It was October the last time he'd left for Australia.

'October.' She determined to be cheerful about what was inevitable. 'That means you'll be in the UK for Rowan's birthday. It's on the twenty-seventh of June,' she added, as he couldn't be expected to know or mind-read that fact, could he?

'When she'll be three, is that right?' He gazed across to where their daughter sat galloping a bright pink My Little Pony across the kitchen floor. 'I wouldn't miss it for the world.' He squinted at Polly. 'Isn't that a few days before yours? You'll both be Leos – now isn't that grand. I might've guessed – a lioness and her cub.'

Well, this is pretty civilised, she thought, rather pleased at how grown up they were being. 'Care to stay for tea?' she asked. 'I'm sure Rowan will like it.'

'I don't mind if I do, thanks. Shall I be staying for my tea then, Rowan?' he asked, but Rowan was busy stuffing My Little Pony underneath the dresser, and as she had her back to him, she didn't hear. 'I'll give Bam a call and let her know,' he said, pulling his mobile out from his inside pocket. 'I'm sure,' he added, waving his phone at Polly, 'that once you and Bam get to know each other, you'll get on like a house on fire. Everybody likes her. She's a grand girl.'

Well, whoopy-doo, she thought, unable to stop her face from falling.

*

As Polly sorted the food, Spike lifted Rowan into her child seat (much to Rowan's surprise), but once ensconced, she merrily chatted away to him. Polly made herself busy while surreptitiously watching the two of them, thinking how this was a scene she'd never envisaged. The three of them, almost like a happy family. As. If.

'Hurry up there, Poll,' Spike said, good-humouredly. 'We're starving, aren't we, Rowan?'

Polly dished up their plates of fish fingers, oven chips and peas.

'See your cooking's improved,' he said, with a conspiratorial wink at Rowan. Gripping his knife and fork, he made yum yum noises – which highly amused the child.

'Tomato ketchup?' Polly plonked the sauce bottle on the table.

'Shall I join you in a dollop of the red stuff? What do you say, Rowan? Yes?'

Ro was demurring like a right little coquette. *Guess I'd better start saving now for the years of therapy she's clearly going to need*, thought Polly. *What with her incipient absent-father crush coming along nicely.*

Spike was giving his daughter a thoughtful look. 'Rowan. That's a beautiful name. I think I shall also be calling you Roly Poly for short. How would that be?'

'Water?' said Polly, pouring him a glass.

They ate the rest of the meal – ice cream for afters – with accompanying small talk: what was the weather like in Australia this time of year? Did water really drain down the plughole in the opposite direction? (It did! She knew it! That was twenty quid Mel owed her.) At turns they were awkward and relaxed, while Spike barely took his eyes off Rowan, and she, in turn, chattered away – mostly nonsense – while he listened, as rapt as if she were imparting the wisdom of the Dalai Lama.

'So, you and Bam?' Polly managed to get in. 'Serious, is it?'

'Oh, you know. Let's just say we get on.' He gave her an inscrutable look. 'How about you and yer Max fella?'

'Early days,' she muttered, deciding to leave things at that – if he wasn't forthcoming then why should she be? It was hardly any of her business if he and Bam were love's young dream or not. Unless of course Bam was to become some sort of unofficial stepmother to Rowan. She began to clear away their plates, thinking this could get complicated. *Still,* she told herself, *small steps. We have all summer.*

'I plan on paying my way, Polly. With the maintenance.'

'There's no need,' she said, collecting up the glasses. 'You weren't around when I decided to keep the baby, so I don't see why you should have to pay for my decision.'

He linked his hands in front of him. 'I would have been over the moon to know about a baby,' he said, giving her an inscrutable look. 'I'm not someone to shirk their responsibilities.'

'You were very young then.'

'I've grown up a lot since,' he said, looking her in the eye. 'And as I remember, you didn't think I was that much of a kid…' The tension in the air sparked between them, and she half expected her hair to stand on end, like when you rub it with a balloon. Then he looked away and broke the spell. 'There's plenty of time for us to sort things amicably.' His voice softened. 'It must have been tough for you. Bringing up a baby on your own.'

You'll never know, she thought, and had no intention of telling him about all the worries, the fears, the sheer terror some nights that she was getting it all wrong, the feeling guilty about going to work, guilty if she stayed at home, about Rowan's hearing loss, being unable to comfort a little girl screaming with earache, the nights she sat on the kitchen floor, exhausted, with a glass of wine and just sobbed and sobbed as she didn't know how she was going to manage to hold it all together for one more day. Ah, but the days with sunny smiles and little chubby arms reaching out for a hug made it all worthwhile. She wouldn't have changed a minute of it.

He sat up straight. 'So. How's the shop doing? In this recession an' all.'

'Doing just fine and dandy, thanks,' she said, filling the washing-up bowl with soapy hot water. No need for him to know, either, that if it hadn't been for Suze stepping in and buying her house, covering the shop's lease and business rates, she would have gone under a long time ago. She barely had enough to pay Donna's salary as it was. Still, she thought, rinsing a plate under the tap, it didn't sit comfortably, being beholden to her mother, and she had no intention of being beholden to Spike, either. She was proud of how well she'd done without any help from her child's father, and saw no reason why that might change just because he was on a flying visit. She wiped her hands on a tea towel and placed it on the back of a chair.

'I mean it, Polly. About the money.'

'I'll not change my mind.'

He looked as if he was about to say something else but instead turned to Rowan. 'Right ye are, young lady, let's get you out of this contraption. If that's okay with your mother? Good.'

Once firmly on the floor, Rowan pulled him towards the sitting room – 'Help, I'm being kidnapped,' he called – as Rowan ordered him to sit next to her on the floor, and play Sylvanian families and Lego, by the sound of it, thought Polly as she finished the clearing-up.

Once done, she stood in the doorway to watch the father of her daughter playing with their child. Nothing was ever going to be the same ever again, was it?

Spike said he'd wait downstairs while Polly gave Rowan her bath and put her to bed. 'I'll finish off the crossword for you, shall I?' He smiled as he picked up the *Guardian* from where Polly had abandoned it. 'I was always better at it than you,' he reminded her.

'Yes, well.' She placed a hand on Rowan's head and gave her a little push towards her dad. 'Give Spike a kiss goodnight, Ro.'

So much for telling Rowan not to talk to strangers, she thought, now watching her toddle over to his arms. *Because even though they've clearly taken to one another – which is good*, she grudgingly acknowledged – *Spike is – let's face it – a stranger to Rowan*. He gave Polly a grateful look over the top of Rowan's head as he embraced his daughter before lowering her to the floor.

In the bath, Polly set about washing Rowan's hair; her thoughts going over the afternoon.

'Mummeee!' complained Rowan.

'Whoops. Sorry, darling.'

Spike had unnerved her. She'd been expecting angry, but instead he'd oozed his Irish charm. Pouring a jugful of water over Rowan's head, she thought it a bit of a nerve. How he'd waltzed into the back garden as if… well, just… as if…

Rowan splashed the surface of the water, some bubble bath catching Polly in the eye. 'Oi, madam. Watch it,' she said good-naturedly.

Spike might have been able to come and go as he pleased in the old days – when they were together. But these were new days. She lifted Rowan's arm: rub-a-dub-dub. *He can't just swan in and out whenever he pleases… upsetting Rowan's routines… ground rules, that's what's needed.*

She took the flannel to her child's face. 'Owww!'

'Sorry, Ro Ro.'

Polly sat back on her heels. There again, she'd been the lucky one, hadn't she, while Spike had missed out on getting to know their daughter. Their beautifully delightful daughter. She contemplated her child, happily splashing away, all deliciously slippery with bubble bath. Irresistible. She collected foam into her hands then plopped it onto the end of Rowan's nose.

'Mummeee!' Rowan giggled and wrinkled her nose to huff it off. But Polly scooped more foam, blowing it at her so that it dotted all over her face, her hair, her chest; Rowan now squealing with delight as she sploshed the water, drenching Polly in the process. 'Silly Mummy,' – splash splash – 'Silly Mummy!'

Daughter tucked up for the night, and story read, Polly made her way downstairs.

'I see you've been making changes in here,' Spike said, as he turned from where he'd clearly been carrying out an inspection of her sitting room.

'The whole world doesn't stand still waiting for your return, you know,' she said, rather more tartly than she meant. 'I'm sorry, I shouldn't have said that.'

The doorbell interrupted them with its loud ring. Both stared at each other and, for a split second, she couldn't think who on earth it could be. And then she recalled. 'Oh my God, is that the time? Max. That'll be Max.' She looked about her, as if for inspiration. 'I'm not ready or changed or anything. God, look at me, I'm still soaked.'

Spike raised an eyebrow at her. 'Shall I let him in?'

'No. Don't be ridiculous!' she couldn't stop herself saying. 'I'll… umm… I'll do it.' Dashing over to the mirror above her fireplace, she ran her fingers through her hair. Where was her brush?

'Just coming,' she called out.

'You look fine,' offered Spike.

Ignoring him, she smoothed down her skirt. 'Wait. Lippy – Bum. Where's my lippy?' Doorbell ringing again. 'Hang on!' she shouted, as she rooted around in her handbag. 'Ah, there it is!' Holding her lipstick aloft then quickly applying it to her lips with a 'That'll have to do,' she hurried to her door. 'Max!' she said, throwing it open.

There he stood, all spruced up with a just-shaved glow about his face.

'You are expecting me, aren't you?' he said, uncertainly, as she didn't appear to be letting him in. 'I'm not going to be sent down the pub like last time, am I?'

'Yes. I mean No. I mean Yes. Of course.' She opened the door wider. 'I am indeed expecting you. Come on in. Umm. Spike's here… he's…'

She turned to discover Spike just a few steps behind her, wearing an expansive smile, looking for all the world as if he owned the place. She ushered Max inside as Spike advanced, hand held out before him. 'We weren't properly introduced last night. I'm Spike.'

Max stepped past Polly to shake his hand. (*It's all getting rather crowded in the hallway*, she thought.)

'Yes, I know who you are, Spike. I'm Max.'

'So I heard.'

*

Good grief, she thought, looking from one to the other as they stood in the kitchen, sizing each other up. If not squaring up. She wasn't quite sure what the difference was but thought she ought to keep a beady eye on them both. Meanwhile they sidestepped around each other, as light on their toes as two fencers in a tournament – or a duel! She had a fleeting image of frock coats, floppy shirts, a rising mist just after dawn, and herself riding over the brow of a hill to stop them… but too late… and… we're back in the room.

'I do hope I wasn't interrupting anything,' Max was saying.

'You're all right,' parried Spike. 'Polly and I have concluded our business. For now.'

Polly threw Max a look that said *Sorry*. This wasn't lost on Spike.

'In any case,' Spike added, with a wry smile. 'I believe it's me who's in the way.'

Polly stepped forward. 'I'll see you out,' she said to Spike and, turning to Max, added, 'There's wine in the fridge. Why don't you help yourself? I'll only be a moment.'

Spike stood on her doorstep.

'Hey, while I have the chance here, I wanted to say…'

'Yes?'

'I wanted you to know that I do forgive you. You know. For not trying harder to contact me an' all. Even though,' he said with a devilish air about him, 'it was a terrible thing keeping the knowledge that I had a child from me.'

She could have said it was a terrible thing he did, leaving her, but deep down she knew he was right. She could have made more of an effort. How much of that – at least on some subconscious level – had been down to her wishing to punish him? *Oh, great time for this revelation, Polly.*

As if on cue, an overhead cloud parted.

'I did try,' was all she could find to say.

There was a pause.

'So I'll be taking Rowan out for the day on Saturday, will I? Like we agreed.'

We did? She must have missed that somehow...

'We have agreed that I ought to get to know her. Before we both tell her that I'm her daddy.'

'I don't know...' She was unsure what the etiquette might be for access with visiting fathers.

'I do know about kids, Polly.' He wore a determined look on his face. 'She'll be perfectly fine with me. I'm an old hand these days.'

She stared at him. Kids? Did Spike and Bam have kids? *Don't be daft, they've no time to have kids. Plural. But they could have squeezed one out...*

He gave a broad smile. 'I can practically hear those rusty cogs in your brain going round there, Poll. I'm talking about my Uncle Dermot, not me. I've not got any children – other than Roly Poly. Auld Dermot got married again, and it's him who has a kid. A little two-year-old girl. Wee bit younger than Rowan here.'

The relief on her face must have been obvious, and she could feel herself begin to colour up. 'Oh right. Good. I mean good for Dermot – that your Uncle Dermot has a child. Not that you can't or couldn't have a child...' (*what? Stop now, while you're ahead*) '...and... good that you've had some practice.'

'Quite.'

Her mind appeared to have undergone some sort of brain-freeze, as she couldn't fathom what might be the thing to say next. Spike leant in towards her and, what with his being on the step below and now roughly her height, she thought for one giddy moment that he was going to kiss her. Instead, he reached up for something in her hair.

'Got it!' he said. 'Spider. There you go, little fella.'

'Oh.'

'Saturday it is, then. Yes?' He had an annoying grin all over his face.

'Erm, yes. Of course,' she said. 'Oh, and when you're out with Ro, do make sure you keep a tight hold of her hand, won't you?' He gave her a quizzical look. 'I'm not being overprotective or anything. It's because of her hearing, you see. It's so bad that she can't hear traffic, and she might run off, not hearing you call her. She doesn't fully get the danger, you see. I'll be trusting you with her, and it's very, very important.'

'I promise I'll keep a good hold on her, and I'll make sure Bam knows too. How's that?'

'Hmm. Yes, okay. Saturday it is, then. I'm working all day so Rowan is at Daisy's in the morning and then Mel collects her at twelve. I'll ask Mel to bring her back here, if that suits? What time are you thinking of collecting her?'

He appeared to be considering this, so she waited. Finally he said, 'You work often then, Polly?'

What was he implying? 'Of course I do. *Someone* has to support us.' Unnecessary, she knew, and she could see him flinch.

'Which is why,' he insisted, 'I fully intend to contribute to Rowan's upkeep.'

Belatedly, she was acutely aware that Max was inside; she didn't want him listening so lowered her voice. 'I neither need nor want your money. Truly. Is that clear? Okay?'

'Clearly now's not the time to be discussing this.'

She stared at him. He could be so infuriating. 'No,' she started, 'now's not the time—'

'Right you are,' he interrupted – all affable. 'That's settled for Saturday, and I'll collect Rowan from here at one o'clock. From Mel.'

'Yes, that's fine,' she said, glancing over her shoulder as if expecting Max to be standing there, listening to make sure she'd got it right, and that she wasn't a mercenary conniving cow like he'd said his ex, Claire, was.

'Make sure you have her back by five.'

'I'm thinking a picnic if the weather's fine.'

'Okay, but don't give her Coca-Cola or chocolate. Makes her hyper.'

He gave her a quizzical look. 'I'm not some Willy Wonka's Chocolate Factory child snatcher, here.' He almost cracked a full-on smile, made to leave then stopped, and in pure Detective Columbo-style added, 'Just one more thing...'

'What?'

'Aren't you at work 'til six o'clock?'

'Mel will be—'

'Tell you what, why don't I give Rowan her tea as well? That way I could bring her back at seven? Give you time to have a cuppa and a couple of Jammie Dodgers.'

(*Damn him for remembering her addiction to those biscuits...*)

'Why not. Yes, seven will be fine – now scoot – go!'

He touched her arm, and those familiar electrical currents excitedly zip-zapped up and down it. (*Muscle memory*, she told herself. *That's all it is.*)

'See you Saturday,' he called with a cheery wave, and set off down the path.

No going back now, she thought, sensing that a rubric had been crossed, and that hers and Rowan's world had tipped on its axis. *Because*, she thought as she closed the door, *when there's a child involved, you're forever linked, aren't you? One minute you're sailing along and the next – urrhh – creak and roll as some head wind forces you to set sail in a different direction. Why do I always think in seafaring terms when Spike is around?*

Turning, she noticed Max skulking in her kitchen doorway. Just how much had he overheard?

That night she discovered what all the fuss was about Max. After Spike had gone, there was wine, kissing, and touching and flirting – until Polly pulled Max upstairs to her bedroom, for their very first shag. And what with all the pounding, the roiling, the wet and the salt, the ebbing and flowing, the tossing and heaving, then the undulating, Polly was finally left softly murmuring like a spent mermaid. Yes, she knew. Still with those bloody sea analogies!

17

The day after her night of passion with Max, she walked to work with a spring in her step and a Minnie Ripperton song trilling away in her head. She wouldn't have been at all surprised if zip-a-dee-doo-dah bluebirds had landed on her shoulder. It was amazing what an irrefutably splendid shag could do.

'You look fantastic!' said Donna.

Polly gave her a broad grin.

'You haven't!' said Donna – looking as if she was busting for a squeal.

'I have!' declared Polly, causing her assistant to release The Squeal.

'Eeeeeeeee!'

I mean, Oh My God, thought Polly, as she squealed back at Donna. *Five times! Five glorious again-and-again shags. Three last night, and two this morning!* That had to be a record.

Polly looked up as Max strode into the shop, just as she was serving two schoolgirls who were in the process of buying a vintage teacup filled with lavender-scented wax. Max sidled up behind her to place a kiss behind her ear. 'Max!' she admonished him. The girls shoved each other, giggling. He gave them a wink, which made them giggle even more.

'Sorry,' Polly said to them, pushing Max away with her hip. He feigned interest in a rack of baby clothes as she placed the fushsia-pink-crepe-paper-wrapped girls' purchase into a bag stencilled with her shop logo.

Nudging each other, the schoolgirls made their exit.

'Right, I'm all yours,' Polly said, then half wished she hadn't as it caused Max to pull her towards him – much to her embarrassment.

'Excuse me, why don't you?' announced Donna as she emerged from the basement where they kept their stock, carrying a mug of coffee in her hand. 'I'll leave you two lovebirds alone, shall I?' and she moved to the back of the shop where she did a bad job of pretending not to eavesdrop.

'You smell divine,' Max whispered into Polly's hair. Polly was feeling much like a giddy schoolgirl herself and, before she could tell him to behave, Max had pulled her in for a full kiss on the mouth. When he finally let go, she felt rather giddy and unsteady on her feet but could see Donna giving her the thumbs-up behind his back.

'I've missed you,' he said.

'Don't be daft,' she said, pushing him away. 'I only saw you just last night – a few hours ago.'

'I had to come in and see you,' he said, turning and giving Donna a wink and then making a sad face at her. 'I also have to impart some very sad news. No, listen. I'm off filming for a couple of days.' That was sad, she thought, especially as he was now stroking her arm and causing all her little hairs to stand on end. 'You must stop being quite so delicious, Polly,' he murmured, now running his hands down the length of her body. 'You know how much you turn me on, you minx.'

'Stop it,' she mouthed.

'Stop it yourself,' he said. 'And now look,' he added, peering down at his obvious erection. 'See what you've done to me?' Mischievously he stared into her eyes. 'I can't go yet, can I? Not until this bad boy has gone down.'

She had to admit that it was pretty spectacular, and even though smutty, she couldn't resist feeling smug at the effect she was having on him, or being pleased that her allure had returned. Donna – not missing a thing – gave her a mock shocked face then threw up her hands, before moving behind the curtain at the back of the shop.

'I've got a brilliant idea,' he said, his face all close and blurry. 'How's about me, you and the kids all get together on Sunday? Hmm? You could meet my son, Ben.' He took a step back. 'Will Sunday afternoon suit you? And Rowan? Even better – how about lunchtime? That way we can combine a walk with a picnic.' (What was it with weekend fathers and picnics?)

'Sounds lovely,' she said, beaming at him, because she was feeling – hang on, she did a quick check – yes, she was actually feeling happy. *This could work; me, Max and our children. I don't need Spike. Who's Spike, anyway, but a ghost from the past?*

As Max backed out of her shop, camera bag held in front of his crotch area, he gave her a cheeky salute, just as Donna came out of hiding to stand alongside Polly. 'He's like a dog with two dicks, that one,' she said, causing Polly to snort with laughter.

'So?' said Donna. 'How was he in the sack, eh?' Looking her up and down, she added, 'Ooh, you dirty mare,' then pulled her to the back of the shop. 'Right, come on, madam. Spill the beans.'

On her drive home, Polly saw her mother – yes, it was definitely Suze – crossing the road and heading into the Nuffield Hospital in Clifton Village. Bit weird. Because if Suze was in town, why

The Trouble With Love

hadn't she arranged to meet up with Polly? Or arrange to see her granddaughter? Maybe Suze was booked in to have more work done on her face and didn't want Polly to know – as Suze knew how her daughter disapproved. She'd been vocal on more than one occasion about the fact that her mother was beginning to get that pillow-face look from too many fillers and Botox.

I suppose I should ring her and check that nothing untoward is happening, she thought, as she indicated right to turn down the hill. And then immediately forgot all about it.

*

Polly made a start on tidying up. *New boyfriend/ new start/ tidy house. Right. Things are going to change – for the better – starting with this mess.*

Enlisting the help of Rowan to put away her toys in the gaily painted pine chest, they made a start, but Rowan was soon distracted by the Fisher Price garage she'd discovered on clambering inside the chest. 'C'mon, Ro Ro,' Polly said, reaching down to lift out both Rowan and her prize – firmly grasped between Rowan's pudgy fists. 'Oof. You'll have to cut down on those Jammie Dodgers, young lady.'

She decided it was probably best if Rowan was left to quietly entertain herself with her garage and toy cars. At least it might distract her from posting bits of paper into the DVD slot on the side of the television, or down her favourite gaps in the floorboards – into which she was particularly fond of slotting pieces of Lego, or even a whole book! She blamed Rowan's favourite TV character – Postman Pat. The theme tune started to play in her head, just when her mobile rang.

Phone, phone, where did I put my phone? Ringing coming from the direction of... hall... inside bag... scrabbling around inside... *Why don't they ever ring long enough?* she thought, as it rang off the very moment she located it. Caller ID said "Vanessa" and she rang her voicemail.

'Hi, it's Vanessa here. I do hope you're free next Wednesday as we want to film you at home – at your house, yes? We'll see you then – round about eight o'clock. Great. Okay. Bye.'

Honestly, that woman.

Back in her sitting room, Rowan was banging a plastic skittle on the feet of Cap'n Jack. Polly sighed and, abandoning her tidy, mooched over to the dining table, where she fired up her laptop as Rowan vroom-vrrooomed a newly found toy pick-up truck across the floor. Logging onto her Facebook account, Polly told herself she was merely going to check the shop's site, that's all. She was not going to check her old boyfriend's Facebook account. Oh, who was she kidding? She clicked onto Spike's page where his status read "In a relationship with Bam Tyler". Of course it would. What did she expect? His cover photo of Spike and Bam sitting at a beachside bar sipping cocktails while smiling happily in front of a glorious sunset. Slowly she closed the lid shut. *Enough*, she told herself. *Enough already.*

*

Max sent her flowers from Manchester – where he was filming – and they now took centre place on her kitchen table. A good and constant reminder that she was part of a couple too. *So there*, she thought, emphatically nodding her head.

Over the course of the next few days, Max sent her text messages when he could, and they even indulged in a naughty phone conversation late one night. It was exciting – it was wicked, and more importantly it did a good job of driving silly thoughts of Spike from her mind. Plus, there was the picnic on Sunday to look forward to, she reminded herself. Frequently.

The Trouble With Love

*

Saturday, the day of Spike's access visit with Rowan, arrived. All afternoon Polly was on tenterhooks in the shop, knowing that Mel or Daisy would have done the handover and that Rowan was now with Spike and Bam. As time wore on, she couldn't help but worry about how things were going, and especially whether Spike had remembered to keep tight hold of Rowan's hand if they should walk anywhere near traffic. She'd sent him a long text that morning reminding and giving him instructions (again), and since then a couple more text messages (just to be on the safe side and) to check that nothing untoward had happened. In return she'd received his cheery assurances. Would phoning as well be too much? Yes, she decided, it would.

Finally, it was time to shut up shop for the day and her phone beeped as she was locking up. *We're all at Daisy's house*, the text read. *Rowan fine. Come right over. Laters. Mel xx*

It was Bam who greeted Polly at the door; kissing her on both cheeks as if they were best buddies. 'Come in, come in.' Turning her head, she shouted, 'Hey, everyone, Polly's here! Rowan! Mummy's here!' Then addressing Polly, added, 'I think the kids are out in the backyard. C'mon through, hon.'

Well, she's certainly made herself at home, thought Polly, as she stepped over the threshold. Bam was wearing a light blue jersey dress which clung in all the right places and ended just above her knees. Angular boy-like knees; the sort Polly wished she had instead of her hated round ones.

Daisy called, 'We're in the kitchen!'

Daisy's house was two doors down from Polly's. It had bigger proportions, with a longer tiered garden, and the kitchen expansive enough to house a welcoming and well-used kitchen table, an Aga cooker, plus a breakfast bar at which Daisy sat, cutting fresh-out-of-the-oven brownies into squares. 'Fancy a cuppa or a glass of wine?' she asked as she glanced up at Polly. 'Can I tempt you with a brownie? The kids made them, so I have no idea what they'll taste like!' Daisy gave one a sniff – 'Smells all right.'

Bam headed for the French doors – 'I'll let the others know you're here,' she said with a smile to Polly.

'Come on…' said Daisy, passing her friend a tall glass '… have a Bellini.'

Polly took a sip of its smooth peach juiciness mixed with Prosecco bubbliness and immediately felt better. 'Cheers,' she said, plonking herself down on a stool opposite her friend. 'I've had a pig of a day, full of awkward customers, and I'm trying my best to be all cool about Spike's first access visit with Rowan.'

'Poor you. I'd have been worried sick all day,' said Daisy. 'Still,' she dropped her voice to a whisper, 'I hear it all went fine. No dramas. And Rowan seems to have really taken to Spike.' Daisy made large beckoning signs to her husband, Phil, who Polly could see was in the garden swinging a giggling Morwenna around by her arms, her feet narrowly missing Spike, who was coopied down next to Rowan. Spike got to his feet as Bam approached. Still absorbed, and clearly oblivious that her mother had arrived, Rowan was poking dandelion leaves through the bars of the hutch of Dexter – the psycho-killer rabbit (so called because he tried to bite the children whenever he was picked up). Polly watched Bam slip her arm through Spike's and then indicate towards the kitchen. Spike gave Polly a wave and tapped Rowan on the shoulder. But Rowan was having none of it. She shook off his hand, muttering something. Probably insisting that Nothing Means No, thought Polly. Spike gave a Gallic-type shrug at Polly then bounded into the kitchen to envelop her in a hug. Unprepared, she flushed a deep rosy colour.

'I'm afraid Rowan's more interested in Dexter than you,' he

grinned, standing back to look at her, as Phil bustled past Spike and delivered a peck on the cheek. 'Hey, Polls. How's tricks?'

'Give the poor girl a drink,' ordered Daisy, fingers chocolately from the brownies. 'I've nearly finished dividing these up.'

'Righty-ho,' said Phil, full of his usual bonhomie, as befitted his restrained boarding school upbringing, thought Polly – as polite and cheerful were two words that would spring to mind if she ever had to describe Phil.

Spike was watching Polly rather too intently for her liking; for Bam's too, she surmised, as Bam moved in to whisper something – clearly intimate – into his ear. Spike placed his arm around her waist, and Bam leant into him. Polly turned away, wishing Max was there. She'd never felt like such a spare part before, not even when Mel was in a couple. By the way, where was Mel?

'Filthy Lidl plonk, okay?' Phil waved an already opened bottle at her.

'Yes please,' she said, thankful for the cold glass and the wine's crisp chillness. 'Cheers!' She lifted her glass as if toasting her two pairs of friends. 'That's better,' she said, after taking a large sip then wiping her brow with the back of her hand.

Determined to put a brave face on things, she was glad she'd applied lippy and zhooshed up her hair in the car. And also that earlier – after Mel's text announcing that Bam and Spike would still be at Daisy's – she'd popped back to her shop and borrowed one of the frocks newly in from a tea dance range: a floaty if not flighty little number, with pretty flower pattern, capped sleeves and low-cut bodice. She'd thought it cute, but now – next to Bam – she felt more frump than fab.

Taking another gulp of wine and pulling her pink angora fluffy cardigan around herself, she thought, *Stop it – you're having a lovely time.*

With a deep breath, she turned to Spike. 'So, did everything go all right with Rowan?'

'Grand. We all got along swimmingly, didn't we, Bam?'
'We sure did.'
'Although…' he said, looking a tad worried '…and I hope you're not going to go off the deep end here, Polly… but there was that incident when I took my eyes off Rowan for a minute there, and she ran right out in front of a bus…'

Her face was a picture of horror mixed with outrage and a touch of *I knew it*.

Then Bam guffawed. 'Honestly, you are awful, Spike. Look at poor Polly's face. You've scared her half to death with your teasing.'

Polly goggled at Bam, her brain having not yet caught up.

'He's pulling your leg, Polly.' With a broad beam she turned to Spike. 'You truly are a terror.'

'Sorry, Poll,' said Spike, doing his best to look contrite. 'I didn't mean to give you a heart attack. I was just playin' with ya. Honest. She was fine. Better than fine. She was a little angel.'

'We had loads of fun,' said Bam, refilling her glass and reaching for a handful of crisps.

'I promise you I took good care of Roly Poly,' he continued. 'We made sure she could see our faces when we spoke to her, didn't we, Bam?' Bam nodded; her mouth full. 'And I held tight to her hand, just as you instructed. I tell you what, though, she can't half run, can't she? When she's a mind to. Maybe we should train her up for the hundred-metre dash.' He noted Polly's face. 'In the park is where she was running, Polly. She had a race with me in the park.'

Before she could say anything else, Daisy was offering up a plate of flapjacks. 'Sorry. Bit burnt,' she said. Both Spike and Bam took one, just as Rowan bowled into the kitchen. 'Mummee!' she squealed, running to grab both her mother's legs.

'Hello, darling.' Polly rubbed the top of her precious daughter's head. 'Hi, Tiggs,' she added to Tiggy, who'd followed in Rowan's wake and suitably rewarded Polly with a teenage grunt.

'Up, up,' demanded Rowan, as she bounced up and down on her sturdy legs.

'Here we go.' Polly reached down. 'Ups-a-daisy!'

Pulling her daughter onto her lap, she asked, 'Did you have a good day, Ro Ro?'

''Ess,' Rowan emphatically declared. Then, looking up from underneath her long eyelashes, said, 'Mum? Bam says Spike is my daddy.' Rowan beamed at her mother, who in turn stared in shock at Bam. 'Is he my daddy?'

'Sorry, mate.' Bam offered an apologetic shrug. 'It just sort of popped out.'

'Right then,' said Mel, as she waltzed into the kitchen, clapping her hands together. 'I'd leave that toilet for ten minutes, if I were you. Hi there, Poll.' Then she clocked everybody's faces. 'What? What did I miss?'

*

Daisy, Mel and Polly lounged on wooden steamer chairs in Daisy's pretty backyard, which was planted with a myriad of the sort of plants more commonly found in a Cornish garden: terracotta pots gay with geraniums, hardy palms and perennials, and semi-tropicals brought back from the Scilly Isles, where they holidayed each year on the Isle of Bryher. In the summer these plants would burst forth in a profusion of reds, yellows, blues, purples and oranges. Now all was green and lush, with the occasional white flower poking through here and there: the ones with thrusting sharp leaves, which would have orange flowers in the summer, were out (*whatever those are called*, thought Polly, who knew nothing at all about gardening). Daisy's back wall was hedged with ornamental grasses and bamboos, and a couple of sturdy evergreen bushes. White gravel covered the ground. On a sturdy table, opposite the back door, pots of herbs – carefully labelled – were within easy reach for cooking. No wonder Daisy's kitchen was so full of heavenly aromas, whereas hers exuded the stench of burnt oven chips. Polly admired Daisy's skills in all things domestic – oh, and she had a good eye for timeless classic clothes… and tasteful internal décor – okay, Polly admired Daisy on many levels, full stop.

She suspected her own culinary prowess – limited as it had always been – had diminished in direct proportion to her own mother's rise to television celebrity chef stardom. Suze's shows were practical and down to earth, specialising in utilising the sort of ingredients that could just as easily be bought in Aldi as Waitrose. That was her USP. Common-or-garden recipes for cash-strapped mums. It went down a bundle in these times of austerity, when even the well-heeled baulked at the idea of trying to track down truffles from the foothills of Kazakhstan, or bottled dragon's breath, or whatever other exotic ingredients seemed to pepper celebrity chefs' books. Like most daughters (she reckoned, and herself even more so…), Polly dreaded anyone saying she was "just like" her mother. She determined to steer a different course in life – even if she did on occasion use her mother's recipes. Thinking of Mum now, she remembered she'd meant to ring her. What with Suze not getting on top of Donna's plumbing problems, and then that unexplained sighting of her in Bristol. Hmm, Polly was starting to wonder if something might be afoot.

'You okay?' asked Daisy, evidently referring to Bam's indiscretion about blabbing to Rowan that Spike was her father. 'Look, maybe it's for the best,' Daisy continued, sitting up and shielding her eyes from the sun, now low in the sky. 'Rowan had to find out sooner or later.'

'I suppose so,' said Polly, who'd decided not to cause a scene, there being nothing she could do faced with this *fait accompli*. 'But it should have been me who told her. Not Wham Bam in there.' She nodded towards the kitchen, hopefully far enough away that they were unlikely to be overheard.

'Well, I like her,' announced Mel.

'Hmm.' Polly could see Bam with the two men, throwing back her head to laugh at some joke, swigging from a bottle of beer, touching Spike ever-so-lightly on the arm.

'Bam is very down to earth, actually,' said Mel, as she swatted a fly. 'Good fun too. You should have seen her when we took Rowan to the rock slide up on the Downs…'

'You took Ro to the rock slide?' The 'without me' hanging unsaid in the air. Because she was decidedly put out, having wanted to be the one to take Rowan there for her first time. Mel knew full well that it was on her list of must-dos, for when she wasn't so busy. The rock slide being a Bristol institution!

'Yeah, well, Bam was great, clambering over rocks, going down the slide with Ro, chasing her all over the play area.'

Getting on the good side of Spike, I'll be bound, Polly thought ungenerously, and feeling rotten about it too.

'Made me exhausted just watching them.' She shielded the sun from her eyes. 'I guess that's being twenty-three. While she dashed around after Ro Ro, me and Spike sat on the grass eating ice cream like a right pair of old age pensioners.'

'How cosy.' Polly could not stop herself from sounding snippy.

'Don't be daft.' Mel reached out to touch her friend's hand. 'I do get it, you know,' she said, giving Polly's hand an extra squeeze. 'It must be very difficult for you, hon. Having your old boyfriend back – and with someone else…'

Before they could discuss it further, Phil came over to join them. 'Thought we might fire up the barbie in honour of our guests. What d'you think, Daise?'

'Sounds lovely,' she said, giving him an affectionate smile.

'I could eat a scabby horse,' declared Mel.

'Seeing as the burgers are from Asda, that might very well be what's in them,' he said, grinning away.

'I expect the kids are hungry too,' said Daisy.

'Righty-oh.' He bent over to give his wife a kiss. 'I'll get right on to it once I've popped along to the Spar shop with Spike. We're running out of beer.'

'Okay, better get more buns for the burgers while you're there. Sausages too.'

'Man go hunt, man light fire, wo-man stay home with children,' said Mel, in a fake Neanderthal way.

Spike called out, 'Anyone need anything from the shop?'

Polly stood up. 'You couldn't grab me a pint of milk while you're there, could you? Only I've run out,' she said, guiltily regarding her friends.

'What?' she said, once the men had left. Both of her girlfriends were giving her a quizzical look. 'Well, he did ask.'

The men returned and the barbie was in full swing when Daisy's friend Annabelle arrived. Tall and blessed with Swedish blonde good looks from her mother's side, she waved two bottles of Cava above her head. An Adele CD blasted out from the sound system. 'I come bearing gifts. Let's have something lively on, shall we?' She clocked Spike and Bam outside in the backyard and stage whispered, 'That the child bride, is it?'

'Yep. Although not bride,' hissed Mel.

'Hmm. Give her time…' said Anna, interrupted by Spike seeing her, waving hello and then hurrying inside, holding Bam by the hand.

Anna flung both arms around his neck. 'Hello, handsome. I heard you were back in town. Causing mayhem, as ever, I expect.' She winked at Polly, who promptly reddened. 'Ah, and you must be Bam. Good to meet you. Be a love and change the music. This lot's dead dreary.'

Bam rooted around Daisy's eclectic horde of Mark Ronson, R&B, Phil's jazz, classical, CBeebies, and Tiggy's drum and bass, and pulled out a Paulo Nutini.

'Yeah, that'll do,' said Anna, slipping the album into the CD player. Soon sunshiny reggae beats and cheeky lyrics burst forth, and nobody much minded that the late-afternoon air had turned chill, especially as Daisy had fetched a pile of red fleecy Ikea blankets and was handing them out.

Annabelle called across to Phil, who was still flipping burgers and sausages outside. 'C'mon, big man, get me a tea towel so I can open one of these babies.' She waved a bottle in his direction. He obliged, and in no time, she'd popped the cork. 'Shampoo all round!'

'That the doorbell?' said Daisy, looking up.

'I'll go,' said Phil as he went to answer it, soon returning with Fen.

'There she is!' declared Mel. 'My Fender Bender,' and gave her girlfriend a full-on kiss on the lips.

'Glass of champagne?' offered Phil, as he handed one to Fen.

'Cheers,' she said. 'And...' giving Mel a pointed look '...this is the perfect opportunity for us to share our own good news. Eh, Mel? We have something to celebrate too, don't we?' Everyone was looking at them both. Mel threw Polly an "I'm sorry" look...

'We – that's Mel and I – are going to have our very own...'

The pause was almost as bad as waiting for the results on *Strictly Come Dancing...*

'...baby!'

The whole room fell silent, just as Paulo Nutini sang about having lots of lead in his pencil. *Mel?* Polly thought but didn't say. Her friend gave her an embarrassed shrug.

'Does this mean… You're not pregnant, are you, Mel?' asked Daisy.

'No. No, I'm not. Well, not yet.'

'Then what?'

'I might as well tell you all, seeing as how Miss Big Mouth here can't keep it to herself,' said Mel, giving Fen a pointed glance, 'but we've decided to go for donor insemination.'

'What's that when it's at home?' said Phil.

Tiggy, who was passing through, muttered, 'Ugh, gross.'

Fen draped a protective arm across Mel's shoulder.

'Oh, come on, everybody,' said Anna. 'Don't look so serious. Instead,' she raised a glass, 'let's drink a toast to the happy couple. To Mel and Fen!'

'To Mel and Fen!'

'Looks like you're all having babies,' said Bam, glancing at Spike.

'Well, I think it's all rather wonderful,' Daisy said. And being slightly tipsy, she turned to Anna. 'How about you, sweetie? Do you think you might ever settle down and have babies too?'

'What, me?' said Anna. 'No thanks.'

Suddenly all went quiet as the others listened intently. 'Don't get me wrong,' she continued, 'I love all of your kids. Truly. But (a) I am not the maternal type, and (b) there are enough people on this planet already, without adding to their numbers. No offence.' She smiled at her friends. 'Now, who's hogging all that fucking champagne!'

*

Polly wandered by herself to the bottom of the garden. What on earth was wrong with her? Why couldn't she just be happy for Mel? Was she perhaps the teensiest bit jealous that Mel was getting her happy ever after and was moving on without her… just like…

'Can I join you?'

She didn't need to turn to know it was Spike. 'Yeah sure,' she said.

They were standing in the corner of the garden. Just behind a bush, out of plain sight of the rest of the party-goers.

'You okay?' he asked. 'About Mel and Fen doing the whole baby thing?'

'I think so,' and then because of the intimacy that dusk brings with it, and because it felt so familiar to be talking to him, and maybe also because they used to talk about anything at all, she added, 'I know it's silly, but I just kind of feel… I dunno… like my best friend is slipping away from me.'

She felt ashamed now that she'd said it out loud.

'Things change, Polly. It's perfectly natural that people move on,' he said, leaning back against the garden wall, and apparently not noticing how loaded his statement had been. 'So, just look at us. Who'd have thought we'd have a child?' he said, looking up into the gathering dark. 'None of us are the single carefree people we once were.'

Polly said nothing. The sounds of the others filtered down to the two of them: Daisy good-naturedly ordering Phil about, Fen and Mel laughing and talking, Anna loudly saying something or other… And here in the quiet of the evening's gloaming was Spike. Who wasn't her Spike anymore but was with Bam instead. She shivered, suddenly feeling chilly.

'Here, have my coat.' He placed it about her shoulders and as she pulled it around her, she could smell his scent on his jacket. And there he stood, ruffling his hair in the old way he did when he was nervous.

'Thanks,' she muttered.

'But you and Mel, you're solid, right? I mean she'll always be your very best friend, won't she?'

Polly stared at him, and in the half-light his eyes seemed to burn with an intensity. 'That's what scares me,' said Polly, 'that she won't be my Mel anymore. Because...' and her eyes filled with tears '...I don't know who I am without Mel,' she said quietly. Softly, she began to cry.

'Hey,' said Spike as he moved closer.

'No, don't.' She put up her hands. 'I'm fine, honest I am. I'm just being bloody stupid, that's all. And maudlin. Stupid stupid. I'm tired and feeling a bit sorry for myself. Don't take any notice.'

'Ah Polly, you've nothing to feel sorry about,' he said. He pulled a paper handkerchief from his pocket and gave it to her to dry her eyes. 'I came prepared with plenty of tissues,' he added. 'Thought I might need them for Rowan. You know. Runny noses, stuff like that. I can't tell you what it's meant to me – spending time with my daughter. Even having a daughter!'

'She seems to have taken to you,' said Polly, her crying stint over with. She braved a smile.

'Doesn't she? I was worried, I can tell you. What if she hated me, that kind of thing.'

Nobody could hate you, she thought, as she looked up into his face. The dark was doing its trick with time, and it could have been three years ago.

'She's a darling and no mistake. I'll bet she's like you were at her age.' He gave her a half-look and swatted at a mosquito buzzing past then turned his attention back to her. 'You've done a grand job of bringing her up on your own, so you have. You should be proud.'

'Thanks.' There was nothing else to say, really.

'It suits you, you know,' he said gently. 'Being a mother. You look even more beautiful, Polly.' His eyes were large as they steadied on her.

'Don't be daft,' she said, feeling all flustered as he was so close she could catch the aroma of the soap he'd showered with

The Trouble With Love

– it was heady – and when he gave her his broad old-Spike-like smile, it was almost like they were back when.

'This is kind of weird, though, isn't it? In some ways, it's like I never left. Do you know what I mean? You, me, Bristol. We'll always have Bristol,' he said, in a Humphrey Bogart voice. 'And Rowan,' he was saying as he moved closer, or was it her leaning in, drawn towards him by some invisible thread. She kissed him, feeling his soft lips part and then… He drew back and pushed her a step away from him.

'No, Polly. We…' He looked about him, but they were still hidden from view.

'Oh shit,' Polly said, her hand going up to her face as she realised her stupid, stupid mistake. She'd misread the signs. Stupid Polly.

'Bam… I…' he began. 'I'm with Bam, Polly. Look, I didn't mean to give you the wrong idea…'

'You didn't. Oh God, I'm so sorry. So sorry.' *What did you go and do that for?* she thought, as she took in a gulp of the night air, thinking how she might be sick, or die from humiliation.

'Look, Polly, you've got your Max, and I've got my…'

'Bam – yes, I know.'

'And she's a grand girl.' Before anything else could be said, they heard footsteps approaching on the gravel. It was Bam holding Rowan by the hand.

'That's where you've been hiding,' she said, good-naturedly. 'I was beginning to think you two might have been kidnapped.' She smiled at them both.

'Daddeee!' said Rowan, as if trying out his name once more. He lifted her up and into his arms and gave her a kiss on the cheek. She slapped either side of his face with her two hands.

Polly moved to take her off him. 'It's time we went,' she said, ignoring Rowan's protests as she strode back up to the house.

*

'We have to go, Daisy.'

'So soon?'

'Yes.' Even though Daisy tried to insist that Rowan stay the night for a sleepover with Morwenna, Polly was adamant. They needed to be up early for their picnic with Max and Ben, she said, and left, kissing everyone but Spike goodbye, beyond caring if anybody noticed.

Daisy accompanied her friend to the door; Polly carrying a now sound asleep Rowan over her shoulder.

As Daisy held the door open, she said, in a low voice, 'By the way, Polly, this Spike and Bam. It won't last.'

Polly turned and seemed about to say something when Daisy continued. 'I'm not at all convinced that they're love's young dream. I was watching them carefully tonight, and it's clear that Bam is more keen on Spike than he is on her.' She held her hand up. 'I'm just saying.'

'You don't know…' Polly began.

'You must have noticed,' Daisy said, as she quickly looked back over her shoulder, 'how he couldn't take his eyes off you. All evening.' She leant forward and added, 'There's clearly something still there. You mark my words.'

You couldn't be more wrong, thought Polly, as a gust of wind blew her hair about her face.

She was wondering whether she ought to come clean with her friend when she heard Mel shout out from behind them, 'Out of the way! Lesbian coming through!' as she dashed past Daisy to envelop Polly in a huge hug.

'Mind the kid,' said Polly with a smile.

'Ta ta, you old tart. I do love you, you know. Even though you can be a right muppet.'

'I love you too, you old lezzer.'

The Trouble With Love

Behind them Fen stood, in the background. 'Bye, Polly,' she called out.

*

Rowan safely tucked up in bed, Polly couldn't resist one last check of Facebook. Nothing fresh on her shop page, but there was a new Max status update: "In a relationship with Polly Park". She sat back staring at this, not sure if she was all that keen on his declaring their status to all and sundry. After all, they'd only just started seeing each other. Wasn't it too soon for them to be boyfriend and girlfriend? She didn't know the dating rules anymore.

Her mobile rang. Max. She let it go straight to voicemail, not bothering to analyse just why she didn't want to have a chat with Max. (Shouldn't she if he was her boyfriend? *Remember – you're not going to analyse. Not tonight.*)

Like giving into the inevitable, she clicked on Spike's Facebook profile – not at all stalkerish, she told herself. (*Yeah right*, said that annoying voice in her head that always sounded like Mel.) She clicked on Photo Album of Picnic with Rowan and began trawling through. There was Spike with Rowan on his shoulders; Spike swinging Rowan upside down, by her legs; Spike throwing Rowan up in the air; Spike, Rowan and Bam sitting at a wooden table grinning at the camera; Spike chasing Rowan in and out of the climbing frame with Mel watching and pointing; Spike plonking ice cream from a cone into the laughing face of Bam; and Bam giving Spike a kiss on the cheek as he held onto Rowan's hand – looking for all the world like… well, like a happy family, thought Polly, miserably.

At the bottom in the Comments box was written *Spike's cute daughter. We heart Rowan. Bam xxx*

That night she dreamt of the sea, of swimming through weeds, trying to escape a giant clam that opened and shut its jaws. Open and shut. Open and shut. She woke, drenched in her own salt sweat.

18

Donna phoned first thing the next morning. 'Look, babe, I know it's Sunday, and I'm sorry to hassle you on your day off an' all… but your muh still hasn't arranged to fix my boiler.'

'Still? Right. Gosh, I'm so sorry, Donna. I did call her. She's usually right on the case.'

'Yeah, but not this time, lover, innit. Look, is embarrassin'…' her voice dropped to a whisper "Me and Jez did the biz last night and can't even have a shower. Is right minging."

'Leave it with me.'

Polly could do without this, as she was in a rush. Max would be arriving any minute to take them out. The day looked set to be one of those freakishly hot April days when all and sundry stagger outside blinking into the glaring sun and go, 'Phew, what a scorcher!'

He'd phoned about an hour ago to announce that they were all off to the seaside. 'What a fabulous idea!' she'd said, feeling a thrill as going to the beach always made her feel like a big kid. Even if it was Berrow Sands just up from Weston-super-Mud.

'Woo hoo! Come on, lazy bones,' she'd said to Rowan, waking up her sleepy daughter and rubbing her face with a flannel. 'We're going to the seaside!'

With Rowan dressed, sandwiches made, wrapped and packed, Polly set about trying to calm down her daughter, who was practically beside herself, running about squealing, asking if she could take this (her favourite My Little Pony – yes, she could) and that (her big box of Duplo – no, she couldn't), and demanding to know just when it was they were all going.

'Is it now?'

'No.'

'Now?'

'No. Go and watch a DVD until Max arrives.' To be fair, Polly was excited too. The morning had dawned with her in a positive frame of mind. She'd decided to put Spike and that whole kiss thing right out of her head and to concentrate instead on the fact that for the first time in ever such a long while she had her own bona fide boyfriend! Who was gorgeous and sexy, and well into her. Spike wasn't the only one who could move on.

Still, mundane matters called. Just enough time to give her mum a bell.

'Yes. That you, Polly?' Suze sounded uncharacteristically hoarse down the line.

'Morning, Mother. Look, I've had Donna on the phone because her boiler is still not fixed.'

'Don't go on, darling. I've had other things on my mind.'

Polly couldn't believe how self-centred her mother could be at times. (Well, she could, but it still caught her by surprise.)

'Shall I call a plumber this end?' Polly gave a sigh of exasperation.

'No. It's fine. I'll get Brian on to it.' Which was unusual, as Suze – being a control freak – liked to sort everything herself rather than delegate. Even to Brian, her live-in lover. Perhaps she was mellowing.

'Right you are. So long as that's sorted. Only I must dash,' said Polly. 'Am off to the seaside. With my new boyfriend.'

'That's nice,' said Suze, sounding as if it wasn't particularly.

As Polly replaced the receiver, she was left with a nagging feeling that something was amiss. Her mother had not insisted on a blow-by-blow account of how, when and why Polly had a new boyfriend – or even what his name was. Also, Polly was irritated with herself that she'd forgotten to ask Suze about her visit to the Nuffield Hospital in Clifton last week.

Oh well, the sun was shining and she had sandwiches and bucket and spade all ready. Toot toot. Max had arrived.

'Come in, come in,' she said, opening her front door. 'I've nearly got everything ready.'

Max propelled a ginger-haired boy into the house. 'This is Ben.'

'Oh, hello, Ben.' (*He has got rather a weaselly face,* she thought. *Nothing at all like Max. Poor boy probably takes after his mother.*) Polly must have been staring as Max was giving her a decidedly quizzical look.

'I am just catching up with how yummy you are,' she said, affecting a speedy recovery.

'Stop it,' Max whispered into her ear. Placing his hand on Ben's head, he told him to say hello to Rowan, who was now peeking round the door frame of the sitting room, unusually shy. Ben, however, had no such reservations, running straight for Rowan and bellowing 'Yaaarrgghh!' in her face before wrestling a rainbow My Little Pony out of her hand.

'Ben!' Max swiftly took it off him to hand to Rowan, who was rooted to the spot, not sure quite what to do. There was never any rough play allowed at her Montessori nursery.

'Now play nicely,' Max instructed Ben.

'Righty-ho!' said Polly – forcing jollity into her voice. 'Let's get this show on the road, shall we?'

'Look! I can see the sea!' Polly called over her shoulder to Rowan and Ben, who were both safely strapped in child seats in the rear of Max's car. She wouldn't be sorry to arrive as Ben had been kicking the back of Polly's seat for most of the journey, and no amount of her asking him not to had made a blind bit of difference. Still, she was determined that they'd all have a lovely day, so she gritted her teeth. 'Look, there!'

'Where?' said Rowan, craning her neck to try and see around the confines of her seat. 'Where?'

Soon they were parked up on the beach in front of the high dunes of Berrow Sands, and all piling out of the car. The wind blew hard off the Bristol Channel as Max set about knocking in the pegs of their windbreak. Polly watched a man on a kite surfboard in the middle distance whizz across the wet sands at a fast lick; his board rising up in the air, then back down to hit the sands with a soft slap. The sea was a long way out, the colour of brown from mud and churned-up sand in a channel where tides swirled treacherously, Polly knew. Her dad, Jeff, used to bring her here with Gillian for Sunday outings.

Polly shivered, pulling her fake leopardskin car coat (authentic '60s buy from a friend's retro shop) around her. She zipped up a protesting Rowan's brightly coloured jacket.

'It's freezing,' Polly called over to Max, her voice nearly carried away by a sharp south-westerly. Although sunny, those April gusts had a bite to them.

'It'll be fine once we're out of this wind!' he called back.

Just like a real family holiday, thought Polly, as she smiled and took some snaps. *There, I'll load these up onto Facebook when I get back. Ha! See? Two can play that game, Spike*

The Trouble With Love

Monaghan. Oh stop it. She'd promised herself she was going to enjoy this trip and not fret about the whole making-a-right-pillock-of-herself-with-Spike thing. After all, here she was with her fabulous boyfriend, and his son. (*Okay, his devil-child son*, she thought, now looking across to where Ben was charging around going 'Raaaaar!' – for no apparent reason. Should have called him Damien!) Ben had far more freckles than Max; his hair stuck up, giving him the look of someone who'd run from a barber's clutches before he could finish his haircut; his nose was snub, and he had a mischievous- looking turned-up mouth and a tight wiry body. In short, he resembled an archetypal scamp.

When she glanced across fondly at Max, he gave her a thumbs-up. Her very own proper boyfriend doing manly boyfriend stuff like hammering. *I could get used to this*, she thought, even though her hair kept blowing across her face in tatty rats' tails as she tried to push it back. (*Soon be thick with salt and sand… Oh, do stop moaning! Just enjoy!*)

She decided to enjoy a bit of chasing Rowan into the sand dunes. Cue much squealing on Rowan's part and fun had by the two of them, until Damien/Ben stuck his foot out, sending Rowan headlong – 'Oof!' – onto the hard windblown sand.

'Ha ha ha!' he said, sticking out his chest before scampering off.

Rowan let out a good long cry as Polly scooped her into her arms and proceeded to carry her – sand sinking and soft with each step – back to Max. Ben arrived before them in a sliding stop any baseball player would be proud of.

She decided to ignore Ben. 'Phew! You weigh a ton, missy,' she said, placing her daughter next to Max, who tickled her under the chin before standing to dust off his jeans, clearly chuffed at his hammering-in of windbreak pegs.

'There,' he said, as proud as if he'd just knocked up a house.

'That should do the trick. Coffee?' Screwing the top off a thermos flask, he poured some out for her.

'Ta. Just what I needed,' she said, cupping her hands around the beaker, and when Max moved in to place his arm about her shoulder, she thought how lovely it was to have a boyfriend she could go on family outings with, and how clever she was to land a single dad who was a dab hand at windbreaks and thermos flasks, and who wasn't going to want her to stay out late watching his band, or get bladdered on drink and recreational drugs. She smiled up at him. Yep. Max was a real catch. Gorgeous, and fabulous in bed.

'Stop smiling at me like that,' he said, then whispered, 'You've given me another stiffy.' Polly had to admit there was some impressive straining-at-the-jeans going on down there. She felt a bit squirmy herself.

'It's no good... I'm going to have to recite the whole of Bristol City football team in my head. Unless,' he said, grabbing her hand, 'you want to help me out...'

'Oi,' she said, skipping out of his way, 'behave, you' – before reaching into the car for the blankets and picnic basket. He gave out a groan... 'Stop showing me your bottom, then.'

'Not now... Later.'

'I'll hold you to that.' He walked a little way then turned. 'You know your friend Mel?'

'What about her?'

He walked back and, lowering his voice, added, 'She's a lesbian, isn't she?'

'Well?'

'Have you two ever – you know...' He gave her a small nod and wink. 'I could just watch...' Polly gave him a shove. 'Or join in – if you like?' he added.

'Oh, for heaven's sake! Boys and their fantasies!'

The Trouble With Love

Rowan was diligently digging with her spade just on the periphery of their windbreak boundary. It was quiet on the beach and their nearest neighbours were a good fifty yards away.

'Where's Ben?' said Polly, looking about her. A seagull hung in the sky like a spotter plane. She caught sight of Ben. 'Ah, there he is. I can just see his feet,' she called to Max. Ben's feet were poking out from behind a sand dune. She strolled over, just in time to see him tunnelling into the dune with his spade. 'Oh no, you don't,' she said, reaching in to pull him back out.

'Get off!' he screamed in a loud voice. 'Get off, get off!' and tried to scrabble in further. But Polly had him by the waist now and was just about to pull him free when Max appeared to see what all the commotion was about.

Right at that moment, a nude sunbather chose to saunter past, his tackle in full dangle smack-bang in Polly's eyeline. 'Good morning,' he said, and she was so startled she let go of Ben and fell backwards – hard – onto her coccyx. 'Ouch!'

Max had his son out of the makeshift tunnel and onto his feet in front of him as he set about dusting him down.

'Right, there we are,' he said. 'No harm done.'

'Did you see that?' said Polly.

'Chill, Poll,' said Max. 'So Ben dug a tunnel. All boys do that.'

'No. I meant the nudist.'

'Naturist, they're called,' he said. 'Better leave the digging, Ben. Now go and join Rowan, there's a good boy.' He stood up. 'This part's the naturists' beach, Poll.'

'Well, you could have said, because I wouldn't have brought Rowan if I'd known.'

'Whyever not? I didn't have you down as a prude.'

'I'm not,' she said. 'But everyone knows that paedophiles try and join naturists' clubs to get an eyeful of naked children.'

'That's very un-PC of you, Polly, and I'm sure it's an urban myth. Or rubbish, more like.'

She felt rather ashamed. He was probably right. Poor man was just enjoying a bit of a breeze around his nether regions.

'You shouldn't worry so much,' said Max, guiding her back to their spot where Ben now appeared to have snatched Rowan's spade and was whacking the sand – a spade in each fist – close to where she sat, hanging onto her bucket.

'Want to dig a tunnel!' Ben whinged.

'Not now, mate, okay?' said Max.

'In any case,' Polly said, addressing Ben, 'it's not safe. A boy was killed here a couple of years ago. He got buried alive on this beach, because he was digging a tunnel in the dunes – just like you were – when it collapsed on top of him.'

Ben's eyes lit up. 'Cool,' he said. 'Did he die?'

'Yes. I'm afraid he did.'

'Did anyone see it? Did they, like, dig and dig, with their bare hands, but they couldn't reach him? Was he like this?' and Ben put both hands around his neck and made a choking sound. 'Blahhhh.' Rowan watched – rapt. 'Did he turn blue…' Ben continued 'and—'

'Ben! Enough!' Polly said, rather more sharply than she intended. 'Rowan's listening, and you'll scare her.'

Ben looked at Rowan in disgust. 'But Dad said she was deaf!'

Max suggested Polly take Ben to the ice-cream van while Max helped Rowan build a sandcastle. She wasn't sure it was a good idea but he insisted, saying, 'I think I can manage to keep an eye on your daughter, Polly.' About ten yards from the car was a dip in the wet sand – forming a natural pool – from where Max could send Rowan to collect sea water in her bucket. 'She'll be fine,' he insisted. 'Off you go.'

*

'Can I have two flakes with my 99?' Ben demanded loudly once they'd reached the window of the van. The man looked expectantly at Polly.

'You'll have one flake like everybody else,' she said, returning the man's look. 'Sorry.'

'Why are you saying sorry to that man? What have you done to him?'

'Nothing.'

'If you buy me an extra flake then he'll have extra money, and you'll have made it up to him.'

'Ben, I don't have to make amends.' She gave the man an embarrassed shrug. 'I've not done anything to him.'

'Then why are you sorry?'

The man finished loading the four cones with ice cream, poking a flake into each, and stood awaiting Polly's decision.

'Just the one flake,' she said, sticking to her guns, as she knew full well it was not a good idea to change your mind once you'd said No to a child.

'I'll pay for the extra flake with my own pocket money,' Ben insisted. Ice-cream man frozen to the spot, ice cream starting to melt and dribble down the cones. Ben continued. 'That's fair, isn't it?'

'Seems fair to me,' said the man, smiling encouragingly at Polly. 'Sometimes it's best not to dig yer heels in, love,' he added, as he reached for the contentious extra flake.

'And strawberry syrup?' said Ben, a triumphant look on his face.

Triumphant yet angelic, thought Polly, as she contemplated Max's son. *That's a hard look to carry off.*

Job done, money paid, Ben charged through the dunes ahead of her, guzzling his double-flake-99 as he pelted along.

As Polly rounded the sand dune to where they were parked, she could see Max patting the sandcastle and, as she cast about for her daughter, she handed him his cornet. Shielding her eyes from the sun peeking out from behind a grey cloud, she asked, 'Where's Rowan?'

*

Everything seemed to slow down as she took in Max's dawning realisation, felt her head turn – hair slewing round in slo-mo – as she scanned her eyeline. Max, to her left, was saying, 'Where is she? I sent her for some water!'

No. No. This is not going to happen. Not today. Not ever, thought Polly, then – There! A tiny figure, a long way off, was heading steadfastly out to sea – the tide a long way out. Oh God! Oh God! Polly dropped her ice cream, kicked off her shoes and began to run, then running backwards, she shrieked to Max, 'If it looks like we're stuck – call the coastguard! 999!'

She didn't wait for his reply but turned once more to face the sea, head up, feet firmly on the ground, as she took off like the sprinter she used to be at school, bursting out of the blocks. Running through her mind was the accident at Weston-super-Mare when a small child got stuck in the quicksand and mud, and how her father had tried to rescue her, but they'd both been sucked down and held fast by the sand and mud so that they were drowned by the incoming tide. *Not my Rowan!*

Polly's feet pounded the sand. Thud, huh huh huh. Thud, huh huh huh. Her daughter growing in size as Polly gained on her: bigger and bigger as she got closer and closer. The sand wetter now, giving slightly under her toes with each step. Each slap of her feet flattening surface whorls, made by burrowing creatures – cockles? – who knew, who cared? Then as Polly neared Rowan, her daughter spun round, saw her mother and – clearly thinking it was a game of chase – chortled and ran, giggling, away from her. Towards the sea!

The Trouble With Love

'Ro! Stop! Ro! Stop!' No good. Polly knew her daughter couldn't hear her, and in any case, Polly needed her breath for running. She had to catch her before the quicksand; the ground now sucking ever so slightly at her feet as she ran, trying to slow her, trying to pull her to a stop.

The image of the white horse in that film *The NeverEnding Story* sprang to Polly's mind. Floundering in a bog, going under while his boy owner cried and wailed, unable to keep its head up, unable to stop it being pulled down.

Well, the mud isn't going to get my daughter. Fuck off, you bitch, she thought as she stepped things up into Ripley-from-*Alien* mode, adrenaline pumping her legs and heart as she flew across the sand; flying to her daughter's rescue.

As she reached her, caught her and swung her into her arms, Polly shouted, 'Don't you ever! Ever do that again!'

Rowan, startled, patted her mother's cheeks in best Eric Morecambe-style and went, 'Ahhh. Mummee.'

'Never ever run off to the sea again,' said Polly, directly into her smiling child's face. Knowing she'd have to explain it all to her daughter later, she hugged her tight, pent-up emotion nearly bursting her chest as she checked there was no damage anywhere. Then, holding her daughter's hand, she began to walk back. Thanking God, and whoever, that there was going to be a later.

Max and Ben were waiting for them. 'There you go,' said Max. 'No harm done.' Polly had never felt so alone.

*

They drove back in relative silence, apart, that is, from Polly having to turn round every now and then to stop Ben from sticking his finger up Rowan's nose, or bonking her on the head with his toy car, or kicking the blinking back of Polly's seat again. Honestly. That boy. Did he have ADHD or what?

Max was due to drop Ben off at Claire's, but first he helped Polly indoors with her things: basket, rugs, picnic, child seat. He asked if he could use her loo.

'Sure,' she said, wondering why he couldn't have hung on until he got home – they'd stopped off at a service station on the M5 where he'd taken Ben to the toilets and she'd done the same with Rowan. Hadn't he gone then? Or was this some kind of male-marking-territory thing? She tried not to imagine him spraying her bathroom with his wee, like some big two-legged tomcat, and instead she switched the kettle on and left the kids playing in the front room.

It began to dawn on her that whereas before the kids had been pretty noisy – what with running about and screeching – now all was quiet. Unnaturally so. Better go check, she thought, as in her experience, quiet and young children invariably equalled trouble.

Careful not to make a noise – hoping to catch them at whatever it was they were doing – Polly gently pushed open the sitting-room door. There stood Rowan, with her back to Polly. Ben was bent in front of her with his head up and under her dress. Rowan must have heard Polly enter, as she looked over her shoulder. Ben quickly ducked out and stood to attention, giving Polly a defiant it-wasn't-me-guv look. It was then that she noticed he wasn't wearing any trousers – or pants! She couldn't have been more surprised at the little scenario she'd just witnessed if the Phantom Flan Flinger had leapt out from behind her Cap'n Jack pirate and splatted her face with a custard pie.

What the...? 'Ben!' she shouted.

Ben jumped up and down on the spot a few times, his little willy jiggling up and down as he let out a squeal, and then

The Trouble With Love

rushed to sit in front of Rowan's box of Lego, where he noisily rummaged around in it as if that was what he'd been doing all along.

Rowan turned to face her mother, a puzzled look on her face. 'Mummy?' she said. 'Ben tickled my china!'

'Come on,' said Max – at her door with a fully trousered Ben. 'You've got to admit, it was pretty funny.'

'Funny?' she said, unable to credit that Max appeared unfazed by the behaviour of his son.

Max was helping Ben into his jacket. 'You're having a serious sense of humour failure, here.' He straightened up, gripping Ben by the shoulder.

She regarded Ben. He was only a kid; Max was right. 'I'm sorry,' she said, her shoulders drooping. 'I guess I'm not used to boys.'

He leant forwards to give her a kiss on the cheek. 'Shall I come by later, as arranged?'

Feeling somewhat reassured that there was nothing to fear, and that Ben was not a budding pervert, Polly smiled back at Max. 'Yes. That would be lovely.'

'Okey-doke. We'll be off, then. Say goodbye to Polly, Ben.'

'Goodbye, Polly,' said Ben, as he fidgeted from one foot to the other.

'Better get this young man back to his mother,' said Max.

But truth be told, Polly still had some nagging doubts.

*

After they'd gone, she decided it would be a good thing to talk through the whole boy thing. Get more perspective on whether she had overreacted. She punched Mel's number into her mobile. No reply. Instead it went to voicemail.

'Ring me when you can, Mel. Be good to speak.'

She wandered back into the sitting room, where Rowan had her back to her, doggedly completing a large-piece jigsaw.

Perhaps – and she had no idea why – she'd taken an instant dislike to Ben for no reason, and that was colouring her opinion. *Daisy*, she thought. *She'll be in. Yes. Daisy knows all about boys. She's raised one of them, after all.* And very successfully too – Zak was a lovely boy: polite and respectful… Unlike Max's prince-of-darkness child.

She tapped her daughter on the shoulder and, as Rowan turned her open face to her mother's, Polly was struck by how like her father she looked.

'C'mon, sunshine,' she said, and was rewarded with a beam from Rowan. 'Let's go see Daisy and Morwenna.'

19

Zak, Daisy's tall and clearly-going-to-be-handsome-once-he-grows-into-his-looks son, was clattering out of the house with a guitar case when Polly and Rowan arrived. He held the door open for them. 'Mum's in the kitchen,' he muttered, in that embarrassed teenage boy way.

'Cheers, Zak,' she said, backing Rowan in through the door. 'You got band practice? How's it all going?'

'Fine, thanks,' he said with a cheery wave.

Daisy looked up from where she was about to push the plunger on her cafetière. 'You're just in time for coffee.' Daisy took Rowan by the hand and, bending down, said directly to her – 'Morwenna's up in her room. Do you want to go and find her?'

'Ess pees,' and she charged out of the room. Soon they could hear her call 'Morwenna! Morwenna!' and then thumps and squeals from above.

'That's them settled for a while. How's tricks?'

'I need some advice, Daise.'

'Oh yeah? Mel's been bending my ear too. I ought to start charging,' she said. 'Coffee?' proceeding to pour them both a cup.

'Is everything all right with Mel?' Polly asked, wondering why whatever it was, Mel hadn't confided in *her*.

'Oh, just something about Fen wanting them to go visit her mother. That sort of thing. So,' said Daisy in a lighter, more breezy tone, 'what can I do for you? Is this about Spike?'

'Spike? No! God no! And you're wrong, by the way, about there being something – anything – there between us.' She didn't fancy telling Daisy about the whole kissing- Spike thing. Far too mortifying.

'Hmm,' said Daisy, passing Polly her cup. 'Methinks the lady doth protest too much.'

'Trust me,' said Polly, giving what she hoped was an earnest look. 'There's nothing. Apart from affection, of course. After all, we do share a child.' She added milk to her coffee. 'We've all moved on, and I'm very happy with Max.' ("Moving on" seeming to be the theme of the week.)

'If you say so,' said Daisy, throwing her an I'm-still-not-convinced look. 'So go ahead, what else would you like my advice about, if it's not Spike and his obvious crush on you?' Polly poked her tongue out at her.

'Mum! Mum!' Morwenna came charging in, holding Rowan firmly by the hand. 'Can Ro Ro sleep in my bed? Can she? Can she?' Morwenna had her perfect little rosebud mouth pursed as she waited for her mother's verdict.

Daisy turned to her friend. 'That's up to Rowan's mum.'

'Peeeese,' said Rowan, jumping up and down on the spot.

'Please,' begged Morwenna.

'I couldn't possibly, Daise. You've been doing far too much babysitting for me.'

'Nonsense, we love having Rowan. She's an absolute delight.'

Polly smiled her thanks then turned to the girls. 'All right. Rowan can stay over.'

The girls excitedly shouted 'Yay!' and dashed out of the room before anyone could change their mind.

Once the women were both sure the two girls were well out of earshot, Daisy turned to Polly. 'I'm glad you're getting on well with Max. And now that you've got the evening off, you can invite him round to yours, can't you? Do whatever you want – swing from the chandeliers or re-enact *Fifty Shades of Grey* – without being interrupted by a little girl. Oh, and don't worry about the morning, either. I can take them both to the Montessori nursery, and that way you won't have to worry about collecting her until after work tomorrow. How's that suit you?'

'You are a saint,' said Polly – and with Daisy's light brown hair framing that fine cheek-boned face, Polly thought she did bear more than a passing resemblance to the plaster Saint Barbara that Polly had on her landing table, just outside the bathroom. But Saint Barbara was kept in a tower or something waiting for her lover to return, wasn't she? Whereas Daisy was more like a saint to the rescue – *Wonder which one that was.*

'Mel tells me that Max has a reputation for being quite the stud!' said Daisy, giving Polly a suggestive look. 'You lucky girl.'

Polly paused. 'God, yes, okay. He *is* actually.'

'Good for you! You could do with some fun.' She gave Polly a steady stare. 'Is it just fun or do you think it might become something more serious?'

'Truth? I just don't know. It's not like he's being cool or anything. Quite the opposite. He seems pretty keen. But you know me, I'm rubbish at relationships.' She pulled at her cardigan. 'I'm beginning to wonder if Spike –and this whole fantasy thing I've got going on about him being the one I could have loved, but sadly he's always out of reach? Perhaps it's some sort of get-out clause. You know, a good reason not to get involved with anyone else.' She reached for a chocolate biscuit. 'I've been giving it some thought and was starting to come round to the idea of giving Max a chance: having a real go at being a couple… But now the fly in the ointment appears to be his kid. Ben the devil child. Or am I making Ben a new reason for not getting involved? I can't tell anymore. And I feel like a right cow for feeling this way about a small child. I could do with some advice, Daise.' She looked at her friend. 'Basically I need to pick your brains about boys.'

'I see.' Daisy went to the fridge and pulled out an opened bottle of Prosecco. 'Reckon this still has bubbles in it? What the hell, we'd better finish it off. To hell with coffee – what we need is a proper drink while you tell me all about it.' She indicated that they sit on the more comfortable and rather tasteful armchairs, covered in a white with large vibrant purple lilies pattern. 'Go ahead,' she said, handing over a full glass. But before Polly could begin on her day with Max and Ben, and the no-pants incident, in wandered Tiggy boy in tow. A tall, skinny one in skinny jeans, Converse trainers, bedraggled jumper and floppy hair almost covering his face.

'Ignore us.' Tiggy gave a fulsome smile to the women. 'We're after food. Studying, you know.'

'Yes, of course. Studying,' said Daisy, fixing her daughter with an I-do-know-that's-not-all-you're-getting-up-to stare.

'Shut up, Mum!' said Tiggy. She turned to the boy. 'Don't mind her. She's being annoying,' and then pulled open the fridge door as the boy smiled sheepishly at the two women.

'Hello, Mrs Hyde.'

Tiggy, head in the fridge. 'White, you mentalist. I'm Hyde, she's White. Stepdad! Duh!'

The boy blushed.

'Please, call me Daisy,' she said, proffering her hand, which

The Trouble With Love

he gave a firm shake as Tiggy stuck her head out long enough to raise an eyebrow.

'Duh, Mum. Handshakes? Well lame.'

Daisy ignored her child. 'And this is Polly.'

'Right you are, Mrs – umm – Daisy – Polly,' smiled the boy – or young man. Polly thought he looked like that serial-shagger floppy-haired boy from that famous boy band.

Tiggy emerged with a plate piled high with leftovers from the party: cooked sausages, barbecued drumsticks, pizza slices – and a large bottle of Diet Coke in hand. 'Here,' she said to the boy-band lookalike, thrusting the drink at him.

As he headed for the door, he paused, ran his fingers through his luxuriant brown locks and said, 'Dolphin.'

'I'm sorry,' said Polly. 'I thought you said Dolphin.'

'He did, duh,' said Tiggy, in typical teen adults-are-so-thick voice. 'Because that's his name. Nuh.'

The boy-man smiled. 'No worries. My parents are, like, total hippies – brother Ocean, sister Sky. Everyone calls me Fin. I just like to sometimes tell people I'm called Dolphin. It's funny, like.'

'Well, it's very nice to meet you,' said Daisy – completely unfazed.

The teenagers left in a clatter of plates and sniggers as Polly gawped at Daisy. 'What on earth were his parents thinking? I'm surprised he doesn't get the crap beaten out of him every day!'

'Who's this?' said Phil – in his genial way – as he strolled in from another room, stopping to plant a kiss on the top of Daisy's head. He sat on the arm of her chair – looking very uncomfortable in his not-very-bendy-looking rugby frame.

'We were just discussing Tiggy's new boyfriend,' Daisy said, glancing up at her husband, who looked like he might topple over and flatten her at any moment. 'You know. The one with the surfer-dude parents.'

'Ah,' was all he managed to say, before the eponymous Tiggy

came bouncing back in – jiggling around Phil, much like her namesake Tigger.

'Pops! Pops!' He stood up. 'Lend us a twenty, will you? Me and Fin want to go see a movie.'

'Not one of those *Final Destination* slasher-type movies, is it?' he said, nonetheless reaching into his wallet for a note.

'Honestly, Phil, she hasn't tidied her room,' said Daisy. 'You know the rules. No tidy, no money.'

Tiggy stamped her foot – 'Mum…!'

Daisy turned to Polly. 'Honestly, her room looks like someone emptied a skipload of rubbish all over it.'

'Mu-u-u-u-m!'

'Here's an idea,' said Phil, placing the note on the kitchen counter. 'If you tidy it in – say – half an hour, the money's yours and I'll run you both to the cinema. How's that?'

Daisy had already unpeeled one then two black bin bags from their roll. 'Here you are,' she said, before slipping them into the kitchen drawer.

Tiggy, looking from Phil to Daisy, accepted her fate. 'Oh, all right,' and hurried from the kitchen, clattering up the stairs, shouting, 'Fin! Fin! Help me tidy my frickin' room! Fin!' Followed by a slam of her bedroom door.

'Kids, eh?' Phil collected up his newspapers and tucked them under his arm. 'Leave you two to it, shall I?'

Tiggy and Phil clearly got on well. But it hadn't always been so.

Daisy's first husband, Steve – the father of Tiggy and Zak – had died tragically in a freak car accident five years ago. Tiggy was ten and Zak twelve at the time. Zak never talked about it, despite Daisy's best efforts. She supposed he talked it through with his counsellor, which their Steiner School had arranged for both children. Tiggy, though, became full of rage; misbehaving at school, smoking, getting drunk. The school persevered, and

The Trouble With Love

Daisy – although numb – had a reason to carry on – her kids needed her. Phil, as Steve's best friend, was increasingly there for her until – even though Steve was supposedly the love of her life – she fell for Phil.

At the time, both Polly and Mel were convinced that Daisy was settling.

But on the morning of Daisy and Phil's wedding, less than two years after Steve's death, Daisy – radiantly beautiful, and wearing a tastefully glorious ivory satin dress – had turned to Polly and said, 'I know you think I'm settling, but I'm not. I'm truly happy. Oh, it's okay,' she added, grasping Polly's hands in hers. 'Don't look so embarrassed. I know Phil isn't as handsome or as witty as Steve. And that I loved Steve with a grand passion...' she let go of her friend '...but... Phil is a *good* man, and he loves me. He makes me feel safe and I love him and I'm lucky to have found him.'

But Tiggy hadn't felt the same.

Still, now witnessing the affectionate exchange between stepfather and daughter, Polly could see that Daisy's conviction that all would turn out fine in the end had indeed been spot on. Phil's kind and humorous devotion to them all had won over even Tiggy. Polly glanced at her friend, all happy and complete with her family, and for a split second she found herself wishing she too could find some of that.

'So,' said Daisy, once they were alone, 'come on, spill the beans. What is it you need to talk about? Is it Max, or is it his child?'

'Both.'

'Oh dear. Do tell,' said her friend, as she refilled their glasses.

Daisy snorted wine through her nose, she was laughing so much.

'Is it funny, Daise? Only I didn't think it was funny at the time,' said Polly.

'Oh, Polly, Polly, you are daft. Seriously, he was just being a boy. I'm sure Rowan's fine and she'll have forgotten all about it.'

'I don't think I handled it very well at all. And now Max might be off with me because I...' she said, realising that what she was about to say would sound stupid '...because I more or less accused a little five-year-old boy of being a pervert!'

Daisy did another snort.

'Don't laugh. Max wants to "talk about it" later tonight.' Polly slumped in her chair. 'I don't know. I guess I like my own way of doing things. Max and I clearly have different ideas about parenting. He's too lax for my liking, and he thinks I'm a fusspot. But look what happened today when he took his eye off Rowan at the beach. She could have drowned, and he just shrugged it off!'

'You might not want to hear this, darling. But relationships – real relationships – are all about compromise. If you care enough about each other then you'll find some middle ground.'

'And if you don't?'

'Then you hold out for someone who does share your values and who you *do* want to compromise with. Pass me that big knife, will you?'

Daisy began chopping veg to go into her large turquoise Le Creuset casserole dish. 'You don't mind if I carry on getting supper ready, do you?' she asked. She was cooking some Nigella recipe which she'd adapted herself, she told Polly, who was more of a bung-stuff-in-and-hope-it-turns-out-all-right kind of cook.

Who on earth has the sort of ingredients Nigella insists on, in any case? Apart from Suze – and clearly Daisy.

Polly watched as Daisy moved about her kitchen; the glow from the dimmed lights, the smell of the food and the drawing-in of the night outside as it did its hug about the kitchen all served to give Polly a warm and cosy feeling.

'I wish I could marry you.'

'Shame you can't stay for supper,' said Daisy, giving her friend a peck on the cheek.

'Yes, it is a shame.' Polly's voice had more than a tad of wistfulness about it as she moved across to Daisy's Aga to inhale the yummy aromas emanating from inside its cast iron doors. 'God, that smells delicious. So, you do think it's worth my persevering with Max? Or should I cut my losses? There again, if we carry on, how am I going to deal with devil child and other myriad things involved…?' Polly sunk her head into her hands.

'Do you really want to know what I think?' Daisy asked, as she smoothed her apron. Polly nodded. 'Okay then, for what it's worth, I think you *should* give Max a chance. He seems like a nice man, he clearly likes you, though goodness knows why…' she added, grinning away.

'Oi. Thanks a lot.'

'Max doesn't understand yet that you're extra careful with Rowan because of her hearing loss. And you'll see, things will settle down with Ben. Boys are different to girls; that's all. Ben probably feels a bit weird about his dad dating. He sounds like a lively little chap, and a typical boy. At that age, they're all fascinated by the fact that girls don't have willies.'

'Not just at that age! Ha ha. Seriously, you really don't think there's any cause for concern?'

'I really don't.' She narrowed her eyes at her friend. 'You could do a lot worse than Max, you know. He ticks a lot of boxes, doesn't he? First, he's a single dad – which means he knows what it's like to have a child. Second, he's attractive – oh, and bright. And I hear he's a very good bonk…!'

Polly sighed. 'You're right, you're right.'

'Of course I am. I am always right.' She opened her oven door, checking on the pot inside, before adding, quietly, 'I know he's not Spike.'

'No. Well. That boat's well and truly sailed.' Polly picked up a raw carrot and waved it about as she continued. 'Even if I *was* interested – which I'm not. I… I dunno, Daise… maybe I'm just wired up differently to everyone else.' She took a bite of carrot.

'What on earth do you mean?'

'When I try *not* to fall in love with someone – yes, yes, okay, with Spike – then I go and fall head over heels. But I'm not now, okay? And when I meet someone who, as you say, ticks the right boxes and should be someone I could *easily* fall in love with, then I'm – well – just not. That's the trouble with love, I guess. Not bloody convenient but bloody contrary.' She gave a wry smile.

'It can indeed.' Daisy reached to give Polly a reassuring touch on the shoulder. 'Just give it time. You probably would have been well away with Max if Spike hadn't turned up. I'm right, aren't I?'

'Suppose so.'

'Take me and Phil. Who'd have thought a few years ago that we'd end up together? But our love grew – on my side, anyway. And who's to say that yours won't with Max, too? Why not give him a chance? Stop analysing everything and instead take things as they come. Love might very well blossom.' She leant back against her Butler sink. 'Have you ever thought it might be difficult for you to trust – because of your mum?'

'Not you too. That's the sort of stuff Mel comes out with. I hate all that self-help psycho-babble shit.'

'But she might have a point. Or, you could have a go at proving her wrong?' Daisy gave her a devilish look before lifting the casserole from the Aga. 'Mmm. This smells great, even though I say so myself. Are you sure you don't want to stay and join us for dinner?' But Polly shook her head.

'I hope you don't mind my asking. But don't you ever get lonely? Being a single parent must be tough. I don't know how you do it, because I couldn't manage if I didn't have Phil.'

Did she get lonely? Polly wondered. She'd always considered

herself a free spirit who didn't want to get tied down and considered that was why she didn't want to commit, to compromise, or to settle. She'd always been happy with her own company... But now that Rowan was in bed fast asleep by 8 pm every night and the evenings tended to stretch before her, then, well yes, there were times... And having Mel to stay had reminded and given her a glimpse of how things could be – with a significant other. Maybe a little loneliness was no longer a price worth paying for her freedom.

Then a small voice inside reminded her that there was one other person – beside Mel – whom she could have imagined sharing hers and Rowan's life with. But there again, perhaps she only thought that because he was "safe" because it would never be an option because he was either moving to Australia or had a girlfriend. Overanalysing again, Polly. Overanalysing.

*

Once she was back home, she rang Mel.
'Mel? It's me.'
'Hello, you,' Mel whispered down the phone.
In the background, Polly could hear Fen call out, 'Who is it?'
'It's okay, it's only Polly,' was Mel's reply.
Charming. Only Polly. No one important. Oh, do stop being a ninny.
'So what is it?' Mel said, not unkindly.
Polly briefly filled her in on her conversation with Daisy.
'Daisy said you should compromise? Well, she would say that, wouldn't she? She's Mrs Middle Class Smug Married. I'm sorry – you know I love her, but she is... Why didn't you ask me?'
'You weren't around.'
'Just answer me this, Polly. Who would be doing the

compromising? With you and Max, eh? It would be you, that's who, and you know it. Anyway, darling, Fen's calling and I must go. Love you.'

All her life, Polly had done things her and Mel's way – and look where that had got her! Ditched for the new girlfriend, that's where. Well, now she was going to give Daisy's way a try.

*

Max came over, and before he could say anything at all, Polly pulled him inside by his lapels and gave him a big kiss, which promised a lot, lot more.

'Let's forget about today, shall we? I'm really sorry. I overreacted,' she said, rather breathlessly.

'I expect you can make it up to me,' he said, pulling her tighter into him, with the sort of smile you'd normally associate with the twiddling of moustache and flourishing of cape.

'We've got all night,' she said.

'We have?'

'Yes. Rowan's on a sleepover at Daisy's… so… let's go down the pub, get well and truly bladdered and then have lots of filthy, dirty sex. You can stay over.'

He couldn't get her out of the house quickly enough.

They had a great night at the Nova. Polly thought there might well have been some singing of sea shanties in the bar – involving her and a couple of sailors – at some point, but she couldn't be absolutely sure as she'd drunk too much scrumpy. Much, much later, what she was sure of was that the next day she'd be walking like John Wayne minus his horse, because sex with Max proved Epic – with a capital E.

20

Tuesday morning, and a package arrived with a thud on her doormat. Inside was a nature storybook on eels, of all things. It had a beautiful green iridescent cover, and inside exquisite illustrations of eels in different stages: glass eels as thin and flat as leaves, buffeted by the ocean's tides; ribbon elvers entering rivers, excited by the smell of fresh water as they wriggled up rapids and climbed around rocks; maturing eels with their large saucer-like eyes hiding in mudholes; eels thick as snakes dining on stickleback eggs; eels clambering overland crunching the shells of snails; eels with the biggest grins ever, as if laughing at the funniest joke in the world!

Fascinated, Polly turned page after page. In the back was a pocket for its accompanying CD, which promised an eel song. *Mind boggles*, she thought, deciding to play it that night with her daughter. Who was it from? She had a pretty good idea as she reached inside the brown padded envelope and pulled out a note, immediately recognising her mother's scrawl:

Polly, I saw this in a shop in Totnes and thought Rowan would love it. Make sure when you read it to her that you tell our darling Ro Ro that it's from her grandma, who loves her very, very much. Suze xxx

Strange, thought Polly, as she put the book to one side. Suze was more an email and iPad kind of person than an actually writing-a-note one. Oh well. Polly shrugged, collected her coat and dashed out the door.

Later that day, she tried her mother's phone, but it went straight through to voicemail.

'Umm, Suze, it's Polly. Thanks for the gift. I'm sure Ro Ro will love it. Umm. Everything okay your end? I've gone ahead and organised a plumber for Donna's flat. And, Mum, whatever were you doing at the Nuffield Hospital the other week? I saw you in Clifton but couldn't stop. Anyway. Call me.'

*

The following Friday, Polly and Max went to the cinema. 'Like a proper date,' Polly whispered, and Max said, 'Okay, if we must, we can go see this Colin Firth film.'

Afterwards, in the car, Max said, 'I fancy some fish and chips. How about you?'

'Lovely. I'm starving.' She slid into the passenger seat of his car. 'What did you think of the film?'

'Not really my sort of thing. I prefer French films. They often show them at the Watershed. Fancy going next time?'

'Oh. Yes,' she said, and let it go at that, because she couldn't abide films with subtitles. If she wanted to read a book then she'd have stayed at home. If that made her a philistine in his eyes, there was no need to tell him just yet. She sat back in the comfy leather seats. She could regard it as an opportunity for him to teach her all about foreign film. Like Richard Gere introducing Julia Roberts to opera in *Pretty Woman*. Max could point out the story, the details, while she let the beauty and emotion wash all over her.

'What do you think of Richard Gere?' she said.

'Who?' he answered, as he looked over his shoulder to back his car out of the space. 'Must take this old girl to the garage tomorrow,' he said, giving the car's dashboard an affectionate tap.

Max's old pale blue Mercedes was his pride and joy. A classic car – so he kept telling her – she didn't have to take his word for it as whenever they passed another Merc, the owners would wave hello at Max. Same as with 2CV owners – and 2CVs were definitely classic. Even had their own rallies.

'Yeah right,' he'd said when she told him. 'They're hardly classic cars, though, are they? They've the engine of a sewing machine, are made from tin, and threaten to tip over each time you take a sharp bend.'

'I'll have you know they race them in the Sahara Desert,' said Polly, distinctly miffed as she didn't like her car being insulted. 'For your information, you can't roll a 2CV.'

'Yeah, and you can't get one to do sixty, either.'

Polly had humphed at this point, sailing pretty close to an argument. Yet he could be very sweet. Could spend hours just pleasuring her, she reminded herself, smiling. Yes, he'd been very giving in bed. Had a body to die for, and she loved his cock. She squirmed just thinking about it and slid her hand onto his thigh. 'Steady on,' he said. 'Don't want to crash the car.'

Sitting in the dark of the cinema and hugging her coat about her knees, she smiled thinking of what was to come. Later they drove along the familiar Bedminster streets in companionable silence as she peered out into the night, her mind wandering until it alighted on her mother, and how she'd left Polly and her dad when the going got tough. *I'm not going to be like Suze. Ever.*

Her mother was just seventeen when she fell pregnant with Polly. Okay, now she was a mother herself, she had an inkling of how tough that must have been. She couldn't imagine being anywhere near ready if she'd been expecting at that age. She hadn't felt ready at thirty! Suze's own parents had wanted Suze to have an abortion or the baby adopted, but Suze, determined to keep her baby, felt her only option was to stick with Jeff. He'd been more than happy to take her and the baby on, as he was besotted with the strikingly pretty and feisty Suze. When Polly – in her teens – had finally got up the courage to ask Suze why she'd left them, her answer was plain – she'd thought it for the best. 'I had a nervous breakdown, hun. Took to the streets. Did drugs. You can guess the sort of thing – blah di blah. You were better away from all that.'

'You're quiet there,' Max said, glancing briefly in Polly's direction. 'You okay?'

'Yes,' she answered. 'Just tired.'

'Not too tired, I hope.'

*

Weeks passed in relative harmony and soon acquired a rhythm – much like the tides that washed to and fro at the front of her house.

Polly saw Max a couple of times a week, and Spike would take Rowan out for the day, either on Saturday or Sunday – sometimes fitting in an extra visit during the week. Spike didn't mention "the kiss", and as he was clearly determined to ignore it, she decided to do the same. Max was fine when Polly asked if he minded not staying over when Rowan was at home, as she didn't want Rowan to get confused. Could they leave it until it felt right? 'Sure thing,' he'd said, which gave Polly extra confidence that he was a solid bet. The two of them settled on either staying in, watching a DVD and then having sex on the sofa, or sneaking up to her bed for a while, or going out and having sex in his car (and once even on waste ground that was soon to be turned into flats and bars – which had been terribly exciting and made her feel like a teenager). Whatever they did, their dates would end with Max wandering home alone.

'I quite like it,' he said, snuggling down under her covers for a cuddle before getting dressed. 'Feels kind of illicit. Like we're having an affair.'

'Oh,' said Polly, not sure if this was a good thing or not.

'Really, Poll,' he'd reassured her, 'I like going home on Shanks's pony. The streets are quiet and it clears my head. Know what I mean?'

Polly gave herself a mental pat on the back at how civilised they were all being – she and Max, Spike and Bam. She was totally cool, she assured herself, with the whole Spike and Wham Bam thing by now – although not as comfortable as Mel, who'd taken to collectively naming the couple Spam – causing Polly to guffaw out loud each time she uttered, 'Here comes Spam.'

Yes, they were all being grown up about it. Rowan was loving spending time with her father, and Max was polite if wary around Spike – but that was to be expected with two macho males – the wariness, that is. Spike and Bam fitted in sightseeing around visits to Rowan and visits to London to do with the sorting of Elspeth's effects. Polly's heart contracted when he told her that he'd sold his boat to Leo. (*Talk about burning boats*, thought Polly – *oh no, that's burning bridges, isn't it? Same difference.*) She'd flinched a little whenever Spike mentioned his return to Australia. In October. Each time finding it hurtful that he seemed unmoved by the fact that he was more or less re-enacting his last departure from Polly's life. Still, she couldn't expect everyone to be as daft and sentimental as her, now, could she? All in all, things were going well.

There had been that moment when they'd both reached – at the same time – for Rowan's little backpack, and their hands had accidentally touched, and she'd felt electricity zing up her fingers; her heart galumphing like a big posh girl galloping along a boarding school corridor. She tried not to imagine that Spike felt something too, even though she hadn't imagined him staring at her hand, or that he had left his there a moment longer than was absolutely necessary… Or perhaps she was being fanciful and daft? She gave herself a mental shake. Whatever. Made no difference either way. She was totes cool – as Donna would have said – hashtag totes.

21

The wind was brisk coming upriver from the Atlantic, as Polly stood leaning out over the rail of her balcony, much like a figurehead on the prow of a tall wooden sailing ship, mid-ocean. She closed her eyes, letting the wind flap her shirt and wet her hair as drizzle whipped like sea spray. She adored her home – and on days like this she could easily dream of adventure… Her doorbell rang and, taking in a lungful of ozone-spiked air, she reluctantly turned to go back inside.

Upstairs, Rowan was safely tucked up fast asleep as she let in Vanessa, who'd arrived to complete the last piece of filming at Polly's house. She hadn't rung for a while, and Polly had all but forgotten about it – or more like had been wishfully thinking that Vanessa had. But no. Here she was. Larger than life, and not sporting double denim this time but a skirt of indeterminate age and an old washed-out blue Jigsaw cardigan drawn tight across her matronly bosom.

'Very arty,' Vanessa was saying, as she cast her eye over Polly's sitting room. 'In here,' she said to the camera man and sound guy, without waiting for Polly's permission. Polly knew that Max wouldn't be the camera man as he said he'd dropped much of his work with Vanessa following a better offer from a different production company.

'I suppose you can't afford a cleaner, dear,' Vanessa was now saying, as she cast a critical eye about the place. 'I suppose that's what being a strapped-for-cash single parent does for you. Well, you mustn't worry as I'm sure we can miss the untidy bits. I tell you what; let's shove that box of toys into the kitchen. Sam, can you be a love and move this for me.'

Bloody cheek, thought Polly, who had swapped shifts with Donna just so she could spend all afternoon cleaning and tidying away. But she held her tongue as she suspected that any comebacks would be water off a duck's back. Polly wished she'd never agreed to the whole film thing in the first place and was glad this would be the last session.

Vanessa clapped her hands together. 'Right then, we'll shoot the whole thing in here, yes?' It was then she noticed Captain Jack. 'Oh My God!' She beckoned the camera guy. 'You have got to get shots of him. How terribly *Pirates of the Caribbean*! Polly, I must have you over by the pirate. What is his name? Did you get him from a film props company? Of course, he's magnificent. We must have you here, with your imaginary boyfriend. You could gaze at him, looking all wistful and lovelorn. This is sooo mental.'

Polly had no intention being filmed as if she was some saddo with no boyfriend of her own other than one made of fibre glass! 'I'd rather not,' she said, with an I-mean-it fixed smile. She knew from Anna how films got edited and cut to suit the producer's overall theme – or to get revenge on someone who'd been rude – so she tried again.

'I'd just rather not, if it's all right with you.' She gave Vanessa her sweetest smile, as she had no intention of being cast as Jilly-No-Mates as some form of spiteful revenge.

The Trouble With Love

But Vanessa was now peering at her face. 'Oh, no no no. This won't do... Do you have any face powder? Only you do have rather a shiny face, don't you? A tad too red as well. All that ginger hair. Have you thought of dying it brown? Now, I might well have some here in my bag if we're lucky,' rummaging around. She looked up. 'Your gorgeous daughter around, is she?'

'No, she's in bed,' said Polly, inwardly seething at the ginger insult. She almost wished she'd gone on that Ginger Pride march she'd heard about in Edinburgh, imagining herself and little Rowan carrying banners stating: "Rather Red than Dead" and "Gingers Forever!"

'Well, never mind,' Vanessa was saying, as she fluffed a powder puff over Polly's forehead and nose. 'Try this lipstick... It still would have been nice to get some footage of your little girl. She's so photogenic, isn't she? Have you ever thought of modelling work? For her, that is, only they're always crying out for little blonde girls. Now, you just sit here while we set up the lights.' Snapping fingers. 'C'mon, Simon, we haven't got all night.' Polly was not going to get her daughter into the world of modelling. No way. Vanessa dabbed and swept at Polly's face with bronzer. Dab dab, sweep sweep. 'Lip gloss? No? Oh here, try this.'

Polly took the proffered mirror and lip gloss, and began to apply. The sooner she got on with it, the sooner Vanessa and her crew would be out of her hair. She caught Simon trying to give her a slow smile. *Gosh, he's not flirting with me, is he?* She resolutely turned away, not wanting it to get back to Max that she'd been flirting with yet another camera guy – not that she had been...

'Maybe have you over here? Sitting at this table?' Vanessa pointed to Polly's small computer console in front of the window. 'If we pull it out here, we can film you on your laptop. Yes, yes, that looks good. Think lonely...' (*Less of the lonely, thank you very much*, thought Polly) '...yes, lonely single mum on social networking site. Ooh... or even better, we could get you on one of those internet dating sites right now. In real time. Yeah? And then talk about internet dating on camera.'

'I haven't actually done any internet dating,' Polly said. 'Haven't really fancied it...'

'Of course you have. Everyone has these days. No? You seriously haven't? Well, you should try it. I know plenty of people who've found love that way.'

Polly didn't much like the direction this was going and wondered if she ought to refuse the whole going on a dating site, but Vanessa was carrying on regardless; clearly unstoppable when in full flow. 'Great. Internet dating it is then, after we've had a wee interview in your comfy chair. Oh yes, that'll be a great shot. Simon, Simon, shift the pirate so he's just behind... Oh, he won't move – well then, shift the chair...'

Vanessa was now full-on bossing about both the sound and camera guy.

'Shall I make coffee for everyone while you set up?' said Polly.

'Yes please,' said smiley Simon.

'Hmm? Yes, very well, if you're quick and don't smudge your makeup.'

'Biscuits?'

Simon glanced hopefully at Vanessa.

'Not for me. But I expect the boys will.'

*

Vanessa had one hand on the table as she leant over Polly's shoulder. 'There,' she was saying. 'If you google "Hot Dates"...'

'You are kidding! Hot Dates?' *Could there be a more miserable/desperate-sounding site?* she thought.

'Why on earth would I kid? Look, it's just for this scene. We want you to come across as a girl of our time. Savvy about social media. You know… tweeting, shopping online, internet dating. A real twenty-first-century girl. Or what was it you said? Oh yes. A true Renaissance Woman.'

'Ah.' Polly had consigned to the "Embarrassing" folder in her brain the incident of the speed dating night and her speech to camera afterwards about how she was a Renaissance Woman. Inwardly she groaned.

Simon continued fiddling with a white umbrella and lights as they found the Hot Dates site and logged on.

'So women – not desperate or sad women – really do shop for men on sites like these?'

'Of course. Everything's online these days, Polly. I'm serious when I say you should give it a go, for real.'

'But I'm already fixed up, remember?'

Vanessa stared intently at the screen as a menu came up. 'Ah yes, the lovely Max,' she said, rather distractedly, Polly thought. And then – 'There' – Vanessa pointed. 'Log in your details and you can browse for free.' She stood up. 'Tom,' she called to the sound guy, 'is her microphone still fine?'

She wandered over to where Tom and Simon were putting in some final techie touches.

Polly was on the page where there were men in her age group and area. They all had thumbnail full-face pictures of themselves, plus a username and tag line. *Oh, will you look at this*, she thought. *Hilarious.* She began to scroll through her selection. *Oh please*, she thought – *this one's in his forties and looking for a girl who's – what – in her twenties? He should be so lucky… Oh, this one's pretty damn hot, hmm, might come back to him… Oh dear, this fella-me-lad's a right sad case. Doesn't he know it's not a good idea to strip off your top when you've a beer gut the size of Wales! …And just clock that manky grey sofa he's sitting on… Eugh.*

'Will you look at this one, Vanessa. Vanessa?' But Vanessa was busy faffing about with her techie boys. *Shame Mel's not here*, thought Polly. *And why oh why is it that guys think if they say they like extreme sports – cycling, running marathons or climbing mountains– that they'll get laid? As if. I'll bet they're lying, in any case. Oh dear. Reading the start of a profile – "My friends think I'm attractive..." Clearly not, then. Let's have a look. Yep. Not. Hang on, this next one's... What?*

She peered closer at the screen, almost doing a cartoon double take and cartoon rub of her eyes – but – there he was. No doubt about it. *Cute Camera Guy looking for fun* – it was Max.

Vanessa chose that particular moment to come over and take a gander at Polly's laptop screen.

'Ah,' she said.

Polly swivelled her chair round to face her. 'Did you know about this?'

'No, I didn't,' she said – far too shiftily for Polly's liking.

*

I shouldn't ring him, should I? I should wait until we meet up, and then give him a chance to explain. But hang on, why should I wait on tenterhooks until then? No. That's ridiculous! Look, I know it's late – what's the time? Midnight. But. He's bound to still be up. If he's not. Tough. I've got to know what's going on. Is he doing internet dating while seeing me? Is that all right or not? Feels like not. Shit. I've totally forgotten the rules of dating. Are we exclusive? I'd assumed... Let me think.

Polly set her cup of tea next to her laptop, where she was logged onto Max's profile page. *Yes. That's him, all right. Wants fun? (Well, we all know what that means, don't we? Fun? Internet dating speak for meaningless fuck.)*

Right, let me think. I suppose we've only been seeing each other

The Trouble With Love

for a few weeks... No wait, five – six if you count the filming bits. Guess those don't count. Right, five weeks. We've not discussed whether we're seeing anyone else, have we? No. Because I just assumed, didn't I? Idiot. Obviously I'm not seeing anyone else – anybody can tell that... But he could have more than me on the go, couldn't he? Well, you'll never know unless you ask – moron. Oh, hang on... didn't I say that I ought to have more than one lover? At that bloody speed dating night? But I was pissed! You don't think he took me at my word, do you? Deep breaths.

She reached her hand towards her mobile, and then stopped.

Look, Polly, there's nothing wrong with giving him a call and asking him straight out – Hey, Max, is that you on this dating site? Yes, could start there. Or more casual, like. So, I was browsing an internet site... No. No. That sounds like I was trawling for men. Just phone, Poll. It's far better for Polly to get these things sorted here and now – even though you now appear to be addressing yourself in the third person. Aargh!

Okay. Ringing his number.

Half-asleep voice on the other end of phone. 'Uh?'

'Max?' She launched straight in. 'What are you doing on an internet dating site?' *Oh, well done. Very cool way to start*, she told herself sarcastically.

'Polly? Is that you? Hang on a minute.' There followed some muffling and crackling as if he'd placed his hand over the receiver – then – 'Sorry, hang on – Ben wants me. Don't go away, I'll be right back.'

Polly thought she could hear giggling in the background.

'Are you on your own?' she asked

'Hmm? Get off, Ben. Yeah, of course I am – apart from Ben, that is. Just a sec.'

As she waited, she wondered whether he might be playing for time. Whether he might, after all, be standing there, hand over the end of his receiver as he worked out what to say next.

You had to admit that this delay was rather convenient for him. She began to wish she'd suggested they meet face to face so that she could see his response when she challenged him. She shook her head. *C'mon, since when did you become so suspicious? Just wait and hear what the man's got to say.* In the end, it sounded very plausible.

'...so you see, although I've left the site, Polly – like, weeks before I met you – they don't actually take your name and profile off straight away.'

*

'What? And you believed him?' Polly had rung Mel straight after. 'By the way – what time is it?' She was whispering, so Polly guessed she must be in bed with Fen.

'Sorry, did I wake you?'

'Never mind that. I'll just take the phone into the other room...'

Polly waited.

'Right, fire ahead.'

She gave her all the details, including Vanessa witnessing her embarrassment.

'So, what d'you think, Mel? Should I stick to my old motto?'

'You have an old motto?'

'Yes I do – it's: give them the benefit of the doubt and then if they lie to you, that's it. Never ever trust them ever again.'

'Ah, that motto. It's a rather long motto.'

'It's the best I can come up with.'

'Polly?'

'Yeah?'

'Haven't you learnt yet? They always lie.'

'Cynic.'

'Now fuck off before we both wake Fen.'

The Trouble With Love

*

Polly was having a terrible dream. She was on board a galleon – no, a pirate ship – up on the top deck with Max, who was old and wizened and togged up like Johnny Depp's Captain Jack Spratt's grandfather – and looking even older than Keith Richards. He had her firm in his grasp as she struggled to get free. Overhead, the ship's sails hung lifeless – there not being a breath of wind to fill them. For they were stuck in the doldrums, mid-Atlantic. Short of water, and the men starving. Pirate Max stood alongside the ship's wheel as he grappled with a bustled-and-gowned-up Polly, who twisted and turned in his grip, much like a muscled eel trying to escape an angler, so desperate was she to stop what was happening on the deck below, where a motley crew of bedraggled pirates were driving pure white horses over the side of the ship into the sea below. The horses plunged, screaming as they fell, whinnying as they thrashed about in the water, nostrils widely flaring as they swam round and around in circles, frantically seeking a shore to head for. But there was none. As they tired of striving to keep their heads above the water, Polly sobbed. One by one, they went under – the sea shimmering like beaten pewter in the harsh glare of the sun.

'Noooo!' screamed Polly as a mare – being manhandled to the side of the ship – reared up, kicking out at the men who grappled with her foal – a little blonde baby horse with big round eyes. The pirates pushed, shoved and beat the mother until she jumped – like a champion show-jumper – over the side. Then they lifted the stiffly long-legged youngster – eyes wild with fright – and flung her out and into the briny too.

Polly woke in a sweat, the faint echoes of whinnies and cries in her ears. Her dream had shaken her. She loved horses. She struggled into wakefulness, her chest feeling as if it was going to burst with suppressed sobs. *God, fancy dreaming of that.* It was at school when she'd first heard of the sad plight of horses that were chucked overboard mid-Atlantic. Back in the days of tall ships, it was common in that area of the ocean – now known as the Bermuda Triangle and which traversed the Sargasso Sea – for ships stuck in the doldrums to employ this practice to lighten their load. So common that it was called the Horse Latitudes. They'd covered it during history – when they got to the Tudors, Francis Drake and Spanish galleons. Her history teacher thought they ought to hear of real-life tragedies. Polly supposed it would these days feature in *Horrible Histories* and be no big deal. But girls were softer back then. By the end of the lesson, many of the girls – especially the pony-mad ones – were in tears.

What on earth is the time?

She reached for her box of tissues and checked her alarm clock. 3.20 am. What a horrible dream! Blowing her nose, she sighed a deep sigh and snuggled back down underneath her covers, hoping she'd soon get back to sleep. It was then that she heard a noise.

Christ. Is that someone moving about downstairs? She held her breath. *Don't be daft.*

But there it was again. Slipping out of bed, she pushed her feet into her sheepskin slippers and pulled her red silk kimono over Bridget-Jones-style pyjamas. Taking care not to make a sound, she reached around the corner of her bedroom door to turn on the landing light. If the noise was burglars, then a sudden switching on of a light might well be enough to scare them off. She waited. Half expecting to hear a rumpus below as one – possibly two – thieves made good their escape. But no. Nothing. Creeping along the landing to the top of the stairs, she flicked the switch that turned on the downstairs light. Again, she waited for any robbers to leg it. Nothing. Wait, what was that? Was that a rustling sound coming from the kitchen? She couldn't be sure. Could just be her imagination.

The Trouble With Love

She leant over the banisters to peer down into the hallway. All clear. Unless of course a burglar was waiting – with bated breath – for her to give up before he made good his escape. (Or he could be waiting until the coast was clear and she padded back to bed, so he could then climb the stairs and murder both Polly and Rowan in their sleep…)

Oh great. Why not think of the worst-case scenario?

She began to feel a little sick as – tiptoeing down the stairs – she couldn't help but think of all those television murder mysteries (*not so cosy now, eh?*)… or of those dreadful horror movies where you want to shout *Don't go downstairs! Lock yourself in your bedroom! Call the police, you moron! Oh no, she's going downstairs!*

Polly strengthened her resolve with good old British reserve and embarrassment. After all, she didn't want to make a fuss, call the police and say *I think there's a burglar in my house* if it turned out to be nothing. Nope, she knew it was daftness in the extreme, but she'd rather risk being murdered than be laughed at by some copper on her doorstep.

She made her way on tiptoe to just outside the kitchen, counted to three, then flicked on the kitchen light and dashed at full pelt – like some FBI agent with a gun. Stopping in the middle of the kitchen floor, she registered that the balcony door was swinging open on its hinges.

'Fuck me!' a voice said behind her.

She spun round, catching Mel – slice of pizza in hand – in the act of raiding the fridge.

'What the fuck are you doing here?' said Polly.

'Why have you got a pretend gun in your hand?' said Mel, pointing her pizza slice at Polly.

Lowering her pretend weapon, Polly replied, 'Well? What's going on?'

'I've left Fen,' said Mel, smiling rather sheepishly at her friend.

'Any particular reason?' said Polly.

'Yeah, she told me I had to choose between her and you!'

Polly and Mel sat in Polly's sitting room sipping mugs of hot chocolate and munching biscuits.

'Better?' said Polly.

'Yes, I think so.' Mel blew her nose on a tissue so loudly that Polly half expected an elephant to trumpet back in response. She didn't think she'd seen her friend so upset before – well, not since they were kids and her next-door neighbour's Alsatian dog had mistaken Mel's tortoise for a large and extra crunchy meat pie.

'So what now?' said Polly.

Mel had already told her, through sobs and hugs, that this was definitely It. 'I know it's silly, Poll, and that we've told each other everything in the past, but there's a lot I've been keeping to myself lately. I'm so sorry. I guess I wanted to please Fen. She didn't want me to discuss what she called "our private stuff" with you. And then I was embarrassed...'

She went on to say how Fen was too intense, wanting to know where Mel was day and night. 'Honestly, Poll, being in possession of a mobile phone was like being electronically tagged by Fen. I honestly think she would have got one of those tracking devices if she thought she could get away with it.'

'I'm so sorry, I had no idea,' Polly said, outraged for her friend. 'And as for saying you have to choose between her and me – that's ridiculous. The sort of jealous controlling thing some bloke might do.'

Polly knew that Spike would never ever have made her choose – as for Max... he'd probably want a threesome. She dragged her attention back to her friend.

'I dunno,' Mel said, as she ran her hands through her short hair. 'Oh, I know you're right. It's true. I might just as well be going out with a man! I've been so naive. I thought one of the perks of turning lesbian would mean that we'd support each other – you know, women together. Not have all this possessiveness. She even reads my text messages…'

'Oh babe. And she really wanted you to stop seeing me?'

Mel looked Polly square in the eye. 'Yes. She did. And *you* know, don't you, that I'd *never* agree to that. We swore, didn't we? That we'd never let a man come between us.' She gave her friend a shrug. 'Guess we need to include women in that oath now, too.'

Polly smiled at her friend. 'Should I get out my penknife, so that we can swear another oath as blood sisters?' Mel smiled back at her, the two of them remembering how – in that long hot summer before they started at "big" school – they'd been out playing with Mel's brother's penknife and made the decision to become blood sisters. Like native American Indians in one of those cowboy films. They'd taken it in turns to nick their thumbs with the knife – just enough to draw a little blood – and then held their thumbs together so that their blood mingled (smudged, more like). And they'd sworn a most solemn child's oath to be friends forever and ever.

'I've missed not having you around so much,' said Polly.

'I know.' Mel laid her head on Polly's shoulder as Polly drew her towards her, thinking of how Mel had remained the one constant in her life: through all the troubles with her mother, through all her rebelliousness towards her father and stepmother, and through her pregnancy and Rowan's birth. No wonder Polly had been feeling all at sea without her.

Mel sat up and took both of Polly's hands in her own. 'There's something I've not told you yet. Promise you won't hate me.'

Polly knew before she said a word just what she was going to say.

'I asked Spike to be my sperm donor. Sorry.'

Sigh. 'When?'

'At Daisy's party.' She hung her head. 'After you left.'

The next morning, Mel was looking very sheepish over breakfast. 'Sorry about the drama last night,' she said, sipping a glass of Alka-Seltzer and wincing at its fizzy noisiness.

'That's what friends are for,' said Polly, as she wiped Rowan's face with a flannel and cleared away her bowl of Cheerios. 'So, are you going to stay here for a while? Spare room – or should I say, your room – is always ready and waiting for you. You know that.'

There was no reply for a moment, then Mel lifted her head and looked briefly at Polly before looking away again. 'Fen called this morning. We've made up, and I'm going back.'

'You can't!' Polly said, before she could stop herself, sounding harsher than she meant to. She took a seat back at the table. 'What I mean is, are you sure this is the woman you want to have a baby with? She sounds very controlling to me. Jealous, and with a temper too.'

'But I love her,' said Mel, so quietly that Polly wasn't sure at first that this was what she said. She lifted Rowan out of her child seat and let her run out of the kitchen to play at dismembering her latest Barbie doll.

Polly took Mel's hand in her own. 'Sometimes love is not enough, Mel,' she said.

Mel stood up and drew herself up to her full five foot eight. 'It's enough for me. I love her, and even though she can be a right bitch when she wants to be – she's my right bitch.' She gave Polly a rather feeble smile. 'I'll get out of your hair,' she said.

'Don't be silly. Stay. You don't have to shoot off. Whatever you decide to do is fine by me. Honest.'

22

*G*enerations of seagulls have seen many comings and goings on and around the river. Tall ships laden with goods, the harbour bustling with merchants in powdered wigs, and urchins scavenging alongside birds for scraps with much squawking and hollering. They'd seen it all, those gulls. Had seen people in couples, groups or singly, strolling along the side of the river, else sat at tables next to soon-to-be-gentrified dilapidated houses. Or the ruins of Bristol Gaol where the rioters of 1831 were hanged with much cheering from a crowd so deep that they threatened to spill over the walkway and fall into the water.

Yes, they'd seen it all. The gulls and the river. Nothing much changes. A couple of seagulls hung in the air over Polly and Spike, as if listening in on their conversation.

'Will you stop your fidgeting, Polly,' Spike was saying. He'd invited Polly and Rowan to join him at the boatyard where he was repairing a dinghy belonging to a friend of his. Polly had been tapping her foot on the concrete slipway and twiddling her bag handle with agitated fingers.

'I've coffee in that flask over there, if you'd like some,' he said. 'Might give your hands something to do.'

Polly stuck her offending hands behind her back. Spike was the only person (beside Mel) who ever teased her about her fidgeting. 'No, you're all right,' she answered.

He bent down, allowing Rowan – on tippy toes – to reach up both her arms and latch them around his neck, giving him a cuddle – or "huggle" (Rowan and Polly's word for half-hug-half-cuddle).

'How's my darling girl?' said Spike, and was rewarded with Rowan's trademark: a double-handed-Eric-Morecambe-slap-around-the-chops.

'Daddy,' giggled Rowan, as he started to tickle her in response. Then – 'Daddeee!' – writhing, shrieking and squealing as he continued to tickle: first up and under her arms, then her tummy, then her sides. Polly could see that Rowan was starting to turn puce in the face.

'Put her down. That's enough,' she said. 'Seriously, Spike…'

He stopped to look at her – mid-tickle. 'What harm can it do? You're enjoying it, aren't ya, Roly Poly.'

'Spoken by a man who is not ticklish.' Polly took Rowan from his lap, stood her child firmly on both feet and then smoothed down Rowan's little pinafore dress.

'So you remember that I'm not ticklish, Polly?' he said, making her feel uncomfortable under his amused gaze. 'If I remember rightly, you can't abide having your feet tickled. Would insist I'd somehow tickle you to death, if I did. Isn't that right?'

'Yes, well.' She reached inside her bag for a tissue to wipe Rowan's runny nose. 'That was a long time ago.'

'Not so long,' he said and, before she could respond or even register, he turned to Rowan, saying, 'Who's for ice cream?'

The Trouble With Love

Polly sat at one of the small tables outside the Cottage pub, next to the sailing club. Idly she watched Rowan investigate a cat meticulously cleaning itself with spit and paw on a low wall. Spike had gone inside to get them all a drink.

Across her line of vision passed a Bristol dragon boat with a carved wooden dragon's head on its prow. Its rowers, instead of – well – rowing, were paddling like some crew of a Viking ship headed for shore and a spot of pillaging and invading. Except, instead of furs and those horned helmets, they wore T-shirts emblazoned with – Bristol Royal Infirmary. *Must be medics*, thought Polly, as she shaded her eyes with one hand from the rays of the afternoon sun. *Suppose they're getting ready for the Dragon Boat Festival in September.* Would Spike be around for that? Inwardly she flinched, feeling a pang, like the memory of an old wound signalling the return of rain. She turned round at the sound of clattering announcing Spike's arrival, carrying a tray with a pot of tea and cups in one hand and a clutch of crisp packets in the other. She gave him a welcoming smile.

'They were out of sandwiches,' he said, as he set down the tray. 'Here, Roly. Come and sit next to your dah.' She left off stroking the cat to come charging over, arms up for him to lift her onto a chair. 'Shall I give her one of these?' he asked Polly.

Rowan regarded the crisps with all the concentration of a blackbird waiting for a worm to wriggle up from the ground.

'Okay,' said Polly.

'Yay!' from Rowan.

'Which one do you want, Roly?' asked Spike. He opened the cheese and onion one she pointed to, and handed it over. She was rather low to the table, so he pulled her chair next to his in case she fell off.

'Bam not here?' asked Polly, her attempt at nonchalance sounding false even to her own ears.

'Why? You're not planning on getting me on my own and

giving me a kiss again, are you?'

'What?' Polly blustered. *Of all the nerve. Trust him to rub it in when he knows perfectly well that I'm happy with Max...* It was then that she saw the twinkle in his eye. 'Huh. You wish!' she said. Glad at the same time that they could joke about it. 'So, you expecting Bam?'

'We're not joined at the hip, you know.'

'Oh really? Isn't that her coming towards us now?' she said. Spike turned to follow Polly's gaze. There was Bam, all right, striding along the path, raising her hand to them in a cheery greeting.

Polly thought (but wasn't quite sure) that she heard Spike mutter 'Christ!' under his breath as Bam arrived, all smiles and kisses.

'Hey, babes.' She threw her arms around his neck and planted a big kiss on his cheek. 'Hey, Polly – mwah! Roly – mmmm, big smackeroonee for you!'

'I thought we were meeting up later,' Spike part hissed at her. 'You could have texted me, you know.'

'I was bored with shopping. Couldn't find anything at that Cabot Circus.' She held out her arms. 'Look. See? Didn't buy a single thing. I guessed you'd be here so thought I might as well toodle along to join you.' She gave them all a big white-and-straight-toothed grin.

'Polly and I have things to discuss,' insisted Spike.

'We do?' said Polly, trying not to notice how Spike half-heartedly resisted Bam's hugs, much like someone trying to fend off a puppy.

Spike gave in with a half-shrug.

'Bet you're glad to see me really, though, babe, huh?' said Bam, placing her face alongside Spike's as if they were posing in a photo booth together. He looked rather uncomfortable.

'Oh, oh, I get it,' said Bam, pulling up a chair to join them.

'Not a good tactic to speak about stuff in front of Rowan, right?'

Spike gave her a pointed look. She leapt to her feet. 'I know!' she declared, clapping her hands together, causing Rowan to jump at the noise. 'C'mon, Roly Poly.' She turned to Polly and Spike and said, 'No worries. I'll keep her entertained while you two have your chat.'

'Good idea,' said Spike, smiling a stiff thanks.

'Right then, Roly,' said Bam, as she lifted the child from her chair. 'Up you get.' Bending down, she encouraged Rowan to climb up onto her back. 'Hop on!' Rowan didn't need asking twice. With as much skill as a nearly-three-year-old could muster, she clambered up onto Bam's back, concentrating as hard as a freestyle climber scaling the outside of the Empire State Building. Polly kept an eye on proceedings – after all, Bam was nearly six feet tall, without heels, and Polly didn't want her child crashing to the ground. By now Rowan was safely on board, arms clasped tightly around Bam's neck, while Bam had firm hold of her ankles.

'Phew. Better cut down on that chocolate, Roly. You weigh a ton! Just kidding,' she said to Polly's stricken face – after all, no mother likes to be told her child is fat. Bam pranced up and down. 'Look, see? She's as light as a feather.' She twisted her head around to address Rowan. 'Horsey-horsey, yeah? We had great fun playing that the other day, didn't we, Roly?'

'Horsey!' squealed Rowan, as she clapped her hands, nearly falling backwards in the process.

'Hold tight,' instructed Bam, as the two of them took off down the tow path; Bam galloping along and Rowan jiggling up and down, squealing with delight.

Polly and Spike watched them go.

'Guess this is where her polo pony experience comes in handy,' said Polly, who rather admired Bam's cheerfulness. She wouldn't have blamed Bam if she felt threatened – even a scintilla – by the presence of the mother of her boyfriend's child. She knew she would.

She turned to face Spike. 'She's good for you, y'know.'

'Yes. I do know.' He sighed, and smiled fondly in Bam's direction. 'She's a great girl. Just look at her…' Bam was now chasing Rowan up the path, letting her run ahead, little legs pounding, then scooping her into her arms and swinging her round, legs flying, the two of them having so much fun that Polly could hear the laughter from where she was sitting.

'So,' said Polly, shielding her eyes from the sun, 'what is it you want to talk to me about?' She noted how he had a wayward black curl threatening to flop into his eye. She supposed he'd not had a chance to get it cut since arriving back in Bristol. Polly always did prefer it on the long side.

'Are you staring at me, Polly?' he asked, his crinkly smile deepening the dimple in his right cheek. The one that Rowan had inherited.

God, I probably was, wasn't I, she thought, but didn't say. She wondered if there was some primeval force that rendered the father of your child deeply attractive to the mother. *Or are you not as over him as you like to think, eh? Oh, shut up.*

'Hmm? Did you say something, Polly? You look as if you were about to say something.'

'I was wondering if it was arrangements you wanted to talk about. You know? For contact after you've… after you've gone back to Australia. Just when are you planning on leaving us again?' She hadn't meant to blurt it out like that. She looked over to where their beautiful daughter, with Spike's curls – only blonde – and Spike's same-colour eyes played perfectly happily with the woman who was about to make off with her father. For good. She turned back to Spike. 'I think it's only fair that I know. So's I can prepare Ro…' her voice faltered under his steady gaze '… and everything,' she muttered.

He leant back in his chair, stretching out his long legs in their dust-covered jeans. 'Ah yes, there is that, Polly. I can see how we do need to talk about that… and everything…'

For a moment Polly wondered what on earth he might mean by "everything". Did he mean anything at all by everything? Was "everything" just a generic catch-all everything? Or was it something? Her heart went pitter-pat.

'Well,' he continued, 'not to put too fine a point on it… there is something else. Something which, if I'm frank about, did come as a surprise… I've been trying to find the right time to speak to you about it.'

A surprise? What could it be? She tried not to let her mind run riot – but there it was, going off on its own, imagining Spike grabbing her hand, saying how his feelings had taken him by surprise, how he'd never got over her, that she was The One, that seeing her in the flesh once more had made him realise he was going to break it off with Bam…

'Mel has asked me to be her sperm donor.'

'Yes, I know.'

'So you know, do you?'

'Yes, she told me last night. But what I want to know is why didn't *you* mention this to me?'

He shaded his eyes against the sun, low in the sky. 'What, and cause a ruckus between you twos? Would take a stronger man than me, Polly. Now, I can't say I'm not flattered,' he continued, 'but is that how you girls see me? A sperm bank for you to have your babies by?'

*

When Polly returned home with Rowan, there was a note waiting for her – pushed through her letter box.

Thanks for everything, babes. Am sorting things with Fen, and concentrating on her at the moment. I know you think I'm mad – but I do love her so much! You are, and will always be, my best mate and blood sister. Mel xxxxx

Polly screwed it up and threw it in the bin. She still thought Mel was making a mistake.

'Mummy?' said Rowan.

'Is okay, Ro Ro. Why don't you go watch *Peppa Pig* while Mummy cooks the tea.'

'What?'

Polly bent down to Rowan's level. 'Mummy cook tea. You go watch *Peppa Pig*. Yes?'

'Desss.' And, with that, she high-tailed it off to the sitting room.

Polly rubbed her forehead, feeling very alone.

She walked over to the verandah doors, and opening them, she went to stand on her deck; leaning out over the railings to take a big breath of fresh air. She shivered slightly as there was an evening chill and she'd already taken off her coat. She gazed over the water. And now Mel was probably having make-up sex with Fen, while all that was on Polly's menu was chicken burgers.

I'll bet Mel's having a glass of wine with Fen right now, she thought, as she wandered back into her kitchen and put the burgers in the oven. *Probably cooking their adults-only meal too.*

She wiped her hands on a tea towel, thinking how she'd felt fine on her own, before. Had been proud that she didn't need a man. So why the difference now? Because… oh, because before she'd always had Mel.

Come on, she told herself, flicking at a fly buzzing around the room. *Buck up, for fuck's sake.* Flick – *damn, missed it!*

She gave up on the fly and absent-mindedly picked up the

bottle of red that she and Mel had part drunk the night before and placed it on the kitchen worktop. Yes, she'd relied on Mel, and taken her for granted. And just when Mel had needed her the most, she'd disapproved. After all, who was she to tell Mel who she could and couldn't have a baby with? Polly looked around at the mess in the kitchen, the sounds of her child watching television, the thankless task ahead of making something to eat, the endless cooking, clearing up, washing, folding clothes away, spreading out before her forever and ever, amen.

Oh, this won't do.

She began to clear the kitchen worktop, wiping its surface, moving the bottle out of the way. She stared at it. She could just have the one. Ah, but that was how becoming an alcoholic started. Drinking wine on your own. She glanced at the clock. Pretty close to wine o'clock. She shrugged – *what the heck* – and poured herself a large glass then took a gulp. It slipped down her throat like a sigh as she closed her eyes, letting the alcohol deliver its first muted kick. That was better. Turning the bottle over in her hand, she examined the label. Lidl's finest German plonk. She hugged the bottle to her chest.

Gawd. Carry on like this and I'll end up singing along to "All by Myself" in penguin-covered pyjamas. Drunk in charge of a kid.

She poured the rest of her glass down the sink.

'Yes, I'll give it a go with Max. For at least he's here and not about to take off to the other side of the planet with some leggy doe-eyed posh bird!'

'What? What you say?' called Rowan from the sitting room.

'Great,' muttered Polly. 'Am now talking out loud to myself!' She wandered over to stand in the sitting-room doorway to watch her daughter. Rowan had her back to her, engrossed in the television.

'Nothing,' said Polly, coming up behind her. She touched her on the shoulder. 'I said nothing, Ro Ro.'

'Eh?' Rowan twisted her head to look up into her mother's face.

'I said Nothing,' repeated Polly.

'Nothing means No,' said Rowan emphatically, and returned to her programme.

Polly took out her mobile and sent Max a text. *Be good to see you. Now. If you're free. xxx*

The morning after getting tipsy and maudlin and insisting that Max come over and shag her senseless, Polly was feeling foolish. Max, on the other hand, appeared delighted that she'd finally broken their curfew and he had been allowed to stay overnight when Rowan was at home.

As Polly opened first one eye and then the other, she groaned and reached for the glass of water by her bed.

'Morning,' said Max, propped up in bed by a couple of pillows. 'Guess I must be your proper boyfriend now.'

'Guess you must be,' she answered; her tongue like the bottom of the proverbial birdcage, and her hair – she could see in the wardrobe mirror – having acquired all the shape and texture of a bird's nest.

'This is great,' insisted Max, as he snuggled down under the covers to spoon her in bed, his obvious erection pushing against the cheeks of her bottom.

'Hmm. Not now, okay?' she said, squirming out of the way. Because although she would have loved to burrow under the covers and lose herself in their lovemaking, she knew that Rowan would soon be up. 'Rowan. She'll be awake any minute – if she isn't already. What time is it?'

'Nearly seven,' he said, as he kissed the top of her head. 'You know I really would like us to do more of this… ' his hands moved round to tweak her nipple '…and this…' and then slid between her legs.

The Trouble With Love

'No. Sssshhh...' she said, breathless, her body wanting to – oh, so wanting to – but she had to be sensible.

He stopped and pulled her round to face him. 'You delicious creature,' he said, and Polly was almost purring like a cat – she did indeed feel delicious, and soft, and yielding and horny... He sat up in bed and looked down at her. 'I really want to make this work, you know. I mean This. You and me.'

'Me too,' she said, pulling him back down to her, and coiling her leg around his.

'Only you'll have to stop doing that,' he said, rubbing his penis on the inside of her thigh, where it would be oh so easy to just... but no. She pushed him to the other side of the bed. 'Seriously,' he said over his shoulder, as he swung his legs out of bed. 'We could be great together.'

'Let's talk about it later, yeah? Just not right now,' she said, throwing a pillow at him. 'Because – have you seen the time? Rowan...'

'Righty ho. I'd better pop along to the bathroom.' He bent over to give her a kiss on the lips. She watched as he moved across her bedroom floor, admiring the curve of his bum and his long legs.

Why do men have far better legs than women? He made for the door. 'Oi, underpants,' she called, suddenly remembering. She searched under the bed, located his boxers and chucked them at him.

'Why? Oh, I see. Rowan, right? Only I'm used to walking around commando with Ben.'

'Not with a little girl around, you don't.'

He pulled on his boxers and made for the bathroom while Polly slipped into her silk dressing gown and attempted to smooth her hair in the mirror. *Bag,* she thought. *Where's my bag?* She located it just behind the door, pulled out her brush and headed for the bathroom, where she spotted Rowan, standing on the landing in front of the open doorway of their separate toilet, her mouth agape as she stared in fascination at Max's back while he peed into the toilet pan with the full force of a horse that had drunk a whole flippin' lake!

'Door!' cried Polly, pulling it to and taking Rowan by the hand.

After getting herself and her daughter dressed, Polly carried Rowan downstairs to the kitchen, congratulating herself on the fact that – all things considered – the sleepover had gone rather well. She slotted her daughter into her child seat and fetched her a bowl of Cheerios. Polly was feeling not only relaxed but pretty cool with it all – much like the cat that got the creamiest double-clotted creamy cream.

'Hey there, Rowan,' said Max, as he strode into the kitchen, now dressed in his jeans and buttoning up his shirt. He ruffled a startled Rowan's hair and planted a tickly kiss on Polly's neck while she was doing her best to concentrate on buttering a slice of toast. 'Mmm, you smell gorgeous,' he said, nicking the toast from her hand.

'Catch you later, hmm?' he said, leaning over to cup her breasts in his hands. She wriggled out from under him.

'Honestly. Stop it! Child present,' she hissed, all too aware of Rowan, sitting and staring at them open-mouthed. She passed her daughter a beaker of juice.

*

Max shot off soon after. 'I'll give you a call,' he'd called as he skipped down the path, making Polly laugh. She shut the door behind him.

'C'mon, Roly Poly,' she said. 'Finish up your breakfast.'

'Eh?'

'Eat, darling. C'mon or we're going to be late.'

Polly finished her toast and set about facing the rest of her day.

She tried Mel again, leaving messages on her mobile phone, but Mel was proving to be elusive, and Polly needed to let Mel know that she understood about her going back to Fen (even though she didn't). Either Mel was avoiding her or Fen had yet again asserted her wish that Mel choose between Polly and her. Weirdly enough, Suze was being elusive too. And Donna was threatening to withhold her rent.

'I don't want to, Poll,' she'd said, 'but FYI, your muh's not returning my calls, and I can't hang about for ages like last time, Poll. Is not on. Really it's not.'

Polly's own calls went straight through to voicemail, and remained unanswered. Even though she said it was urgent. Emails weren't answered, either. She finally managed to get through to Suze's boyfriend, Brian.

'Sorry, Poll,' he said, 'but your mum's got a lot on her plate right now.'

Polly nearly made a joke about plate and Suze being a chef but thought better of it. At times Brian found Polly's sense of humour strange.

'Shall I go ahead and arrange something this end again?' she asked.

'Yeah, sure. Sorry, babe. Got to go.'

With that, he hung up. How on earth he managed to get acting work when he could hardly string a sentence together was anybody's guess. *Ah well, probably got hidden shallows*, she thought, and nearly made herself laugh… if it wasn't for that nagging feeling…

23

Things were going pretty well, even if she said so herself. Her and Spike were being civilised and accommodating on the organising of access visits to Rowan, Polly was being friendly to Bam (even though she still found her annoying – sorry, but she did), and Max was proving to be a naughty-but-nice boyfriend, and she was enjoying their times together and managing to avoid any discussions about parenting and Ben. So what if Polly's heart fluttered whenever she saw Spike or heard the sound of his voice? That would soon fade, and then he'd be back off, leaving them all to return to normal. Just a matter of time.

One night Polly and Max trooped along to the open mic night at the Angel Café, where Polly was keen to perform a new poem she'd written called "We're All Middle Class Now". It had some lines she was particularly pleased with:

"Keep Calm, Carry On our – *Such Fun* – jolly motto
We'd rather self-harm than fill in the Lotto

The Trouble With Love

Our kitchen's festooned with Union Jack bunting
We don green Hunter wellies for shooting and hunting

We drip with Cath Kidston, with Boden with Toast
Our Phoebe is gifted, we don't like to boast!
We knit Kindle cosies, we're oh so "ironic"
We swear loads at parties, we drink gin and tonic…"

When Polly had finished performing her poem, she returned to her seat. Buzzing. Spike and Bam had arrived earlier, threatening her equilibrium and calm with their presence. Not good to get rattled just before going on; but he'd merely waved at her as he stood alongside the bar, his drink on the counter, turning to watch her perform. Polly was aware of his presence during her performance, yet somehow it hadn't thrown her. Instead the delivery of her poem went down well – even though she said so herself.

Max, on the other hand, didn't say anything. Not a 'Well done,' or an 'I liked it.' No, he just said, 'What d'you want to drink?' She knew she shouldn't mind, and that he probably didn't realise how vulnerable it felt to get up and perform, and how marvellous it was to have support and encouragement from your loved ones. In spite of her best intentions to not mind Max's omission, a wet blanket of disappointment threatened to envelop her. (*You know why he didn't say anything, don't you*, whispered that horrid little voice inside her. *It's because he hated it, that's why.*)

As Max made his way to the bar, passing Spike and giving him a nod of recognition, Spike caught Polly's eye. He turned to say something to Bam and then started to thread his way through the tables, towards Polly.

'Well done, Poll,' he said, leaning over her slightly, causing her to catch a heady whiff of his familiar scent.

'Cheers.' She scrambled to her feet to give him a hug, determined to ignore the way her nerve endings went Ahhh, once she was in his arms. Embarrassed and hoping that he hadn't spotted her discomfiture, she patted him on the shoulder. 'It's always nice to hear when someone enjoys your poem,' she said.

'Sounds like you're back on form. Very witty. You've a way with words, so,' and he gave her a grin. 'I liked the line about glamping. Spot on!'

Polly was positively beaming now. 'Thanks. You're a real pal.'

'I'd better get back.' He cast a smile back over his shoulder to Bam, who raised her glass in salute.

'You want to join us?' said Polly. 'Me and Max, I mean?'

'No, you're all right, Poll. Wouldn't want to be the gooseberries now. We're off in a mo, as it is.'

He kissed her lightly on the cheek and she felt as if she'd been subjected to a small laser burn. She closed her eyes for a moment. *Pull yourself together. Eejit.*

Spike returned to Bam, and soon his laugh – that same old laugh – came drifting over to her, even as she watched Max return, manoeuvring his way back to his seat.

'Was that Spike?' he said, looking over to where both Spike and Bam were taking their leave. Both Spike and Bam mouthing 'Bye.'

'What did he want?'

Polly could have said, 'To congratulate me,' but she didn't. Instead she answered, 'Oh, nothing much.'

Max leant in to nibble her ear. 'I loved your poem. You clever minx, you.' He had a gleam in his eye, and Polly felt rotten that she'd harboured doubts about his support.

*

The Trouble With Love

Polly and Max were trying another picnic with the kids. According to the forecast on the news last night, the weather was set fair. As she threw open her verandah double doors to greet the morning, the morning blew drizzle back in her face.

Brrr. Not to be daunted, she turned to her daughter and set about buttoning – or should that be toggling – up her red duffle coat. 'Don't you look cute, Ro Ro. Just like Little Red Riding Hood.'

But Rowan wasn't listening as she fidgeted and twisted around. 'Hold tight,' said Polly, fastening the last toggle, while Rowan rooted about in her pocket, pulled out a lemon fruit pastille and popped it into her mouth before Polly could take it off her.

'Ugh, Ro. That'll be all mucky.'

Rowan merely chuckled and carried on chewing.

Polly slipped Rowan's pink boots – covered in purple daisies (chosen by Rowan) –onto her feet. In the past, Rowan had not shown much interest in clothes, happy to let her mother choose. But lately, she'd begun insisting on choosing her own; and an increased demand for pink had crept in, which Polly wasn't mad keen on.

Brrrring went the doorbell. *That'll be them.*

She opened the door, and in bound – a wolf!

Polly shrieked, and Rowan threw both hands up in a startle reflex as a dog barked in her face.

For a moment, Polly thought she might well be in an Angela Carter book – but – 'Down, George!' ordered a grinning Max, as he strode after his hound; Ben charging in behind him, pushing past Polly.

'Yaaarrrrr!' Ben shouted as he jumped on George's back.

'God sake, Ben,' said Max, pulling him off. 'Leave poor George alone.'

By now George was sitting on his haunches, giving a

delighted Rowan's face a good licking with his pink tongue. *Oh God, oh God*, thought Polly. She turned to Max.

'A dog? You never told me you had a dog? Or is he some stray that followed you here? And,' she said, gesturing to the dog, 'can you please stop him slobbering all over Rowan!'

Max placed his arm around her shoulder. 'Don't worry. This is George. He's harmless. He's Claire and Ben's dog. She's had to go away overnight, so I'm looking after him, as well as Ben. Aren't I, George?' Max said, ruffling the dog's ears, causing George to set about having a good scratch. Rowan, clearly delighted at such doggy antics, beamed while Ben ran around the kitchen in circles.

'Woof! Woof!' joined in George.

'Christ,' was all Polly could say.

'Stop worrying. Fresh air for George – whoops – and Ben,' added Max, as he grimaced in the general direction of Ben, who was sitting cross-legged on the floor, emptying out the contents of Polly's saucepan cupboard. 'We'll have them tired out in no time.'

'You sure the dog's okay?' she hissed, as if the dog could hear and possibly disapprove. 'Does he like children?' Rowan was bent over, peering straight into George's eyes, while George lifted first one eyebrow, then the other, and finally opted for licking the end of Rowan's nose.

'Like them?' half laughed Max. 'Oh yes. Especially with crunchy dog biscuits!'

'Hilarious.' But Polly wasn't – actually – finding this funny at all. She'd not had a dog when she was a child, and tales of dogs ripping children's faces off all too easily sprang to mind any time she passed a big one – like an Alsatian!

'But it's an Alsatian,' hissed Polly, as she pulled Rowan over to stand next to her. 'And they can – well – they can be vicious, can't they? The police use them and everything...'

'Don't hurt his feelings, Polly,' said Max, as George did his eyebrow-raising thing again in some sort of doggy attempt to look appealing, she supposed. 'George here is a rescue dog. He's a cross between a German Shepherd and a Border Collie. Aren't you, boy?' Ruffling his ears again. 'He's got a sweet temperament. In any case, Claire had his knackers lopped off.' Max gave George an "ouch" look. 'I'm sure she'd have liked to do the same to me an' all.'

And there it was. That slight edge to his voice. But then he turned on his smile. 'Just kidding.'

The dog let out a low rumble.

'He's growling,' said Polly, not moving away from the safety of Max's side, and keeping Rowan close.

'That's not a growl, is it, Ben?'

'No, Daddy,' said devil child, who'd been banging Polly's Jamie Oliver non-stick frying pan on her Belfast sink.

'Put that down, Ben,' said Max. 'Sorry,' he mouthed at Polly. 'That was George speaking to us, wasn't it, Ben?'

Ben chose that moment to charge from the kitchen up the stairs, followed closely by Rowan, with George lolloping behind them.

'It'll be fun,' said Max, turning to Polly, who smiled an uncertain smile back at him.

*

They set off up the path into Leigh Woods, an area of woodland covering acres of land opposite the Clifton side of the suspension bridge. Polly kept smiling to herself. What could be more grown up, and responsible urban family, than a walk with a bona fide boyfriend, his child, her child and a dog? All they needed now was a bottle of pop and a packet of crisps to make it complete, she thought, remembering that daft childhood song the kids around the Greenham Common campfire used to sing. She resisted the urge to text Mel and let her know just what she was up to.

Max strode alongside her, up the rocky path overhung with trees freshly sprung into leaf. He had firm hold of her hand. 'C'mon, slow coach.' She quickened her pace to keep up.

'You try and walk fast in boots two sizes too big.' She'd borrowed the ones Mel had left behind at her house.

Up ahead, a meadow hove into view as they neared the end of the path-cum-tree-lined-tunnel. The clearing was bathed in bright light, its grass long and dotted with wild flowers. As they stepped into the sunshine, Polly was hugging herself about how bloody marvellous it was to have an actual card-carrying boyfriend.

'You okay?' he said.

'Oh yes,' she smiled.

'Polly? Why do you keep smiling?'

'Oh nothing,' she said, all dreamy.

'I'll give you nothing!' And he chased her around the meadow, in the middle of Leigh Woods, kids chasing after them, dog barking and bounding alongside, until they all collapsed on the ground in a giggling heap.

'Phew. This is great,' said Polly, when she managed to catch her breath. She pulled a blanket from the rucksack which Max had so gallantly insisted on carrying, and spread it on the ground. Gesturing at the day, she said, 'The sun is shining, the birds are singing…'

'And by the look of things – the dogs are shitting!' said Max, catching sight of a crouched-down George. 'Poo bags! Quick!' he ordered, clambering to his feet as Polly rooted around in the rucksack. He dashed across, scooped up the deposit and held high the poo-filled bag. 'Lovely and warm,' he called.

'Ugh, that's disgusting.'

The Trouble With Love

He made as if to run towards her, causing her to jump up to her feet with a squeal; then he swerved at the last minute and sprinted across to a bin, where he did the drop. Finally flopping down next to Polly, he said, 'Joys of dog ownership,' and kissed the end of her nose.

'God, nappies are bad enough,' said Polly. 'Here. Hands. Use one of these wet wipes.'

Polly and Max laid out the picnic things. It was quite a palaver, what with George having his nose into everything; and Ben wasn't much better.

'Gerroff,' Polly kept saying, pushing first one then the other away from the sandwiches, while Rowan sat and waited with the patience of a small blonde Buddha.

'Here you are, Ro.' Polly held out a cheese sandwich, but George was quicker. He promptly snatched it from Polly's hand and wolfed it down.

'Bad dog,' said Rowan, wagging her finger at George, who sat with a "Who? Me?" expression on his face. Polly was agog. She had no idea a dog's face could be so expressive.

Ben was already on his third and fourth sandwich: one cheese and one ham grasped firmly in each hand, as he expertly held them in the air out of George's reach. In his excitement, George knocked Rowan over, nicked her sandwich, licked her face and was now standing four-square over her, like a four-legged gazebo. Polly turned to Max, who lay on his back, eyes closed against the sunlight. 'Can you please do something about George?'

He squinted through one eye at her then sighed. 'Okay,' sitting up. 'Keep your hair on.' Clipping the lead onto George's collar, Max held it down until the dog gave up and lay on the rug.

'Better?' said Max.

'Yeah, well. Dogs shouldn't be allowed to lick faces,' said Polly.

'Don't be so precious, Polly,' said Max, who'd managed to catch Ben on a run-past and was now wiping his child's face and hands with a wet wipe. 'You have to expose your kids to dirt. It's good for their immune system.'

'Dirt, yes. But not dog saliva.'

'Fine. You made your point.' He stretched out on the blanket once more. 'You're too protective of Rowan, you know. Can't wrap kids up in cotton wool.' He placed his hands above his head as a cloud passed over the sun.

'Anyone for a drink?' called Polly, trying to sound cheerful while wishing she had something stronger than fizzy pop for herself.

*

Soon, the food was over, the picnic packed away, and the small troupe of Polly, Max, Rowan and Ben – followed by George – set off along the gravelled pathway heading into the trees. Leigh Woods was alive with leaves that rustled, even though there didn't appear to be a breeze, and with birds which chirped away merrily yet were nowhere to be seen. *Sure isn't Kansas*, she thought.

She found woods spooky at the best of times and would never have ventured into them with just herself and Rowan. For Polly could remember only too well the horror of the mother, two little children and a dog who'd set off down a woodland lane where they met a grisly fate at the hands of a hammer-wielding madman. She placed her arm through Max's, feeling the reassurance of his big muscular body. Rowan and Ben were a little way ahead.

They passed a section lined with ancient ferns. Very like those in the film *Jurassic Park*, she noted, where those small bird-like dinosaurs had hidden among pre-historic fronds. She half expected to see one stick its head above the foliage, cock it to one side then leap – talons unsheathed, teeth bared – onto her plumply young Rowan. She shivered. 'Don't go too far, Rowan. Rowan!' But she didn't hear. Ben tapped Rowan on the shoulder and pointed to Polly. Rowan ran back to her mother. 'Stay close,' Polly said, making sure she was talking into her daughter's face. Rowan nodded and ran off to join Ben.

It was getting chilly in the woods, where the sun filtered weakly through oak and ash, and other woodland trees whose names she didn't know.

'I often jog in these woods,' Max said. 'Sometimes I take Ben mountain biking.'

Polly, at all times aware of just where the children were, had seen them charge along a path to their right, she steered Max down it.

Ben and George were up ahead, the dog having found a large puddle from the rain the night before, and was now rushing up and down it, mouth like a shovel as he ploughed through, deluging himself in muddy water, tail wagging, clearly delighted with it all.

'Where's Rowan?' said Polly. 'I can't see her.'

'She'll be with them,' said Max, as he fiddled with the rucksack's straps.

'No. No. I don't see her,' said Polly, struggling with the panic starting to churn her stomach. 'Seriously. She's not there.'

'Rowan?' called Max, stepping ahead of Polly. 'Rowan, come here! Stop messing about!'

They reached Ben. 'Ben?' said Max, a grabbing his son's arm. 'Where's Rowan?'

But Ben was engrossed in poking his stick at the remains of a dead jackdaw at the bottom of a tree; he squirmed in his father's grasp. The dead bird, maggots crawling out of its split guts, was just too good a spectacle for him to ignore.

'Ben!' shouted Max, pulling his child so that he whirled around to face him. 'Ben. Never mind that dead bird. Look at me. I said look at me. Where is Rowan?'

'Boo!' shouted Rowan, as she suddenly popped her head round from behind the tree. With one startled look, she took in her mother's concern and began to chortle. 'Boo!' she shouted again, clearly delighted with the effect she was having.

Max let go of Ben. 'See?' he said, getting to his feet. 'She was fine all along. Nothing to worry about.'

By now Polly had her arms around the bemused Rowan.

'I don't know,' said Max. 'All that fuss about nothing. Have you ever considered that Rowan might choose not to hear you?'

24

Back at the house, and Polly was busying herself in the kitchen. She'd hardly said a word to Max since their return from the picnic.

'Do you want me to go?' said Max.

She turned to face him. 'No,' she said. 'Of course not.'

He gave her a hangdog look, and George slunk over to lick Polly's hand.

'I'm sorry I suggested Rowan's hearing might be selective,' said Max. 'That was insensitive of me.'

'Yes... well...'

'I feel as if I'm in the doghouse, never mind poor George here,' he said, looking down at George, who was now sitting on the floor gazing up adoringly at Polly. 'Say you forgive me. Hey? Girlfriend?'

She stopped unpacking the picnic things and looked up into his contrite face. 'I'm sorry. I guess I'm a big touchy where Rowan's hearing is concerned.'

'Perfectly understandable.'

About to throw the sandwiches in the bin, she turned to Max and said, 'Should I give these to George?' She didn't know what dogs could and couldn't eat.

'Best not,' said Max. 'Claire would go mental. She's got him on expensive dried dog food. No treats or snacks allowed. Isn't that right, boy?' he said, scratching George behind his ear.

'Raaaaarrrr!' Ben bowled in, a nudely dishevelled Barbie clutched in his hand, and Rowan chasing after him. 'Give me! Give meeeee!' she screamed. Max grabbed Ben's arm, causing him to stand stock-still.

'Give Rowan her Barbie, Ben.'

'No,' said Ben, the Barbie held aloft in his hand while Rowan jumped up, trying to reach it.

Polly shot Max a look. 'Okay, okay,' he said, then physically took the Barbie off Ben and handed it back to Rowan, who grasped her dolly tight to her chest and hid behind Polly's legs. Ben aimed a kick at Max's shin. 'Ouch!' And Max smacked Ben on the back of his legs.

Smacked! He's actually smacked his child, thought a horrified Polly. Rowan was stock-still, her saucer-like eyes trained on Max, mouth agape. Max had smacked his much-smaller-than-him five-year-old child.

Ben, now clearly incensed, was lashing out at Max, who in turn exerted an even firmer grip on him. 'Ben! Stop it!'

'Aaaaarrgh!' screamed Ben. George, now beside himself, ran at them, barking and bouncing up and down, while Rowan had tight hold of Polly's legs. And now Ben was trying to bite Max's hand.

Max turned to Polly, giving her a look that signalled he was out of his depth.

'I know!' said Polly, clapping her hands together. 'Why don't you kids go and watch *The Lion King*?' Ben shot her a glance. Clearly she'd piqued his interest. 'I've got popcorn,' she added.

The Trouble With Love

'Yesss!' shouted Ben, as he wriggled free from his father's grasp.

'Mummy?' said Rowan.

'It'll be fine, Rowan. Now you run along and get the DVD down and Mummy will come and put it on. Yes?'

Ben gave Max one final look – which reminded Polly of the way a caged lion might eye its tamer were it determined to bide its time until the trainer's back was turned and then have him!

'For fuck's sake, Max,' hissed Polly, as soon as the children had left the room. 'You actually hit Ben!'

At least he had the decency to look shame-faced.

'It was only a tap. He's not hurt, so no harm done.'

'No harm done? Did you see the way he looked at you? I think you'll have a lot of ground to make up there. Plus,' she continued, as she reached up to her cupboard and fetched a large bag of popcorn, 'Rowan was terrified.'

'Okay, okay. It's not like I make a habit of it. I've never smacked him before. I'm sorry if I scared Rowan. Is there anything I can do to make it up to her?'

'Nothing. Right?' she hissed. 'I don't approve of smacking, Max. I really don't.' She emptied the popcorn into a big bowl and took it through to the sitting room, where the two children sat cross-legged on the floor.

'Here you are, Mummy,' said Rowan, clambering up on her feet and handing her the DVD.

'Thanks, hon.' Polly slipped it into the television slot just as Max sauntered in, lowered his large frame onto the sofa and held out his arms to Ben who, without a word, clambered up onto his father's lap.

'That's it, big man,' said Max, giving his son a cuddle.

'Ahh, better now,' said Rowan, not minding one little bit that George was snaffling most of the popcorn from right under her nose.

Polly watched as Max settled into the sofa, Ben sucking his thumb as he snuggled further under his father's arm. 'Sorry,' mouthed Max to Polly. Rowan was stretched out flat on her tummy, bowl of popcorn under her arm, while George sat patiently, looking from Rowan to Max to the popcorn, and back. Polly sighed, and returned to tidying the kitchen. She didn't know what to make of things but decided in the end to think about all that later.

*

As Polly opened the door to let them out, Max leant in to kiss her on the cheek.

'Better take these two back home,' he said, indicating to Ben and George. 'I'll ring you later, yeah?'

'Yes. Fine.' Polly still wasn't in the mood to let Max off lightly.

'Look, I promise I'm not some child beater.' He gave her an apologetic smile.

'I'm tired, Max. It's been a long day. Let's just leave it at that.'

Max had his hand round the back of Ben's head as he ushered him out of the door. George was trying to lick Rowan's face, but Max held him tight on his leash.

'At least George was a hit – I mean, success,' Max said, trying a half-smile at her.

'Yes,' said Polly, recognising Max's attempt to lighten the mood. 'George can come again.'

'Is that with or without me?'

Polly tried for a smile, but it came out lukewarm.

'Poll?'

'Yes?'

'Oh nothing.' He turned to go. 'I'll leave you to ring me, shall I?'

'Yes, okay,' she said, already starting to close the door.

The Trouble With Love

Max put his hand out to stop her. 'Have you never made a mistake, Polly?' he said, and then headed down the path, Ben skipping by his side and George trotting along behind them.

Have I ever made a mistake? Well, of course I have, she berated herself as she paced up and down her kitchen. *What on earth is wrong with you? You've made tons of mistakes! Remember that time when Rowan dashed out in front of a truck and you'd been so scared that you shouted in her face and smacked her bottom?* Inwardly she cringed as she recalled how a couple walking past had tut-tutted at Polly's behaviour.

And let's face it. Ben's behaviour would try a saint!

Yes, but that smack was an angry one.

So what? Aren't they all angry ones? You know you don't hold with all that "smack your child with love". That whole ridiculous toddler-taming approach. And – c'mon – Max did seem genuinely sorry, didn't he?

Yeah, but only when I took him to task.

Oh, shut up!

Polly rubbed her head, took two ibuprofen, texted Max to say she hoped things were fine with Ben and that she'd call in a couple of days.

You moose, Polly, she told herself. *You have a not-quite-perfect-but-right-age-single-father-sexy-good-company-boyfriend. So what's the problem?*

But deep down, she knew that for her and Max to stand a chance, she had to get a grip, because – at the bottom of it all, way down deep as if on a bed of a weed-infested ocean where sea monsters lurked and Davy Jones kept his locker, was the truth – Max just wasn't Spike.

Outside it was that in-between time. That time of day when the sun's not quite set, and the birds are returning to their roosts for the night, or else out on a late hunt for flying insects. Lights in harbourside apartments were flicking on, curtains not yet drawn, as their occupants moved about doing their evening chores, watching television, getting changed for a night out, not yet conscious that they could be seen by an outside world.

And down below, the river – kept constant and hemmed in by the gates of the harbour locks and the roads lined with houses – moved back and forth, like a caged and silent presence, biding its time.

25

Polly set off on foot to the harbourside where she was meeting up with Mel at the Bicycle Café; Polly had arranged for Daisy to collect Rowan. Thank goodness for Daisy.

It was early evening as Polly settled to wait at a table on a balcony overlooking the river. She checked her watch. She was early. Shading her eyes from the low-lying sun, she wondered if she could see where Spike was working on his friend's boat, from here. She stood up to have a look but couldn't, so she sat back in the uncomfortable-yet-stylish silver metal chair and stared over the water, not thinking of anything in particular. A waitress arrived with her cappuccino. 'Thanks.' Opening a sachet of brown sugar, she poured half into her cup and then reached into her bag for her notebook and pen. She might as well do a spot of freewriting while she waited.

Gazing at the houses opposite, she began to write – *Rows of houses whose balconies resemble pockets on a man's shirt; gulls calling and swooping down over the heads of commuters crossing the small swing bridge on their way home to Totterdown,*

Windmill Hill or Southville. Hmm, could be the start of a poem? Polly paused to listen to the sound of seagulls. To her, their cries were a call to adventure. She scribbled away about Bristol being a seafaring city, where once thrived stevedores, smugglers and explorers setting sail for new worlds.

A ferry boat with a brightly painted red top pushed its way along the river; on its prow, a small light already switched on. The sun was setting, and with the sun went the warmth. Polly shivered as she set down her pen to pull on her faux leopardskin coat.

She looked across to where Mel had reached the top of the steps that ran up the outside of the café to the verandah. As Polly waved, her friend smiled back in greeting and made her way over, puffing a little from the climb.

'Hi. You been waiting long?' Mel gave her a peck on the cheek. 'Want another coffee?' she asked, the fading sun reflecting off her blue-rimmed Wayfarer sunglasses.

*

We've been through a lot, me and Mel, thought Polly, as she watched her friend return with their drinks.

'I'm glad you called, lovey,' said Mel, taking her seat and then getting stuck right in, 'because we need to get a few things cleared up once and for all, don't you think?'

She had that determined-Mel expression on her face. She meant business. Next to them, a seagull sat perched on the rail. *Bit close,* Polly noted.

'Starting with Spike. Now you might think that I shouldn't have asked Spike to be my sperm donor,' she began. 'Not without asking you first.'

'Yes, I do think that.'

Mel gave Polly a look.

'Oh, c'mon, Mel – you must realise it's a pretty stupid idea. Your having a baby with Spike.'

'I do not think it a stupid idea at all,' said Mel, as she leant forwards. 'You forget that you agreed. We have discussed this before—'

'Yes, but that was when Spike was in Australia. It was purely academic. You don't think that if I'd known he was going to turn up larger than life that I'd have agreed?'

Mel humphed.

'In any case – this you and Fen having a baby. Do you seriously think it's a good idea? When she wants to control just who you do or do not see? Hmm?'

The seagull in profile appeared to have its beady eye fixed on the women. Mel shifted in her seat as the gull looked the other way. A vision of Tippi Hedren fending off seagulls in *The Birds* flitted through Polly's mind.

'Fuck's sake, Polly. Fen is my girlfriend. If you cared about me then you'd stop dissing her.' Mel's ice cream was melting in the dish, and her triangular wafer had been fixed on by the seagull's gimlet eye.

'I love her,' Mel continued.

'So you say,' Polly turned her full attention on her friend, 'but is it enough?'

'Right then, missus. If you're going to get all high and mighty, then it's time I put you straight.'

'Oh yeah?'

'It's all right for you – getting yourself pregnant "by accident".' Putting in the quote marks with her fingers. 'Getting knocked up by a commitment-phobic toy boy who was leaving the country. How very convenient for someone with their body clock ticking loudly!'

'You what? Take that back!' (Secretly Polly was rather enjoying having a verbal fight with Mel – nothing like a Mel-fight to clear the air.) 'And I might say, a toy boy who you now want to have a baby with an' all!' she retorted. Yeah, she could give as good as she got.

'At least ours would be planned,' parried Mel. 'At least we're being responsible and exploring the options instead of getting up the duff like some chav on a council housing estate—'

'You know perfectly well it wasn't like that!' *Oh, losing the advantage there, Polly.*

'I don't know what your problem is. It's not like I'd be muscling in on you and Spike, is it? Because as you keep telling me, there is no you and Spike—'

'Of course there isn't!'

'Hmm. Methinks the lady doth protest too much.' Mel scoring an Ace! (Especially because that particular Shakespearean phrase was a favourite of their English teacher Mrs Yabsley, who'd churn it out whenever someone protested that, yes, they had actually, really and truly, forgotten their homework, or yes, the dog definitely did eat it – treasury tag an' all – 'Honest, Miss!')

'Bit below the belt,' said Polly – a foul to Mel Healey. 'You old lezzer!' A grin now threatening to break out.

'You sperm-stealing floozy!' retaliated Mel, as a couple of businessmen at a nearby table glanced over, clearly wondering if it was all about to kick off.

The two women stared at each other, and then Polly leant over to give Mel a pinch on the arm. 'Ouch!'

Mel retaliated with a thump on her friend's arm, grinning a broad grin now as she sat back, surveyed her friend and said, 'Come 'ere, you.' She got up out of her seat and hurried round to give her bestest-friend-in-the-whole-wide-world a hug and kiss.

'Gerroff!' Polly said loudly and then – for the benefit of the men, who were doing a poor job of pretending they weren't listening – 'I told you before! I don't care if you are a transsexual – the baby's yours!'

One of the men spluttered his coffee, and the other shot them a look of disdain.

Polly and Mel burst out laughing, and the seagull launched itself towards their table, snatched Mel's wafer from her dish and then, with a laconic flap of its giant wings, took off into the evening air.

'Did you see that?' said one of the men.

Mel, who'd ducked at the last minute, was now joining Polly in snorts of laughter.

'I'm not giving up on your one day seeing that my having Spike's child makes sense,' said Mel, swigging from a bottle of St Miguel beer.

'It's not just me you'd have to convince,' said Polly, also on beer. 'I've spoken to Spike, and he insists that he's not interested.'

'There's time before he goes back. He'll come round. What? Please think about how brilliant it could be. You know that Rowan is my favourite child of all times. She's gorgeous. Spike's got good genes, you gotta give him that. Our kids could be half-siblings – how cool would that be?'

Polly shook her head sadly. 'There's no guarantee – I mean, look at Max with his *Omen*-like devil child.'

'Never mind all that,' said Mel. 'Think how we could all be a big extended family. My baby a half-brother or half-sister to Rowan.'

Polly knew there was no point arguing when Mel was like this. Clearly she was still hoping to go ahead and use the sperm of Polly's ex-boyfriend to father a child. In the mad hope that she'd produce a replica Rowan.

'Have you thought of counselling, Mel? Someone dispassionate to talk it all through with?'

'What on earth for? I might be desperate, but I don't want just anyone's sperm.' She looked Polly straight in the eye. 'I'm asking you one last time to reconsider and change your mind.'

Polly said nothing.

'Say something. Huh?'

Polly took a deep breath. 'Mel. I'm not the boss of you. Of course I'm not. I do sympathise, truly I do. I mean, there's nothing so wonderful or so knackering as having a child…'

'So you must see that's what I want too. For myself.'

Polly smiled in what she hoped would be a letting-her-friend-down-gently kind of way. 'I hear what you say about us becoming more of a family, and how that might seem on the surface to be a positive thing. But… Spike? Have you thought this through? I can't see him wanting anything whatsoever to do with any child he fathered.' (*Even though we've not talked this through ourselves*). 'And what about Bam? How would she feel? What about donor agencies? There must be some good ones. We could make a list.'

'You don't have to worry about Bam,' Mel said.

Polly leant across the table and took her friend's hand in hers. 'You know I love you. But if you want my blessing then I can't guarantee it, but I will consider it. I can't say fairer than that.'

Mel looked as if she was considering something. 'There's no need for you to draw up a list,' she finally said.

'C'mon, Mel. Don't give up at the first hurdle. It's a brilliant idea to go for a donor.'

'No. You don't understand,' she said, lifting her head. 'We don't want just any donor. I'm going to ask Spike again.'

'I realise I can't stop you…'

'What you don't know,' said Mel, sounding more enthusiastic now, 'is that I've already discussed it with Bam and she is totally cool with the whole idea. Especially as they're going to be returning to Oz anyway.'

The Trouble With Love

'Bam doesn't mind that you want a baby with Spike?'

'No. She understands my predicament.' She gave Polly an unlike-you sort of stare. 'After all, it's only his sperm, not him that I'm after. I'd be having a baby with Fen, and she'll be the other parent, not Spike. I know that once you've had a chance to think this through properly, you will see that it makes sense. It could be brilliant.'

'It feels wrong.'

Mel moved her shoulder out of the way as a waitress came to collect their coffee cups and bowl. Once she'd gone, Mel said – rather grimly – 'Right. Well, if that's your final word...'

She stirred her coffee and, for a horrible moment, Polly thought Mel was going to cry. Mel never cried, and if she did now then Polly would feel it was all her fault. *It is all your fault!*

'I think you're being incredibly selfish, Poll,' Mel said, so quietly that Polly had to ask her to repeat herself. 'I said you're incredibly selfish. I've always been there for you. Right from when you first discovered you were pregnant. I've done nothing but support you.'

'Mel, I am really sorry, and I'm truly grateful—'

'Save it. I don't want your gratitude. It's all right for you,' she said, collecting her bag from underneath the table. 'You've got your baby.' She sat with her bag on her lap. 'I'm not getting any younger. This could be my last chance. Whether or not me and Fen work things out.' At this, she turned away from Polly a little. 'Truth be told, she's already cooling to the idea.'

'Mel, I—'

Mel put out her hand to silence Polly. 'So,' she said, giving a grim smile, 'looks like I might well have to go it alone.' She pushed a stray hair out of her eye. 'Whaddaya know, turns out we could both be destined to end up alone.'

'You and me. Two old biddies wandering around Clifton, muttering about what might have been,' said Polly, raising her bottle in salute at her friend.

'Yeah,' agreed Mel, as she clinked bottles with Polly. 'Like a right couple of Miss Havishams. We'll have badges saying Retired Sex Bombs…'

'…or Spinsters R Us!'

Mel's eyes were starting to fill up once more.

'Don't you dare cry,' said Polly, as she passed her friend a tissue. 'You'll get me started.'

Mel wiped her eyes and blew her nose.

'I love you, Mel. You know that, don't you?'

'Oh, fuck off.' Mel gave her one of her killer smiles and playfully punched Polly on the arm. 'I love you too. Wally.'

The office guys exchanged glances, which Mel noticed. 'Think we've stirred up their girl-on-girl fantasies, don't you?' Then louder, she said, 'Can't wait to get you home. I've got a special leather strap-on dildo from that catalogue we could try out!'

Polly glanced over at the suitably shocked-looking men; the two women burst into laughter. 'Don't mind us,' Mel called over to them. 'We're just larking about.' The men returned, rather too earnestly, to their conversation.

'Mel,' said Polly, 'I don't ever want you to forget that no matter what happens, you will always have me.'

'Ditto, mate.'

'I mean it. Whatever you decide to do about a baby, or Fen, or anyone.'

'You and me together, eh?' said Mel.

'Forever,' smiled Polly.

Mel reached out and lightly touched her friend's hand. 'Look, Polly, there's been something else I've been meaning to say…'

Polly groaned. 'What now?'

'It's about Spike. I know you. You're scared. Scared to tell him how you really feel.'

'Look, Mel—'

'No, don't interrupt me, I've been meaning to tackle this for a while now. This thing with Bam. It won't last. He's meant to be with you, Polly – anyone with half a brain can see that. I've seen the way your eyes light up whenever his name is mentioned. You can't fool me. I know you. Do you still love him? You can tell me.'

'Truly? I don't know, Mel.'

'Perhaps you should talk to him. Spend some time together.'

'But Bam's always around.'

'Do it, Polly. I'm serious. What if he was to go and you missed your chance? Don't let him leave for Australia without knowing how you feel.'

'But I don't know what I feel, Mel. That's the problem.'

A ferry tooted its horn and sailed through the swing bridge while commuters, cars and cyclists all waited for it to pass them by.

*

On her way home, Polly's brain went into overdrive. Was Spike – after all – the answer to Mel's prayers? Had Polly been unreasonable in not seeing her friend's point of view? Did she have the right? *Oh God*, she thought, stopping in her tracks, *I have been selfish, haven't I?* What's more, she had not tried hard enough to get along with Fen. She resumed striding along the riverside path.

If Mel could persuade Spike to be her donor (although Polly didn't think it likely), then who was she to get in her way?

Was Mel right? Did she still love Spike? Surely she didn't – that would be too pathetic. Yet there was no denying that his presence made her feel strange and raised all sorts of questions.

'I'll have to finish with Max, won't I?' she said out loud. 'If I do have feelings for Spike.' But did she? She checked around to make sure no one could overhear her mad ramblings. 'Finish with Max,' she mumbled. 'Is that what I ought to do?' She paused for a while on the dockside as she waited for some – any – emotional response to having just suggested to herself that she finish with her boyfriend. Did she feel upset at the prospect? Nope. Nothing. She felt nothing.

Guess that settles it then, she thought, as she headed off along the path once more. *If I'm not upset at the notion of finishing with Max, then I can't be in love with him. Full stop.*

She nearly collided with a woman walking her dog. 'Whoops!' The woman swerved to avoid her. 'Sorry.' She'd better get herself home before she knocked someone into the river.

Polly trudged up the incline leading to her road. Wouldn't she be mad, to throw away someone like Max, who was perfect on paper? If Spike was merely some echo? Maybe if Spike hadn't turned up then she'd be madly in love with Max by now. So why dump him when he'd not done anything other than spawn devil child Ben and have different ideas on child-rearing?

Traffic whizzed by, causing an airstream which pulled at her hair and tugged at her hemline. *Right. So, what if... what if we had a break instead? Yes, that could work. A break – until Spike left the country? No, that might be too long. Max might meet someone else. Maybe just for a couple of weeks...* She stomped up to her door. In the meantime, she ought to make things better with Mel.

*

Once indoors, Polly rummaged inside her handbag for her mobile. She'd time to make this call before she was due to collect Rowan from Daisy's. Placing a smile on her face (as she'd heard somewhere that difficult telephone conversations were best tackled while smiling – apparently the smile comes through in your voice – worth a try), she pressed Call.

Spike picked up on the third ring, and Polly launched right in.

'I've been talking to Mel.'

'Is that you, Polly?'

'Who else would it be?'

'Any number of people.'

Determined not to be wrong-footed by his teasing, she tried again. 'I've been talking to Mel—'

'So you said—'

'…and I want you to know that I no longer have any objections to your being her sperm donor.'

'Are you a bit tiddly, there, Polly?'

'No, I am not.'

'So you're seriously suggesting that I should rethink my position. Is that right?'

'Well… yes.'

'But haven't I already told you, Polly, that I do not think it's a good idea? Not to put too fine a point on it – the whole idea is downright bonkers. Especially as she's your best friend.'

'What if she wasn't my best friend?'

''Twould still be a no.'

'Mel said she'd spoken to Bam, and Bam was fine with it.'

'Did she now? Whether Mel has or has not spoken to Bam makes no odds. It's my call. I make my own decisions about my wee fellas. Although you and I didn't exactly…'

'No. Quite.'

'Bam does not speak for me, Polly. I'm sure she meant well…'

'Okay. I just… I don't know… You don't think I was being mean, do you? Telling Mel that I was against it? Effectively putting the mockers on everything?'

Gentle laughter – the same laughter she'd once loved, once

dreamt of, and once yearned to hear again – came from the other end of the line, giving her a warm feeling. 'Polly, whatever shall I do with you? You are never mean, Polly Park,' he said, then paused. 'Least ways, not intentionally.'

'Do you love her?' she said quietly into the receiver. But he'd already hung up.

26

Towards the end of the week, Mel and Fen flew off on a romantic trip to Paris – in the hope that they could revive their relationship and reconcile differences (that sort of thing, thought Polly, although Mel had sounded pretty miserable). She gave Polly strict instructions to not call while they were away.

'Yes, okay. No, I won't.'

Polly was no longer sure that having a break from Max was the right course to take; but seeing as he was away filming in deepest Manchester, she didn't have to face him yet. The shop was quiet, and so she was busy staring into the middle distance when her doorbell binged, announcing the arrival of Bam.

'Isn't that Wham Bam?' hissed Donna as she moseyed past, carrying an armful of stock to place back on hangers.

'Shh,' Polly hissed. She turned a smiling face to Bam. 'Bam,' she said, in a cheery voice. 'What a lovely surprise.'

'Can we talk?' said Bam, who looked young and uncertain in baby-blue baggy sweatshirt, rolled-up skinny jeans and black ballet pumps. Her hair was scraped back in a ponytail, her face devoid of makeup. She looked for all the world like a fashion model on her day off. Effortlessly beautiful, yet Polly couldn't fail to notice that she'd clearly been crying.

She felt a twinge of regret for all the times she'd taken the piss out of Bam. After all, Bam had done nothing wrong, except to fall in love with the man who happened to be Polly's own maybe-one-true-love.

Donna was trying to slink past the two women, no doubt to position herself where she could eavesdrop. 'Donna, tell you what,' said Polly. 'I'm going to take Bam next door to the café. You can hold the fort until I get back, yeah?'

'No,' said Bam, pulling herself up to her full height. 'What I have to say I'd rather say here, if you don't mind.'

'Okay. Sure.' Polly gave Donna a pleading look. Not slow on the uptake, Donna cast her eye from one woman to the other and said, 'Why don't I pop out back and make us all a coffee, yeah?'

'Good idea,' said Polly, not taking her eye off Bam for one moment; much like a rookie hiker might keep an eye on a dangerous snake they'd unwittingly disturbed.

'I'll come quickly to the point,' said Bam. As she tossed her head back, her ponytail swung from one side to the other. 'I want you to leave Spike alone.'

'I'm sorry?' Polly felt well and truly blindsided. She'd not seen that coming at all, although Donna – waiting for the kettle to boil – had done. She shook her head at Polly's idiocy.

'I've thought it through,' said Bam, nodding her head as if agreeing with herself. 'I've tried to be cool about the whole thing. I understand that Rowan is Spike's daughter and so of course he must see her...' She lifted her head to gaze at Polly straight in the eye. Words appeared to have escaped Polly. Words were not top on her list of priorities right now. Instead she was trying to stop her brain from dashing about going *What? What? Eh? What?*

'However,' continued Bam, whose small-yet-determined chin was firmly resolute, 'I don't see any reason why he has to spend time with you.'

'Look, Bam,' Polly began, words making an appearance, but not the right ones to sort out this mess. 'I don't know what you think—'

'...is going on?' Clearly Bam was ahead of Polly. 'Oh, don't worry. I know that there's nothing going on,' continued Bam. 'Not as far as Spike is concerned. He's moved on. But the question is – have you? I rather suspect you'd like him back.'

'Well, I—'

Bam held up her hand. 'Please, hear me out, Polly. I've been practising this for ages.' A glimmer of a smile passed over her full, lightly glossed lips. 'You might not realise this yourself yet… I'll give you the benefit of the doubt here…'

Oh dear, this was not going to end at all well, thought Donna out back.

Polly merely stared, open-mouthed.

'I know he's confused because of Rowan. But let me make this quite clear, Polly. Spike loves me. I fully expect him to ask me to marry him, and I don't want you ruining things by messing with his head. You had your chance, sweetheart, and quite frankly you blew it. He told me all about your turning him down when he asked you to come away with him—'

'It wasn't quite like that…' Polly began, but then shut up as she could tell that Bam was in no mood for an interruption.

'When I met him, he was devastated, I can tell you. You really hurt him.'

(*I did? News to me*, thought Polly. Spike was so cool, so convincing that it was no big deal. *Yeah, almost as convincing as you! God. How's that for irony!*)

'It took him a long time to get over your rejection of him,' Bam continued, holding her head as high as a dressage pony.

'And quite a while to be able to trust again.' She shook her head – again, like some filly, thought Polly, distracted by the similarity. 'I've been good for him, Polly, and I shall love him much more than you ever could…'

Polly tried to take it all in. Spike? Devastated? She held on tight to the sides of her high stool, because if there had been any feathers around you could certainly have knocked her down with one.

'I like you, Polly, I really do. Maybe another time, another place, we could have been friends. I'm asking you, woman to woman, to please leave Spike alone. He's going to come back to Australia, and he's going to marry me, and we're going to have babies of our own.'

After Bam had gone – leaving Polly reeling – Donna finally made an appearance with the coffees. She handed Polly a mug. 'Here's your drink, lover,' she said. 'I could have told you there'd be tears before bedtime.' She gave Polly's shoulder a pat. 'Honestly, your life's getting more and more like *EastEnders*,' she said, trying to lighten matters, and adding a wide toothy grin.

But Polly was not for cheering up. 'Thanks, Donna,' was all she could manage to say.

'I'll be shootin' off now,' said Donna, starting for the door and then turning back. 'Changing the subject here, but when you next speak to your muh, tell her to return my calls, yeah?'

'Right. Okay.'

Donna opened the door, letting in a woman customer who held a girl in green school uniform by the hand. Polly watched Donna leave then tried her hardest to bestow her best professional smile on the mother and daughter come in for a browse.

She needed to get away, she decided. Go down to Devon. Yes, that was it. She couldn't think here. What she needed was space, to decide if Mel was right and she was still in love with Spike. And if that was the case, she must talk to him about it. Or should she just accept that she'd missed that particular boat, and persevere with Max? *Persevere. That's not a great word, is it?* No, she'd better finish with Max and then hightail it down to Devon.

Polly would phone Suze. (*Yes, that's what I'll do.*) Because at times like this, a girl needs her mother. Even a rubbish one like Suze. She gave herself a wry smile. She'd arrange a visit with Suze and Brian. What better place to collect her thoughts? She felt a yearning for the solitude of Suze's place overlooking the Tamar Estuary, where it was so peaceful that you could almost hear the tides and winds calling to you. Otters floating on their backs munching fish, curlews calling as they flew low over the water, that soft light bouncing off the river…

Donna could cover for her in the shop – she was always asking for extra shifts, as she was skint – and she could bring in that friend of hers to help out. Then Polly could pack up Rowan, and the two of them could be on the road to Devon by tomorrow, with any luck. Just for a week or two. Sort out just how she felt. It would be tricky, but things could hardly get any worse, could they?

27

On her way home, she encountered a detour at the top of the hill and was diverted along Canynge Crescent. In a slow-moving line of cars, Polly drove past an old lady, with white hair swept into a tight bun, who strode at quite a lick along the pavement. An elderly Cliftonian colonial-type, who owned Polly's dream house. She'd discovered that her name was Dr Edith Sutton – not that she'd been stalking her – but she had looked her up on the electoral roll and then googled her. She'd been a redoubtable female surgeon in the days when there weren't many. Had even raced Bugattis in Monte Carlo, in her day, and was now often to be seen striding through Clifton in her stout shoes and tweed skirts – come rain or shine. She'd been engaged to a pilot during the Second World War, and after he was shot down over the English Channel on his way back, she never recovered – had never been married or had children, so Polly had been told, one night by a barmaid in a Clifton pub. The story went that Edith had been pregnant when his mother got the telegram, and the shock of his death brought on a miscarriage. 'Life's too short,' the barmaid had murmured as she topped up Polly's glass. 'She should have married him while she had the chance, you see. But she didn't, and – well – it's a tragic tale, isn't it?' After that, Polly had tried to smile at Edith in the supermarket but was either ignored or met with a hostile glare.

Yes, life was short. The roadworks traffic lights turned green and she turned into Clifton Vale, where she had to drive past Max's flat, and – oh look – there outside was his car.

She thought he wasn't due back until the end of the week… but – what the hell. 'No time like the present,' she said out loud, as she turned the wheel and executed a perfect piece of parallel parking right outside his house. She took the fact that there was such a space – a bit of a miracle in Clifton Village – well, she took it as a sign that now was as good a time as any to have this "let's take a break" conversation. Yep. Time to pay him a surprise visit.

He was surprised, all right.

*

Polly bounded up the steps to Max's front door, just as one of the other tenants was letting himself into the building. 'Hi. I'm here to see Max,' she said, giving him a gay smile.

The guy smiled back and stood aside. 'Be my guest.'

She clambered the stairs to the first floor where she stood in front of the thickly painted white door of Flat No. 3. *Here goes nothing.* Knock knock knock. She waited. *Guess he's not in after all*, she thought. *Maybe he's popped out for milk, or something.* It was a daft idea to call around unannounced. She rummaged in her bag, hunting for her mobile so she could send him a text message, when the door was opened by –Sarah the paramedic actor! Minus her television paramedic uniform. Minus anything at all, actually, except for what Polly recognised as one of Max's blue shirts – the one that Polly particularly liked because it brought out the blue of his eyes. Oh, and – yep – Sarah was also wearing a pair of Max's hiking socks by the look of things.

'Whoops,' said Sarah (not even bothering to look apologetic, noted Polly, whose brain was playing catch-up). 'Hello there. It's Polly, isn't it?' Sarah languidly leant against the door frame like she was posing for a *GQ* magazine model shoot.

'Who is it?' came Max's voice from within the flat. Sarah shrugged, and Polly – now more than capable of coming up with two plus one equals cheater – thought, *Unreal, I can't believe this is happening. What a fuckin' cliché.* She turned tail and scurried back down the stairs.

'Oh fuck, oh fuck,' she could hear Max say behind her, followed by Sarah saying, 'Let her go, Max.'

But Max was thundering down the stairs after Polly, catching up with her on the pavement outside. 'Wait! Polly!'

She turned to see that he'd only managed to wrap a towel around his waist. A hand towel at that – one which he was having problems holding together with the one hand as he reached for her arm with his other.

'Don't touch me!' she shouted, pulling her arm away from him. 'You're pathetic!'

The afternoon sun bounced off Polly's loose hair, giving her the appearance of a flame-haired medusa. In this clear light, she couldn't help but notice how Max had a large angry-looking zit on his right shoulder, and how white and pasty his skin was. He'd a red flush creeping all over his face, neck and upper chest, too. Not so handsome naked (well, practically naked) in the harsh light of day. Polly felt more like laughing than being angry.

Two elderly ladies in matching raincoats, one of them pushing a tartan shopping trolley, were passing by on the opposite side of the narrow road. They stopped to watch the action.

Max, making a move towards Polly, stepped on a small stone and was now hopping from one foot to the other. 'Ouch. Shit. Look. Don't go, Polly. Please. It's not—'

'Oh do me a favour, Max,' she said, hauling herself up to her full height. 'It's exactly what it looks like!'

'But, but, Polly,' he tried again, his one free hand stretched out, palm upwards. 'We had a few drinks after the filming and she'd had too much to drink—'

One of the ladies turned to the other and said, 'I think this young man has got himself into hot water.'

'Ooh yes,' said the other. They both stared openly at the scene unfolding across the road.

'Let me guess. I suppose she slept on the sofa,' said Polly, not bothering to keep the yeah-right sarcastic tone out of her voice. She was feeling angry now – but more at herself for being so blind and bloody stupid.

'Well, no, okay, she didn't,' said Max, arm down by his side as he rubbed the sole of his foot up the length of his shin. Clearly still smarting from the stones.

Good, thought Polly.

He squinted at her through the glare of the sun. 'You know how it is,' he said.

'Oh, I know how it is, all right,' said Polly, wondering if fate was having a laugh or deciding to intervene. After all, she'd not been one hundred per cent sure whether she ought to dump Max and… well… and now her mind had been made up for her.

'Look, Polly,' he continued, 'I've known Sarah for ages. And sometimes we – you know…'

'She's your fuck buddy. Why not just come out and say it, Max!'

'Fuck buddy? What's a fuck buddy?' whispered one of the old ladies.

'Shh,' hissed the other one. 'Don't you watch *Sex and the City*?'

'God's sake, Poll,' said Max, who'd spotted the old ladies listening. 'Keep it down, will you? Yes. Okay. If you want to put it like that, then I suppose she is.'

Polly glanced across at their audience – the two ladies now joined by a younger man (clearly someone they knew). A white van drove past and tooted its horn at Max – 'Oi, flasher! Put yer clothes on!'

'C'mon, Polly. Don't be daft. You're overreacting. It's you I love…' Max was saying.

She just stared at him.

'I'll stop seeing Sarah, I promise. It was insecurity on my part. Yes, that's right,' he said, clearly feeling he was on firmer ground here. 'I felt insecure. This whole Spike thing. It's been making me crazy.' He was advancing towards her, as she backed into the gap between hers and another parked car. 'Because I don't have you, Polly, do I? Not really…'

'What's he saying?' one of the ladies asked the other.

The man said, 'He's saying he doesn't have her.'

'Who?'

'Shh.'

A squirrel chose that moment to make a dash for freedom underneath Polly's car as she fumbled in her pocket for her car keys. 'So,' she said, looking up into his face, 'you're saying it's my fault, is that right? That your shagging Sarah is somehow down to me? How very bloody convenient!'

'I was always going to be playing second fiddle to Spike.' He held out his hand. 'But that's all right. I understand. We can work it out.'

One of the ladies nudged the other in the ribs – 'So, is he her Mr Big, then?'

The Trouble With Love

'I don't think so...'

'D'you know what, Max?' Polly stepped into the road to make her way round to the driver's side, jingling her keys in her hand. 'You've helped me make my mind up.'

'Good... because I—'

'No! We're over. Us. I deserve better than this. I deserve better than you.'

'You tell him, love!' one of the women called across. The man gave Polly an impromptu round of applause.

'What? What?' the other lady was saying, cupping her ear with her hand.

'Oh, and that's Spike, is it?' Max called after her. 'He doesn't want you. He's got Bam!'

Polly clambered into her car and fired up her engine – which shot out a satisfying puff of black smoke right into Max's face. She drove off, leaving Max to hold up both his arms in frustration – which caused his towel to fall to the ground and reveal that he had on no underpants.

'We're not over, Polly! You don't mean it!' he shouted after her.

'Ooh,' said one of the women, unable to take her eyes off Max's "impressive wedding tackle" as she'd later tell her cat.

In her mirror, Polly could see Max pick up his towel, salute to his audience and then walk back inside – buck naked.

28

The sky glowered darkly as she parked her car in the bay outside her front door. She so wanted to call Mel but she'd blinkin' well promised not to call her while she was in Paris. She needed to tell her about Max doing Ms Ambulance Drawers behind her back, and that she'd finished with him for good. Spike was on her mind too. And Max's passing shot. Polly had now gone back to thinking that it was too late – and in any case, if it wasn't too late, why on earth would she want to put herself through the turmoil of getting close to him again, and him then leaving? Better if she was done with both Max and Spike. Far better to be on her own. Free of all the trouble – and alone with Rowan.

Polly slammed her car door and pelted down the road to Daisy's to collect Rowan, just as the sky opened and rain bucketed down.

'Phew!' she said, when Tiggy opened the door to her. 'Your mum and the girls in?'

'Yeah, in there,' said Tiggy, in her Kevin-the-teenager voice.

Walking through, she saw that there in the kitchen – as

if she'd just conjured him up by thinking of him – was Spike, sitting at the breakfast counter, having a cup of tea and a chat with Daisy. Polly felt a quickening of her heart.

'Hey, Polly,' he called, with a little wave.

'I didn't expect to see you here,' she said in a voice that rang out in the echoey room, sounding more harsh than she intended it to.

'Was totally my fault, Polly,' said Daisy. 'I saw him walking up to your door and it was raining, so I invited him round here to wait. I knew you'd turn up sooner or later to pick up Rowan.'

Polly turned to Spike. 'You were coming to see me? Why was that?' He gave her a look as if he could read what she'd been thinking of earlier, and – hating herself for it – she began to colour up.

'Why, to see if I could spend some time with my gorgeous daughter. Daisy here took pity on me, invited me in. Yet as soon as I arrived, Rowan dashed upstairs and hasn't been seen since,' he said, with a questioning look in his eyes.

'Is anything the matter?' said Daisy. 'Only you do look rather flustered.'

Polly's initial desire to tell Daisy what had happened with Max was tempered by the presence of Spike. She also didn't want him to know that she was thinking of travelling down to Devon. He might well raise some objections. She made a snap decision to wait until her trip was a done deal.

'It'll keep,' she said.

'Don't mind me,' said Spike, clearly guessing that he might well be in the way. He hopped off his stool and added, 'I can always go and find Miss Nibs.'

Polly paused. Would it really hurt? She didn't have to mention her trip – yet she was dying to tell someone about what had just happened with Max. 'Oh, what the hell,' she said. 'I might as well tell you both. I've just had a bust-up with Max.

On the way over here. We've split up. I was going to tell him anyway that I thought we should have a break…' (*don't give me that look, Spike Monaghan*) '…what with this and that. But then, well, let's just say that something happened that convinced me it was never going to work.'

'What?' said Daisy.

'Yes, what? You can tell us, Poll,' said Spike, sounding eager to hear.

'Oh okay,' said Polly, who was – according to Mel – a world champion blabbermouth. Briefly, and without going into too much detail, she told them about catching Max and Sarah "at it".

'No!' said Daisy.

Spike said nothing – although he seemed to find the towel episode amusing. Daisy had gasped, 'No! Oh dear. That's hilarious,' and laughed a good deal.

'So that's it,' said Polly. 'Over. Finished. Finito.' She flopped onto the small white leather sofa in the corner.

'Oh dear,' said Daisy. 'Just when I thought he might be good boyfriend material.' She cast a look in Spike's direction, but his face was giving nothing away.

'I dare say I'll survive,' said Polly, feeling much more cheerful now that she'd unloaded herself. 'We were hardly a match made in heaven, were we? Done and dusted.' She sat up straight. 'Look, I hope you don't mind. But now that I've bored you rigid, can we change the subject?'

'Sure,' said Daisy.

'I'll be shooting off soon in any case,' said Spike. 'Leave you girls to it.'

Polly gave him a steady stare. 'No Bam?'

He raised his eyebrows at her. 'No, Polly. She's gone to visit her mother – in Kettering?'

'Ah right,' said Polly, having no idea where Kettering was. Geography and maps and stuff not being her strong point.

'You have no idea where Kettering is, do you?' said Spike, an ill-disguised smirk on his face.

Polly was not in any mood for verbal sparring. 'Rowan around?' she asked Daisy, ignoring Spike's question.

'She's upstairs…' both Daisy and Spike said together, and Daisy said, 'Snap,' smiling at him rather indulgently, Polly thought. Jolly cosy too. She looked at Daisy, who was casting coy looks in Spike's direction.

'Rowan?' Polly said, reminding her.

'Oh sorry,' said Daisy. 'She's upstairs playing with Morwenna. Do you want me to give her a call?' Daisy placed a beautifully crafted cup filled with tea in front of Polly.

'Good idea,' said Polly, as she lifted the cup to examine it – it was painted with pink roses and gold twiddly bits. 'These cups are lovely.'

'D'you like them? My friend Thalia made them at our pottery class. Gorgeous, aren't they?'

'Mmm. Yes.'

'I didn't know you were a potter,' said Spike.

Daisy gave a soft laugh. 'Oh God, not me. Mine are terrible! I daren't even bring them home. Phil has threatened to have a Greek night where we all chuck my pots on the floor and down loads of Ouzo!'

'Ah, c'mon, I'll bet they're not as bad as all that,' said Spike, with his characteristic twinkle.

God, thought Polly. *Daisy's positively simpering! Spike ought to bottle it, you know, he'd make a fortune. Spike's Irish Blarney!*

Daisy rose out of her chair – but not before she'd twiddled with her hair, Polly noticed. 'I'll go tell Rowan her mummy's here.'

'So,' said Polly, the moment Daisy left the room.

'So yerself,' said Spike. 'You sure you've not come with a request from another of your friends for my sperm?'

'I'm tired, Spike. Can we forget all that for the time being?'

'Fine by me,' he said, taking a slurp of his tea. 'She does a fine brew, does Daisy.'

'You can wipe that stupid grin off your face. She's not after your sperm, either!' Polly couldn't help saying, and then mentally (yes, very mental) kicked herself.

'A man never knows with you girls!' His face broke into a dimpled grin.

'Mummeee!' Rowan came charging into Polly's legs without engaging any toddler brakes.

'Oof!' said Polly.

Daisy followed behind, muttering, 'Honestly...' She turned to the others. 'Sorry. Tiggy's got boy trouble.'

Haven't we all! thought Polly.

'You know Tiggy and Fin have been having sex?'

'What? No! She's just a child.'

'She's sixteen, Polly.'

'She is? Oh God, I've missed her birthday, haven't I? I'm so sorry. I'll get her a present. But... God. Tiggy having sex? How on earth do you know?'

'We've been letting him sleep over.'

'In her room, you mean?' Polly's mind was boggling. 'In her bed?'

'Shh, she'll hear us.'

Spike was saying nothing. Daisy reached for the bottle of red on the side. 'Anybody want one?'

'No thanks.'

Spike shook his head.

'Well, I hope nobody minds if I do,' said Daisy, pouring herself a hefty glug.

Rowan still had hold of Polly's legs while Polly fervently hoped – given the subject matter – that Rowan's ears were well and truly bunged up.

'Shall I take Roly to get her coat?' said Spike.

'Hanging up in the hall,' Daisy said, waving her hand. 'Thanks.' She gave him a thin smile then turned back to Polly. 'Just you wait until Rowan is older. It's a nightmare knowing what to do for the best. Me and Phil talked it over and decided a long time ago that if she had a boyfriend and was going to have sex with him, better in our house where we can keep an eye on them than in the back seat of a car...'

What's wrong with the back seat of a car? Polly was thinking. Wasn't that, like, a rite of passage everyone had to go through?

'...or in some alleyway, or the backroom of a club...'

'Backroom of a club?' said Polly. 'God, I feel old. Is that what they get up to in their clubs nowadays?'

'So, yes, Fin has been spending a couple of nights a week here.'

'But... but... isn't that, like, horribly embarrassing?'

Daisy took a slug of her wine. 'You get used to it,' she half shrugged.

'Oh God,' said Polly. 'I'm going to make sure Rowan doesn't have sex until she's at least thirty! Tell me you haven't heard them – you know. Doing it?'

'Whoah, too much information there,' said Spike, entering the kitchen with a Rowan suitably coated and booted.

'Anyway,' stage whispered Daisy, 'Phil took her to the STI clinic this morning. Seriously, Polly. He wasn't best pleased, either. And Tiggy's furious with Dolphin. She insists he's the one who's given her crabs as she's not slept with anyone else for months!'

'Months?' Polly'd understood that Dolphin was Tiggy's first boyfriend.

Spike covered Rowan's ears and then said to Polly, 'Sorry to interrupt this chinwag. But shouldn't this one be getting off home?'

'Yes. Of course,' said Polly, rising up off her stool.

'All right if I come back with yous two, Poll?' asked Spike. 'Give this little monster – I mean cherub...' as Rowan wriggled in his grasp '...her bath? Would that be okay?'

'Hmm? Yes, I'm sure she'd love that,' she said, distracted by Daisy's tale of teen sex and pubic lice. She still found it hard to fathom... 'I'll call you,' she said to Daisy.

As Rowan merrily skipped along the road, holding onto her father's hand, she asked, 'What are mabs?' The rain had stopped long enough for them to get home and dry. 'Why has Tiggy got mabs? Can I have some?'

'Would you like to stay for something to eat?' Polly called up the stairs. It seemed daft not to invite him.

'Is it safe or is it something you've cooked yerself?' he called back.

'Cheek! Even I can't go wrong with vegetarian chilli,' she yelled back. He came to the top of the stairs. 'I only have to boil rice, fry onion and garlic and bung in chilli powder, tinned tomatoes and tinned kidney beans!' she added.

'So long as you don't boil the onion and fry the rice instead,' he said, arms folded across his chest and his eyebrows joining in with his amused smile.

'Very droll.'

A squealing and naked Rowan streaked across the landing behind his back, and he turned to give chase. 'Come here, you!'

Polly retired to the kitchen and the task of wielding a can opener.

All was simmering away nicely as he entered the kitchen. 'Rowan safely tucked up and fast asleep,' he reported, with a salute.

'How many times did you have to read her *Meg and Mog*?'

'Twice,' he said.

'You got off lightly.'

He came to stand next to her at the oven, took the wooden spoon she'd been using for the stirring and leant across her to take a taste – just brushing Polly's arm as he did so – the little hairs on her forearm going ping!

'Hmm,' he said, as he stood back upright. 'I'm getting tomato, I'm getting garlic, I'm getting burnt onion...'

'Oi!' Giving him a playful shove. 'I have not burnt it.'

'Guess that burnt flavour must be ingrained in the pan, then.'

'Bloody nerve,' she said, flicking a tea towel at him as he jumped out of the way and then fixed her with a glance.

'Sorry about yer Max fella. Seems he acted like a right pillock. I'd—'

'Yeah well,' she interrupted, trying not to return his unsettling gaze. Instead she concentrated on the pan, hoping against hope that she could calm the flush threatening to rise from her chest and up over her face. 'I don't want to talk about it,' she murmured, 'if it's all the same with you.'

'Righty-ho, Polly. If you're sure that's what you want.'

Miserably she thought that what she might actually want – what she could see in her mind's eye – was for him to throw himself at her feet and declare his undying love. But that wasn't going to happen, was it? Not now. Not ever. *God's sake, Polly. What's got in to you?*

She began to plate up the food, setting out bowls of chilli and a small bowl of yoghurt to share.

'So,' she said, as she took her place opposite him. 'Guess that's me on my own again. You know. No Max. Oh, don't give me that look. I like it. As Hugh Grant said, "I know that no man's an island..."'

'"...but if I have to be one then better make it Ibiza!"' finished

Spike. The pair of them not quite getting the quote word for word but close enough.

'*About a Boy*,' she said, as they both paused, remembering happier times when they used to stay in, snuggled up on the sofa and watch that very same DVD... one of their favourites back then... before Spike left... before Rowan... just before everything, she thought. Disconcerted, she gave a small cough. 'Yeah well.'

He reached across to take her hand, and when she looked up into his eyes, they were dark and dilated. 'Polly?' he began... but that was when the phone in the hall started ringing.

When she returned to the kitchen, her face was deathly pale.

'That was Brian,' she said, clearly shocked. 'It's Suze.' She grabbed hold of a chair as her knees didn't feel capable of keeping her upright. 'She's had an accident. Nearly drowned. Is in hospital. Brian said there's nothing we can do tonight. And to come down tomorrow. Oh, Spike.' He caught her just in time and held her tightly to his chest, as she cried.

'Shh, shh,' he said, reminding her of the sound of waves coming in on the shore.

All that night, she tossed and turned as if approaching the eye of a storm. While Spike slept below, like a sailor preparing to steady the helm of a ship.

29

They were in deepest Devon, travelling along the sort of country lanes that John Steed and Emma Peel might have careered along in an episode of *The Avengers*; what with their tall green hedgerows, narrow tracks with pull-over places to let tractors pass and tiny crossroads with white signs pointing the way to West Hoe, Weir Quay, Milton Combe, Hoe's Hole. Finally they were at the small dirt track leading down to the river's edge and Ruby Red Farm. Suze's country hideaway on the banks of the Tamar Estuary.

Even though she'd promised she wouldn't – but this was an emergency – last night Polly had rung Mel in Paris to let her know what was happening. 'Christ, Poll, I'm so sorry. I wish I could be there. When are you going down to Devon? Tonight?'

'No. In the morning. Spike's going to drive. He's insisted. I don't think I'm in a fit state.'

'Of course you're not. Good for him. See? I told you he's a good bloke, and I'm always right.'

Now Polly looked across at Spike, trying his best not to

crunch the gears of her 2CV as they headed down the track. Donna and her friend were to look after the shop between them, so all Polly had to concentrate on was visiting her mother and finding out what on earth had happened. Because a near drowning wasn't the only news Brian had imparted to Polly. And why, she wanted to know, if it was true, hadn't her mother told her?

'She didn't want to worry you,' Brian said during their phone call. 'I tried to get her to call you. But you know what she's like. Stubborn. She's been avoiding this whole breast lump thing for weeks, Poll. Like a bleedin' ostrich.'

Cancer. The word that filled hearts with dread. Polly's mother might have breast cancer, Brian said. *But why wouldn't she want to get it properly checked out?* Polly thought, gazing out of the car window. After her first consultation in Bristol (yes, that was what she'd been up to), she hadn't been back for a scan or a biopsy.

The travellers passed a field where a neighbouring farmer was grazing his large square beasts: the cattle a dark ginger, giving their name to the breed Ruby Red Devonshires. As they rounded a bend, the estuary swung into view, its waters calm and as flat as a board, with boats of varying sizes appearing pinned by their masts to its surface, much like butterflies in a Victorian display cabinet. As the car crunched across the gravelled approach, Brian emerged from the house to greet them.

Brian. As solid and square as if he were a Devonshire farmer himself, and he might have passed for one, what with his country get-up of a Barbour jacket, were it not for his blue Paul Smith shirt, black jeans and black winklepickers nailing him as a townie at heart.

'Aw right, twinkle,' he called out to Polly, as he reached their car.

'Hey, Brian,' she said, clambering out of her seat to plant a kiss on his cheek and allow herself to be enveloped in his big bear hug.

'You okay?' he said, shaking Spike by the hand. 'Journey down all right in that excuse for a car? Honest to God, Poll, it looks like a frickin' skip on wheels!' He patted Spike on the back. 'Really good to see you, mate. You staying long? In the UK, that is?'

'Only time will tell,' said Spike, as he stretched his legs, taking in his surroundings. 'Bit cramped in that old jalopy of Polly's there.'

Brian was giving him the once-over. 'I'm not surprised. Still, you're looking well,' he said. 'More grown up, like. What?' he said, catching Polly giving him a look. 'You know what I mean. Australia clearly suits you, Spike.'

'Yeah,' he replied, in a non-committal way.

'Here, let me help you with this little darlin'.' Brian shifted the front seat forwards and reached in for Rowan.

Polly said nothing. There was nothing to say. Everything felt so trivial, so forced. She couldn't get her head around the fact that the sun still shone, the earth still turned, birds chirped away, as if there was not a care in the world, while inside, Polly was screaming that her mother may have cancer and that she'd nearly drowned.

''Ello, Princess,' Brian said, placing the child on her feet. 'Cor, look at you. Right Bobby Dazzler. You've grown an' all. What they been feeding you on? Popeye's spinach?' He gave a smile to Polly and Spike, but neither really had the heart to smile back.

''Lo, Byan,' Rowan said in a sleepy way, looking rather overwhelmed at being woken from her car nap to find herself transported to a different place with different sounds and smells.

'Shall we find Blue?' Brian took her by the hand and gave a soft whistle. Soon, Brian's brown Labrador came waddling out to say hello. Blue was ancient; at fourteen years old, he had grey around his muzzle and a touch of arthritis in his hips. He gave Rowan a lolloping doggy lick and wagged his fat otter-like tail at her. A delighted Rowan threw her arms about his neck.

'That's the babysitting sorted,' said Spike.

Brian beamed at Rowan. 'Ain't she beautiful,' he said, and turning to Spike added, 'She's the spit of you, mate. But with Suze's blonde hair.'

Polly took in the chocolate-box cottage, the blue sky dotted with fluffy white clouds, and inhaled a deep breath of country air. 'I keep forgetting how glorious it is here.'

'You should come an' visit us more often, Poll. We don't see enough of you and this little treasure, as it is. I don't think we've seen you since last Christmas, have we? "Ere, let me take those.' He clutched their two cases in his ham-sized fists. 'I know your mum wishes you'd come visit more often.'

Well, perhaps if she'd come to see me more often when I was growing up, flashed through Polly's mind. Which she knew was unfair. Especially now. Water under the bridge an' all that.

'There's things you don't know about, Poll,' Brian said, in a most intriguing manner. But not for Polly, as she was used to Suze's dramas and supposed he must be referring to one of those. Probably some new venture of her mother's. A new television programme. A lot going on, would if she could, blah di blah di blah. She'd heard it all before.

She smiled wanly at Brian. 'So how is Mum?'

She was disconcerted to see that Brian's eyes filled with tears. He reminded her of a large sad lion waiting for Androcles to take the thorn out of his paw.

'Let's get you all inside, first, shall we?' he said.

The house was a beautiful Georgian one, of large and square proportions. It overlooked the Tamar, like some Jane Austen rectory. The garden tiered down to a small beach and jetty, where Poly could see Suze's small boat tied up. Suze liked to take it out now and then. 'All very *Swallows and Amazons*, darling' she liked to say. A bird – whose name Polly didn't know – flew low across the water, appearing to skim its surface.

She followed the others as the whole five of them – Brian, Polly, Spike, Rowan and Blue – all trooped indoors. *Although we're nothing like the Famous Five*, thought Polly, and now wasn't the time for jolly japes and lashings of ginger beer.

*

'So, what happened, Brian?' Polly asked, once she and Spike were sitting at the large kitchen table and Brian had set a fat old kettle on the hob of the Aga. The sort of Aga Polly used to wish they had when she was growing up. The sort of Aga where she could have imagined a version of Suze, dressed in Cath Kidston apron, just like her ideal portrait of a mother who would stir her cake mix in a large earthenware bowl, laughing tinkly laughter as she passed the spoon to a young Polly to lick.

Polly blinked. Suze had never been like that. She'd come late to cooking – surprising Polly greatly when she displayed any talent – because all Polly could remember of her mother's cooking back then was pots simmering with vegetables of some sort, and lentil something or other, all with the texture and taste of old socks. Sometime in the early '90s, Suze had fallen into working at a trendy restaurant in Covent Garden, where she'd had an affair with the sous chef, discovered a flair for all things culinary and soon struck out on her own.

The kettle was coming to the boil. Brian rubbed his big paws together and said, 'Right. Who's for a nice cup of Rosie Lee?'

Polly looked over to where Rowan sat, cross-legged on the floor, attacking her colouring book with large chunky crayons.

Blue was spread out next to her, waving his tail every now and then. Polly made herself a promise to start baking cakes with Rowan, offering up a silent prayer that she would be a better mother to her daughter than Suze had been to her. *Which, let's face it, wouldn't be that difficult.*

The kettle boiled, the tea was made in a beautiful large hand-crafted teapot, adorned with cockleshells. Suze had great taste; she'd give her that. She thought about her last telephone conversation with her mother.

'You really ought to think about a school for Rowan,' she'd said. 'Plan ahead. After all, they don't come cheap. How about Clifton High? I'll pay.' But Polly had never really got over her mother's insistence on buying her house and shop for her. Even though, and she had to give her her due, she never rubbed Polly's nose in it.

'She'll be going to the Steiner School,' had been Polly's reply, and she'd practically heard her mother biting her tongue over the phone.

'Shall I be Mother?' Spike was saying, causing Polly to momentarily baulk at his unintentional mother reference. Spike gave her an apologetic smile and shrugged.

'Yes please,' said Brian, in his gruff Ray Winstone voice. 'You do the honours, mate. I'm all at sixes and sevens meself. I'll be shooting off to the hospital soon.'

'Shall we come with you?' Polly made as if to rise from her chair, but Brian placed his hand on top of hers.

'I'll pop along first, if that's okay with you, Poll. I've got to see the doctor.' He gave a half-smile as a thought came to him. 'Tell you what, though, you could help by getting together some things. For Suze – umm, your mum – like. You know. Pretty things to cheer her up. Makeup, moisturiser, nightie; things like that. I wouldn't have the foggiest.'

'Of course.'

'Then I thought you could come by at visiting hour. It's between two and three, yeah?'

'You sure we can't come before then?' Polly experienced an urgent need to see and touch her mother.

'Best not. She's exhausted. And they're dead strict.'

'But...'

Spike placed his hand on her arm. 'Of course, Brian. That'll be fine.'

As Brian moved about, preparing lunch, he filled the whole space with his bulk. He had a large handsome head, and the kind of hands which looked meaty enough to wield a sledgehammer yet were as beautiful as any pianist's. He rubbed one hand across his closely shaved head. He liked to shave his head – even though he wasn't at all bald – as it kept his tight Afro curls at bay. His absent father was Nigerian, his wayward mother a Polish Jew, which meant that he looked more Middle Eastern than half black. ('Mind you, his father has given him the best half,' her mother once told her, with a lascivious wink. 'If you know what I mean?' 'Do you have to?' she'd answered back.) Brian had more or less cornered the actors market of cockney gangsters and Middle Eastern terrorists, having had several small parts in shows like *EastEnders* and *Spooks*; he'd been in several films, and he and Suze had attended swanky premiers, rubbing shoulders with the likes of Angelina Jolie, Spielberg, Harrison Ford, and once Tom Cruise ('Kept us all waiting, dear, while he did his meet and greet the crowd bit. Smacks of desperation, if you ask me,' Suze had said.)

Polly looked up from sipping her tea. Now was as good a time as any to broach the subject. 'You'd better fill us in, Brian,' she said. 'Just what was Mum doing in the water? Was it an accident or something else?'

Brian turned his doleful brown eyes on Polly. 'It's all my fault, Poll. I'll never forgive meself.' He sniffed back a tear. 'We'd had a row, see? She kept cancelling her hospital appointment. I said she was being selfish and she said she'd do it in her own good time. So I shot off to London for this audition. A television commercial. Suze didn't want me to go.' He put his head in his hands. 'She said I had no need to work as she's got more than enough money. But,' and he lifted his head, 'I won't be kept like some ponce. 'Scuse my language,' he said, glancing at Rowan, who was furiously covering a page of her book in red squiggles.

'S'all right,' said Polly.

'Yeah, well.' Brian toyed with his cup. Not taking a sip, he instead stared into its depths as if an answer could be found there. He took a deep breath, filling out his barrel chest. 'She started drinking in the morning, I suppose. I found an empty bottle of vodka and two empty wine bottles. I don't know what she was thinking of. She must have decided to have a swim. Took the rowing boat out onto the water, after lunch. But she was fully clothed, Poll. That's what I don't understand. Luckily Andy was scooting about in his new motor launch. He saw her stand up, and she must have lost her footin' or somefin' 'cos she fell right in.' He wiped his eyes.

'Oh God,' said Polly. Spike said nothing.

'So there we have it. Andy saved the day. Bloody saved my Suze, he did, Poll. Dived in head first and pulled her out. She'd swallowed a lot of water. Was nearly a gonner. Honest to God, I don't know what I'd do without her.' He began to sob, and Polly stood to place an arm about his shoulders.

*

Polly opened the door to her mother's room, feeling rather like a sneak who had no business to be in there. Suze had a separate bedroom to Brian. She insisted it was because he snored like a polar bear in hibernation, but Polly suspected it was all to do with her mother's pathological need for space. Suze had her own study downstairs too, where she liked to sit and read, and write her best-selling cookery books. She had the same set-up in her house in Notting Hill.

Suddenly tired, Polly sat on her mother's bed. The room was tastefully plain, with its old stripped pine dressing table and mahogany tall chest of drawers and matching wardrobe. The bed, an antique Victorian brass bedstead, was high, with authentic French cotton-stuffed mattress. The bed linen – finest white Egyptian cotton, with pretty lace cushions and bolsters – adding a feminine touch to its plain aesthetic. The walls were a creamy white, dotted with a few original paintings of large bright and bold flowers by a local artist her mother favoured. The floor thickly carpeted in soft beige, and on the dressing table, a tortoiseshell-backed hairbrush with its accompanying mirror and comb. White curtains billowed in a soft breeze from an open casement window, and apart from the muffled voices of Brian and Spike chatting in the kitchen below, all was quiet and soothing. Polly loved this room.

A book on her mother's bedside table caught her eye, and as she picked it up she could see it was Suze's much-loved copy of Virginia Woolf's *A Room of One's Own*. A piece of paper fluttered out from between its pages, and Polly bent to pick it up. On it, in Suze's familiar handwriting, was written the words: *I can't be a burden. I only ever wanted to be free.*

Polly stared at it. It bore no date. Was it significant? Just when had her mother written it? 'Oh, Mum,' she said out loud.

*

Having collected some of Suze's expensive satin and lace underwear, and a pair of silk pyjamas, silk kimono dressing gown and fluffy white slippers into an overnight case – plus makeup and stuff – she made her way back down to the kitchen where Brian had laid out a lunch of cold meats, cheese, salad from the garden, olives, homemade wonderfully yeasty-smelling bread, and grapes. Rowan was busily tucking in as Polly entered. Both Brian and Spike looked up.

'Everything okay?' asked Brian.

'Yes,' she said, as chirpily as she could, deciding not to tell Brian about the note.

'Good girl.'

Spike helped himself to a plate. 'Better get some of that there food before Rowan eats it all,' he said, smiling his broad smile at her, as her heart filled with – what? She wasn't sure. Gratitude? It felt more like love. *Now is so not a good time for this*, she told herself.

She stood by a chair, not pulling it out. 'Thanks for the spread, Brian.' Taking a deep breath, she turned to him and said, 'Just what is wrong with Mum? Is it cancer, do you think?'

'We don't know. Not yet. I have to talk to her oncologist. I promise I'll fill you in on all the details later, but right now I have to go. Can't eat a bleedin' thing in any case,' and he gave her a lost-boy look, as if the years had been stripped away and Polly could glimpse the little Barnardo's boy he must have been – waiting for a new mummy and daddy who never came. A lump gathered in her throat at the thought, and for the first time – because Brian was normally the strong and silent type when Suze was around – she could see what a genuinely nice bloke he was, and understand the attraction he must hold for Suze. She felt bad about all the times she'd taken the piss out of him. Reaching for his hand, she gave him a reassuring smile and felt glad – so very glad – that a clearly reliable Brian was here.

Polly wandered the garden, feeling unsettled. One minute she was angry with her mother for being such a bloody great drama queen, then worried about this lump in her breast, and the next terrified that the accident with the boat might not have been so accidental. She just couldn't get that note out of her mind.

She'd shown it to Spike, who'd said, 'Now don't go jumpin' to any conclusions, Polly. This could have been written years ago.'

'But what if it hadn't? What if she'd deliberately thrown herself into the river and this was her suicide note?'

He'd stared directly into her face. 'You won't know until you ask her.'

They were just killing time really: Spike swinging Rowan about by the arms, chasing her across the lawn. Polly sat on an old and weathered bench overlooking the estuary, shading her eyes from the sun as she watched Spike throw a chuckling, kicking Rowan high above his head, where she hung for a moment in mid-air, like an angel, before falling to be caught.

'Hallo!' – came a call.

She turned to see Andy, her mother's rescuer, sauntering up the drive. He waved a greeting at Spike and made his way over to Polly.

'How's your mother?' he asked, as he took a seat beside her.

'Fine, I think. Thanks to you, Andy. They've kept her in hospital, and we're popping along to see her any minute.'

'I won't hold you up then,' he said. 'Gave us a fright, she did. I can tell you.'

'Just what happened, Andy?' She'd met Andy – and his partner, Simon, who was a fair bit younger than him – at one of her mother's parties. Andy had the solid look of an ex-rugby player, with his Jack Wills-type clothes of chinos, deck shoes and comfortable light mustard rugby shirt.

Andy gave a sigh. 'She was lucky we were out in my boat. Simon wanted to get in some water skiing.' He gave a half-smile. 'The water's pretty flat up here. Luckily the tide wasn't in too far, or we'd have never found her in the water. I don't know how it happened. One minute she was standing up in her boat – that was what alerted me at first. The fact that she'd stood up, you see. Not a very clever thing to do.'

'No,' Polly said, in a voice so quiet that it was barely a whisper above the insects busying themselves in and out of the small hedge frilled with pink climbing roses in differing shades of pink. A wood pigeon gave a throaty coo.

'Next thing, she was in the water. Had gone under, and clearly wasn't coming up, either. We could tell she was in trouble, so we scooted across and Simon jumped in. I don't know how he found her. You can hardly see your hand in front of your face down there, it's so murky. But on the second dive, Simon located her and somehow managed to pull her up to the surface. He had a lot of trouble getting her free of the weeds and such, Polly. For some reason, she had stones in the pockets of her cardigan.'

'Right,' said Polly. *Stones. Of course she would have her pockets full of stones – like Virginia Woolf did when she committed suicide… More or less settles it, doesn't it?*

'Are you all right, old girl?'

'Yes, I'm fine, Andy. Do carry on. I want to know everything.' She placed her hand on his arm in encouragement.

'Like I said, luckily she wasn't too far out so we were able to drag her to shore – once we'd got her out of that ruddy cardigan – oh sorry.'

'No, that's fine, Andy.'

'She'd stopped breathing, you see…'

Spike, holding Rowan by the hand, slowly approached them, clearly listening to what Andy had to say.

'…Simon did a good job of resuscitating her while I called an ambulance. We thought she was a goner, Polly. She'd swallowed a great deal of water. Dreadful business.'

'Yes. I can imagine.'

The Trouble With Love

She could imagine all too well her mother under the water, weeds wafting like slow-motion gymnasts' ribbons as she turned slowly, sinking to the river's muddy bottom. The water soft as an embrace.

'Gave us all a ruddy fright! Hello there, Spike. You here with the little one?'

Spike joined Polly on the bench, pulling Rowan onto his lap. 'I'm here to give Polly moral support,' he said.

'Ah, good, good. Well, I won't take up any more of your time. No, you stay there,' he said, as she made to get up. 'Just wanted to make sure your mother was recovering well. Do give her my love. And Simon's too.'

'We will,' said Spike.

Polly gave Andy a wan smile. 'Thanks, Andy. For everything.'

30

They easily found a parking space at Exeter Hospital, and soon discovered where Suze's ward was. Polly was subdued, saying little on the journey down, while Spike attempted to keep their spirits up by chatting away to Rowan, singing songs and pointing out moo cows and the like. Polly insisted on driving, not being able to bear Spike's mishandling of her car's gears.

'Sure it's all upside down and back to front,' he'd said of the gear stick.

As the lift door in the hospital opened and the three of them headed for the nurses' station on the ward, Polly's legs gave way. It was as if she'd been zapped by some turning-legs-to-jelly ray gun; like her legs had decided to do the Funky Gibbon all on their own. She stopped to lean a hand on the wall for support.

'I've got you,' said Spike, as he grasped her under the arm to help her upright. A tricky manoeuvre since he was carrying Rowan, whose four limbs clung onto him like one of those toy monkeys Polly'd had as a child.

Rowan regarded her mother with all the confusion and

worry that a nearly-three-year-old could muster. 'Mum, Mum.'

'I'm fine now,' said Polly, smiling down at her daughter. 'Just feeling queasy. Hospitals.' She shook her head as if freeing a wasp from her hair. 'They give me the heebie-jeebies.'

'Know whatcha mean,' said Spike, 'but I can't carry you both. This one weighs a ton, as it is.' He took Polly's hand and threaded it through his other arm. 'C'mon, Polly. Best foot forward, yeah?'

'Which one is best foot?' enquired Rowan, as she leant over to peer down at Polly's feet.

Polly wouldn't have recognised her mother if she hadn't spotted Brian next to her bed. Suze was lying half propped up by pillows, and dressed in a most unflattering hospital gown, looking much like a shrunken and older version of herself. Her normally plumped and shiny-with-health-and-botox cheeks were sunken, she had dark rings around dull and slightly yellowed eyes, and her skin was white, almost powdery, as if somebody had been at it with one of those giant talcum powder puffs. Her hair – normally coiffed within an inch of its life – was greasy and flat to her head. *Things must be bad*, thought Polly, as a wave of nausea rose up from her stomach. She had an urge to turn and take flight but carried resolutely crossing the ward floor to her mother's bedside, a rictus grin fixed on her face.

'Fuckin' hell, Polly,' Suze said when she saw her. 'Will you wipe that horrible smirk off your face.' Turning to Brian, she said, 'I told you not to worry her,' and gave him an I-could-kill-you glare.

'Just as well he did,' said Polly, as she bent to embrace her mother then took the one and only chair at Suze's bedside. She needed to sit down.

'Rowan!' said Suze, holding out her arms to the tot. She turned to Polly and hissed, 'You really shouldn't have brought Rowan along. A hospital is no place for a child.'

'Ah, she's fine,' said Spike. 'Good to see you, Suze. Although not like this, obviously.' He untangled Rowan from his torso and planted an awkward kiss on Suze's cheek.

'Spike,' she said, acknowledging him with a small nod. Suze had clearly not forgiven him for – in her eyes – deserting Polly (even though she knew he'd not known about the baby). 'Come here, Rowan,' she said, turning to her granddaughter. 'Give your gran'ma a kiss.'

Oh God, it must be bad, thought Polly. *She hates being called Grandma.*

'Where's my grapes?' asked Suze.

'Oh, umm, I didn't…'

'Just pulling your leg,' said Suze, with the hint of a smile. 'My throat's far too sore to eat in any case. They had to put one of those ghastly tubes down my throat.'

'Oh Mum,' said Polly, and surprised them both by bursting into tears and throwing herself across her mother's chest.

'There, there,' said Suze, as she patted Polly on the back.

Spike had Rowan firmly by the hand as he turned to Brian and said, 'Why don't we both go and get Polly a cup of coffee, and something for this little cherub. Leave the two women to have a chat in peace, shall we?'

'Good idea,' said Brian. 'You want anything, love?' to Suze, who shook her head while cradling a still-sobbing Polly.

'I'm fine now,' she said, with a soft smile. 'Got all I need, thanks.'

Eventually Polly dried her eyes and looked about the ward. The woman in the bed opposite gave her a reassuring smile which said, *Don't worry, we're used to seeing all sorts in hospital.*

'So, why didn't you tell me, Mum? About your lump? Why?'

Suze shrugged. 'No point in worrying everyone, now, was there? Not until we knew what's what.'

'Was that what you were doing when I saw you going into the Nuffield Hospital in Clifton? Having your breast checked?'

'Now, now. Like I said, you've got enough on your plate bringing up Rowan on your own. And now that Spike's come back… well, that can't be easy, either.'

'For God's sake, Mum. This is huge. Why must you shut me out of your life?'

And there it was. The thing she'd promised herself she wouldn't say, because her mother was ill. But also the thing she had to say.

She gave her mother a steady stare. 'Come on then, Mum. You better tell me now. You owe me that much. Just what happened?' said Polly, pulling her chair closer so that people in the next beds couldn't hear.

'Just silliness on my part. I'm so sorry, darling. I got a bit tipsy, went out in the boat and fell in, that's all.'

'Fell in, my arse,' said Polly, her annoyance surfacing. 'Perhaps you'd like to explain what this is all about, then?'

From her pocket she pulled out the note she'd discovered in the book and handed it over to Suze.

'Ah,' she said, giving it a desultory look. 'You don't want to take any notice of that, darling.'

'You don't get off that lightly, Mum. Is this why your pockets were full of stones? Were you trying to do a Virginia Woolf and drown yourself? You were, weren't you?'

Her mother shifted uneasily in her bed. 'Pass me that glass of water, Polly, will you? My throat's parched. Honestly, such a fuss about nothing. I'm fine. More importantly, how are things between you and Spike? He's looking as handsome as ever, I see. Still messing with your head? What are the chances he'll—'

'Don't change the subject, Mum,' she hissed. 'Just what were you doing, going out in the boat like that? With your pockets weighted down? You meant to go in the river, didn't you? It wasn't an accident. Admit it.'

Suze took a long draught of water. 'None of that matters now.'

'It does to me!' said Polly, her eyes flashing sharp blue. 'You don't get off that easily. How could you, Mum? How could you do this to me? To Brian? He adores you. How could you think of leaving us like that? It's so bloody selfish!'

Suze leant back against her pillows and momentarily closed her eyes. 'I know. I'm sorry.' She sat up and grasped Polly's hand, her grip surprisingly strong for a woman who'd been through what she had. 'You don't know this, but my mother – your grandmother…'

'Grandma Jones? What about her? What on earth does she have to do with anything?'

'You'd be surprised the stuff passed on from mother to daughter,' said Suze, letting go of Polly's hand with an exhausted-sounding sigh.

'What?' hissed Polly. 'Are you trying to say she topped herself?'

'No,' said Suze, as she plucked at her bed sheets, seeming small and fragile once more. 'As you know, my mother died when I was ten. What you don't know is how horrible it all was. Just awful. I'll never forget it. You see, she didn't die suddenly like I said, Polly…'

No? The family story was that Suze's mother had died suddenly in her sleep. Some sort of brain virus.

'She died slowly and in horrendous pain. You see – she had breast cancer.'

Breast cancer? Things began cranking into place for Polly.

'When I found this lump…' continued Suze '…and we all know how breast cancer runs in families – so when I found it, I just knew I couldn't put everyone through what Dad and I had to endure. And the pain. I'll never forget the look in her eyes, nor the day when she gripped my hand and begged me to kill her. Me! A ten-year-old!' Tears oozed out of her eyes and down the grooves of her face to the sides of her mouth. 'I was only a kid, for Chrissake. I felt so… so… helpless. And then I was glad when she died. Doesn't that sound dreadful? But I was glad it was over. Not just for her. But for me too.' Suze turned her face away from Polly's. 'So there you have it. I've said it, and now you know.'

Polly threw her arms around her mother and held her as she sobbed. The daughter become the mother, the mother become the daughter, round and round over the generations. She knew all about cycles of shame and abuse from those long-ago days of accompanying Suze to women's groups. It had practically been fed to her as mother's milk. There and then, in that hospital, Polly vowed not to be part of that cycle. Not to be filled with fear (as her mother had) that everyone would leave her. Not to expect that as her due. She held her mother's face in her hands.

'Just because your mother had breast cancer and died horribly does not mean that the same fate awaits you, Suze. It's not written in stone. You don't even know for sure if you do have cancer, do you?'

Suze shook her head, slowly, reminding Polly so much of Rowan it nearly broke her heart. 'If it does turn out that you have cancer,' Polly continued, 'well… you're not alone, are you? And treatment is far better than it was back then, Mum. Really.'

She pulled a handful of tissues from the box and wiped Suze's face. 'Now dry your eyes. Us Jones girls are strong, yeah? Not descended from Welsh miners for nothing.'

'We're not at all.' Her mother gave her a weak grin.

'We should be,' Polly smiled back at her. 'Look, I've brought you some pretty things, and your makeup.' She placed the small case she'd packed for Suze on her bed. 'Let's draw these curtains and get your slap on so that you're ready to face the world, shall we?'

Suze looked intently into her daughter's face. 'That note, Polly. You won't tell Brian, will you?'

'No,' she sighed. 'I won't tell Brian.'

'Good. Let's keep it our secret. For the time being.'

And even though Polly believed that secrets were not a good thing between people you love, she agreed. 'Just so long as you don't do anything like this ever again.'

'I promise.'

'If you ever feel that down or desperate, you'd better call me. Or I'll kill you myself. Yes?'

'Yes, okay.'

'I'm not a kid, Mum. You don't need to protect me from life, the universe and everything.'

Suze smiled at the reference to the *Hitchhiker's Guide to the Galaxy* trilogy books she'd bought for Polly one Christmas, a long, long time ago, complete with a towel wrapped around the three of them.

'And,' continued Polly, 'in the unlikely event that it does turn out to be cancer, and you end up losing what little hair you have…'

'Oi!'

'…then we'll buy you some fabulous wigs and scarves. If Kylie Minogue and Jennifer Saunders can beat this, then you can too. It's practically de rigeur among female celebs these days…'

'Ooh. Actually I know Jen Saunders. She lives not far from us.'

'There you are then. You'll be in good company!'

'Shut up,' said Suze, good-naturedly.

*

The Trouble With Love

By the time Brian, Spike and Rowan returned, Suze was transformed. Sitting in her aubergine silk pyjamas, hair brushed and teased into its familiar short spiky style, colour painted onto her face, eyes bright from liner and mascara.

'Hello, boys,' she said to the two men with her husky voice.

'Wow, look at you,' said Brian – big cheesy grin all over his face.

Spike gave a low whistle. 'Suze, if you weren't the grandmother of my child, I'd fancy you myself.'

'Banma!' declared Rowan, a chocolate bar held firmly in her hand.

Suze beamed. She even remained cheerful when Brian said, 'I've been along to oncology and booked you in for that scan tomorrow.'

'Thank you,' she said, reaching for his hand.

Spike's mobile phone rang, and he glanced at caller ID. 'Better take this outside,' he said. 'Won't be long.'

Polly watched him go. Striding up the aisle in his skinny jeans and loose white shirt, looking like a rock star. Women's heads turned to watch as he passed, but Polly was more concerned about who was calling him. She could easily guess.

When he returned, he had a frown on his face.

'Everything all right?' Polly asked, as nonchalantly as she could.

'Girlfriend trouble?' said Suze, as Brian shot her a warning glance.

'Could say that.' The set of Spike's jaw showed that he wasn't in the mood for elaborating.

Looks like he's been Wham Bammed, thought Polly, wishing her mind wouldn't come up with such glib remarks. Especially when it wasn't in the least bit funny.

*

On their way back to the car park, Polly couldn't help herself. 'Was that Bam on the phone? Everything okay?'

'Yes, Polly,' he said, looking resolutely ahead. He carried a half asleep Rowan in his arms, her head resting on his shoulder. 'Bam was worried she couldn't reach me, is all. She'd been calling and texting, wanting to know where I was, so I thought I'd better take her call.'

'Of course,' said Polly, wishing now that she hadn't brought it up.

Spike gave her a quick sideways glance. 'She wasn't happy when I said I was with you.' He wore an inscrutable look on his face but an "oh well" tone to his voice. 'I said I'd get back to her tomorrow. I told her about Suze and that you all needed me today.'

'No, it's—'

'Polly.' He stopped in his tracks, causing her to turn and face him. 'You're the mother of my child. You'll always be family to me,' he said, holding her gaze for a moment. 'And I'll be there for you and Rowan whenever you need me. Bam has to get used to that. Besides,' he added, a slow grin now brightening his face, 'you don't get rid of me that easily.'

And although she knew she shouldn't, deep inside, a small part of her gave a little squeal of delight.

'C'mon,' he added, before she might well have said something she'd have cause to later regret. 'I think the meter's about to run out.'

31

Waiting to be cleared away were the remnants of their Indian takeaway (which Brian had brought back with him – 'Don't tell Suze, she'd kill me!'). Rowan had been tucked up for the night, and the three grown-ups were chatting away, catching up on Spike's trip to the UK so far, as Brian regaled them with his acting tales and his chances of being in a new Spielberg movie, and Polly swapped tales about her shop and recent falling-out and making-up with Mel over the whole baby thing.

'Bloody hell,' Brian said, grinning at Spike. 'You ought to consider setting up your own sperm bank, mate. I'm deadly serious. Good lookin' bloke like you. Could get serious dosh from some of those single celebs desperate to have a kid. I could introduce you to one or two. Serious.'

'No feckin' chance,' came Spike's good-natured reply. He gave Polly a bit of a stare, which she was far too tiddly to bother to try and fathom out. After their emotionally trying day, they'd been knocking back the wine as if it was going out of fashion.

'Just saying. Quick flick through a dirty mag, a little how's yer father, and Bob's yer uncle.'

Polly immediately got the giggles, ending up snorting some of her wine through her nose.

They retired to the comfortable sitting room, where earlier Brian had lit a log fire, as even though it would soon be June, there was a chill in the air. Polly sat on their old squishy sofa next to Spike, who lounged, stretching out his long legs, one arm casually laid across the back of the seat. The threesome were about to embark on their third (or possibly fourth – Polly wasn't sure) bottle of red, when Brian clearly decided it was time to start delivering some home truths.

It began gently enough, with Brian saying to Spike, 'How old are you now then, Spike?'

Polly shifted in her seat so she was more upright. 'That's a funny question. He's not a child, you know.'

Spike gently laughed. 'That's all right. I'll be thirty in October, Brian.'

'October? Same as Polly. You a Libra too?'

'Well yes.'

Brian was into New Age stuff these days, since he'd qualified as a shiatsu master to keep him occupied in between acting jobs.

'That'll explain it then,' Brian said, rather cryptically, Polly thought. 'Scales, you see,' he continued. 'Find it difficult to make decisions, do Libras, 'cos they like to weigh up the pros and cons.' He mimicked the movement of tipping scales. 'Once they do make up their minds, they stick to it. Now, Suze, she's a Leo. Like our little Rowan. Heart of a lion, the pair of them, and no shilly-shallying, either.'

Polly was all too aware of Spike's arm resting on the top of the sofa, just above her shoulders. She imagined she could feel the heat radiating between them, almost sense the electricity building, then arcing across the gap like an old Victorian experiment in a Hammer Horror movie. She wondered if her hair might be standing up on end. *Don't be daft*, she told herself, *it's too long...* Yet she didn't need to reach up to touch those telltale hairs on the back of her neck (where her hair was pinned up with a tortoiseshell clip), nor the downy ones on her arm, to know they had all pinged to attention.

'We're lost orphans, see, ain't we?' said Brian. 'Spike here lost his parents, I never really knew mine...' He stopped, and stared intently at Polly. 'Isn't it about time you pulled yourself together, Poll, and stopped blaming your mother for what happened all those years back?'

'I beg your pardon,' she said, sitting bolt upright. 'Blame her for what?' She began to feel like a petulant teenager. 'Abandoning me as a kid, you mean?'

'She feels bad about all that, truly she does.'

'I'll bet,' said Polly, not bothering to keep the sarcasm out of her voice. 'But clearly not bad enough to have stayed at home! I'd never in a million years leave Rowan.'

Brian topped up his glass and poked the logs back into life. 'All this negativity, Poll. It's not good karma.' He returned to his armchair. 'Suze felt she had no choice – at the time.'

'Yeah right. Look, no offence, Brian, but you weren't there.'

'No, I know I weren't, Poll, but Suze... well, she's told me all about it. There are things you don't know. Things she's kept from you.'

'Like what? I guess she's had enough time to concoct some sort of excuse. But let me tell you that nothing could account for what she did.'

Brian sighed. 'I know your mum would kill me for saying all this, but it has to stop. It really does. For her sake, and for yours too. She already thinks she's got cancer as punishment for what she did to you. And that's not right.'

'You may think I'm being harsh, Brian. And it's awful – we're all devastated – to even think that she might have cancer. But it's hardly my fault, is it, if she thinks it's some kind of karmic payback?' She shook her head. 'I don't believe in all that karma shit, in any case. But let's not forget that I was only ten when she left…'

'The same age as she was when her mother died…' Brian said to her, like this was of some significance – but Polly, although feeling stone-cold sober, was rather befuddled by the wine and the fire and the way the evening was going.

Spike moved his arm from behind Polly and, leaning forwards, he said to Brian, 'Is this the time and place for all this?'

'If not now, when, eh? Now seems the ideal time to me.' He turned an earnest face to Polly. 'Your father was no saint, Poll.'

'I know he's a difficult man,' Polly conceded.

'Back then, you see, your mum… well, she was young, and we all do silly things when we're young. Make decisions we later come to regret. She was only a kid herself when she had you, and she felt trapped…'

Polly snorted.

'Trapped with your father, who didn't get her one little bit. Didn't give a monkey's about how she's a free spirit an' all that…'

'Free spirit? Ha! A convenient excuse for not taking responsibility.' Polly was now sitting upright.

'She thought that what she did was for the best.'

'Best for her, you mean.'

'No. Best for you. She thought leaving you with your father was the best for you, Polly. She knew he could give you a stable home. In any case, he threatened to take her to court, do all sorts if she took you with her. She felt she had no choice. See, things were different back then. Being a single mother was more of a stigma. She had no folks to go home to. She'd run away from her dad when she was fifteen...'

'I didn't know.'

'No. She don't like talking about it. Back then, she lived in squats, or on people's floors. Then she got into art school, met your father, and before too long was pregnant. When she fell for you – well, he seemed like a good option. He played along as if he wanted the same things from life as her. But he was just acting at being an art school teacher and living an alternative lifestyle. He couldn't wait to become a civil servant – suited him down to the ground. What he really wanted was the whole wifey at home with a kid. He wanted to clip her wings, Poll. But that's not Suze. We both know that – and, well, she needed to be free.'

'So she left me behind.'

'As I understand it, she did try and see you whenever she could. She hoped you'd come live with her once she was settled in London. She begged your father. But he was havin' none of it.'

'Because he loved her! He was heartbroken when she left!' Polly could remember only too well her father crying openly, in front of her. Clinging onto little Polly, so that she felt like running and running and not stopping until she found her mum. How he'd listen out for the click of the gate, signalling that Suze had returned. How they both had.

'She did her best. But she was stony broke. She had you to stay holidays and stuff when she could...'

Yes, but you have no idea how a nomadic lifestyle affects a child, Polly thought, but didn't say. She'd never ever do that to Rowan.

'She was into drugs an' stuff too,' he said. 'She'd had issues with her own father after her mother died... He... well, you can imagine. I don't need to draw pictures, I guess, do I? Let's just say he expected her to fill her mother's shoes in more ways than one.'

Polly couldn't believe what she was hearing. Was this true? Yet she knew at some deep level that it was. Of course. Now she could understand why Suze had run away at fifteen. And presumably why she'd mistaken Jeff for the one thing she needed – a father figure. Someone to take care of her and to love her as she was. Instead she got boring Jeff, who wanted her to stay at home and look after him, just as her father had.

'She tried to stay with your dad. But she didn't love him.' He shook his head like a wounded bear. 'She's had loads of therapy since...'

'Right,' muttered Polly.

'So have I. That's how we met. At NA meetings. She's been going to them on and off for years. I guess I'm luckier than most. I'm alive, and I've come to terms with my issues through therapy. I like to think I've been good for your mother. Helped her through rehab an' stuff.'

'Yes,' said Polly, her brain carrying on doing its own sifting, own rearranging. 'I know, Brian. Suze told me. You're doing brilliantly, and I know you've helped her. Truly. You're great for her.'

'Five years clean, now. Mostly down to Suze. She's kept me on the straight and narrow. Strong, see. She's strong, Polly. Like you.'

I am? thought Polly.

'So there we have it. Thought you oughta know. Course, I dare say you and Suze will have a lot to talk about once she's over this blip. Don't look at me like that.' He smiled a slow smile. 'I'm sure it is a blip and that she'll be fine. But you see how much she's blamed herself, and has more or less taken it as her due that you'd hate her...'

'That's stupid. I don't hate her. She can be infuriating...' she said, a wry smile playing about her lips.

'She sure can,' said Brian giving a full-on grin.

'...a right pain in the arse...' Polly smiling some more, and then serious face. 'But...oh, I don't know. It's a lot to take in.'

Spike rubbed her hand in his, and she was so glad that he was there.

'And Spike, here,' said Brian, turning his affable face towards Spike. 'You're more sorted, aren't you, son? Not running off to Australia anymore, I hope.'

'Well, I...'

'Nah, I mean, not running away from our Poll here.'

'I wasn't aware that I was running away,' Spike said, a thoughtful tone to his voice. In the grate, the fire settled into a cosy orange glow.

Polly said nothing.

'You know what I'm saying,' added Brian. 'Got yer wanderlust out of the way, I expect. Must be ready to settle down yourself, eh?'

Polly wondered if Brian had acquired the skills of a spellmaster. (What are they called again? Ah yes, male witches... no, that's not it... warlocks... wonder why "war". And if they're meant to have flowing locks – if so, Brian hardly fits the bill...) Polly was feeling all glowy from the warm fire as the wine finally wove its soporific effect on her.

'Maybe I am done with wandering,' said Spike. 'Maybe I could be ready.'

Polly gave him a sideways glance, her heart thundering in her chest, but Spike was staring into the depths of the fire. *Ah, you silly twit. With Bam, he means, doesn't he? So Bam was right. He is about to ask her to marry him. And I can never tell him how I feel.*

Brian cut across her thoughts. 'There's one other thing about your mother, Polly. She worries about you all the time, you know.' Polly could feel herself bristle. 'Suze hates to see you struggling on your own. Would it hurt to let her give you money now and then? All she's trying to do is help.'

'I like to stand on my own two feet,' Polly said, feeling decidedly uncomfortable getting into all this with Brian.

'There it is,' he said. 'That independent streak you've got from your mum. But ask yourself this, Polly. If you had more money than you knew what to do with, wouldn't you want to use it to secure Rowan's future?'

Well, yes, she would, thought Polly. That's right. She would. Slowly she began to nod her head.

'After all, if she doesn't give it to you now, the taxman will only take it from her when she's dead.'

A heavy silence fell, all solemnly acknowledging that Brian had used the dreaded "d" word.

'Not that it will come to that – not just yet,' said Brian. 'Not while I'm here to look after her. We all need looking after, Poll. You know – like that song – I love this song –' and to Polly and Spike's immense surprise, Brian burst into a short rendition of "Someone to Watch Over Me". He had a fine, surprisingly soulful voice. He beamed at them both – 'I often sing it to Suze. She loves it.'

Polly got to her feet to lean over and give Brian a hug. 'Mum's very lucky to have you, Brian.'

'On the contrary, twinkle,' he said, 'I'm very lucky to have her. And I intend to keep her, an' all.'

Right then, Polly was convinced that Brian would move heaven and earth for her mother. She felt envious, and ashamed that she did so. Outside an owl screeched.

'So, changing the subject here. If you two ain't together, how about this Max fella? Might he be a likely candidate, Poll? For your happy ever after?'

'Honestly, Brian!'

'Just askin', like.'

'No, he's not my "happy ever after" as you put it,' she said, thinking how, if she tucked her legs up underneath her, she'd

The Trouble With Love

be close enough to snuggle into the crook of Spike's arm – but couldn't. He was off limits, she knew. 'We're over.'

'That's sad, Polly. Are you sure you're not doing your own running away? Too scared to let yourself love?'

Polly was stung. If this was Brian all "touchy-feely", she might well prefer his more usual "strong and silent". He didn't know her well enough to offer up such an opinion of her.

'You know, Suze does understand where your hostility towards her comes from. But hasn't it been long enough? I'm just saying this because I love you both, and it breaks my heart to see you sniping at each other. Course, she thinks it's all she deserves, but I reckon it's time you let her off the hook, don't you?'

'Brian, I know you mean well, but I'm not sure…'

'Perhaps own your own problems with your failure of trust? Why not let love in, Polly?'

Ah, but once she had, and Spike had broken her heart. Now Brian had not only brought back the pain of her mother leaving but also the loss of the one and only man she could ever truly love. Tears threatened to fill her eyes, and without further ado, Polly rose to her feet and made for the French windows.

'I've gone too far, haven't I?' said Brian.

She opened the doors and stepped outside. Behind her she heard Spike say, 'Leave her, Brian. She'll be fine. Give her some space.'

*

Polly wandered down towards the river, letting the night weave its magic, as she came to stand on the lawn, where large trees lurked at the edges and a breeze rustled their leaves. She looked up at a sky dark with lighter-coloured clouds daubed across its surface, like a 1980s paint effect: downstream the riverbank was dotted here and there with the odd building, each with one or two lights switched on. They cast their shadows through the mist, giving a ghostly glow reminiscent of gas streetlamps and a gentler age. Polly couldn't decide if the glimmering expanse of estuary was all water or part wet mud as lighter runnels ribboned its surface. In the near distance came the call of a bird returning to its roost.

Turning, she sensed first and then saw Spike walking across the lawn towards her, the white flashes on his Converse trainers bright.

'Watch out for the – whoops!' she called, too late, as he'd not noticed the slope, and what with the soles of his shoes having little to no grip, he slipped and slithered and with a 'Whoah!' slid right into her, sending them both tumbling to the ground.

Polly managed to sit up first. 'You're just not kitted out for the country, are you?'

'Oh, and you are?' he said, pointing to her Ugg boots. 'Out here in yer slippers.'

'I'll have you know Kerry Katona speaks very highly of them!'

'Oh, is it Kerry Katona, now?' he said. 'Only I don't read *Heat* magazine these days, Poll, not since...'

Not since we were together, hung in the air between them.

'C'mon,' he said, breaking the spell as he got to his feet. He held out his hands. 'You don't want to be stayin' down there or you'll get the collywobbles.' He pulled her to her feet. 'Whoops-a-daisy.'

She brushed her skirt down, and they both stood side by side, looking out over the night scene.

'Beautiful, isn't it?' she said in a half-whisper.

''Tis from where I'm standing.' He was gazing down at her, and her heart leapt into a gallopy-gallop. She could just make out his smile in the light spilling through the French windows.

'Sorry about all that,' she said. 'You know. Inside. Brian and whatnot.'

'Don't be.'

'Dragging you into our family stuff.'

She heard him sigh. 'Have I not told you before, Polly?' he said, looking up at the sky. 'We have Rowan now. Whatever happens, we are family.'

She couldn't stop it, but a quick burst of Sister Sledge's "We Are Family" jumped into her head, and she giggled softly.

'Polly?' he said, looking at her with an intensity she could feel but not see. 'What are you sniggering at? Are you drunk, now?' He had a cheeky tone to his voice, too.

'A bit squiffy perhaps,' she said, and hiccupped.

'What are you like? C'mon here.' He stepped forwards. 'You must be freezing.' He pulled her to him, wrapping her in his embrace as she savoured his unique Spike smell, as warm and comforting as toast. 'What am I going to do with you?'

She looked up into his face. Into his gorgeous, manly Spike face, and softly whispered, 'Make love to me.'

That was when he kissed her. She closed her eyes, knowing that this was what she'd been waiting for all these weeks since his return. He took her by the hand and led her inside, up the stairs, and outside the door to his room.

'What about Rowan?' she said.

He opened Polly's bedroom door so they could both see that Rowan was sound asleep. 'She'll be fine,' he said, gently closing the door.

'How about Brian?'

Spike put his fingers to his lips, and in the quiet they could both hear Brian's snores emanating from his room along the landing. 'Out for the count,' whispered Spike.

He turned to face Polly, gazing at her as though feasting his eyes. 'You never looked lovelier.'

'Talk about cheesy,' she said, feeling bashful.

'Are you teasing a man when he's opening up his heart to yeh?' he said. 'I've Jammie Dodgers in me bag.'

'You trying to lure me in?'

He took her hand once more. 'I am. If you're sure about this.' And she nodded.

Then they were inside his room. In the dark half-light. The kind of light you get in the countryside when there are no streetlamps but a bright moon.

'I suppose you'll want to talk?' he said, kissing her neck and taking her breath away. 'Discuss what's going on here, with us?'

'No,' she half whispered. 'Later perhaps.'

He led her towards the bed.

'They do say, don't they,' Polly was prattling, nervously, 'that when there's death – not that Suze – not that Mum is going to die, touch wood, but you know, I heard on Radio 4 once that it makes you horny… something about nature's need to procreate…'

'Will you stop your babbling, Polly,' said Spike, with more than a twinkle in those Irish eyes of his. 'Oh. Hang on. You're not after me sperm again, are you?'

She thumped him on the arm. 'Don't be daft,' she said.

'Good.' His mouth was on hers, and as they kissed she felt herself go, as if she was falling, falling down Alice's rabbit hole, as she savoured his taste, his mouth. She arched her back and he nibbled her neck, just up by her ears where she liked it, his hands reaching up under her dress…

'What the…?' he said, as he encountered her Spanx knickers. 'Big Bridget Jones pants?'

'Shut up.' She unbuckled his belt as they both fell back on the bed.

'I don't have any condoms,' he said.

'It's okay,' she answered, 'I've just had my period. It'll be fine.'

They were making love. Not fucking. It was beyond that, beyond the big-dick-show-off-pounding that Max was so fond of. Instead this was so tender that at one point, Polly began to cry.

'Don't cry, Polly,' he said.

'I can't help it.'

He covered her mouth with soft kisses as he moved inside her; Polly was close to coming... she was going to come... but Spike slowed right down, deliciously taking his time, resting on his elbows as he smiled into her face. 'Not yet. There's no rush.' As they moved together, Polly thought of how she so wanted this – this moment – this feeling – this whole giving of herself – languorous, hot honey breaths; short, sharp gasping; fingers entwined, turning, smooth and slippery – as finally she came in a burst of everything, and felt him come inside her too.

'I love you, Polly,' he murmured, and she thought she might explode with happiness, her face wet with soundless tears, which he wiped away with his thumbs.

'I love you too,' she whispered.

'Well, that's all right then,' he said. 'So long as you respect me in the morning.' And she thought how there was nothing more wondrous than the smile on his face. She rubbed the stubble that was coming through on his chin. If she was a cat, she might well have purred.

He touched the side of her face, next to her right eye. 'I love this part of your face after we make love. Right there. You look so happy.'

She had to say it. 'I thought you loved Bam.'

He leant on one elbow. 'Not like I love you, Polly. It sounds terrible, I know, but I think I must have needed Bam to get over you.'

Could that be true?

'I couldn't stop thinking about you, Polly, and what might have been had I stayed.'

'You couldn't?'

With his finger, he brushed a lock of her hair from her eyes. 'Why do you think I kept my boat here in Bristol?'

'Umm, renting it to Leo?'

'Because, silly, I had an excuse to return.'

'But—?'

'No more ifs and buts, Polly. We've got tonight. Let's consider all the rest tomorrow, because…' he added, with a broad lascivious smile '…I've got some energy left, and it would be a shame to waste this.' He pulled back the covers.

'Shame indeed,' she said, reaching for him.

She must have fallen asleep, as she woke with a start and saw that he was gone. A note on the pillow next to her read:

Polly, don't worry about Rowan. I'm sleeping in your room tonight so you won't be disturbed. Enjoy your sleep, gorgeous.

Spike xxx

A bright moon shone through her window: the sort of moon you could wish on, to make dreams come true.

32

Polly woke to the chirping of birds, and a soft breeze tapping the branch of a rambling rose against her windowpane. Her mouth was dry so she poured herself a glass of water from the bedside jug and drank its cool, slightly metallic taste. She didn't feel tired, even though… she remembered with a slow smile … even though they'd made love three times before she drifted off into a sleep as soft as feather eiderdown. She stretched out, languorous and loose. She felt strong, and alive, ready to face the fallout that would come once Spike had broken the news to Bam: the news that he and Polly were meant to be together. She wouldn't think about Bam now. She did like her. Truly. Even though she'd called her Wham Bam, she thought, ashamed now.

Still, Mel had been right all those years ago when she said that Spike and Polly were like two swans, mating for life. Oh, they might have been separated by misunderstanding and oceans, but he'd come home. Home to Polly. Everything was going to be all right now. They'd sort it. The two of them.

She touched the pillow where his head had lain just a few

hours earlier, and hugged herself with delight, reliving his touch, his kisses, his… oh, she couldn't wait to see him again.

A soft tap came on her door. She sat up and zhushed her hair, in case it was Spike – who else could it be? She didn't want him to see her with bird's nest hair.

'Come in, lover boy,' she said, and Brian opened the door, cup of tea in hand. He gave her a sheepish grin.

'Whoops,' she said, pulling the sheet around her as she sat up.

'Someone had a good time last night,' he said with a wink. 'Here y'are.' He placed a cup by her bedside. 'Nice cuppa Rosie Lee.'

'Thanks, Brian,' she said, unable to keep from beaming back at him – because today she was happy with the whole wide world.

'I'm gonna be shootin' off soon. Gonna take your mum to have her scan and whatnot done, an' then I'm bringing her home. Where she belongs.'

'That's great, Brian. Can I wait here at the cottage until she returns?'

'Of course you can, Poll. She'd like that.' He gave her a light kiss on the forehead, and made as if to leave. 'Oh,' he added, turning to face her, 'and don't you go worrying about that stones-in-the-pocket thing. Andy rang and told me all about it. Me and Suze are going to work through things. It'll be fine. Don't you go worrying yourself on our account, Princess.'

'Thanks Brian.'

'Means the world to her, having you here.'

'She's lucky to have you, Brian.'

And if he could have blushed, Polly was pretty certain that he would have.

*

The Trouble With Love

When Polly came downstairs, the breakfast things had been cleared away, and Rowan was outside running around on the lawn with Blue. Spike turned as she entered the kitchen, but he didn't look her full in the face – that was the first thing she noticed.

'Would you like some toast?' he asked, his back turned as he slipped two slices of bread into the Dualit toaster.

'Yes thanks,' she said, puzzled by his seeming distance. Did this mean he was having second thoughts? Had she got it all wrong? Was last night... Oh God, please don't let last night have been a mercy shag because he felt sorry for her. A knot of panic formed in her stomach. Please no. She could still smell him on her skin, on her hair. She hadn't showered yet as she wanted to keep the traces of him with her for as long as she could. Daft, she knew. She'd dressed carefully in a dress covered with sprigs of summer flowers. She knew it flattered her curves. Her hair was pinned up, with tendrils falling ever-so-accidentally-on-purpose, giving it a sexily tousled look. Her eyes had needed only a slick of mascara, so bright they were, and her lips the merest touch of red to highlight where he'd kissed her, mussing up her mouth, his stubble making her lips, her chin, ever so slightly raw. Hell, she looked good. Didn't she?

She moved towards him, longing to be held in his arms, but instead he put out his hands to stop her.

'I've had a phone call from Bam,' he said, letting his hands drop by his side.

She swallowed hard. 'Oh.' Not knowing quite how to react.

'I'd switched my phone off. She's been trying to reach me.'

'Right.' The next words, she knew, were going to decide their fate. The next words were going to be very, very important. She stood, ready to receive them.

'There's no easy way to say this.' She watched his Adam's apple bob as he swallowed. 'Bam's pregnant.'

Polly grasped the back of a chair. Momentarily baffled. These weren't the words she'd been expecting at all. She'd guessed – of course she had – that something was up, from the phone call he'd received from her in the hospital… but never in a million years would she have guessed… Tears pricked her eyes. A baby. She pulled out a chair to sit down.

'Are you… is that why she called you at the hospital?'

'No! No, of course I didn't have any idea then.'

'Is she sure?' Polly's voice was barely above a whisper.

'Yes. She insists she is.' He took a deep breath, shooting Polly a quick glance. 'She went to the chemist this morning – to get one of those there kits.' He shook his head. 'I don't know how on earth it happened.'

'In the usual way, I suppose,' she couldn't help saying. Now she was wondering if last night had been all about the sex and nothing else. Things were said, it's true, but they'd both been more than a little drunk. She'd meant what she said. But was he now regretting… and if so, what now?

She steeled herself for what must come.

'No. I don't understand,' Spike was saying as he paced the kitchen. 'We were so careful. I was careful.' He ran his fingers through his hair, which flopped forward in his eyes.

'Did you not use condoms?' she said. Unconsciously, she rubbed her own belly.

'Of course I used condoms, Polly.'

Into Polly's mind flashed the memory of Bam's visit to her in the shop. Of Bam saying, 'He will ask me to marry him, you know,' and of that self-satisfied smirk she'd had on her face. Had she planned this? Would Bam do something like prick tiny little holes in condoms with a fine needle? She'd heard tell of determined women taking desperate measures like that. But surely not Bam. Polly stared at Spike, not trusting herself to speak.

'I have to go to her, Polly.'

'To Kettering?' she said, not knowing where the fuck Kettering was.

'It's in Northampton, Polly,' he said with half a smile, as if he'd read her mind. 'Up North.'

She resisted the urge to go – *Duh.*

'Mummy! Daddy!' Rowan was standing in the doorway, a clod of earth in her left hand. 'I got a worm!'

Spike collected her into his arms and nuzzled her neck. 'Daddy has to go, darling.'

Rowan twisted in his arms as she reached out for her mother, dropping the earth-plus-worm onto the floor in the process. They all turned as they heard a car crunch up the gravel and toot its horn.

'That'll be my taxi,' he said. 'I'm catching a train.'

'But you can't catch a train,' said Polly. Thinking, *What a daft thing to say*, but she couldn't think straight.

He opened his arms, folding both mother and daughter in his tight embrace as he kissed Polly's head. 'I'll be back,' he said to Rowan, who clearly had no idea what this all meant.

Instead she gave him a wide grin. ''Kay, Daddy.'

'I have to go, Polly. You do see that, don't you?'

'Of course,' she said, unable to quite fathom what was unfolding.

'I'll call you. I promise. Soon as I can. I meant every word I said last night.'

'What? About your trainers being wet from the grass?' she said, unable to not tease in moments of crisis.

He gave her a long wide smile – the sort that only he could ever give her – then kissed her hard on the lips, and was gone. Leaving Polly to stare at the huge Spike-sized hole he'd left behind.

When Brian's car pulled up, Polly and Rowan were there to greet it. Polly watched as her mother gingerly got out of the car. Polly had been going for a welcoming smile, but she clearly failed, as the first thing Suze said was, 'Whatever is the matter, darling? Where's Spike?' Suze and Brian exchanged a glance.

'Oh, Mum' was all Polly could manage as she tried not to cry – Rowan holding tight onto her skirts.

'Hey,' said Brian, as he placed his arm about Polly's shoulder and gave it a squeeze, 'let's get Suze indoors first, shall we? Then you can tell us all about it.'

'Yes, yes, of course.' Polly took her mother's arm to help her walk, with Rowan scampering in front of them, then skipping to the side, so that in the end Polly had to tell her, 'Careful you don't knock Grandma over.'

Suze patted Polly's hand. 'That's all right, love. Let her be.' She stopped for a moment to catch her breath.

'Are you sure you're all right, Mum?' asked Polly.

'Yes, yes,' insisted Suze.

Polly was struck by how thin her mother looked, and how frail. She felt a rush of love for her, and would have liked to pick her up and carry her indoors herself, if Suze would have let her. But she knew how fiercely independent her mother was. It was a measure of how weak she felt that she was leaning on Polly at all.

'The radiographer said everything looks benign,' said Suze. 'So that's good. I'm to see the doctor next week for a follow-up.' She managed a smile at her daughter. 'Silly me, getting into a tizz.' They reached the large oak-panelled hall, where Polly helped her mother off with her jacket and hung it on the wooden coat stand.

'Put the kettle on, will you, Brian,' said Suze, as she turned to Polly. 'Is Spike not here, then?' Brian led Rowan to the kitchen.

The Trouble With Love

'No, Mum,' Polly said. 'He's left to catch a train. He's had to go back.'

Suze allowed Polly to usher her into one of the chairs, and once Polly was satisfied that her mother was settled, she added, 'It's all gone horribly wrong, Mum.'

'It can't be as bad as all that, surely,' said Suze, as she leant forwards to gently wipe a tear from her daughter's eye. 'You'd better tell me what happened. Brian thought it looked like the two of you might get back together.'

'No chance of that now.'

As a blackbird sang in a tree outside, and the sun shone down on bees buzzing in and out of flowers nodding in the midday, Polly told Suze the bare bones of what had occurred: that she'd finished with Max and thought maybe Spike had feelings for her, but that he'd had to go and be with Bam.

'But why, darling? Why did he have to go?'

Polly sighed. She wasn't yet ready to tell her mother everything, about sleeping with Spike or about the baby. Instead she said in a small voice, 'Can I stay here with you for a couple of days? If that's fine by you? I want to make sure you're going to be okay and… well, I can't face going back to Bristol just yet.'

'Of course you can stay.' Suze appeared delighted even though she was clearly exhausted.

'I don't want to intrude or anything,' said Polly. 'You must promise that if you're too tired or anything, you will say.'

'Don't be daft. Of course you must stay. Sounds like you could do with a nice break. That's all settled, then, isn't it, Brian?' She smiled up at Brian, who beamed back at her as if his horse had just romped home in first place at Ascot.

'Yes, Polly. You stay with us. Long as you like. Is what family's for, innit?'

That night, Polly dreamt she rowed out into the estuary, where fish swim and eels snake in and out of thick weed. There, in the middle of the river, she checked her pockets were full – not of stones, but of sweets – as she slid over the side of the boat and into the water's embrace, where she spun slowly, eyes open, hair billowing around her, like a latter-day Ophelia, spinning down, down, through the green and clear water. She was not fearful, but calm, and then up ahead, there it was – the hand of a small blonde mermaid reaching out to her: Rowan, smiling like an older version of herself. They held hands and together kicked up, up to the surface.

33

Staying with her mother wasn't wholly idyllic. It wasn't like Polly's mother had undergone a personality transplant or something overnight. That kind of fantastical transformation only ever happened in movies, where the shrewish, errant mother turns into an angelic Susan Sarandon-type mommy. Still, Suze didn't prod and pry over what had happened between Polly and Spike, and she was grateful for that. Instead, over the course of the next few days, it was Polly who was transformed as she began to forgive her wayward mother, as they talked, and shared more of their early stories. Polly glimpsed how a young and inexperienced Suze – all alone, apart from Jeff, and with no parents to speak of – might have felt unable to give her young daughter, Polly, the stability which Jeff, with his steady job and then his reliable (if dull) wife, Gillian, could provide.

'God, d'you remember those awful macramé wall hangings Gillian used to make?'

'Yeah. What was that all about?'

'You were lucky you didn't have years of knitted gifts and handmade dangly jewellery.'

'Oh dear, we shouldn't laugh. Poor Gillian.'

No, Suze hadn't undergone a total makeover. She still seemed determined to interfere in Polly's life and lecture her on her mothering skills – but Polly didn't mind so much.

'Oh, I wouldn't do that, darling,' etc.

Yes, they were on far better terms than before, and instead of Polly flouncing off or suffering in silence, she was able to say (with a degree of good-naturedness), 'Thanks, but that's the way I do it, okay?'

'Fair enough.'

Wonders would never cease. There were even times when she silenced her mother with a back-off look, and no accompanying stand-up row ensued!

Brian gave to wandering about grinning from ear to ear, so happy to see 'his girls' getting along. Plus, he was thoroughly relishing the role of step-grandfather, as he took Rowan off in his old black Mercedes car, on trips to the seaside, or to the local wildlife park, or for a walk in the woods. 'We was looking for fairies,' he'd said, big grin on his face. 'No. Not that sort,' he added, before either Suze or Polly could crack a joke. Or else he'd take Rowan to the riverside to practise skimming stones. Rowan – who'd taken to calling a delighted Brian "Ban'dad Byan" – would return from their trips happy, muddy, and with a smile that matched Brian's, while he took every opportunity to hoist her up onto his shoulders and carry her about, like St Christopher toting the Christ child safely across the water.

All of which allowed time for Polly and Suzy to chill out, relax in the garden or cook cakes (Suze). Polly would read or pen lines of poetry while Rowan and Suze took their respective afternoon naps. If it wasn't for the turmoil and uncertainty of what was going on with Spike, she'd have felt even more refreshed and healed than she did. Still, bridges were being mended with Suze, and Polly was appreciating and – yes – enjoying her time spent in both Suze and Brian's company.

One night the adults sat down to a simple hearty lamb tagine cooked by Brian. He'd had to order Suze out of the kitchen as he would broach no interference from her.

'Suze! Stop sniffin' around, will ya! Get outa here!' he'd said, shooing her into the sitting room.

'Don't forget the coriander!' she said, standing in the doorway with her hands on her hips.

'Oi!' He turned her round and playfully slapped her bottom. 'You let me worry about that. You girls just wait in there. Lookin pretty.' Brian gave Suze a full kiss on the lips while she made a grand show of pushing him away.

Watching from her vantage point of an armchair, Polly enjoyed their interplay and couldn't help but feel an ache for Spike. *Oh bugger.* She warmed her toes in front of the stone fireplace, where a couple of logs smouldered away in a wrought iron basket, as Suze took her place in the chair opposite her.

'Now,' began Suze, 'I know I promised not to bring up Spike—'

'Oh, Mum...'

'But listen, darling. You've been moping about this place for days now. You need to do something. From the moment I saw you two in the hospital together... well, any fool with eyes in their head can see that you are obviously in love with each other – and Brian agrees with me. What I can't understand is what on earth the problem is, then. He must prefer you to that Bam creature – I mean, what a stupid name! And so why did he go rushing off like that?'

It was no use. Suze had that determined set to her jaw. She'd wheedle it out of Polly one way or the other, so she might as well tell her. Part of her wanted Suze to know, in any case. If she was wholly honest with herself, it was probably a major reason for staying on.

'Very well,' she said, her tummy responding in a gurgling way to the glorious smells emanating from the kitchen. 'I just hope that Brian's not ready to set the table just yet. This could take a while…'

As the sun set low over the estuary and the shadows outside the window edged across the lawn, Polly began at the beginning: from when Spike returned to Bristol with Bam, right up to Bam's bombshell and Spike's departure "oop north" to Kettering.

At one stage, Brian entered quietly, turned on the table lamp, added another log to the fire and tiptoed out again. The lamplight spilled its orange and cosy glow onto Labrador Blue, who sat outside, watching a goose fly overhead as it honked and swooped across the estuary. Further downriver, a pub nestled in an inlet where weekenders from Bristol, Exeter and further afield kept their boats. They'd be sitting outside in their fleeces and anoraks, tired and content from the combination of a day spent messing about on the water and the intoxication of fresh sea air and nutty real ale; sitting at those weathered wooden trestle tables as the gaily painted pub sign swung ever-so-slightly whenever a gust of wind blew upstream.

'A baby, you say?' Suze took an iron from the companion set and poked at the fire.

'Yes.'

'That changes everything, doesn't it?'

Polly didn't know quite what she'd hoped for. Magic words? A mother's solution that would make everything all right?

Instead her mother had confirmed what Polly already knew. She'd missed the boat and now fate had taken a hand and thrown a baby into the mix. What a mess.

'Don't you worry,' said Brian, as he poked his head around the door. 'I got faith in that boy. He'll sort what's the right thing to do. Things'll work out for the best, you'll see. Now cheer up, there's a good girl. Dinner's served, so come on, gals. To the kitchen.'

But Polly wasn't cheered, because she knew that Spike would indeed know the right thing to do. And the right thing must be for him to stay with Bam and the new baby. No getting away from it. That was the only thing he could do.

In her rush to get down to Devon, Polly had forgotten her mobile phone charger and her battery had gone flat the first day. This meant she couldn't telephone Spike even if she wanted to – which she assured herself she didn't. She'd called Donna a few times from Suze's landline, to check that all was okay at the shop. And – yes – she had rather been hoping that Spike might have tracked down Suze's number by calling Donna or something – but no such luck. She gleaned from Donna that Mel had called. 'Be a doll, babe, and call her mobile to let her know that I'm fine and will be back soon,' Polly asked her.

'No need to rush back, babes,' assured Donna. 'Me and Jade have it all well under control.'

Great, thought Polly. *It's only when you go away that you discover the world carries on perfectly well without you. What a depressing thought.*

Crash! 'My God, Donna. What was that noise in the background...?'

She could hear Donna calling out to someone, 'You dozy mare!' and then back on the phone line. 'S'all right, Polls. Everything's cool. Just chillax. Gotta run. Bye!'

Click.

Polly went online a couple of times to collect and send some work-related emails – and, yes, to check Facebook for anything new on Spike's wall. But no. There was no status update like – Bam's having a baby! – or any other breaking news.

'Oi, turn that off!' Brian barked, when he caught her – nearly making her jump out of her skin as he wagged his big sausage-like finger at her in pretend-telling-off mode.

'Never mind all that going online, darling,' her mother said, walking up behind them both. 'You've had a nasty shock, and you need a rest. Come on. Off. Off.'

So yes. By and large, Polly was somewhat surprised (and perhaps even a little miffed) that the world and her friends could manage perfectly well without her.

In the end, Polly stayed for ten days. Most of her daytimes (thanks to Brian taking Rowan here, there and everywhere) were spent wandering around the grounds (which even possessed a small wood and a disused tin mine); writing poetry or drawing sketches (something she'd not done since a brief stint at evening art classes). The evenings were spent in a companionable way with Brian and Suze as they shared stories. Polly and Suze even laughing at the "radical" old days, when Suze would drag her along to protest rallies and peace camps.

'Happy days,' smiled Suze. And Polly – now things were more sorted between them – was able to look back fondly too.

'Do you remember that woman? You know, the one with the turquoise dreadlocks?'

'God, yes, River.'

'She certainly was wet,' said Polly, and they both giggled as they told Brian about wet River, and her propensity to fart loudly after a supper of lentil stew, making their communal tent a no-go area.

'We had to bunk down in someone else's teepee,' her mother said.

Most nights, Rowan was allowed to stay up later than normal. 'What harm can it do?' Suze had said.

Brian had shot her a warning glance. 'That's up to Poll, Suze. Don't go interfering.'

'It's fine,' Polly had said. 'Rowan loves being around you two.'

Then one day Suze announced, 'That's quite enough lazing about for me. My publisher won't wait forever. Brian, give me my iPad. I have to get back to work.'

'Now, Suze, babe…' began Brian, who'd hidden Suze's iPad for her own good. Polly could see any protests on Brian's part were futile – and that sadly her interlude with Suze was coming to an end. She had hoped to eke it out for a full two weeks.

Suze said, 'You're more than welcome to stay another day or so, darling.'

But Polly felt the pull for home. Time to return to Bristol.

*

'Now drive safely,' Suze said, as she peered through the window of the red Megane Scenic she'd insisted Polly take. Polly's own 2CV had refused to start, and both Suze and Brian had put up a united front, insisting that Polly have Suze's car.

'I'm bored with it in any case,' Suze said. 'Seriously, you'd be doing me a favour. I'm desperate to buy a new one. A nice sport BMW this time.'

'I'd be happier too,' said Brian. 'Is not safe for you and the little 'un to be driving around in that old tin can. I dunno why your mother hasn't given you a proper car before now.'

She had tried, but Polly loved her car. Still, she couldn't deny motorway driving in it could be a nightmare. Her beloved Ruby (her car's name – all 2CVs have to have a name, she'd informed Brian) didn't like driving in the rain – she had such thin tyres – and on motorways Polly had to struggle with the wheel in order to avoid being sucked across the lanes by the slipstream of any overtaking lorry.

'I give in,' she eventually agreed. 'Anything to shut you two up.'

'You know it makes sense. And,' said Brian, 'I quite fancy 'avin' a go at stripping dahn your little car an' driving it across the fields an' that. Be great for pickin' up an' deliverin' stuff – less damaging to the grass than a Range Rover. After all, that's what those little French cars were designed for.'

So it was settled. Her old car officially put out to grass, like some vehicular equivalent of Black Beauty, and Polly and Rowan set off for Bristol in relative (well, for Polly at least) luxury. Bowling along the M5, with Bristol drawing closer, Polly and Rowan singing along to Abba's "Take a Chance on Me", as she wondered if Spike would change *his* mind and take a chance on her.

Oh great, thought Polly. Life's little irony not lost on her, as she thought of Spike and whether or not he'd changed his mind – and if so, in which (or whose) direction?

34

First things first. She'd charge her phone and then call Mel.

'Where the fuck have you fuckin' been?'

'You know where I've been,' Polly sighed. I mean, she loved Mel, but honestly… sometimes…

'Yeah, but no phone call?'

'I forgot my charger.'

'Couldn't you have used your mother's phone?'

'Battery dead? Duh… No numbers?' Polly didn't feel much like explaining to Mel that she'd also been glad of a break from being constantly in touch with everyone. To have some time to think. To let things sift through her mind.

'How are things with you and Fen?'

'Fabulous, Polly. We're all sorted now, and – well – we might have a candidate for the honour of sperm donor.'

'Who?'

'Fen's brother! She's asked him and he's agreed – on principle, anyway. We're all going to meet up in a couple of weeks to talk it through. Don't you think that makes perfect sense? True, it'll be a bit weird. Still, it's the closest we'll get to having our own biological child together. God, I'm so excited. Aren't you pleased for me? Spike will be off the donor list.'

'Yes, of course I'm pleased for you, you doughnut.'

'So how did things go with your mum? How long did Spike stay for? Did you get a chance to speak to him? Properly?'

Where to start? she thought. 'Mel, are you free? Can you come over? You can bore me rigid about your loved-up trip with Fen, and I can fill you in on everything that happened in deepest Devon.'

'Ooh. Something happened, didn't it? Right. Just finishing supper and then I'll be right over!'

Polly and Rowan had picked up a McDonald's at Gordano service station, and after Polly had thrown the cartons into the bin and called Mel, she checked her phone for any voice or text messages. Several missed calls. Dialling 121, she hoped that at least one of those voicemail messages would be from Spike. In the end, there were two.

The first one said:

Polly. I've arrived safely. Look, I can't talk as I'm staying at Bam's parents and I've just sneaked out into the garden... [muffle muffle]. What? [Calling to someone else.] Yeah, sure, in a minute. [Back onto the telephone.] I'll call you soon, Polly. Kiss Rowan for me. Oh, and... [phone line dead].

Second message:

I've just got back from the hospital, Poll. Look. I'm coming back next Saturday. It's the earliest I can get away. Damn. Gotta go... Yes, yes, just coming. Saturday, Polly. I... well, you know. [Click.]

Polly hung up and stared at her mobile. What did all that mean? Hospital? Was he okay? What did he mean, coming Saturday? Was that *this* Saturday, or Saturday next week? Oh God, if it's this Saturday then that's the same day as the screening of Vanessa's film starring yours truly. Polly tapped in her message code once more to listen to them again. Nope. None the wiser.

Still looking at her phone as if it was a traitor, she let the other messages in her voicebox play.

The first one began:

Polly? It's me, Max. Look, this whole Sarah thing. It was a mistake. She means nothing to me. You're the one I love. Surely we can work something out. Ben keeps asking when he can play with Rowan. It's killing me. Ring me. Text me. Bye.

She sighed. The nerve of that man.

Next message:

Polly, what do I have to do? I called round the shop, and Donna wouldn't say where you've gone. C'mon, babe. We're good together. You know we are. Yeah? Don't give up on us. This is silly.

Unbelievable.

And the next and final one:

Polly, Polly [clearly drunk and slurring, sound of pub in background], *don't be such a stuck-up cow. Sorry, sorry.* [Singing Lionel Richie now...] *"I just called to say..."* [Then to someone else – presumably in the pub.] *What? Ah, fuck off, you cunt.* [Into phone.] *Not you, Polly... I... Ah bollocks.*

'Mummeee!' cried Rowan, tugging at her mother's skirts. 'Want Daddee. Where's Daddy?'

She gazed down at her beautiful child, with her big eyes and that dimple on her right cheek. 'He's gone to see Bam's mummy and daddy, darling.' Rowan had never looked more like Spike. 'C'mon,' said Polly, 'it's time to get you washed and ready for bed.'

Later, after more 'Where's Daddy?'s, and a reading of *Spot the Dog*, followed by two *Meg and Mog* books, Rowan was finally asleep. Sneaking out of her child's room, Polly tried Spike's phone, but it went straight through to voicemail.

Spike? she said, leaving a message, *I've only just picked up your messages. Sorry, my battery had run out. Call me.*

She wandered back downstairs to her kitchen, wondering if and when he'd call. Even though she'd only been gone a little over a week, she felt that both she and everything had changed. She'd found her mum and lost Spike all in the course of a few days. And now her home didn't feel like home anymore. She felt disconnected, and dog- tired.

Probably everything catching up with me, she thought, as she surveyed her kitchen, thinking how shabby it looked. How the cupboards could do with painting, and the walls too. She wondered which colour would suit the room best. Maybe blue. Or a Farrow & Ball French grey. The whole kitchen could do with a spring-clean, she decided.

And that was how Mel found her, at a quarter past nine when she let herself in with her own keys.

'Hallooo!' she called out.

'In here!'

Polly, up to her elbows in soap suds. Marigolds on. Tin cans, jars and condiments out of the cupboards and stacked on the worktop, as she scrubbed away at the shelves inside. Full washing machine on the go, dishwasher thrumming away. Mel nearly tripped over the mop next to a bucket of soapy water.

'Watch the floor! Pass that paint brush, would you, Mel?'

Mel stood her ground. 'Stop!' she said. 'What on earth is going on?'

Polly put down her J-cloth and turned an anguished face

towards her friend. 'Oh God, Mel,' she said, not realising what she was going to say until she said it. 'I think I might very well be nesting.'

'Don't be so daft.'

'No really.' Pushing back a stray strand of hair from her face, Polly peeled off her Marigolds. 'My boobs hurt, and suddenly I can't bear the taste of coffee – or tea, either!'

'For God's sake. Sit down, you're making me nervous.'

'I can't,' she said, pacing the floor.

Mel grabbed her arm. 'This is nuts. You can't be pregnant. It's a stomach bug, that's all. Are you feeling sick?'

Polly nodded.

'There you are, then – enteritis!' Mel squinted at her friend. 'Have you missed your period?'

'No.'

'See?'

'I am pregnant, Mel. I just know I am,' Polly insisted.

'Right,' said Mel, putting her hands out in a calming way. 'Have you told anyone else this silly notion of yours?'

Polly shook her head.

'Good. How about Max? You haven't told him, have you?'

'Of course not. I've not done a test to confirm it yet, have I? And, in any case – if I am pregnant...'

'But that's the point, Polly,' said Mel, grabbing her by the shoulders. '*If.* You don't know for certain that you are.'

'No, but if I am pregnant then I'm pretty sure it's not Max's baby...'

Mel now stared goggle-eyed at Polly. 'Sorry, am I missing something here? Should I be calling in the men in white coats because you're up the duff via immaculate conception?'

Polly pulled out a chair to sit at the table, and Mel joined her. 'Okay,' Polly began. 'Here's the thing... If I am pregnant – and I'm pretty sure that I am. One, because I could be, and two, because I had these same symptoms only a couple of weeks after I was pregnant with Rowan. Remember?'

'Yes, I do. And I remember that at the time you thought it was that norovirus. Which could be what you have now. Vomiting virus.'

Polly fixed her with a glare – it didn't matter how much her friend tried to persuade her otherwise, she knew her body. 'The point is,' she continued, 'if I am pregnant then it can't be Max's because we always use condoms. Industrial-strength condoms at that. What with Max being paranoid about not getting anyone pregnant ever again after Claire…'

'I still don't understand…'

'If I am pregnant then I'm ninety-nine per cent certain that the baby is Spike's.'

'Spike's? How—?'

'Shut up and I'll tell you.' Polly relayed the whole story about how her trip to her mother's ended with her sleeping with Spike. And about him taking off in the morning for Kettering – and the reason…

'Where the bloody hell's Kettering?'

'Exactly… that's what I said…'

'Shit. That Spike sure has determined sperm. I always said he'd make a great sperm donor… What? Shut up! Just kidding.'

'I haven't told you the clincher yet.' Polly looked down at the table. 'We didn't use a condom.'

'Oh, Polly. You are such a plonker. Does he know?'

'What? That I'm a plonker?'

'Oh, ha ha.'

'No. He doesn't know. How can I tell him I might be pregnant – when I thought it was safe? And now that he's having a baby with Bam.' Mel watched helpless as her friend burst into tears.

*

The Trouble With Love

In the middle of the night, Polly was woken by Rowan's cries of 'Da-a-a-a-deee!' Polly's heart almost breaking as she entered Rowan's bedroom to find her sitting bolt upright in bed, tears streaming down her face, sobbing for her father.

She hadn't seemed to miss Spike so much or suffered nightmares when she was in Devon, where the fresh air and Brian's attentions had managed to tire her out. But now, as Polly held her child in her arms, it wasn't easy to dispel Rowan's conviction that there were great big spiders lurking in the shadows, and that Daddy was the only person who could dispatch them.

Polly wondered whether it might have been better all round if Spike hadn't returned to the UK. She'd been doing just fine on her own, and Rowan certainly hadn't missed what she never had. Now what was to become of them? How much worse was it going to be when Spike set off for Australia? How would Rowan cope, let alone her?

Polly sat and comforted her child, Rowan's little arms flung about her mother's neck as they rocked back and forth until it was hard to tell just who was comforting whom.

In the corner of the room, a spider snuck back beneath a skirting board, while outside the night gathered around. The lights of a plane, passing far above them, winked in close formation, and a star, which might well have been the planet Venus, twinkled in the sky.

*

The shop was busy the following day, so Polly had little chance to buy a pregnancy testing kit. Even though Mel kept ringing to ask if she'd done it yet.

'Duh,' said Donna – handing over the phone once more to Polly. 'It's your mental friend again.'

'Mel. Go away. I'll do it tomorrow, right?'
'You make sure you do.'

But the next day was every bit as frantic, as Polly caught up with all that had been happening in the shop while she was away, and then there was the stocktaking.

'There's something different about you,' said Donna, squinting at Polly as she unpacked a box of hair slides.

'Don't be daft,' she said. 'Good old country air, I expect.'

Donna stood and closely regarded her, making Polly feel as if she were being scanned by an airport security guard.

'No, it's definitely summat else.'

Anxious to put Donna – who could give a bloodhound a good run for its money when sniffing out a piece of juicy gossip – off the scent, Polly added, 'Maybe I look more relaxed because I've finally made my peace with Suze.'

'Ah,' said Donna, visibly relaxing her guard. 'That'll be it then. Glad she's okay now. Did you hear about…' And as Donna prattled on, in her element, about the latest piece of Clifton-based scandal, filling Polly in on the goings-on at The Arcade, Polly's mind slipped into cruise mode.

It was when she heard Donna say '…and that Dr Sutton has gone and died or something. You know, that batty old battleaxe who lives on… lives on… oh, where is it now?'

Polly straightened up. 'Canynge Crescent?' she said.

'That's the one.'

*

On her way home, Polly drove past her dream house on Canynge Crescent, where outside was staked a For Sale sign. She parked her car up and sat for a few moments gazing at the house she remained convinced should be hers. If she won the lottery. Or was the sort of mercenary cow who could quite happily sponge off her rich mother.

Polly started to wonder about the old lady who'd lived in the house. Had she died at home, or in one of those awful residential homes? Did she have any relatives? Would they be the ones selling up, hoping to maximise their inheritance? Had they even visited during her final illness? Or had it been very sudden?

She pulled out her notebook to jot down the name and number of the estate agent handling the sale, making a mental note to look the house up on the internet. See how much it was on the market for. Because – well, you never know. Yeah, right.

She turned her ignition key to start the car engine and head off home. Tomorrow was Saturday – the day of the screening of the film down at The Scout Hut, on the harbourside. Tomorrow might also be the day when Spike returned for their "Big Talk". Her stomach squirmed with butterflies, and it was a toss-up between whether it was from the anticipation of seeing Spike or the thought of the possible horrors that might entail from Vanessa's film.

35

High Tide

Polly snuck into the *Honeypot Café,* knowing that the waitresses would be too busy serving their Saturday lunchtime customers to wonder why Polly was using their restroom when she had a perfectly good one back at Cutie Pie.

Shutting the door of the Ladies behind her, she took a deep breath to try and steady her nerves. *Here goes nothing.*

*

She stared at the stick. No doubt about it. There was the second blue line. Pregnant. And this was the third stick she'd weed on. She stayed where she was – sitting on the loo seat – staring at the feckin' stick, when – *Beep Beep.* It was a text from Mel.

Have you done it yet? What's the result?

Honestly, there were times when Polly wondered if her friend had supernatural powers.

Opening the Compose Message box on her mobile (instead of the more sensible Reply one), Polly tapped out:

Just did test. Am pregnant! Up the duff!

She scrolled down her list of contacts to Mel's name – located just below that of Max. *Max*, she thought. *What shall I say to Max when I see him? He's bound to be there at the screening later today?* Without thinking, she clicked on Max instead of Mel, and pressed Send.

What? 'Oh no!' she cried out loud. Too late, as the message was already winging its way to the wrong target. 'Oh fuckin' no-o-o-o!'

But yep, she'd only gone and sent the message to Max instead of Mel.

A shy knock came on the door. 'You all right in there?' enquired a female voice.

She couldn't face sending Max another text; she couldn't face another angry call from him, either. She knew it was the coward's way out, but she switched her mobile off. She was bound to see him at the screening, in any case, and by then she would have her friends around her for moral support. Flushing the toilet, she gave herself a feeble smile in the cloakroom mirror and mentally crossed her fingers.

After collecting Rowan from the childminder's, Mel was waiting for her outside her door – suitably done up to the nines in a pair of black cigarette trousers, white top and tailored black jacket.

'Well?' she demanded, as Polly, carrying Rowan in her arms, walked up the path.

'Let's go inside first,' said Polly.

Mel had her impatient face on but said no more as she followed Polly inside, where Rowan was safely settled in front of *The Little Mermaid* on the DVD player. Polly, returning to the kitchen, was met by Mel, who'd been pacing back and forth, ostensibly waiting for the kettle to boil. 'Well?'

'Well, if you're making tea then none for me. Remember, it makes me sick when I'm...' said Polly.

'Oh God, so you are! Is that what you're telling me?'

'Yes.' Polly half turned her face away, still not sure if she was glad or not about her news.

'You really are pregnant? You numpty!' Mel wiped her forehead with her hand. 'Sorry, but honestly you are a stupid mare, sometimes.'

'That's not the worst of it,' said Polly. She told Mel about the text message she'd sent to Max.

Mel burst into laughter. 'Ha ha ha. Oh dear, you don't half get yourself into some scrapes! Ha ha ha ha.'

The doorbell went. 'Dadd-eee!' shouted Rowan, up on her feet and already in the hallway. Polly glanced at Mel. 'Can you answer it, please?' She grimaced at her. 'Just in case it's Max.'

Collecting Rowan into her arms, Polly watched from the kitchen doorway as Mel opened the door. Maybe it was Spike. But no, it was Tiggy, closely followed by Dolphin. Of course, they were babysitting!

'You all right, Poll?' said Tiggy, holding out her arms for Rowan. 'Hey there, Ro Ro!'

'I'd better go and get ready,' Polly announced.

'Yeah, you better had. And fasten your seat belts,' said Mel, in best Bette Davis mode, 'it's gonna be a bumpy night.'

Just then, the doorbell rang again. 'Anna and John, I expect.' They were giving Mel and Polly a lift to the screening. 'Can you let them in?' Polly asked Mel.

'What did your last slave die of? All right, all right.'

Polly grabbed her arm and whispered, 'Not a word, yeah? About the pregnancy. I need to tell Spike first. Okay?'

'Whatever you say, oh mistress.'

*

The Trouble With Love

'Are you sure you don't mind?' Polly said to Anna. 'We could have walked, honest.'

'What, in those shoes?' said Mel, giving a pointed look at Polly's new purchase from *Irregular Choice*.

Annabelle turned around in her seat as John started up the engine of their spanking brand new BMW and said, 'No problem, girls. You have to arrive in style. You are the star, after all, Polly.'

Polly had dressed up for the occasion in one of her new Hawaiian print dresses – with very low cleavage – a Mexican bead necklace and her favourite navy Vivienne Westwood jacket purchased from eBay. It was true that the blue sandals on her feet decorated with ladybirds were ridiculously high, but they made her legs look fabulous, even if she said so herself.

'Just where is this hut thingy?' asked Mel.

'You'll love it,' said John. 'Very trendy.'

'We went to one of those pop-up restaurants in there,' said Anna. 'It's become terribly popular as a small discreet venue. Quite the perfect place for a small screening.'

'How's the musical coming along?' Polly asked Anna.

'It's been cancelled,' she said, not sounding particularly bothered.

'That's dreadful,' said Polly.

'It's not so bad. I get to keep my fee. It happens all the time, you know. Especially as there are so many *Mamma Mia*-type musicals out there, and loads of celebs trying to get in on the act. It's actually worked out quite well, as Handbag Films have optioned my script for *Down the Locarno*.'

'That's brilliant,' said Mel.

'Isn't it just?' Anna beamed with excitement, and John patted her affectionately on the knee. 'I'm delighted actually. There's even a rumour that Tom Hanks might come on board for the production. There's a real feel for '60s music right now. And they say my play is authentic. Yeah? Tamla, Stax, Ska, Bluebeat, Desmond Dekker – Oh, and Prince Buster. All dem rude boys, "Uptown Top Ranking", innit. Set in St Pauls, with its Windrush West Indian population. Be great. The timing is right, and I'm ready to surf that zeitgeist,' she said, doing a surfing motion with her hand and then turning back in her seat to face front. 'Still, we'll see. Things often get commissioned. Scripted. And then stall. But, if they do get Tom…'

'Sounds fab,' said Polly, wishing she could summon up more enthusiasm. She did think it a fantastic project. She'd defo go see the movie. But right now she had other things on her mind, like: would Spike be at the screening? Was Max going to blow his top? Would she come across as a right pillock in Vanessa's film?

'Hey,' said Anna, sensing her friend's unease. 'Don't worry about your little film. If Vanessa has messed it up then not many people will see it – not even if she posts it up on YouTube.'

(Famous last words as it turned out, because the film would go on to win awards all over Europe, and Polly become a bit of a minor celeb. But that was all to happen much, much later.)

As they drove their short drive to park near The Scout Hut, they passed people scurrying home to their families, and Polly's head turned to watch two seagulls squabbling over a piece of burger bun. She wished she hadn't stayed up so late watching *Practical Magic* on Film Four. As she stared out of the car window, her attention was drawn to a small pile of leaves being quickly picked up by a gust of wind which sent them spiralling into the air like a double helix, or some witchy portent.

Mel squeezed Polly's hand. 'Count to ten. Everything is going to be fine.'

'Oh, I nearly forgot to tell you,' said Anna. 'I bumped into Spike yesterday when I was in Bath. He was coming out of Doolally's café.'

'Spike?' said Mel. 'I thought he was in…'

'...Kettering,' said Polly, her voice barely above a whisper, and her heart pounding away so loudly that she was sure people walking past the car must be able to hear it.

'I asked him where Bam was, and he looked most shifty.'

'Shh,' Polly hissed at Mel, shaking her head in warning not to say anything.

'I wouldn't be at all surprised if Spike and Bam were to get married. Would you?' said Anna. 'She'd be great with kids.'

'Oh, oh,' Anna continued, as she pointed out of the window. 'Over there' – indicating a parking space to John. 'I invited Spike along to the screening tonight.' She twisted round to smile at Polly. 'Hope that's okay with you, Polly. Maybe he'll bring Bam along too.'

Oh goodee, Polly thought, miserably. *Spike, Bam and their little bun in the oven. Won't that be great!*

*

From where they parked, it was a short walk across the cobbles to The Scout Hut, which stood on the edge of Redcliffe Wharf, directly opposite a converted boat-cum-bar-cum-club called *The Thekla*. Polly had spent many a carefree night boogieing away to a live band or DJ in there – before Rowan. It used to be one of her favourite haunts, but she'd not noticed the hut before. Approaching, she could see that The Scout Hut did what it said on the tin, being a large dark-stained wooden shed – much like a scout hut. It put her in mind of the place where she'd briefly had ballet lessons as a child.

Inside, the venue was full of people milling around, chatting, getting drinks, standing in groups, or finding their seats in the forty or so stackable chairs which had been arranged in rows to face the white film screen at one end. 'I wasn't expecting so many people,' Polly whispered to Mel.

A trestle table served as a bar, where people happily queued for beers and wine. *Maybe most of the audience are Vanessa's friends*, she thought, although she hadn't spotted anyone that she knew – yet. (A few she did vaguely recognise…)

'This is a fine mess you've gotten us into,' Mel half whispered back, as she elbowed Polly and pointed to where Max was standing – up front, next to Vanessa, who wore a broad grin on her face and a voluminous red kaftan on her body.

Spotting them, Vanessa rushed to give Polly a kiss on each cheek. 'Lovely, lovely,' she said.

'Sarah here, is she?' said Polly, looking around her. She was determined to not let Sarah see that she was at all fazed by their embarrassing doorstep encounter.

'Why would she be? Oh, you don't know, do you? We decided to drop Sarah and edit the film so that it's just you alone. Isn't that fun?'

Polly gave Vanessa a lukewarm smile. She'd run out of conversation or any other type of smile herself.

'I think you'll like it,' said Vanessa, giving Polly's arm a squeeze as she dashed off to buttonhole somebody else.

Mel whispered in her ear, 'Let's find a seat,' and guided Polly in Daisy's direction, who was waving them over.

'Did you hear that?' Polly said to Mel. 'About the film just featuring me?'

'Yeah,' Mel pulled an oh-dear face. 'This promises to be interesting. Not.'

Polly shuffled along, past Daisy, to her seat. 'Where's Phil?' she asked, shrugging out of her jacket and folding it neatly on her knees.

'Babysitting Morwenna. He sends his love. Zak's out at band rehearsal.'

Briefly, Polly scanned the room, searching for Spike. Because it wasn't wholly beyond the realms of possibility that he might be there – and with Bam too. But she couldn't see either of them. She avoided searching out Max, as his face had been like thunder last time she looked.

'Did you see Max?' whispered Mel in her ear. 'Looked well pissed off.'

'Oh God.' Polly risked a glance over at him, then looked away sharpish. If looks could kill. 'You won't leave me alone with him, will you?' she hissed to Mel.

'Don't worry, Batman. Robin's got your back.'

Mel was actually grinning at her. She always liked a drama, did Mel.

'Everything fine?' asked Anna, who was sitting the other side of them.

'Yes, just nervous,' Polly said, although she was more nervous about her imminent showdown with Max than about the film.

Daisy gave her arm a little shake. 'You'll be fine,' she said.

And Polly thought how much she loved her friends, and how glad she was to have them around her.

Vanessa was standing in front of the screen. She clapped her hands together for silence, and then after waiting for the buzz to quieten down, she announced, 'Welcome to this little screening of my film *Would Love to Meet*. I hope you all enjoy it. It's a kind of Amelie meets the modern single Bristolian girl about town.' She paused for effect and then continued, 'At the end of the film, if you'd like to collect a feedback form, then we'd love to hear what you think about our little movie.' She lifted her arms expansively. 'Enjoy.' The lights went down and the film's opening credits rolled as accordion music played on screen.

Talk about embarrassing! Polly was so aggrieved about the film, and how – in her eyes – Vanessa had stitched her up, that she plain forgot all about Max. So shocked and mortified was she that she didn't notice the door at the back softly open and close again soon after the start. She watched a good deal of the film through her fingers, in the same fashion she had with scary *Doctor Who* episodes when she was a kid!

She didn't know which part was worse. So much to choose from. The bit with her surfing the net? With Vanessa as the unseen interviewer asking, 'So, Polly, would you say that you've ever met The One?'

And Polly's response: 'I don't know. But there was someone. [Camera zooming in for a close-up on her dreamy-looking face.] I often think of him more as The One That Got Away. [Camera staying in close up.] That's the trouble with love, isn't it?' she was saying. [*God, you can practically see each and every one of my pores!*] 'You can't make love happen, can you? And sometimes – well, sometimes you don't even know it's there… until it's gone.'

Cue music and then cutting to Vanessa in a voice-over saying, 'Polly, in true modern woman style, sets about tracking love down.' [*Who does she think she is? David Attenborough?*] Cue jokey white text across the screen: *The Speed Dating Night.* [*Oh, kill me now!*]

Scenes of Polly pulling faces to camera as various men take their turn at impressing her. Cut to Polly dancing with man in blazer, giving Vanessa 'I'll kill you' looks. [Laughter from the audience.] Cut to Polly outside, one red wine too many, spouting her [deeply embarrassing – cringe] speech about being a Renaissance Woman – 'I don't need a man to make me complete!' [Giggling from the audience.] Cue Polly toddling off on her tod into the night. Cue accordion-bloody-music again. More jokey text. [*I can't bear to look.*] Footage of Polly chasing Rowan across Brandon Hill while her own voice-over goes, 'There aren't many men who'd fancy a woman with a kid in tow.' Then on to the open mic night. [More laughter from the audience when she recites her poem – *small comfort… at least it got a laugh.*]

But honestly, it was like a nightmare version of This is Your Life!

More filming of Polly at home – internet dating – sitting at her laptop on MatchMadeInHeaven.com. 'Why not shop for men online?' she was saying to camera. In a chirpy sort of way, even she had to admit. 'After all, it's the way I do most of my shopping.' [More laughter from the audience.]

Finishing off with Polly sitting outside a café on Park Street. All alone, as the shot panned out and accordion-bloody-music started up again. The End.

The audience clapped, and the lights went up.

'Oh God, is it over?' Polly asked Mel.

'Yes,' she whispered.

Vanessa walked up to the front and called out, 'Stand up, please, Polly Park. The star of our film.'

Heads turned and strained as they tried to clock where Polly was. Reluctantly she rose to her feet, acknowledged the polite applause and sat down again.

'Oh dear,' said Anna. 'That was a bit – weird.'

Daisy reached across to pat Polly's hand. 'I think you came across as very warm and sweet.'

'More like some saddo,' said Polly, who certainly didn't want to chat to any of the punters. Too embarrassing. 'I need to get out of here. Get some fresh air.'

Before Mel could say 'Hang on,' Polly was pushing her way through people starting to leave, collecting bags and coats, chatting… She particularly wanted to avoid Vanessa, who at any moment would be heading her way like a galleon at full sail. As Polly made her way towards the exit, she heard someone say, 'Good piece,' someone else 'Most entertaining.' Polly had gained the door and was stepping outside into the early- evening light before anyone could stop her.

Thank goodness she was out of there. She'd thought she was going to faint. Wandering over to the quayside, she stopped to watch, without wholly seeing, a ferry boat chug by.

She wasn't all that surprised when she heard her name being called by Max (it had to happen).

'Polly!'

Reluctantly she turned to face him as he stood a few feet away from her. She wished now that she'd waited for Mel.

'So what the hell are you playing at?' he said, and as she tried to duck past him, he grabbed her wrist.

'Not so fast!' he said, and she nearly laughed – it was such a corny dastardly type of line. 'You're going nowhere until you tell me just what's going on,' he said, as she tried to twist her arm away from him. 'I've been trying and trying to call you,' he blustered. 'And what? Now you're saying you're pregnant? What is this? Some sort of cheap trick? I'm not going to fall for that again. Not after Claire. You women are all the bloody same.'

Polly stood her ground, thinking how he was a stranger to her. Once he'd set her heart all pitter-patter; once she'd thought him handsome, that he might even have been someone to take a risk with. Now he reminded her of Phil Mitchell with a touch of Les Dennis thrown in – what with his red face, receding hairline (which she'd not noticed before) and red spots by the side of his nose. He still had hold of her wrist and was twisting it in a most painful way.

'Don't be an idiot, Max. Let me go. You're hurting me.'

He released his grip, and she tried to sidestep him. But he blocked her way.

'Look,' she tried again. 'I'm sorry. Okay? That text I sent was for Mel – not you! Your contact details just happen to be right next to Mel's. It was a silly mistake.' It sounded lame even to her. 'That text was not meant for you. End of. No big deal.'

But instead of him smiling and going – 'Oh, I see. That was

silly, was it?' – or words to that effect (yeah, she knew it was a long shot), he got even redder in the face, and for a moment Polly thought he might be having a heart attack or a stroke, and was trying to remember what the drill was if one or other were to happen? CPR or mouth-to-mouth? She hoped it was CPR, as that would give her an excuse to give him a good thumping.

'No big deal?' His voice increasing in volume. 'What? You are pregnant with my child and you say it's no big deal? What sort of woman are you?' His stare was full of contempt, and Polly – to her shame – could feel a titter if not a full-blown giggle coming on. (She was nervous, all right?)

'Unless,' he continued, in high dudgeon. (*Funny word, "dudgeon", isn't it? she thought. Sounds like dungeon...*) 'Yes, of course, that's it.' Max was still ranting on. 'It's somebody else's brat, isn't it? You've been sleeping with someone else. I might have known. You're nothing but a whore!'

It really was no good; Polly was going to burst out laughing because she had this awful tendency at times of high drama to want to break into gales of merriment. She tried to concentrate on keeping a serious face, biting her lip in the process but, really, it was like she was starring in her own B movie.

'You fucked somebody else, didn't you?'

(Polly had her hand over her mouth now, shoulders beginning to shake – yes, she knew it wasn't funny...)

'And now you are trying to pass whoever's kid off as mine!'

It was no good. She let out a guffaw.

Max, incensed, took a step towards her, with his hand raised. This stunned Polly into silence.

'That's enough!' came a voice behind Polly. 'Leave her alone.' Spike. It was Spike's. She'd recognise his voice anywhere – whether from the top of a cliff or across the oceans... *For Chrissake, pull yourself together, Polly. You're not out of hot water yet.*

Max squared up to Spike, who had stepped in between him

and Polly. She caught her breath, thinking how Spike had never looked more gorgeous. Standing there, in his skinny jeans and blue checked shirt, like a model from Urban Outfitters. Where was Mel when she needed her?

'I might've guessed,' Max was saying. 'Polly's expecting your baby, I suppose!'

Spike turned briefly to Polly with a "What baby?" look.

'You wanna watch it, mate,' Max sneered. 'She's been trying to pass your kid off as mine. Hoping I'll cough up for the price of an abortion.'

'I haven't… I wouldn't…' she began. But Spike tucked her safely behind him and, without any preamble, punched Max in the face. He went down hard on his bottom, just as Mel and the others arrived.

'Oh my God, it's a fight,' said Mel, doing a cartoon-like screech to a halt. She watched, slack-jawed, as Max gave Spike a baleful glare and clambered to his feet, by which time John had pulled Polly away, passing her to Mel, who had a tight hold of her.

'John, do something,' called Anna.

'Don't you worry,' he said. 'I'll make sure this doesn't get out of hand.' He stood on the side, keeping a careful eye on things as Spike held out a hand to Max, but Max batted it away. Spike made to move towards Polly, when all of a sudden Max rushed at him, bellowing like a bull.

Whoomph! There proceeded some shoving and poorly aimed kicks, with John trying to keep them apart. Polly was about to make some comment to Mel when she saw what no one else had yet fully comprehended. That the two men – with their scratching, biting, twisting, fighting – were getting closer and closer to the edge of the quayside. In fact, she suspected that Max, who had a good ten pounds – and the rest – on Spike, and who used to play rugby for his uni, was heaving Spike towards the edge on purpose,

The Trouble With Love

much like pushing a scrum. The rest she saw as if in slow motion. Spike trying to get a purchase on Max. A man walking hand in hand with his girlfriend, dropping her hand as he too realised what was about to happen. Polly could only have looked away for a nanosecond, as when she looked back, there was Spike teetering on the edge, holding onto the lapel of Max's leather jacket while – too late – John made a run towards them. Spike's eyes locked onto Polly's as she heard his 'Whoaaa!' – and he fell backwards into the water, taking Max with him.

Next, Polly was at the water's side, and someone was screaming and screaming so loudly that she had to put her hands over her ears. As she called out 'Spike!' she realised that the screamer was herself!

Oh God, oh God, where was he? He couldn't swim! Should she jump in? What about the baby? But John had already dived in. Polly fell to her knees, not caring if she ended up with great big holes in her new stockings, as she frantically scanned the river's surface. And then Mel was there, holding onto her shoulders as she pointed and said, 'Look. It's all right,' as first Spike bobbed up, spluttering water, followed by John, who had hold of a dazed-looking Max. John struck out for the side, swimming on his back, as he pulled Max along by the chin in good old-fashioned life-saving style.

A man who'd been rummaging around on his houseboat ran over to Polly and handed her a blanket. 'I don't need…' she began.

'No,' he pointed to Spike, who was hauling himself out of the river, 'it's for him, love.'

'Yes, of course, thanks.' She took it from him and ran to Spike.

'Brrrr. I'm bloody cold,' said Spike, his teeth chattering as she placed the blanket over his shoulders. People with blankets appeared and were tending to the other men.

'You terrified me,' she said. 'I thought you were on your way down to Davy Jones's locker.'

He gave her a quizzical look. 'Now what would I be doing going in the closet of one of those there Monkees?'

'Shut up!' she said, as he gave her a broad grin.

'Is Max okay?' he asked, and glancing over his shoulder, he could see that Max was indeed fine. Both him and John sitting on the dockside while Anna fussed about and someone plied them with brandy.

She gave Spike a little push. 'I was scared, Spike! You said you couldn't swim!'

'Just what did you think I was doing on all those surfer beaches, Poll? Surfing, that's what! Of course I can swim – I didn't used to like it. The most important thing is, I didn't drown.'

'So,' said Polly, as she looked hesitantly about her, 'where's Bam? Is she here with you?'

'No, Polly. She's not here. We've called it a day. That's what I came to tell you.'

He stood before her, dripping wet in spite of the blanket, and shivering.

'But what about the baby?' she said. 'I mean Bam's baby, not…' She looked shame-faced, as he gave her a quizzical look.

'There is no baby.'

'What?'

He held his hand out to her. She didn't need asking twice. Or care about getting wet. Once she was in his arms, he said, 'I'll tell you about it later. Wait 'til I get you home. You can explain then whether or not you are pregnant yourself.'

36

Home, in front of a few logs burning in Polly's grate, Spike sat on the sofa waiting for Polly to join him; his hand nursing a mug of hot chocolate laced with brandy, while a fast-asleep-yet-happy Rowan sprawled next to him. Even in her sleep, she had a smile on her face.

Earlier, when Spike and Polly burst through Polly's front door, accompanied by all the others – Mel, Anna, John and Daisy – they were greeted by Tiggy and Dolphin (who'd plainly been canoodling – or worse – on the sofa). 'Mum!' said Tiggy, hurriedly straightening her clothes as the assembled group grinned at their embarrassment.

Upstairs, Rowan was wide awake. Alerted by the kerfuffle of the arrivals, she heard her father's voice, clambered out of bed and made her way along the landing – Winnie the Pooh dangling in her grasp – to the top of the stairs, where she stood at the locked stair gate and called, 'Daddy, daddy, da-a-a-a-a-deee!'

Spike – dressed in clothes kindly lent by "houseboat man" – turned to the others and said, 'Hang on a sec. Daughter calling.' Although still stiff and sore from his dunk in the harbour, he took the stairs two at a time, to haul Rowan and Pooh up into his arms, Rowan clinging to his body like a koala bear to a eucalyptus tree.

'Tomorrow...' Polly was saying to Annabelle as she tried to herd them all out of the door. 'C'mon, you lot. Spike and I haven't had a moment to ourselves.'

'Yes, but what about Bam?' asked Mel, straining over the top of Polly's shoo-out-you-get-arms.

'That's for me and Polly to discuss, big ears,' said Spike, descending the stairs. 'I dare say you'll find out soon enough.'

'Ill ring you tomorrow,' Polly said, with a smile as warm and content as if she'd just been out delivering Christmas presents to all and sundry, rather than screaming and wailing as her loved one near drowned. Because, somehow, there was Spike. Rocking that whole manky jeans and moth-eaten sweater combo he'd had donated to him. She couldn't wait to get him to herself.

'Now out! Get out, all of you!' she ordered. Remembering how, when Spike was on the docks, soaking wet, he'd held her face between his hands and said, 'I love you, Polly Park, and I'm not going to be your One That Got Away. All right?'

As she shut the door, Spike – with Rowan still in his arms – led her through to the sofa, where they all three sat down.

So here they were. Polly and Spike. Alone, save for their child lying beside them – *and the one in here*, she thought, patting her belly.

She tucked her feet up underneath her as she cosied up next to Spike – with his lovely handsome face, his hair all sticky-up and curled like bedhead hair, those blue eyes framed by thick lashes, that dark hint of stubble spreading across his chin, upper lip and jaw. Those large manly hands, gripping his mug of —

'Polly?' He interrupted her thoughts. 'Will you stop sizing me up like a prize piece of beef?'

'Hmm?' She shook her head, telling her hormones to behave. 'Sorry. Am concentrating now, I promise.'

He pulled her towards him for a deep kiss – not a passionate tongues-and-stuff kiss, but a melting-inside kiss, full of love and the promise of more to come.

Pulling apart, and taking a sip from his chocolate drink, Spike told Polly how, after he left her that day in Devon, the uppermost plan in his mind was to somehow sort things out and to tell Bam that he didn't love her anymore.

'So, you don't love her?' Polly's voice barely above a whisper.

'No, Polly Park. Isn't that what I've been trying to tell you? I might have thought I loved Bam, but it's you I love – eejit that I am.' He gave her a wry smile. 'Always have, always will.'

Polly squirmed with delight while in her mind's eye she was up on her feet, punching the air, going 'Yesss!' Back on earth, she waited for what he had to say next. Her Spike. Hers, not Bam's.

'Pay attention now, Polly,' he was saying, 'and leave off looking at me like that or I'll have to ravish you right here on the carpet.'

'What?' she said, hand on heart in pretend shock. 'In front of Rowan and Cap'n Jack?'

'We could blindfold the old fella… and as for Rowan…' he said, gazing lovingly at his daughter '…bless her heart. She's out for the count.'

Polly snuggled up, enjoying the feel of him through his sweater, the smell of him – oh, she could now admit fully to herself that she adored everything about him. 'Go on then,' she said. 'You'd better tell me the rest.'

And so his story unfolded. How Bam's parents were pleased as punch to see him at first. How there were plenty of hints about a wedding, and how he'd been alarmed to see given pride of place on the coffee table a stack of bridal magazines. Spike kept trying to find an opportune moment to get Bam alone so he could break the news that they couldn't be together, but that of course he'd be there for the baby – and for her too – as much as he could, but that his life lay ahead with Polly and Rowan.

'I suspect she had an inkling,' he said, 'because she was doing her darnedest not to have a "talk" with me.' And, of course, uppermost in his mind was the existence of a baby and how this made it all the more important to have a heart-to-heart about arrangements and whatnot now that Spike was absolutely sure he was returning to Polly. But Bam – 'Like she had some sixth sense or something' – managed to head him off each time he tried. Both Spike and Bam were staying at her parents' house, in separate bedrooms: again, meaning fewer opportunities to be alone. 'I like her parents, Polly.'

'Shame you'll now have to make do with Suze and Brian,' she said, rather cheekily.

'C'mon, I love Suze – she's very… umm… spirited. And Brian, well, he's grand.'

He didn't tell Polly how awful it had actually been. The tears and recriminations when he did manage to explain as gently as he could that it was over. Bam's father throwing him out into the night; trying to find a taxi, a hotel, feeling like a right heel, but deep down knowing it was the right thing to do.

'Frankly, Polly, I was stunned that she was pregnant. We'd not had sex in weeks.'

Polly threw him an "As if" stare.

'Cross my heart and hope to die,' he said. 'Hardly any since that first night I bumped into you outside Mike's bar and I first learnt about Rowan.' He rubbed his forehead. 'Bam insisted she understood. Said I was probably confused, and that things would get back to normal once we returned to Australia. She's a grand girl, is Bam.'

'So everyone keeps telling me. You can still pick her over me, you know,' she said. He gave her arm a pinch. 'Ow!'

'Don't go teasing me at a time like this, Polly.'

She longed to reach out and touch his face, but she'd not heard the whole of his story yet.

'Before all this, she'd given me an ultimatum,' he sighed. 'To choose either her or you. I thought she was nuts. As far as I knew then, there was no choice to be made. You'd made it clear you were happy with Max...'

'But I wasn't, not really... I thought you were happy with Bam!'

He gave her a rueful smile. 'Guess we were both at cross purposes, then.' He took hold of her hand and lifted it up to his lips. 'Ah, Polly, you have the hands of a skivvy.' She tried to pull it away, wishing she had manicured hands, like any sensible person her age. But Spike held on tight, turned it over and kissed her palm. 'Love this hand.' He put that one down and picked up the other one. Kissed that on the palm, too. 'Ah look, a spare one. That'll come in handy...'

She gave him an 'oh-ha-ha' look.

'This hand's pretty scrumptious too,' he said.

Polly placed both her hands firmly in her lap. 'So? What happened next?'

'You know what happened, because that was when I started to hope it might be worth my while asking you to consider giving us another go, when the whole thing with your mother happened, and then,' he gave her a goofy smile, 'well, then we had our glorious sex.'

'It was good, wasn't it?'

'So-so,' he said, breaking into a broad grin, which she soon wiped off his face by launching herself at him, to give him a small thump on the chest. 'Be gentle with a part- drowned man, Polly.' She then began to tickle him under the arm. 'Aargh! Stop that right now. Okay. The sex was stupendous. Fabulous. Are you happy now?'

She let go, her hair all dishevelled, both of them laughing. He placed his palm on her flat tummy. Polly's pale tummy, which would soon grow more and more rounded until her innie became an outie. Absent-mindedly, he began tracing the outline of her belly button with his finger, causing her muscles to contract deliciously.

'Seriously mind-blowing sex, Polly. I dare say there'll be plenty more where that came from.' His stare was downright sizzling… but Polly stopped him by handing over his half-drunk hot chocolate.

'Come on,' she insisted. 'Tell me the rest.'

'Ah well,' he said, lying back, letting his head rest on a cushion. She took his now finished cup from him, while he peered at her intensely. 'Honestly, Poll. Are you sure you're pregnant? It's not just a Jammie Dodger belly?'

'Yes, I'm sure,' she said, in a small voice.

'Jeez, it's like being involved in some crazy version of pregnancy musical chairs!' he said, with an affectionate smile. 'Isn't it too early for you to be certain?'

'I knew the moment I got back from Mum's.'

He gave her a look.

'Duh…' she said. 'I have been pregnant before, you know.'

'Ah.'

'And, before you ask, yes, I did do the test. Did three, as it happens, and they were all positive.'

'Three, you say? Hope that doesn't mean we'll be having triplets.'

'Idiot!'

They were both silent for a while until Polly half whispered, 'What if it's Max's child?'

He looked her straight in the eye and said, 'It's you I want.

Makes no mind whose the child it is. This child,' and he placed his hand on her tummy, 'will be a part of you, and that's all that matters. As far as I'm concerned, a child is an added bonus.'

She thought she might burst with happiness.

'So what happens about Bam? It's not like you can clone yourself so that one of you can live here with me and our children, and the other can move to Australia with Bam and her child.'

'No clones needed, Polly.' He took hold of her hand once more. 'I'm sad to say that fate intervened, and Bam had a miscarriage.'

A sob caught in Polly's throat. Okay, a part of her (a really mean part!) was relieved, but the bigger and better part felt desperately sorry, for Bam and for Spike.

'That's why I couldn't properly call to let you know what was happening. Why it took longer than I'd hoped. I couldn't just up and leave Bam to it, could I? It was deeply sad, and Bam – well, she was devastated. Her parents – as you can imagine – were well pissed off with me,' he said, looking rueful. 'I thought her dad was going to punch me.' He rubbed his knuckles, still sore from where he had punched Max earlier. 'Maybe it's what I deserved. But not as much as that Max fella.'

Polly's mind was still brimful of Bam's predicament. Yes, she knew she hadn't warmed to Bam, but that was more to do with her being a rival. Polly suspected had they met under different circumstances, they might well have got on famously.

'How far along was Bam?' she had to ask.

Spike sighed. 'Eight, maybe nine weeks, they think. I was surprised she was pregnant at all because she was on the pill.'

Ah, thought Polly, deciding not to inform Spike how some women can forget to take the pill – accidentally on purpose. *Mind you, I'm a fine one to talk, aren't I*, she chided herself. Giving Spike the go-ahead to not use a condom, knowing full well that going by period dates was not reliable. She felt ashamed of thinking such thoughts of Bam. Poor Bam, who'd lost her baby and Spike all in one go.

'So I couldn't leave. Not right away. Both Bam and I needed time. The doctor said many babies miscarry before twelve weeks. Guess we were unlucky – or lucky – I don't really know. I'm still trying to get my head around it. And Bam – well, she was brilliant in the end. Strong. She said that of course I must go.' He thought of how she'd seen him off with a brave smile, which had made his heart squeeze with sorrow. Yes, he'd been sad for them both, but he was meant to be with Polly. He and Bam wouldn't have stood a chance.

'What were you doing in Bath, when Daisy saw you?'

'Truth? After I left Bam, I went to London first, stayed in Elspeth's house and sorted things with the sale, and then on to Bath. I'm sorry I kept you waiting, and that I didn't phone or anything, but I needed time to think things through. If we're to forge a good life together then I needed to be absolutely sure that I was choosing to stay for you, Polly, and not just for Rowan. That I wanted you, whether or not you were the mother of any of my children. I'm not sure I've put that very eloquently, but does that make sense?'

'Yes,' she said, as he looked intensely down into her eyes. 'It makes perfect sense.'

He pulled her towards him so that her head rested on his chest. She could feel his heart go boom-diddy-boom as she breathed in time to his breaths. Her eyelids were heavy, and she closed her eyes.

'Hey,' he said, gently giving her a nudge. 'Don't you go to sleep on me. I've got other things planned for us. Once we get this wee one off to bed,' he said, nodding at Rowan on his other side. Fast asleep with her mouth open, snuffling away like a little woodland creature.

Spike bent forwards to kiss Polly's not-there-yet bump. 'What shall we be having, do you reckon? A boy or a girl?'

'I don't mind,' said Polly.

'I think a boy next, don't you? We'll call him Sonny.'

'Oh, will we?'

'Not that I'd say no to another gorgeous little girl. We can always have a boy the baby after that.'

He pulled Polly to her feet.

'The one after?' she said.

'Yes, Polly. I'm thinking four's a good number. Or how about five?'

'Five?'

'Too few? Okay then. Six. Although you've probably not got enough child-bearing years left for more than six, eh?'

Polly, being a bit slow on the uptake, didn't get that he was teasing her until he gave her a slow wink.

'Oh you!' she said, attacking him with a cushion.

'No! Get off! I'm an injured man, remember! Oof! I fought for your honour! Aargh! Get off!'

Rowan, stirring, rubbed her eyes and held her arms out to Spike.

'I'm starving,' he said to Polly. 'What've you got to eat?'

'Erm. Cheese on toast do you?'

'See that the cooking hasn't improved in my absence,' he said, as he rose to carry Rowan up to bed.

*

After placing the cheese and toast under the grill, Polly popped back upstairs to where she joined Spike to stand in Rowan's doorway, watching her sleep.

'You know that house in Canynge Crescent, Polly?' he said.

'House?'

'Yes, your all-time favourite house.' He was smiling his laconic smile at her.

'But how did you...'

'I remember everything about you, Polly Park.' He took her hand, turned her wrist over and kissed her faint scar. 'Like this scar, which you got from trying to stop a dog eating Mel's tortoise like it was a Fray Bentos pie.' Polly felt heady with his scent. He was close to her, lifting his head as if to kiss her – then – BEEP BEEP BEEP BEEP shrilled her smoke alarm.

They looked at each other then both shouted, 'Cheese on toast!' and charged downstairs to the kitchen, where Polly grabbed the smoking grill pan and dropped it on the floor as she'd forgotten her oven gloves, and burnt her fingers. Spike opened the French doors and windows and flapped at the alarm with a tea towel, until it stopped.

'Phew,' he said, holding Polly's fingers under a running cold tap. 'Some things never change. Thank goodness.' He kissed her fingertips. 'As I was saying, Polly...'

'Yes?'

'The house. Your house.' He took a deep breath as if steeling himself. 'I've bought it.'

'You what?'

'Bought it, Polly.' Her face was a picture of surprise, crossed with even more surprise. 'The money came through from the sale of Elspeth's house in Islington. I had no idea they could fetch that much.' He gave her a sheepish look. 'I'm hoping it can be our home now, Polly. You, me, Rowan and the little 'un.'

Polly could hardly believe her ears. 'But how did you know that I'd want you... that I'd want us... to all be together?'

'I didn't, Polly. But, sometimes, you just gotta have faith!'

As if they were telepathic, they both burst into a few bars of George Michael's song "Faith", and then cracked up laughing.

'Better than that Will Young one,' she said – remembering.

The Trouble With Love

'What on earth are you on about now?' said Spike. Outside, the night drew in, peeking through her window.

'Tell you afterwards,' said Polly, as she pulled him towards her.

Later in bed, they made the slow kind of love that Polly had dreamt of since returning from Devon. Not just sex – but love. Making – making – love. Polly was singing "All You Need is Love" in her head, complete with brass section.

'Polly?' said Spike, stopping to gaze down at her.

She opened her eyes, all languorous and dreamy. 'Mmm?'

'You're humming again, Polly.'

'Hmm?'

'Humming, Polly, humming,' he was saying, whispering into her neck. 'So, shall we be getting married, now, Polly?'

'I don't know. Marriage is such an outmoded institution.'

'Ah, there ya go again with that Renaissance Woman thing.'

She couldn't help smiling in the dark. 'I think we ought to do a Helena Bonham Carter/Tim Burton thing, don't you?'

'I can't afford to buy the house next door, Polly.'

She nuzzled into his shoulder.

'Just so long as you don't make me wear a monkey suit like in that there *Planet of the Apes*!' he added. 'Mind you, I think a monkey costume might suit you.'

'Oh, very funny!'

'Hey, Polly,' he said, gazing down at her. 'Are you crying?'

'Shut up.' She kissed him and he kissed her as they coiled around each other, entwined and as undulating as fronds of kelp pulled by the rhythms of tides and oceans.

Epilogue

It's October when winds are up, tides are high, and calendars signal a fast-approaching All Hallows' Eve, when witches are abroad, riding the night skies.

At the top of Spike and Polly's new house are two attic rooms. Polly stands at the window of the one she calls the Spy's Nest, as it's where Spike has rigged up a telescope right next to Cap'n Jack, who stares permanently towards the docks. Outside the window there is a small balcony where two chairs can just fit, side by side and, on nights when there's not a cloud in the sky, Polly and Spike like to sit together, drink wine and gaze at the stars, as so many star-crossed lovers have over the years, centuries, millennia. They chat, kiss and look up to the heavens. Sometimes they take a blanket and make love out there in a quiet awestruck way, knowing that they have come home.

She'll go down in a minute. Spike is below with their baby, Sonny, whose crying threatens to wake Rowan. Polly takes a moment to stand and stare into the night; a sudden gust whips her hair, and she can taste the salt on the wind's breath.

Author's Note

When I first had the idea for this novel, I was a single mum of two young children and found myself writing about the family of friends on whom many of us rely. It's said that it takes a whole village to raise a child, Polly is surrounded by her own hotchpotch village. Although mainly a tale of Polly and Spike, the beating heart of this novel are Polly's friends and family.

Although substantially a romcom – I prefer to see it more as a Jane Austen-esque comedy of errors, exploring the modern dilemmas of women, men too, in what are different and changing relationships. An important one being the changing dynamics between Polly and best friend Melanie when Mel realises she's gay.

I hope I've given a flavour of Bristol. It's my home city: one which mixes the folk lore of the West (easily seen in places like Glastonbury) with an Afro-Caribbean vibe (reflected in Bristol's music scene). It's laid back and urban at the same time, with many beautiful gateways to lush countryside and woods.

Initially published at a time when the publishing industry

was getting to grips with digital, this novel was first taken on by Sphere as an e-book and I'm now happy to have this opportunity, with The Book Guild, to re-issue Polly and Spike's story in both digital and paperback form.

I live on the banks of the Bristol Channel which has the biggest tidal drop of any waters in Europe. Sometimes the waters are brown, sometimes grey, sometimes blue with streaks of red. Ever changing it brings its flotsam and jetsam in on tides where eels wend their way.

Ok, some information about me. I began writing this novel soon after gaining a master's degree in creative writing at Bath Spa University. I am a published writer of short stories and poetry. An erstwhile Bristol poetry slam champion, I've been involved in Bristol's poetry scene since the late 1990s. These days I teach creative writing at an adult education centre in Bristol as well as undergraduate and masters degree courses at The Open University. I also tutor residential writing courses at Retreats For You in Devon – a lovely place in the depths of Devon, yet close enough to the sea for anyone to pop along for a mooch and a paddle.

Annoyingly, I live alongside various chronic illnesses which, whilst challenging, have not stopped me writing. I finally possess my dream writing shed, dedicated to the alchemy of writing novels (i.e. the walls are covered with Post-It notes and scraps of paper, etc.). I'm often joined by my cockapoo who snoozes under my desk, dreaming her doggie dreams.

Acknowledgements

Writing is a lonesome (rather than lonely) pursuit. Even so, if we're lucky there will be people to hold our hands: mentors will turn up, as will writers who've been where you are, and friends to give steadying advice.

When my novel was in the "pink and wobbly" early notes and ideas stage, I enrolled in a Cornerstones Literary Consultancy day-course with Julie Cohen and Liz Weatherley. At the end, Julie asked me to stay behind – and told me I could write. Sometimes it takes one person you respect or admire, to have some faith in you, so big thanks are due to Julie who mentored me on subsequent projects. She's an angel.

Next came my (then) agent, Kate Hordern, who taught me that sometimes we need tough love. Without her pithy notes, this novel may not have developed into one I'm proud of.

Thanks are due to Manpreet Grewal, my editor at Sphere who had faith in this book and took a chance when the publishing industry was getting to grips with e-books. I must also thank all the crew at The Book Guild: Carolina Santos, Emily Gett, Holly Porter, and Rosie Lowe. Without their help and support, this re-release would not have happened.

I'd also like to acknowledge the love and support I've received from Lola Jaye. She's been a wonderful cheerleader and giver of advice.

And how can I forget my colourful friend Queenie, who's sadly no longer with us. Her wonderful and wacky shop provided inspiration for Polly's emporium. Thanks to all my past and present friends (especially my besties). You know who you are – and I'm not saying if any of you are in this novel! All my novels include the love of best friends as these are special relationships for women.

Big thanks to Polly and Spike and their family of friends. It's truly magical when your characters become so real that you can hear them talking in your head and they never quite leave you. I often wonder what they might be getting up to. Publishing this, their first story a second time around, has made me wonder if it isn't high time I revisited the gang and penned a sequel. (So, watch this space.)

A writer needs a tribe of fellow writers, and I'd like to acknowledge some of mine, especially Polly Moyer, Jane Purcell, Debbie Flint, Helen Thomas, Lola Jaye, Julie Cohen, Tom Bromley and many more plus my first agent Maggie Noach who is sadly no longer with us but never lost the faith. And thanks to the Bristol Harbour Master who answered many of my daft questions. Bristol is such a magical place with its folk lore, tidal waters, and its chilled vibes.

Finally, thanks to my beloved daughters Kate and Morgan, who've had to put up with me – particularly if in the car when I'm driving and I suddenly shout – "Quick, write this down before I forget it." Because one never knows when ideas may pop up as, much like Life, ideas can happen when you're doing something else.

I hope you have enjoyed this tale of Polly and Spike and little Rowan, and they promise to see you again, soon.